THE #1 SPINE-TINGLING PAGE-TURNER IN MANY A YEAR!
JAMES PATTERSON'S
CAT & MOUSE

"A RIDE ON A ROLLER-COASTER WHOSE BRAKES HAVE GONE OUT."
—*Chicago Tribune*

"*CAT & MOUSE* IS A PULSATING GAME. . . . THE ACTION IS FAST AND FURIOUS. . . . The pages turn in a blur. . . . You might just finish this in one sitting. It's that kind of book."
—*Rocky Mountain News*

"A QUICK-PACED ADVENTURE . . . WITH A PROTAGONIST WORTHY OF ADMIRATION. Alex Cross is a hero. Patterson moves readers along with short chapters, snappy dialogue, and creepy chills. . . . Read it at your own risk."
—*Pittsburgh Post-Gazette*

"FANTASTIC READING ENTERTAINMENT . . . does not disappoint. . . . The reader is deluged with horror. . . . If you have been a James Patterson fan in the past then you are just waiting for *CAT & MOUSE*. If you have never read any Patterson books then you should go back to *Along Came a Spider* and read all of the intervening stories. If you don't have time for that you can still enjoy *CAT & MOUSE* as a stand-alone story."
—*Daily Sun*

more . . .

"PATTERSON IS A MASTER at creating scary murderers, but his hero has what it takes to pursue them. . . . Don't start this book on a night you have to turn in early, because you won't be able to put it down."
—*Newark Star Ledger*

"Patterson gives his fans two thrillers for the price of one . . . delivers THE SWIFTLY PACED FARE THAT HAS MADE HIM A CHAMP OF THE CHARTS."
—*Publishers Weekly*

"A BREAKNECK CHASE."
—*Lexington Herald-Leader*

"A MUST-READ AUTHOR . . . reaches out and grabs you from the opening page and doesn't let go until the last drop of blood . . . a great job of developing characters. . . . Alex Cross is a lovable, down-to-earth hero that anyone could relate to. . . . An incredible thriller that keeps you flipping from one chapter to the next. It's not the kind of book you can easily put down, and even when you're done you're left hungry for more. Thankfully, Patterson has paved the way for another sequel starring Alex Cross. Many of his readers will be waiting."
—*Providence Journal*

"HE'S UNBEATABLE. . . . In *Jack & Jill* [Patterson] again proves himself master of the hair-raising thriller with a climactic, double-twist ending, the trick that made his *Along Came a Spider* and *Kiss the Girls* memorable nail-biters."
—**Buffalo News**

"CHILLING. . . . THIS BOOK IS HARD TO PUT DOWN."
—**Associated Press**

"QUICK AND SCARY."
—*New York Daily News*

Kiss the Girls

"TOUGH TO PUT DOWN. . . . TICKS LIKE A TIME BOMB, ALWAYS FULL OF THREAT AND TENSION."
—*Los Angeles Times*

"AS GOOD AS A THRILLER CAN GET . . . . WITH KISS THE GIRLS, PATTERSON JOINS THE ELITE COMPANY OF THOMAS HARRIS AND JOHN SANFORD."
—*San Francisco Examiner*

"THIS ONE'S HOT!"
—**Liz Smith**, *New York Newsday*

"HORRIFIC . . . SKILLFULLY PUT TOGETHER!"
—*Cosmopolitan*

Novels by James Patterson

CAT& MOUSE

JAMES PATTERSON

WARNER BOOKS

A Time Warner Company

WARNER BOOKS EDITION

Cover concept by Rory Phoenix
Cover illustration by Joe Ovies
Hand lettering by James Montalbano

Warner Books, Inc.
1271 Avenue of the Americas
New York, NY 10020

Visit our Web site at
http://warnerbooks.com

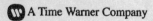 A Time Warner Company

Printed in the United States of America

Published by arrangement with Little, Brown & Company.
First Warner Books International Paperback Printing: April, 1998
First Warner Books U.S. Paperback Printing: November, 1998

10 9 8 7 6 5 4 3 2 1

For Suzie and Diamond Jack

Prologue
Catch a Spider

CHAPTER 1

Washington, D.C.

THE CROSS house was twenty paces away and the proximity and sight of it made Gary Soneji's skin prickle. It was Victorian-style, white shingled, and extremely well kept. As Soneji stared across Fifth Street, he slowly bared his teeth in a sneer that could have passed for a smile. This was perfect. He had come here to murder Alex Cross and his family.

His eyes moved slowly from window to window, taking in everything from the crisp, white lace curtains to Cross's old piano on the sunporch, to a Batman and Robin kite stuck in the rain gutter of the roof. *Damon's kite*, he thought.

On two occasions he caught sight of Cross's elderly grandmother as she shuffled past one of the downstairs windows. Nana Mama's long, purposeless life would soon be at an end. That made him feel so much better. *Enjoy every moment—stop and smell the roses*, Soneji reminded himself. *Taste the roses, eat Alex Cross's roses—flowers, stems, and thorns.*

He finally moved across Fifth Street, being careful to stay in the shadows. Then he disappeared into the thick yews and forsythia bushes that ran like sentries alongside the front of the house.

He carefully made his way to a whitewashed cellar door, which was to one side of the porch, just off the kitchen. It had a Master padlock, but he had the door open in seconds.

He was inside the Cross house!

He was in the cellar: The cellar was a clue for those who collected them. The cellar was worth a thousand words. A thousand forensic pictures, too.

It was important to everything that would happen in the very near future. The Cross murders!

There were no large windows, but Soneji decided not to take any chances by turning on the lights. He used a Maglite flashlight. Just to look around, to learn a few more things about Cross and his family, to fuel his hatred, if that was possible.

The cellar was cleanly swept, as he had expected it would be. Cross's tools were haphazardly arranged on a pegged Masonite board. A stained Georgetown ball cap was hung on a hook. Soneji put it on his own head. He couldn't resist.

He ran his hands over folded laundry laid out on a long wooden table. He felt close to the doomed family now. He despised them more than ever. He felt around the hammocks of the old woman's bra. He touched the boy's small Jockey underwear. He felt like a total creep, and he loved it.

Soneji picked up a small red reindeer sweater. It would fit Cross's little girl, Jannie. He held it to his face and tried to smell the girl. He anticipated Jannie's murder and only wished that Cross would get to see it, too.

He saw a pair of Everlast gloves and black Pony shoes tied around a hook next to a weathered old punching bag. They belonged to Cross's son, Damon, who must be nine years old now. Gary Soneji thought he would punch out the boy's heart.

Finally, he turned off the flashlight and sat all alone in the dark. Once upon a time, he had been a famous kidnapper and murderer. It was going to happen again. He was coming back with a vengeance that would blow everybody's mind.

He folded his hands in his lap and sighed. He had spun his web perfectly.

Alex Cross would soon be dead, and so would everyone he loved.

CHAPTER 2

London

THE KILLER who was currently terrorizing Europe was named *Mr. Smith*, no first name. It was given to him by the Boston press, and then the police had obligingly picked it up all over the world. He accepted the name, as children accept the name given by their parents, no matter how gross or disturbing or pedestrian the name might be.

Mr. Smith—so be it.

Actually, he had a thing about names. He was obsessive about them. The names of his victims were burned into his mind and also into his heart.

First and foremost, there was Isabella Calais. Then came Stephanie Michaela Apt, Ursula Davies, Robert Michael Neel, and so many others.

He could recite the complete names backward and forward, as if they had been memorized for a history quiz or a bizarre round of Trivial Pursuit. That was the ticket—this case was *trivial pursuit*, wasn't it?

So far, no one seemed to understand, no one got it. Not the fabled FBI. Not the storied Interpol, not Scotland Yard or any of the local police forces in the cities where he had committed murders.

No one understood the secret pattern of the victims, starting with Isabella Calais in Cambridge, Massachusetts, March 22, 1993, and continuing today in London.

The victim of the moment was Drew Cabot. He was a chief inspector—of all the hopelessly inane things to do with your life. He was "hot" in London, having recently apprehended an IRA killer. His murder would electrify the town, drive everyone mad. Civilized and sophisticated London loved a gory murder as well as the next burg.

This afternoon Mr. Smith was operating in the tony, fashionable Knightsbridge section. He was there *to study the human race*—at least that was the way the newspapers described it. The press in London and across Europe also called him by another name—*Alien*. The *prevailing* theory was that Mr. Smith was an extraterrestrial. *No human could do the things that he did.* Or so they said.

Mr. Smith had to bend low to talk into Drew Cabot's ear, to be more intimate with his prey. He played music while he worked—all kinds of music. Today's selection was the overture to *Don Giovanni*. Opera buffa felt right to him.

Opera felt right for this *live* autopsy.

"Ten minutes or so after your death," Mr. Smith said, "flies will already have picked up the scent of gas accompanying the decomposition of your tissue. Green flies will lay the tiniest eggs within the orifices of your body. Ironically, the language reminds me of Dr. Seuss—'green flies and ham.' What could that mean? I don't know. It's a curious association, though."

Drew Cabot had lost a lot of blood, but he wasn't giving up. He was a tall, rugged man with silver-blond hair. A never-say-never sort of chap. The inspector shook his head back and forth until Smith finally removed his gag.

"What it is, Drew?" he asked. "Speak."

"I have a wife and two children. Why are you doing this to me? Why me?" he whispered.

"Oh, let's say because you're Drew. Keep it simple and unsentimental. You, Drew, are a piece of the puzzle."

He tugged the inspector's gag back into place. No more chitchat from Drew.

Mr. Smith continued with his observations as he made his next surgical cuts and *Don Giovanni* played on.

"Near the time of death, breathing will become strained, intermittent. It's exactly what you're feeling now, as if each breath could be your last. Cessation will occur within two or three minutes," whispered Mr. Smith, whispered the dreaded *Alien*. "Your life will end. May I be the first to congratulate you. I sincerely mean that, Drew. Believe it or not, *I envy you*. I wish I were Drew."

Part One
Train Station Murders

CHAPTER 3

"I AM the great Cornholio! Are you challenging me?
I am Cornholio!" the kids chorused and giggled.
Beavis and Butt-head strike again—in my neighborhood.

I bit my lip and decided to let it go. Why fight it?
Why fan the fires of preadolescence?

Damon, Jannie, and I were crowded into the front
seat of my old black Porsche. We needed to buy a new
car, but none of us wanted to part with the Porsche. We
were schooled in tradition, in the classics. We loved
the old car, which we had named "The Sardine Can"
and "Old Paintless."

Actually, I was preoccupied at twenty to eight in the
morning. Not a good way to start the day.

The night before, a thirteen-year-old girl from Ballou
High School had been found in the Anacostia
River. She had been shot, and then drowned. The gunshot
had been to her mouth. What the coroners call a
"hole in one."

A bizarre statistic was creating havoc with my
stomach and central nervous system. *There were now
more than a hundred unsolved murders of young,
inner-city women committed in just the past three
years*. No one had called for a major investigation.
No one in power seemed to care about dead black and
Hispanic girls.

As we drove up in front of the Sojourner Truth School, I saw Christine Johnson welcoming kids and their parents as they arrived, reminding everyone that this was a community with good, caring people. She was certainly one of them.

I remembered the very first time we met. It was the previous fall and the circumstances couldn't have been any worse for either of us.

We had been thrown together—*smashed* together someone said to me once—at the homicide scene of a sweet baby girl named Shanelle Green. Christine was the principal of the school that Shanelle attended, and where I was now delivering my own kids. Jannie was new to the Truth School this semester. Damon was a grizzled veteran, a fourth grader.

"What are you mischief makers gawking at?" I turned to the kids, who were looking back and forth from my face to Christine's as if they were watching a championship tennis match.

"We're *gawking* at you, Daddy, and you're *gawking* at Christine!" Jannie said and laughed like the wicked child-witch of the North that she can be sometimes.

"She's Mrs. Johnson to you," I said as I gave Jannie my best squinting evil eye.

Jannie shrugged off my baleful look and frowned at me as only she can. "I know that, Daddy. She's the *principal* of my school. I know exactly who she is."

My daughter already understood many of life's important connections and mysteries. I was hoping that maybe someday she would explain them to me.

"Damon, do you have a point of view we should hear?" I asked. "Anything you'd like to add? Care to share some good fellowship and wit with us this morning?"

My son shook his head no, but he was smiling, too. He liked Christine Johnson just fine. Everybody did. Even Nana Mama approved, which is unheard of, and actually worried me some. Nana and I never seemed to agree about *anything*, and it's getting worse with age.

The kids were already climbing out of the car, and Jannie gave me a kiss good-bye. Christine waved and walked over.

"What a fine, upstanding father you are," she said. Her brown eyes twinkled. "You're going to make some lady in the neighborhood very happy one of these days. Very good with children, reasonably handsome, driving a classy sports car. My, my, my."

"My, my, back at you," I said. To top everything off, it was a beautiful morning in the early June. Shimmering blue skies, temperature in the low seventies, the air crisp and relatively clean. Christine was wearing a soft beige suit with a blue shirt, and beige flat-heeled shoes. Be still my heart.

A smile slid across my face. There was no way to stop it, to hold it back, and besides I didn't want to. It fit with the fine day I was starting to have.

"I hope you're not teaching my kids that kind of cynicism and irony inside that fancy school of yours."

"Of course I am, and so are all my teachers. We speak Educanto with the best of them. We're trained in cynicism, and we're all experts in irony. More important, we're excellent skeptics. I have to get inside now, so we don't miss a precious moment of indoctrination time."

"It's too late for Damon and Jannie. I've already programmed them. A child is fed with milk and praise. They have the sunniest dispositions in the neighborhood, probably in all of Southeast, maybe in the entire city of Washington."

"Oh we've noticed that, and we accept the challenge. Got to run. Young minds to shape and change."

"I'll see you tonight?" I said as Christine was about to turn away and head toward the Sojourner Truth School.

"Handsome as sin, driving a nice Porsche, of course you'll see me tonight," she said. Then she turned away and headed toward the school.

We were about to have our first "official" date that night. Her husband, George, had died the previous winter, and now Christine felt she was ready to have dinner with me. I hadn't pushed her in any way, but I couldn't wait. Half a dozen years after the death of my wife, Maria, I felt as if I were coming out of a deep rut, maybe even a clinical depression. Life was looking as good as it had in a long, long time.

But as Nana Mama has often cautioned, "Don't mistake the edge of a rut for the horizon."

CHAPTER 4

*A*LEX CROSS *is a dead man. Failure isn't an option.*

Gary Soneji squinted through a telescopic sight he'd removed from a Browning automatic rifle. The scope was a rare beauty. He watched the oh-so-touching affair of the heart. He saw Alex Cross drop off his two brats and then chat with his pretty lady friend in front of the Sojourner Truth School.

Think the unthinkable, he prodded himself.

Soneji ground his front teeth as he scrunched low in the front seat of a black Jeep Cherokee. He watched Damon and Janelle scamper into the schoolyard, where they greeted their playmates with high and low fives. Years before he'd almost become famous for kidnapping two school brats right here in Washington. Those were the days, my friend! Those were the days.

For a while he'd been the dark star of television and newspapers all over the country. Now it was going to happen again. He was sure that it was. After all, it was only fair that he be recognized as the best.

He let the aiming post of the rifle sight gently come to rest on Christine Johnson's forehead. *There, there, isn't that nice.*

She had very expressive brown eyes and a wide smile that seemed genuine from this distance. She was tall, attractive, and had a commanding presence. *The school principal.* A few loose hairs lay curled on her cheek. It was easy to see what Cross saw in her.

What a handsome couple they made, and what a tragedy this was going to be, what a damn shame. Even with all the wear and tear, Cross still looked good, impressive, a little like Muhammad Ali in his prime. His smile was dazzling.

As Christine Johnson walked away and headed toward the red-brick school building, Alex Cross suddenly glanced in the direction of Soneji's Jeep.

The tall detective seemed to be looking right into the driver's side of the windshield. Right into Soneji's eyes.

That was okay. Nothing to worry about, nothing to fear. He knew what he was doing. He wasn't taking any risks. Not here, not yet.

It was all set to start in a couple of minutes, but in his mind it had already happened. It had happened a hundred times. He knew every single move from this point until the end.

Gary Soneji started the Jeep and headed toward Union Station. The scene of the crime-to-be, the scene of his masterpiece theater.

"Think the unthinkable," he muttered under his breath, "then *do* the unthinkable."

CHAPTER 5

AFTER THE last bell had rung and most of the kids were safe and sound in their classrooms, Christine Johnson took a slow walk down the long deserted corridors of the Sojourner Truth School. She did this almost every morning, and considered it one of her special treats to herself. You had to have treats sometimes, and this beat a trip to Starbucks for café latte.

The hallways were empty and pleasantly quiet—and always sparkling clean, as she felt a good school ought to be.

There had been a time when she and a few of her teachers had actually mopped the floors themselves, but now Mr. Gomez and a porter named Lonnie Walker did it two nights a week, every week. Once you got good people thinking in the right way, it was amazing how many of them agreed a school should be clean and safe, and were willing to help. Once people believed the right thing could actually happen, it often did.

The corridor walls were covered with lively, colorful artwork by the kids, and everybody loved the hope and energy it produced. Christine glanced at the drawings and posters every morning, and it was always something different, another child's perspective that caught her eye and delighted her inner person.

This particular morning, she paused to look at a simple yet dazzling crayon drawing of a little girl holding hands with her mommy and daddy in front of a new house. They all had round faces and happy smiles and a nice sense of purpose. She checked out a few illustrated stories: "Our Community," "Nigeria," "Whaling."

But she was out here walking for a different reason today. She was thinking about her husband, George, and how he died, and why. She wished she could bring him back and talk to him now. She wanted to hold George at least one more time. *Oh God, she needed to talk to him.*

She wandered to the far end of the hall to Room 111, which was light yellow and called *Buttercup*. The kids had named the rooms themselves, and the names changed every year in the fall. It was *their* school, after all.

Christine slowly and quietly opened the door a crack. She saw Bobbie Shaw, the second-grade teacher, scrubbing notes on the blackboard. Then she noticed row after row of mostly attentive faces, and among them Jannie Cross.

She found herself smiling as she watched Jannie, who happened to be talking to Ms. Shaw. Jannie Cross was so animated and bright, and she had such a sweet perspective on the world. She was a lot like her father. *Smart, sensitive, handsome as sin.*

Christine eventually walked on. Preoccupied, she found herself climbing the concrete stairs to the second floor. Even the walls of the stairwells were decorated with projects and brightly colored artwork, which was part of the reason most of the kids believed that this was "their school." Once you understood something was "yours," you protected it, felt a part of it. It was a simple enough idea, but one that the government in Washington seemed not to get.

She felt a little silly, but she checked on Damon, too. Of all the boys and girls at the Truth School, Damon was probably her favorite. He had been even before she met Alex. It wasn't just that Damon was bright, and verbal, and could be very charming—Damon was also a really good person. He showed it time and again with the other kids, with his teachers, and even when his little sister entered the school this past semester. He'd treated her like his best friend in the world—and maybe he already understood that *she was*.

Christine finally headed back to her office, where the usual ten-to-twelve-hour day awaited her. She was thinking about Alex now, and she supposed that was really why she had gone and looked in on his kids.

She was thinking that she wasn't looking forward to their dinner date tonight. She was afraid of tonight, a little panicky, and she thought she knew why.

CHAPTER 6

AT A little before eight in the morning, Gary Soneji strolled into Union Station, as if he owned the place. He felt tremendously good. His step quickened and his spirits seemed to rise to the height of the soaring train-station ceilings.

He knew everything there was to know about the famous train gateway for the capital. He had long admired the neoclassical facade that recalled the famed Baths of Caracalla in ancient Rome. He had studied the station's architecture for hours as a young boy. He had even visited the Great Train Store, which sold exquisite model trains and other railroad-themed souvenirs.

He could hear and feel the trains rattling down below. The marble floors actually shook as powerful Amtrak trains departed and arrived, mostly on schedule, too. The glass doors to the outside world *rumbled*, and he could hear the panes *clink* against their frames.

He loved this place, everything about it. It was truly magical. The key words for today were *train* and *cellar*, and only he understood why.

Information was power, and he had it all.

Gary Soneji thought that he might be dead within the next hour, but the idea, the image, didn't trouble him. Whatever happened was meant to, and besides, he

definitely wanted to go out with a bang, not a cowardly
whimper. And why the hell not? He had plans for a
long and *exciting career after his death.*

Gary Soneji was wearing a lightweight black jump-
suit with a red Nike logo. He carried three bulky bags.
He figured that he looked like just another Yuppified
traveler at the crowded train station. He appeared to be
overweight and his hair was gray, for the time being.
He was actually five foot ten, but the lifts in his shoes
got him up to six one today. He still had a trace of his
former good looks. If somebody had wanted to guess
his occupation, they might say *teacher.*

The cheap irony wasn't lost on him. He'd been a
teacher once, one of the worst ever. He had been *Mr.
Soneji—the Spider Man.* He had kidnapped two of his
own students.

He had already purchased his ticket for the Metroliner, but he didn't head for his train just yet.

Instead, Gary Soneji crossed the main lobby, hurrying away from the waiting room. He took a stairway
next to the Center Café and climbed to the balcony on
the second floor, which looked out on the lobby, about
twenty feet below.

He gazed down and watched the lonely people
streaming across the cavernous lobby. Most of these
assholes had no idea how undeservedly lucky they
were this particular morning. They would be safely on
board their little commuter trains by the time the "light
and sound" show began in just a few minutes.

What a beautiful, beautiful place this is, Soneji thought. How many times he'd dreamed about this scene.

This very scene at Union Station!

Long streaks and spears of morning sunlight shafted down through delicate skylights. They reflected off the walls and the high gilded ceiling. The main hall before him held an information booth, a magnificent electronic train arrival-and-departure board, the Center Café, Sfuzzi, and America restaurants.

The concourse led to a waiting area that had once been called "the largest room in the world." What a grand and historic venue he had chosen for today, his birthday.

Gary Soneji produced a small key from his pocket. He flipped it in the air and caught it. He opened a silver-gray metallic door that led into a room on the balcony.

He thought of it as *his room.* Finally, he had his own room—*upstairs* with everyone else. He closed the door behind him.

"Happy birthday, dear Gary, happy birthday to you."

CHAPTER 7

THIS WAS going to be incredible, beyond anything he'd attempted so far. He could almost do this next part blindfolded, working from memory. He'd done the drill so many times. In his imagination, in his dreams. He had been looking forward to this day for more than twenty years.

He set up a folding aluminum tripod mount inside the small room, and positioned a Browning rifle on it. The BAR was a dandy, with a milspec scoping device and an electronic trigger he had customized himself.

The marble floors continued to shake as his beloved trains entered and departed the station, huge mythical beasts that came here to feed and rest. There was nowhere he'd rather be than here. He loved this moment so much.

Soneji knew everything about Union Station, and also about mass murders conducted in crowded public places. As a boy, he had obsessed on the so-called "crimes of the century." He had imagined himself committing such acts and becoming feared and famous. He planned perfect murders, random ones, and then he began to carry them out. He buried his first victim on a relative's farm when he was fifteen. The body still hadn't been found, not to this day.

He *was* Charles Starkweather; he *was* Bruno Richard Hauptmann; he *was* Charlie Whitman. Except that he was much smarter than any of them; and he wasn't crazy like them.

He had even appropriated a name for himself: Soneji, pronounced *Soh-nee-gee*. The name had seemed scary to him even at thirteen or fourteen. It still did. *Starkweather, Hauptmann, Whitman, Soneji.*

He had been shooting rifles since he was a boy in the deep, dark woods surrounding Princeton, New Jersey. During the past year, he'd done more shooting, more hunting, more practicing than ever before. He was primed and ready for this morning. Hell, he'd been ready for years.

Soneji sat on a metal folding chair and made himself as comfortable as he could. He pulled up a battleship gray tarp that blended into the background of the train terminal's dark walls. He snuggled under the tarp. He was going to disappear, to be part of the scenery, *to be a sniper in a very public place. In Union Station!*

An old-fashioned-sounding train announcer was singing out the track and time for the next Metroliner to Baltimore, Wilmington, Philadelphia, and New York's Penn Station.

Soneji smiled to himself—*that was his getaway train.*

He had his ticket, and he still planned to be on it. No problem, just book it. He'd be on the Metroliner, or bust. Nobody could stop him now, except maybe Alex Cross, and even that didn't matter anymore. His plan had contingencies for every possibility, even his own death.

Then Soneji was lost in his thoughts. His memories were his cocoon.

He had been nine years old when a student named Charles Whitman opened fire out of a tower at the University of Texas, in Austin. Whitman was a former Marine, twenty-five years old. The outrageous, sensational event had galvanized him back then.

He'd collected every single story on the shootings, long pieces from *Time, Life, Newsweek*, the *New York Times, Philadelphia Inquirer, Times* of London, *Paris Match, Los Angeles Times, Baltimore Sun*. He still had the precious articles. They were at a friend's house, being held for posterity. They were *evidence—of past, present, and future crimes*.

Gary Soneji knew he was a good marksman. Not that he needed to be a crackerjack in this bustling crowd of targets. No shot he'd have to make in the train terminal would be over a hundred yards, and he was accurate at up to five hundred yards.

Now, I step out of my own nightmare and into the real world, he thought as the moment crystallized. A cold, hard shiver ran through his body. It was delicious, tantalizing. He peered through the Browning's telescope at the busy, nervous, milling crowd.

He searched for the first victim. *Life was so much more beautiful and interesting through a target scope.*

CHAPTER 8

YOU ARE *there.*

He scanned the lobby with its thousands of hurrying commuters and summer vacation travelers. Not one of them had a clue about his or her mortal condition at that very moment. People never seemed to believe that something horrible could actually happen to *them.*

Soneji watched a lively brat pack of students in bright blue blazers and starched white shirts. Preppies, goddamn preppies. They were giggling and running for their train with unnatural delight. He didn't like happy people at all, especially dumb-ass children who thought they had the world by the nuts.

He found that he could distinguish smells from up here: diesel fuel, lilacs and roses from the flower vendors, meat and garlic shrimp from the lobby's restaurants. The odors made him hungry.

The target circle in his customized scope had a black site post rather than the more common bull's-eye. He preferred the post. He watched a montage of shapes and motion and colors swim in and out of death's way. This small circle of the Grim Reaper was his world now, self-contained and mesmerizing.

Soneji let the aiming post come to rest on the broad, wrinkled forehead of a weary-looking businesswoman in her early to mid-fifties. The woman was thin and nervous, with haggard eyes, pale lips. "Say good night, Gracie," he whispered softly. "Good night, Irene. Good night, Mrs. Calabash."

He almost pulled the trigger, almost started the morning's massacre, then he eased off at the last possible instant.

Not worthy of the first shot, he thought, chastising himself for impatience. *Not nearly special enough. Just a passing fancy. Just another middle-class cow.*

The aiming post settled in and held as if by a magnet on the lower spine of a porter pushing an uneven load of boxes and suitcases. The porter was a tall, good-looking black—*much like Alex Cross*, Soneji thought. His dark skin gleamed like mahogany furniture.

That was the attraction of the target. He liked the image, but who would get the subtle, special message other than himself? No, he had to think of others, too. This was a time to be selfless.

He moved the aiming post again, the circle of death. There were an amazing number of commuters in blue suits and black wing tips. Business sheep.

A father and teenage son floated into the circle, as if they had been put there by the hand of God.

Gary Soneji inhaled. Then he slowly exhaled. It was his shooting ritual, the one he'd practiced for so many years alone in the woods. *He had imagined doing this so many times. Taking out a perfect stranger, for no good reason.*

He gently, very gently, pulled the trigger toward the center of his eye.

His body was completely still, almost lifeless. He could feel the faint pulse in his arm, the pulse in his throat, the approximate speed of his heartbeat.

The shot made a loud cracking noise, and the sound seemed to follow the flight of the bullet down toward the lobby. Smoke spiraled upward, inches in front of the rifle barrel. Quite beautiful to observe.

The teenager's head exploded inside the telescopic circle. Beautiful. The head flew apart before his eyes. The Big Bang in miniature, no?

Then Gary Soneji pulled the trigger a second time. He murdered the father before he had a chance to grieve. He felt absolutely nothing for either of them. Not love, not hate, not pity. He didn't flinch, wince, or even blink.

There was no stopping Gary Soneji now, no turning back.

CHAPTER 9

*R*USH HOUR! Eight-twenty A.M. Jesus God Almighty, no! A madman was on the loose inside Union Station.

Sampson and I raced alongside the double lanes of stalled traffic that covered Massachusetts Avenue as far as the eye could see. *When in doubt, gallop.* The maxim of the old Foreign Legion.

Car and truck drivers honked their horns in frustration. Pedestrians were screaming, walking fast, or running away from the train station. Police squad cars were on the scene everywhere.

Up ahead on North Capitol I could see the massive, all-granite Union Station terminal with its many additions and renovations. Everything was somber and gray around the terminal except the grass, which seemed especially green.

Sampson and I flew past the new Thurgood Marshall Justice Building. We heard gunshots coming from the station. They sounded distant, muffled by the thick stone walls.

"It's for goddamn real," Sampson said as he ran at my side. "He's here. No doubt about it now."

I knew he would be. An urgent call had come to my desk less than ten minutes earlier. I had picked up the phone, distracted by another message, a fax from Kyle Craig of the FBI. I was scanning Kyle's fax. He desperately needed help on his huge *Mr. Smith* case. He wanted me to meet an agent, Thomas Pierce. I couldn't help Kyle this time. I was thinking of getting the hell out of the murder business, not taking on more cases, especially a serious bummer like *Mr. Smith*.

I recognized the voice on the phone. "It's Gary Soneji, Dr. Cross. It really *is* me. I'm calling from Union Station. I'm just passing through D.C., and I hoped against hope that you'd like to see me again. Hurry, though. You'd better scoot if you don't want to miss me."

Then the phone went dead. Soneji had hung up. He loved to be in control.

Now, Sampson and I were sprinting along Massachusetts Avenue. We were moving a whole lot faster than the traffic. I had abandoned my car at the corner of Third Street.

We both wore protective vests over our sport shirts. We were "scooting," as Soneji had advised me over the phone.

"What the hell is he doing in there?" Sampson said through tightly gritted teeth. "That son of a bitch has always been crazy."

We were less than fifty yards from the terminal's glass-and-wood front doors. People continued to stream outside.

"He used to shoot guns as a boy," I told Sampson. "Used to kill pets in his neighborhood outside Princeton. He'd do sniper kills from the woods. Nobody ever solved it at the time. He told me about the sniping when I interviewed him at Lorton Prison. Called himself the pet assassin."

"Sounds like he graduated to people," Sampson muttered.

We raced up the long driveway, heading toward the front entrance of the ninety-year-old terminal. Sampson and I were moving, burning up shoe leather, and it seemed like an eternity since Soneji's phone call.

There was a pause in the shooting—then it began again. Weird as hell. It definitely sounded like rifle reports coming from inside.

Cars and taxis in the train terminal's driveway were backing out, trying to get away from the scene of gunfire and madness. Commuters and day travelers were still pushing their way out of the building's front doors. I'd never been involved with a sniper situation before.

In the course of my life in Washington, I'd been inside Union Station several hundred times. Nothing like this, though. Nothing even close to this morning.

"He's got himself trapped in there. Purposely trapped! Why the hell would he do that?" Sampson asked as we came up to the front doors.

"Worries me, too," I said. Why had Gary Soneji called me? Why would he effectively trap himself in Union Station?

Sampson and I slipped into the lobby of Union Station. The shooting from the balcony—from up high somewhere—suddenly started up again. We both went down flat on the floor.

Had Soneji already seen us?

CHAPTER 10

I KEPT my head low as my eyes scanned the huge and portentous train-station lobby. I was desperately looking for Soneji. Could he see me? One of Nana's sayings was stuck in my head: *Death is nature's way of saying "howdy."*

Statues of Roman legionnaires stood guard all around the imposing main hall of Union Station. At one time, politically correct Pennsylvania Railroad execs had wanted the warriors fully clothed. The sculptor, Louis Saint-Gaudens, had managed to sneak by every third statue in its accurate historical condition.

I saw three people already down, probably dead, on the lobby floor. My stomach dropped. My heart beat even faster. One of the victims was a teenage boy in cutoff shorts and a Redskins practice jersey. A second victim appeared to be a young father. Neither of them was moving.

Hundreds of travelers and terminal employees were trapped inside arcade shops and restaurants. Dozens of frightened people were squashed into a small Godiva Chocolates store and an open café called America.

The firing had stopped again. What was Soneji doing? And where was he? The temporary silence was maddening and spooky. There was supposed to be lots of noise here in the train terminal. Someone scraped a chair against the marble floor and the screeching sound echoed loudly.

I palmed my detective's badge at a uniformed patrolman who had barricaded himself behind an overturned café table. Sweat was pouring down the uniformed cop's face to the rolls of fat at his neck. He was only a few feet inside one of the doorways to the front lobby. He was breathing hard.

"You all right?" I asked as Sampson and I slid down behind the table. He nodded, grunted something, but I didn't believe him. His eyes were open wide with fear. I suspected he'd never been involved with a sniper either.

"Where's he firing from?" I asked the uniform. "You seen him?"

"Hard to tell. But he's up in there somewhere, that general area." He pointed to the south balcony that ran above the long line of doorways at the front of Union Station. Nobody was using the doors now. Soneji was in full control.

"Can't see him from down here." Sampson snorted at my side. "He might be moving around, changing position. That's how a good sniper would work it."

"Has he said anything? Made any announcements? Any demands?" I asked the patrolman.

"Nothing. He just started shooting people like he was having target practice. Four vics so far. Sucker can shoot."

I couldn't see the fourth body. Maybe somebody, a father, mother, or friend, had pulled one of the victims in off the floor. I thought of my own family. Soneji had come to our house once. And he had called me here—invited me to his coming-out party at Union Station.

Suddenly, from up on the balcony above us, a rifle barked! The flat crack of the weapon echoed off the train station's thick walls. This was a shooting gallery with human targets.

A woman screamed inside the America restaurant. I saw her go down hard as if she'd slipped on ice. Then there were lots of moans from inside the café.

The firing stopped again. *What the hell was he doing up there?*

"Let's take him out before he goes off again," I whispered to Sampson. "Let's do it."

CHAPTER 11

O UR LEGS pumping in unison, our breath coming in harsh rasps, Sampson and I climbed a dark marble stairway to the overhanging balcony. Uniformed officers and a couple of detectives were crouched in shooting positions up there.

I saw a detective from the train-station detail, which is normally a small-crimes unit. Nothing like this, nothing even close to dealing with a sharpshooting sniper.

"What do you know so far?" I asked. I thought the detective's name was Vincent Mazzeo, but I wasn't sure. He was pushing fifty and this was supposed to be a soft detail for him. I vaguely remembered that Mazzeo was supposed to be a pretty good guy.

"He's inside one of those anterooms. See that door over there? The space he secured has no roof cover. Maybe we can get at him from above. What do you think?"

I glanced up toward the high gilded ceiling. I remembered that Union Station was supposed to be the largest covered colonnade in the United States. It sure looked it. Gary Soneji had always liked a big canvas. He had another one now.

The detective took something out of his shirt pocket. "I got a master key. This gets us into some of the antechambers. Maybe the room he's in."

I took the key. He wasn't going to use it. He wasn't going to play the hero. He didn't want to meet up with Gary Soneji and his sharpshooter's rifle this morning.

Another burst of gunfire suddenly came from the anteroom.

I counted. There were six shots—just like the last time.

Like a lot of psychos, Soneji was into codes, magical words, numbers. I wondered about *sixes*. *Six, six, six?* The number hadn't come up in the past with him.

The shooting abruptly stopped again. Once more it was quiet in the station. My nerves were on edge, badly strained. There were too many people at risk here, too many to protect.

Sampson and I moved ahead. We were less than twenty feet from the anteroom where he was shooting. We pressed against the wall, Glocks out.

"You okay?" I whispered. We had been here before, similar bad situation, but that didn't make it any better.

"This is fun shit, huh, Alex? First thing in the morning too. Haven't even had my coffee and doughnut."

"Next time he fires," I said, "we go get him. He's been firing six shots each time."

"I noticed," Sampson said without looking at me. He patted my leg. We took in big sips of air.

We didn't have to wait long. Soneji began another volley of shots. *Six shots. Why six shots each time?*

He knew we'd be coming for him. Hell, he'd invited me to his shooting spree.

"Here we go," I said.

We ran across the marble-and-stone corridor. I took out the key to the anteroom, squeezed it between my index finger and thumb.

I turned the key.

Click!

The door wouldn't open! I jiggled the handle. Nothing.

"What the hell?" Sampson said behind me, anger in his voice. "What's wrong with the door?"

"I just locked it," I told him. "*Soneji left it open for us.*"

CHAPTER 12

DOWNSTAIRS, a couple and two small children started to run. They rushed toward the glass doors and possible freedom. One of the kids tripped and went down hard on his knee. The mother dragged him forward. It was terrifying to watch, but they made it.

The firing started again!

Sampson and I burst into the anteroom, both of us crouched low, our guns drawn.

I caught a glimpse of a dark gray tarp straight ahead.

A sniper rifle pointed out from the cover and camouflage of the tarp. Soneji was underneath, hidden from view.

Sampson and I fired. Half a dozen gunshots thundered in the close quarters. Holes opened in the tarp. The rifle was silent.

I rushed across the small anteroom and ripped away the tarp. I groaned—a deep, gut-wrenching sound.

No one was underneath the tarp. No Gary Soneji!

A Browning automatic rifle was strapped on a metal tripod. A timing device was attached to a rod and the trigger. The whole thing was customized. The rifle would fire at a programmed interval. Six shots, then a pause, then six more shots. No Gary Soneji.

I was already moving again. There were metal doors on the north and south walls of the small room. I yanked open the one closest to me. *I expected a trap.*

But the connecting space was empty. There was another gray metal door on the opposing wall. The door was shut. Gary Soneji still loved to play games. His favorite trick: He was the only one with the rules.

I rushed across the second room and opened door number two. Was that the game? A surprise? A booby prize behind either door one, two, or three?

I found myself peering inside another small space, another empty chamber. No Soneji. Not a sign of him anywhere.

The room had a metal stairway—it looked as if it went to another floor. Or maybe a crawl space above us.

I climbed the stairs, stopping and starting so he wouldn't get a clear shot from above. My heart was pounding, my legs trembling. I hoped that Sampson was close behind. I needed cover.

At the top of the stairway, a hatchway was open. No Gary Soneji here either. I had been lured deeper and deeper into some kind of trap, into his web.

My stomach was rolling. I felt a sharp pain building up behind my eyes. Soneji was still somewhere in Union Station. He had to be. *He'd said he wanted to see me.*

CHAPTER 13

SONEJI SAT as calm as a small-town banker, pretending to read the *Washington Post* on the 8:45 A.M. Metroliner to Penn Station in New York. His heart was still palpitating, but none of the excitement showed on his face. He wore a gray suit, white shirt, striped blue tie—he looked just like all the rest of the commuter assholes.

He had just tripped the light fantastic, hadn't he? He had gone where few others ever would have dared. He had just outdone the legendary Charles Whitman, and this was only the beginning of his prime-time exposure. There was a saying he liked a lot. *Victory belongs to the player who makes the next-to-last mistake.*

Soneji drifted in and out of a reverie in which he returned to his beloved woods around Princeton, New Jersey. He could see himself as a boy again. He remembered everything about the dense, uneven, but often spectacularly beautiful terrain. When he was eleven, he had stolen a .22-caliber rifle from one of the surrounding farms. He kept it hidden in a rock quarry near his house. The gun was carefully wrapped in an oilcloth, foil, and burlap bags. The .22-caliber rifle was the only earthly possession that he cared about, the only thing that was truly his.

He remembered how he would scale down a steep, very rocky ravine to a quiet place where the forest floor leveled off, just past a thick tangle of bayberry prickers. There was a clearing in the hollow, and this was the site of his secret, forbidden target practice in those early years. One day he brought a rabbit's head and a calico cat from the nearby Ruocco farm. There wasn't much that a cat liked more than a fresh rabbit's head. Cats were such little ghouls. Cats were like him. To this day, they were magical for him. The way they stalked and hunted was the greatest. That was why he had given one to Dr. Cross and his family.

Little Rosie.

After he had placed the severed bunny's head in the center of the clearing, he untied the neck of the burlap bag and let the kitty free. Even though he had punched a few airholes in the bag, the cat had almost suffocated. "Sic 'em. Sic the bunny!" he commanded. The cat caught the scent of the fresh kill and took off in a pouncing run. Gary put the .22 rifle on his shoulder and watched. He sighted on the moving target. He caressed the trigger of his deuce-deuce, and then he fired. He was learning how to kill.

You're such an addict! He chastised himself now, back in the present, on the Metroliner train. Little had changed since he'd been the original Bad Boy in the Princeton area. His stepmother—the gruesome and untalented whore of Babylon—used to lock him in the basement regularly back then. She would leave him alone in the dark, sometimes for as long as ten to twelve hours. He learned to love the darkness, to be the darkness. He learned to love the cellar, to make it his favorite place in the world.

Gary beat her at her own game.

He lived in the underworld, his own private hell. He truly believed he was the Prince of Darkness.

Gary Soneji had to keep bringing himself back to the present, back to Union Station and his beautiful plan. The Metro police were searching the trains.

The police were outside right now! Alex Cross was probably among them.

What a great start to things, and this was only the beginning.

CHAPTER 14

H E COULD see the police jackasses roaming the loading platforms at Union Station. They looked scared, lost and confused, and already half beaten. That was good to know, valuable information. It set a tone for things to come.

He glanced toward a businesswoman sitting across the aisle. She looked frightened, too. White knuckles showing on her clenched hands. Frozen and stiff, shoulders thrown back like a military school cadet.

Soneji spoke to her. He was polite and gentle, the way he could be when he wanted to. "I feel like this whole morning has to be a bad dream. When I was a boy, I used to go—*one, two, three, wake up!* I could bring myself out of a nightmare that way. It's sure not working today."

The woman across the aisle nodded as if he'd said something profound. He'd made a connection with her. Gary had always been able to do that, reach out and touch somebody if he needed to. He figured he needed to now. It would look better if he was talking to a travel companion when the police came through the train car.

"One, two, three, wake up," she said in a low voice across the aisle. "God, I hope we're safe down here. I hope they've caught him by now. Whoever, *whatever* he is."

"I'm sure they will," Soneji said. "Don't they always? Crazy people like that have a way of catching themselves."

The woman nodded once, but didn't sound too convinced. "They do, don't they. I'm sure you're right. I hope so. That's my prayer."

Two D.C. police detectives were stepping inside the club car. Their faces were screwed tight. Now it would get interesting. He could see more cops approaching through the dining car, which was just one car ahead. There had to be hundreds of cops inside the terminal now. It was showtime. Act Two.

"I'm from Wilmington, Delaware. Wilmington's home." Soneji kept talking to the woman. "Otherwise I'd have left the station already. That's if they let us back upstairs."

"They won't. I tried," the woman told him. Her eyes were frozen, locked in an odd place. He loved that look. It was hard for Soneji to glance away, to focus on the approaching policemen and the threat they might present.

"We need to see identifications from everyone," one of the detectives was announcing. He had a deep, nononsense voice that got everybody's attention. "Have IDs with pictures out when we come through. Thank you."

The two detectives got to his row of seats. This was it, wasn't it? Funny, he didn't feel much of anything. He was ready to take both cops out.

Soneji controlled his breathing and also his heart-

beat. *Control, that was the ticket.* He had control over
the muscles in his face, and especially his eyes. He'd
changed the color of his eyes for today. Changed his
fair color from blond to gray. Changed the shape of his
face. He looked soft, bloated, as harmless as your av-
erage traveling salesman.

He showed a driver's license and Amex card in the
name of Neil Stuart from Wilmington, Delaware. He
also had a Visa card and a picture ID for the Sports
Club in Wilmington. There was nothing memorable
about the way he looked. Just another business sheep.

The detectives were checking his ID when Soneji
spotted Alex Cross outside the train car. *Make my day.*

Cross was coming his way, and he was peering in
through the windows at passengers. Cross was still
looking pretty good. He was six three and well built.
He carried himself like an athlete, and looked younger
than forty-one.

*Jesus, Jesus, Jesus, what a mindblower. Trip the
goddamn light fantastic. I'm right here, Cross. You
could almost touch me if you wanted to. Look in at me.
Look at me, Cross. I command you to look at me now!*

The tremendous anger and fury growing inside him
was dangerous, Soneji knew. He could wait until Alex
Cross was right on top of him, then pop up and put half
a dozen shots into his face.

Six head shots. Each of the six would be well deserved for what Cross had done to him. Cross had ruined his life—no, Alex Cross had destroyed him. Cross
was the reason all of this was happening now. Cross

was to blame for the murders in the train station. It was all Alex Cross's fault.

Cross, Cross, Cross! Was this the end now? Was this the big finale? How could it be?

Cross looked so almighty as he walked, so above-the-fray. He had to give that to Cross. He was two or three inches taller than the other cops, smooth brown skin. *Sugar*—that's what his friend Sampson called him.

Well—he had a surprise for Sugar. Big unexpected surprise. Mindscrewer for the ages surprise.

If you catch me, Dr. Cross—you catch yourself. Do you understand that? Don't worry—you will soon enough.

"Thank you, Mr. Stuart," said the detective as he handed Soneji back his credit card and the Delaware driver's license.

Soneji nodded and offered a thin smile to the detective, and then his eyes flicked back to the window.

Alex Cross was right there. *Don't look so humble, Cross. You're not that great.*

He wanted to start shooting now. He was in heat. He experienced something like hot flashes. He could do Alex Cross right now. There was no doubt about it. He hated that face, that walk, everything about the doctor-detective.

Alex Cross slowed his step. Then Cross looked right in at him. He was five feet away.

Gary Soneji slowly moved his eyes up to Cross,

then very naturally over to the other detectives, then back to Cross.

Hello, Sugar.

Cross didn't recognize him. How could he? The detective looked right at his face—then he moved on. He kept on walking down the platform, picking up speed.

Cross had his back to him and it was an almost irresistibly inviting target. A detective up ahead was calling to him, motioning for Cross to come. He loved the idea of shooting Cross in the back. A cowardly murder, that was the best. That's what people really hated.

Then Soneji relaxed back into his train seat.

Cross didn't recognize me. I'm that good. I'm the best he's ever faced by far. I'll prove it, too.

Make no mistake about it. I will win.

I am going to murder Alex Cross and his family, and no one can stop it from happening.

CHAPTER 15

IT WAS past five-thirty in the evening before I even got to *think* about leaving Union Station. I'd been trapped inside all day, talking to witnesses, talking to Ballistics, the medical examiner, making rough sketches of the murder scene in my notepad. Sampson was pacing from about four o'clock on. I could see he was ready to blow out of there, but he was used to my thoroughness.

The FBI had arrived, and I'd gotten a call from Kyle Craig, who had stayed down in Quantico working on Mr. Smith. There was a mob of news reporters outside the terminal. How could it get any worse? I kept thinking, *the train has left the station*. It was one of those wordplays that gets in your head and won't leave.

I was bleary-eyed and bone weary by day's end, but also as sad as I remembered being at a homicide scene. Of course this was no ordinary homicide scene. I had put Soneji away, but somehow I felt responsible that he was out again.

Soneji was nothing if not methodical: He had wanted me at Union Station. Why, though? The answer to that question still wasn't apparent to me.

I finally snuck out of the station through the tunnels, to avoid the press and whatnot. I went home and showered and changed into fresh clothes.

That helped a little. I lay on my bed and shut my

eyes for ten minutes. I needed to clear my head of everything that had happened on this day.

It wasn't working worth a damn. I thought of calling off the night with Christine Johnson. A voice of warning was in my head. *Don't blow it. Don't scare her about The Job. She's the one.* I already sensed that Christine had problems with my work as a homicide detective. I couldn't blame her, especially not today.

Rosie the cat came in to visit. She cuddled against my chest. "Cats are like Baptists," I whispered to her. "You know they raise hell, but you can't ever catch them at it." Rosie purred agreement and chuckled to herself. We're friends like that.

When I finally came downstairs, I got "the business" from my kids. Even Rosie joined in the fun, racing around the living room like the family's designated cheerleader.

"You look so nice, Daddy. You look *beautiful*." Jannie winked and gave me the A-OK sign.

She was being sincere, but she was also getting a large charge out of my "date" for the night. She obviously delighted in the idea of my getting all dolled up just to see the principal from her school.

Damon was even worse. He saw me coming down the stairs and started giggling. Once he started, he couldn't stop. He mumbled, "beautiful."

"I'll get you for this," I told him. "Ten times over, maybe a hundred times. Wait until you bring somebody home to meet your pops. Your day will come."

"It's worth it," Damon said, and continued to laugh like the little madman that he can be. His antics got Jannie going so bad that she was finally rolling around on the carpet. Rosie hopped back and forth over the two of them.

I got down on the floor, growled like Jabba the Hut, and started wrestling with the kids. As usual, they were healing me. I looked over at Nana Mama, who was standing in the doorway between the kitchen and dining room. She was strangely quiet, not joining in as she usually does.

"You want some of this, old woman?" I said as I held Damon and lightly rubbed my chin against his head.

"No, no. But you're sure nervous as Rosie tonight," Nana said and finally started to laugh herself. "Why, I haven't seen you like this since you were around fourteen and off to see Jeanne Allen, if I remember the name correctly. Jannie's right, though, you do look, let's say, rather dashing."

I finally let Damon up off the floor. I stood and brushed off my snazzy dinner clothes. "Well, I just want to thank all of you for being so supportive in my time of need." I said it with false solemnity and a hurt look on my face.

"You're welcome!" they all chorused. "Have a good time on your date! You look *beautiful!*"

I headed out to the car, refusing to look back and give them the satisfaction of one final taunting grin or another rousing huzzah, I did feel better, though, strangely revived.

I had promised my family, but also myself, that I was going to have some kind of normal life now. Not just a career, not a series of murder investigations. And yet as I drove away from the house, my last thought was, *Gary Soneji is out there again. What are you going to do about it?*

For starters, I was going to have a terrific, peaceful, exciting dinner with Christine Johnson.

I wasn't going to give Gary Soneji another thought for the rest of the night.

I was going to be *dashing*, if not downright *beautiful*.

CHAPTER 16

KINKEAD'S IN Foggy Bottom is one of the best restaurants in Washington or anywhere else I've ever eaten. The food there might even be better than home, though I'd never tell Nana that. I was pulling out the stops tonight, trying to, anyway, doing the best I could.

Christine and I had agreed to meet at the bar around seven. I arrived a couple of minutes before seven, and she walked in right behind me. Soul mates. So began the first date.

Hilton Felton was playing his usual seductive-as-hell jazz piano downstairs, as he did six nights a week. On the weekends, he was joined by Ephrain Woolfolk on bass. Bob Kinkead was in and out of the kitchen, garnishing and inspecting every dish. Everything seemed just right. Couldn't be better.

"This is a really terrific place. I've been wanting to come here for years," Christine said as she looked around approvingly at the cherrywood bar, the sweeping staircase up to the main restaurant.

I had never seen her like this, all dressed up, and she was even more beautiful than I had thought. She had on a long black slip dress that showed off nicely toned shoulders. A cream-colored shawl fringed in black lace was draped over one arm. She wore a necklace made from an old-fashioned brooch that I liked a lot. She had on black flat-heeled pumps, but she was still nearly six feet tall. She smelled of flowers.

Her velvet brown eyes were wide and sparkling with the kind of delight I suspected she saw in her children at school, but which was absent on the faces of most adults. Her smile was effortless. She seemed happy to be here.

I wanted to look like anything but a homicide detective, so I had picked out a black silk shirt given to me by Jannie for my birthday. She called it my "cool guy shirt." I also wore black slacks, a snazzy black leather belt, black loafers. I already knew that I looked "beautiful."

We were escorted to a cozy little booth in the mezzanine section. I usually try to keep "physical allure" in its place, but heads turned as Christine and I walked across the dining room.

I'd completely forgotten what it was like to be out with someone and have that happen. I must admit that I sort of liked the feeling. I was remembering what it was like to be with someone you want to be with. I was also remembering what it was like to feel whole, or almost whole, or at least on the way to being whole again.

Our cozy booth overlooked Pennsylvania Avenue and also had a view of Hilton tinkering away at his piano. Kind of perfect.

"So how was your day?" Christine asked after we settled into the booth.

"Uneventful," I said and shrugged. "Just another day in the life of the DCPD."

Christine shrugged right back at me. "I heard something on the radio about a shooting at Union Station. Weren't you involved just a little bit with Gary Soneji at one point in your illustrious career?"

"Sorry, I'm off-duty now," I said to her. "I love your dress, by the way." *I also love that old brooch that you turned into a necklace. I like that you wore flats just in case I needed to be taller tonight, which I don't.*

"Thirty-one dollars," she said and smiled shyly, wonderfully. The dress looked like a million on her. I thought so anyway.

I checked her eyes to see if she was all right. It had been more than six months since her husband's death, but that isn't really a lot of time. She seemed fine to me. I suspected she'd tell me if that changed.

We picked out a nice bottle of merlot. Then we shared Ipswich clams, which were full belly and a little messy, but a good start to dinner at Kinkead's. For a main dish, I had a velvety salmon stew.

Christine made an even better choice. Lobster with buttery cabbage, bean puree, and truffle oil.

All the while we ate, the two of us never shut up. Not for a minute. I hadn't felt so free and easy around someone in a long, long time.

"Damon and Jannie say you're the best principal ever. They paid me a dollar each to say that. What's your secret?" I asked Christine at one point. I found that I was fighting off an urge simply to babble when I was around her.

Christine was thoughtful for a moment before she answered. "Well, I guess the easiest and maybe the truest answer is that it just makes me feel good to teach. The other answer I like goes something like this. If you're right-handed, it's really hard to write with your left hand. Well, most kids are *all left-handed* at first. I try to always remember that. That's my secret."

"Tell me about today at school," I said, staring into her brown eyes, unable not to.

She was surprised by my question. "You really want to hear about my day at school? Why?"

"I absolutely do. I don't even know why." *Except that I love the sound of your voice. Love the way your mind works.*

"Actually, today was a great day," she said, and her eyes lit up again. "You sure you want to hear this, Alex? I don't want to bore you with work stuff."

I nodded. "I'm sure. I don't ask a whole lot of questions I don't want to hear the answers to."

"Well then, I'll tell you about my day. Today, all the kids had to pretend they were in their seventies and eighties. The kids had to move a little more slowly than they're used to. They had to deal with infirmities, and being alone, and usually not being the center of attention. We call it '*getting under other people's skin,*' and we do it a lot at the Truth School. It's a great program and I had a great day, Alex. Thanks for asking. That's nice."

Christine asked me about my day again, and I told her at little as possible. I didn't want to disturb her, and I didn't need to relive the day myself. We talked about jazz, and classical music, and Amy Tan's latest novel. She seemed to know about everything, and was surprised I had read *The Hundred Secret Senses*, and even more surprised that I liked it.

She talked about what it was like for her growing up in Southeast, and she told me a big secret of hers: She told me about "Dumbo-Gumbo."

"All through grade-school days," Christine said, "I was Dumbo-Gumbo. That's what some of the other kids called me. I have big ears, you see. Like Dumbo the flying elephant."

She pulled back her hair. "Look."

"Very pretty," I said to her.

She laughed. "Don't blow your credibility. I *do* have big ears. And I do have this *big* smile, lots of teeth and *gums*."

"So some smart-ass kid came up with Dumbo-Gumbo?"

"My brother, Dwight, did it to me. He also came up with 'Gumbo Din.' He still hasn't said he's sorry."

"Well, I'm sorry for him. Your smile is dazzling, and your ears are just right."

She laughed again. I loved to hear her laugh. I loved everything about her actually. I couldn't have been happier with our first night out.

CHAPTER 17

THE TIME flew by like nothing at all. We talked about charter schools, a national curriculum, a Gordon Parks exhibit at the Corcoran, lots of silly stuff, too. I would have guessed it was maybe nine-thirty when I happened to glance at my watch. It was actually ten to twelve.

"It's a school night," Christine said. "I have to go, Alex. I really do. My coach will turn into a pumpkin and all that."

Her car was parked on Nineteenth Street and we walked there together. The streets were silent, empty, glittering under overhead lamps.

I felt as if I'd had a little too much to drink, but I knew I hadn't. I was feeling carefree, remembering what it was like to be that way.

"I'd like to do this again sometime. How about to-morrow night?" I said and started to smile. God, I liked the way this was going.

Suddenly, something was wrong. I saw a look I didn't like—sadness and concern. Christine peered into my eyes.

"I don't think so, Alex. I'm sorry," she said. "I'm re-ally sorry. I thought I was ready, but I guess maybe I'm not. There's a saying—scars grow with us."

I sucked in a breath. I wasn't expecting that. In fact, I don't remember ever having been so wrong about how I was getting along with someone. It was like a sudden punch to the chest.

"Thanks for taking me to just about the nicest restaurant I've ever been to. I'm really, really sorry. It's nothing that you did, Alex."

Christine continued to look into my eyes. She seemed to be searching for something, and I guess not finding it.

She got into her car without saying another word. She seemed to efficient suddenly, so in control. She started it up and drove away. I stood in the empty street and watched until her car's blazing brake lights disappeared.

It's nothing that you did, Alex. I could hear her words repeating in my head.

CHAPTER 18

BAD BOY was back in Wilmington, Delaware. He had work to do here. In some ways, this might even be the best part.

Gary Soneji strolled the well-lit streets of Wilmington, seemingly without a care in the world. Why should he worry? He was skillful enough at makeup and disguises to fool the stiffs living here in Wilmington. He'd fooled them in Washington, hadn't he?

He stopped and stared at a huge, red-type-on-white poster near the train station. "Wilmington—A Place to Be Somebody," it read. What a terrific, unintentional joke, he thought.

So was a three-story mural of bloated whales and dolphins that looked as if it had been stolen from some beach town in Southern California. Somebody ought to hire the Wilmington town council to work on *Saturday Night Live*. They were good, real good.

He carried a duffel bag, but didn't draw any attention to himself. The people he saw on his little walk looked as if they had outfitted themselves from the pages of the Sears catalog, circa 1961. Lots of twill that didn't exactly flatter girth; putrid-colored plaid; comfortable brown shoes on everybody.

He heard the grating mid-Atlantic accent a few times, too. "I've got to phewn heum" ("I've got to phone home"). A plain and ugly dialect for plain and ugly thoughts.

Jesus, what a place to have lived. How the hell had he survived during those sterile years? Why had he bothered to come back now? Well, he knew the answer to that question. Soneji knew why he'd come back.

Revenge.

Payback time.

He turned off North Street and onto his old street, Central Avenue. He stopped across from a white-painted brick house. He stared at the house for a long time. It was a modest Colonial, two stories. It had belonged to Missy's grandparents originally, and that was why she hadn't moved.

Click your heels together, Gary. Jesus, there's no place like home.

He opened his duffel bag and took out his weapon of choice. He was especially proud of this one. He'd been waiting for a long time to use it.

Gary Soneji finally crossed the street. He marched up to the front door as if he owned the place, just as he had four years ago, the last time he'd been here, the day Alex Cross had barged into his life along with his partner, John Sampson.

The door was unlocked—how sweet—his wife and daughter were waiting up for him, eating Poppycock and watching *Friends* on television.

"Hi. Remember me?" Soneji said in a soft voice.

They both started to scream.

His own sweet wife, Missy.

His darling little girl, Roni.

Screaming like strangers, because they knew him so well, and because they had seen his weapon.

CHAPTER 19

IF YOU ever began to face all the facts, you probably wouldn't get up in the morning. The war room inside police headquarters was filled beyond capacity with ringing telephones, percolating computers, state-of-the-art surveillance equipment. I wasn't fooled by all the activity or the noise. We were still nowhere on the shootings.

First thing, I was asked to give a briefing on Soneji. I was supposed to know him better than anyone else, yet somehow I felt that I didn't know enough, especially now. We had what's called a roundtable. Over the course of an hour, I shorthanded the details of his kidnapping of two children a few years earlier in Georgetown, his eventual capture, the dozens of interviews we'd had at Lorton Prison prior to his escape.

Once everybody on the task force was up to speed, I got back to work myself. I needed to find out who Soneji was, who he really was; and why he had decided to come back now; why he had returned to Washington.

I worked through lunch and never noticed the time. It took that long just to retrieve the mountain of data we had collected on Soneji. Around two in the afternoon, I found myself painfully aware of *pushpins* on the "big board," where we were collecting "important" information.

A war room just isn't a war room without pushpin maps and a large bulletin board. At the very top of our board was the name that had been given to the case by the chief of detectives. He had chosen "Web," since Soneji had already picked up the nickname "Spider" in police circles. Actually, I'd coined the nickname. It came out of the complex webs he was always able to spin.

One section of the big board was devoted to "civilian leads." These were mostly reliable eyewitness accounts from the previous morning at Union Station. Another section was "police leads," most of which were the detective's reports from the train terminal.

Civilian leads are "untrained eye" reports; police leads are "trained eye." The thread in all of the reports so far was that no one had a good description of what Gary Soneji looked like now. Since Soneji had demonstrated unusual skill with disguises in the past, the news wasn't surprising, but it was disturbing to all of us.

Soneji's personal history was displayed on another part of the board. A long, curling computer printout listed every jurisdiction where he had ever been charged with a crime, as well as several unsolved homicides that overlapped his early years in Princeton, New Jersey.

Polaroid pictures depicting the evidence we had so far were also pinned up. Captions had been written in marker on the photos. The captions read: "known skills, Gary Soneji"; "hiding locations, Gary Soneji";

"physical characteristics, Gary Soneji"; "preferred weapons, Gary Soneji."

There was a category for "known associates" on the board, but this was still bare. It was likely to remain that way. To my knowledge, Soneji had always worked alone. Was that assumption still accurate? I wondered. Had he changed since our last run-in?

Around six-thirty that night, I got a call from the FBI evidence labs in Quantico, Virginia. Curtis Waddle was a friend of mine, and knew how I felt about Soneji. He had promised he'd pass on information as fast as he got it himself.

"You sitting down, Alex? Or you pacing around with one of those insipid, state-of-the-artless cordless phones in your hand?" he asked.

"I'm pacing, Curtis. But I'm carrying around an old-fashioned phone. It's even black. Alexander Graham himself would approve."

The lab head laughed and I could picture his broad, freckled face, his frizzy red hair tied with a rubber band in a ponytail. Curtis loves to talk, and I've found you have to let him go on or he gets hurt and can even get a little spiteful.

"Good man, good man. Listen, Alex, I've got something here, but I don't think you're going to like it. I don't like it. I'm not even sure if we trust what we have."

I edged in a few words. "Uh, what do you have, Curtis?"

"The blood we found on the stock and barrel of the

rifle at Union Station? We've got a definite match on it. Though, as I said, I don't know if I trust what we have. Kyle agrees. Guess what? It's not Soneji's blood."

Curtis was right. I didn't like hearing that at all. I hate surprises in any murder investigation. "What the hell does that mean? Whose blood is it then, Curtis? You know yet?"

I could hear him sigh, then blow out air in a *whoosh*. "Alex, it's *yours*. Your blood was on the sniper rifle."

Part Two
Monster Hunt

CHAPTER 20

I T WAS rush hour in Penn Station in New York City when Soneji arrived. He was on time, right on schedule, for the next act. *Man, he had lived this exact moment a thousand times over before today.*

Legions of pathetic burnouts were on the way home, where they would drop onto their pillows (no goose down for these hard cases), sleep for what would seem like an instant, and then get back up the following morning and head for the trains again. Jesus—and they said *he* was crazy!

This was absolutely, positively, the best—he'd been dreaming of this moment for more than twenty years. *This very moment!*

He had planned to get to New York between five and five-thirty—and here he was. Heeere's Gary! He'd imagined himself, *saw* himself, coming up out of the deep dark tunnels at Penn Station. He knew he was going to be out-of-his-head furious when he got upstairs, too. Knew it before he began to hear the piped-in circus music, some totally insane John Philip Sousa marching band ditty, with an overlay of tinny-sounding train announcements.

"You may now board through Gate A to Track 8, Bay Head Junction," a fatherly voice proclaimed to the clueless.

All aboard to Bay Head Junction. All aboard, you pathetic morons, you freaking robots!

He checked out a poor moke porter who wore a dazed, flat look, as if life had left him behind about thirty years ago.

"You just can't keep a bad man down," Soneji said to the passing redcap. "You dig? You hear what I'm saying?"

"Fuck off," the redcap said. Gary Soneji snorted out a laugh. Man, he got such a kick out of the surly downtrodden. They were everywhere, like a league these days.

He stared at the surly redcap. He decided to punish him—to let him live.

Today's not your day to die. Your name stays in the Book of Life. Keep on walking.

He was furious—just as he knew he would be. He was seeing red. The blood rushing through his brain made a deafening, pounding sound. Not nice. Not conducive to sane, rational thought. *The blood? Had the bloodhounds figured it out yet?*

The train station was filled to the gills with shoving, pushing, and grumbling New Yorkers at their worst. These goddamn commuters were unbelievably aggressive and irritating.

Couldn't any of them see that? Well, hell, sure they could. And what did they do about it? They got even more aggressive and obnoxious.

None of them came close to approaching his own seething anger, though. Not even close. His hatred was pure. Distilled. He *was* anger. He did the things most of them only fantasized about. Their anger was fuzzy and unfocused, bursting in their bubbleheads. He saw anger clearly, and he acted upon it swiftly.

This was so fine, being inside Penn Station, creating another scene. He was really getting into the spirit now. He was noticing everything in full-blast, touchy-feely 3-D. Dunkin' Donuts, Knot Just Pretzels, Shoetrician Shoe Shine. The omnipresent rumble of the trains down below—it was just as he'd always imagined it.

He knew what would come next—and how it would all end.

Gary Soneji had a six-inch knife pressed against his leg. It was a real collector's item. Had a mother-of-pearl handle and a tight serpentine blade on both sides. "An ornate knife for an ornate individual," a greasy salesman had told him once upon a long time ago. "Wrap it up!" he'd said. Had it ever since. For special occasions like today. Or once to kill an FBI agent named Roger Graham.

He passed Hudson News, with all of its glossy magazine faces staring out at the world, staring at him, trying to work their propaganda. He was still being shoved and elbowed by his fellow commuters. Man, didn't they ever stop?

Wow! He saw a character from his dreams, from way back when he was a kid. There was *the guy*. No doubt about it. He recognized the face, the way the guy held his body, everything about him. *It was the guy in the gray-striped business getup, the one who reminded him of his father.*

"You've been asking for this for a long time!" Soneji growled at Mr. Gray Stripes. "You asked for this."

He drove the knife blade forward, felt it sink into flesh. It was just as he had imagined it.

The businessman saw the knife plunge near his heart. A frightened, bewildered look crossed his face. Then he fell to the station floor, stone cold dead, his eyes rolled back and his mouth frozen in a silent scream.

Soneji knew what he had to do next. He pivoted, danced to his left, and cut a second victim who looked like a slacker type. The guy wore a "Naked Lacrosse" T-shirt. The details didn't matter, but some of them stuck in his mind. He cut a black man selling *Street News*. Three for three.

The thing that really mattered was *the blood*. Soneji watched as the precious blood spilled onto the dirty, stained, and mottled concrete floor. It spattered the clothes of commuters, pooled under the bodies. The blood was a clue, a Rorschach test for the police and FBI hunters to analyze. The blood was there for Alex Cross to try and figure out.

Gary Soneji dropped his knife. There was incredible confusion, shrieking everywhere, panic in Penn Station that finally woke the walking dead.

He looked up at the maze of maroon signs, each

with neat Helvetic lettering: *Exit 31st St., Parcel Checking, Visitor Information, Eighth Avenue Subway.*

He knew the way out of Penn Station. It was all pre-ordained. He had made this decision a thousand times before.

He scurried back down into the tunnels again. No one tried to stop him. He was the Bad Boy again. Maybe his stepmother had been right about that. His *punishment* would be to ride the New York subways.

Brrrr. Scar-ry!

CHAPTER 21

SEVEN P.M. that evening. I was caught in the strangest, most powerful epiphany. I felt that I was outside myself, *watching myself.* I was driving by the Sojourner Truth School, on my way home. I saw Christine Johnson's car and stopped.

I got out of my car and waited for her. I felt incredibly vulnerable. A little foolish. I hadn't expected Christine to be at the school this late.

At quarter past seven, she finally wandered out of the school. I couldn't catch my breath from the instant I spotted her. I felt like a schoolboy. Maybe that was all right, maybe it was good. At least I was feeling again.

She looked as fresh and attractive as if she'd just arrived at the school. She had on a yellow-and-blue flowered dress cinched around her narrow waist. She wore blue sling-back heels and carried a blue bag over one shoulder. The theme song from *Waiting to Exhale* floated into my head. I was waiting, all right.

Christine saw me, and she immediately looked troubled. She kept on walking, as if she were in a hurry to be somewhere else, anywhere else but here.

Her arms were crossed across her chest. *A bad sign*, I thought. The worst possible body language. Protective and fearful. One thing was clear already: Christine Johnson didn't want to see me.

I knew I shouldn't have come, shouldn't have

stopped, but I couldn't help myself. I needed to understand what had happened when we left Kinkead's. Just
that, nothing more. A simple, honest explanation, even
if it hurt.

I sucked in a deep breath and walked up to her. "Hi,"
I said, "you want to take a walk? It's a nice night." I almost couldn't speak, and I am never at a loss for
words.

"Taking a break in one of your usual twenty-hour
workdays?" Christine half smiled, tried to anyway.

I returned the smile, felt queasy all over. I shook my
head. "I'm off work."

"I see. Sure, we can walk a little bit, a few minutes.
It is a nice night, you're right."

We turned down F Street and entered Garfield Park,
which was especially pretty in the early summer. We
walked in silence. Finally we stopped near a ballfield
swarming with little kids. A frenzied baseball game
was in progress.

We weren't far from the Eisenhower Freeway, and
the *whoosh* of rush-hour traffic was steady, almost
soothing. Tulip poplars were in bloom, and coral honey-
suckle. Mothers and fathers were playing with their
kids; everybody in a nice mood tonight.

This had been my neighborhood park for almost
thirty years, and during the daylight hours it can almost be idyllic. Maria and I used to come here all the
time when Damon was a toddler and she was pregnant
with Jannie. Much of that is starting to fade away now,
which is probably a good thing, but it's also sad.

Christine finally spoke. "I'm sorry, Alex." She had been staring at the ground, but now she raised her lovely eyes to mine. "About the other night. The bad scene at my car. I guess I panicked. To be honest, I'm not even sure what happened."

"Let's be honest," I said. "Why not?"

I could tell this was hard for her, but I needed to know how she felt. I needed more than she'd told me outside the restaurant.

"I want to try and explain," she said. Her hands were clenched. One of her feet was tapping rapidly. Lots of bad signs.

"Maybe it's all my fault," I said. "I'm the one who kept asking you to dinner until—"

Christine reached out and covered my hand with hers. "Please let me finish," she said. The half smile came again. "Let me try to get this out once and for all. I was going to call you anyway. I was planning to call you tonight. I would have.

"You're nervous now, and so am I. God, am I nervous," she said quietly. "I know I've hurt your feelings, and I don't like that. It's the last thing I meant to do. You don't deserve to be hurt."

Christine was shivering a little. Her voice was shaking, too, as she spoke. "Alex, my husband died because of the kind of violence you have to live with every day. You accept that world, but I don't think I can. I'm just not that kind of person. I couldn't bear to lose someone else I was close to. Am I making sense to you? I'm feeling a little confused."

Everything was becoming clearer to me now. Christine's husband had been killed in December. She said that there had been serious problems in the marriage, but she loved him. She had seen him shot to death in their home, seen him die. I had held her then. I was part of the murder case.

I wanted to hold her again, but I knew it was the wrong thing to do. She was still hugging herself tightly. I understood her feelings.

"Please listen to me, Christine. I'm not going to die until probably in my late eighties. I'm too stubborn and ornery to die. That would give us longer together than either of us has been alive so far. Forty-plus years. It's also a long time to avoid each other."

Christine shook her head a little. She continued to look into my eyes. Finally, a smile peeked through.

"I *do* like the way your crazy mind works. One minute, you're Detective Cross—the next minute you're this very open, very sweet child." She put her hands up to her face. "Oh, God, I don't even know what I'm *saying*."

Everything inside me said to do it, every instinct, every feeling. I slowly, carefully, reached out and took Christine into my arms. She fit so right. I could feel myself melting and I liked it. I even liked that my legs felt shaky and weak.

We kissed for the first time and Christine's mouth was soft and very sweet. Her lips pushed against mine. She didn't pull away, as I'd expected she might. I ran the tips of my fingers along one cheek, then the other.

Her skin was smooth and my fingers tingled at the tips. It was as if I had been without air for a long, long time and suddenly could breathe again. I could breathe. I felt alive.

Christine had shut her eyes, but now she opened them. Our eyes met, and held. "Just like I imagined it," she whispered, "times about four hundred and fifty."

Then the worst thing imaginable happened—my pager *beeped*.

CHAPTER 22

895 • James Patterson

A T SIX o'clock in New York City, police cruisers and EMS van sirens were wailing everywhere in the always highly congested five-block radius around Penn Station. Detective Manning Goldman parked his dark blue Ford Taurus in front of the post office building on Eighth Avenue and ran toward the multiple-murder scene.

People stopped walking on the busy avenue to watch Goldman. Heads turned everywhere, trying to find out what was going on, and how this running man might fit in.

Goldman had long, wavy caramel-and-gray hair and a gray goatee. A gold stud glinted from one earlobe. Goldman looked more like an aging rock or jazz musician than a homicide detective.

Goldman's partner was a first-year detective named Carmine Groza. Groza had a strong build and wavy black hair, and reminded people of a young Sylvester Stallone, a comparison he hated. Goldman rarely talked to him. In his opinion, Groza had never uttered a single word worth listening to.

Groza nonetheless followed close behind his fifty-eight-year-old partner, who was currently the oldest Manhattan homicide detective working the streets, possibly the smartest, and definitely the meanest, grumpiest bastard Groza had ever met.

Goldman was known to be somewhere to the right of Pat Buchanan and Rush Limbaugh when it came to politics but, like most rumors, or what he called "caricature assassinations," this one was off the mark. On certain issues—the apprehension of criminals, the rights of criminals versus the rights of other citizens, and the death penalty, Goldman was definitely a radical conservative. He knew that anyone with half a brain who worked homicide for a couple of hours would come to exactly the same conclusions that he had. On the other hand, when it came to women's right to choose, same-sex marriages, or even Howard Stern, Goldman was as liberal as his thirty-year-old son, who just happened to be a lawyer with the ACLU. Of course, Goldman kept that to himself. The last thing he wanted was to ruin his reputation as an insufferable bastard. If he did that, he might have to talk to up-and-coming young assholes like "Sly" Groza.

Goldman was still in good shape—better than Groza, with his steady diet of fast foods and high-octane colas and sugary teas. He ran against the tide of people streaming out of Penn Station. The murders, at least the ones he knew about so far, had taken place in and around the main waiting area of the train station.

The killer had chosen the rush hour for a reason, Goldman was thinking as the train-station waiting area came into view. Either that, or the killer just happened to go wacko at a time when the station was jam-packed with victims-to-be.

So what brought the wacko to Penn Station at rush

hour? Manning Goldman wondered. He already had one scary theory that he was keeping to himself so far.

"Manning, you think he's still in here someplace?" Groza asked from behind.

Groza's habit of calling people by their first name, as if they were all camp counselors together, really got under his skin.

Goldman ignored his partner. No, he didn't believe the killer was still in Penn Station. The killer was on the loose in New York. That bothered the hell out of him. It made him sick to his stomach, which wasn't all that hard these days, the past couple of years, actually.

Two pushcart vendors were artfully blocking the way to the crime scene. One cart was called Montego City Slickers Leather, the other From Russia With Love. He wished they would go back to Jamaica and Russia, respectively.

"NYPD. Make way. Move these ashcarts!" Goldman yelled at the vendors.

He pushed his way through the crowd of onlookers, other cops, and train-station personnel who were gathered near the body of a black man with braided hair and tattered clothing. Bloodstained copies of *Street News* were scattered around the body, so Goldman knew the dead man's occupation and his reason for being at the train station.

As he got up close, he saw that the victim was probably in his late twenties. There was an unusual amount of blood. Too much. The body was surrounded by a bright red pool.

Goldman walked up to a man in a dark blue suit with a blue-and-red Amtrak pin prominent on his lapel.

"Homicide Detective Goldman," he said, flashing his shield. "Tracks ten and eleven." Goldman pointed at one of the overhead signs. "What train would have come in on those tracks—just before the knifings?"

The Amtrak manager consulted a thick booklet he kept in his breast pocket.

"The last train on ten . . . that would have been the Metroliner from Philly, Wilmington, Baltimore, originating in Washington."

Goldman nodded. It was exactly what he'd been afraid of when he'd heard that a spree killer had struck at the train station, and that he was able to get away. That fact meant he was clearheaded. The killer had a plan in mind.

Goldman suspected that the Union Station and Penn Station killer might be one and the same—and that now the maniac was here in New York.

"You got any idea yet, Manning?" Groza was yapping again.

Goldman finally spoke to his partner without looking at him. "Yeah, I was just thinking that they've got earplugs, bunghole plugs, so why not *mouth* plugs."

Then Manning Goldman went to scare up a public phone. He had to make a call to Washington, D.C. He believed that Gary Soneji had come to New York. Maybe he was on some kind of twenty- or thirty-city spree killer tour.

Anything was a possibility these days.

CHAPTER 23

I ANSWERED my pager and it was disturbing news from the NYPD. There had been another attack at a crowded train station. It kept me at work until well past midnight.

Gary Soneji was probably in New York City. Unless he had already moved on to another city he'd targeted for murder. Boston? Chicago? Philadelphia?

When I got home, the lights were off. I found lemon meringue pie in the refrigerator and finished it off. Nana had a story about Oseola McCarty attached to the fridge door. Oseola had washed clothes for more than fifty years in Hattiesburg, Mississippi. She had saved $150,000 and donated it to the University of Southern Mississippi. President Clinton had invited her to Washington and given her the Presidential Citizens Medal.

The pie was excellent, but I needed something else, another kind of nourishment. I went to see my shaman.

"You awake, old woman?" I whispered at Nana's bedroom door. She always keeps it ajar in case the kids need to talk or cuddle with her during the night. *Open twenty-four hours, just like 7-Eleven,* she always says. It was like that when I was growing up, too.

"That depends on your intentions," I heard her say in the dark. "Oh, *is that you, Alex?*" she cackled and had a little coughing spell.

"Who else would it be? You tell me that? In the middle of the night at your bedroom door?"

"It could be anyone. Hugger-mugger. Housebreaker in this dangerous neighborhood of ours. Or one of my gentlemen admirers."

It goes like that between us. Always has, always will.

"You have any particular boyfriends you want to tell me about?"

Nana cackled again. "No, but I suspect you have a girlfriend you want to talk to me about. Let me get decent. Put on some water for my tea. There's lemon meringue pie in the fridge, at least there *was* pie. You *do* know that I have gentlemen admirers, Alex?"

"I'll put on the tea," I said. "The lemon meringue has already gone to pie heaven."

A few minutes passed before Nana appeared in the kitchen. She was wearing the cutest housedress, blue stripes with big white buttons down the front. She looked as if she were ready to begin her day at half past twelve in the morning.

"I have two words for you, Alex. Marry her."

I rolled my eyes. "It's not what you think, old woman. It's not that simple."

She poured some steaming tea for herself. "Oh, it is absolutely that simple, granny son. You've got that spring in your step lately, a nice gleam in your eyes. You're *long gone*, mister. You're just the last one to hear about it. Tell me something. This is a serious question."

I sighed. "You're still a little high from your sweet dreams. What? Ask your silly question."

"Well, it's this. If I was to charge you, say, ninety dollars for our sessions, *then* would you be more likely to take my fantastic advice?"

We both laughed at her sly joke, her unique brand of humor.

"Christine doesn't want to see me."

"Oh, dear," Nana said.

"Yeah, oh, dear. She can't see herself involved with a homicide detective."

Nana smiled. "The more I hear about Christine Johnson, the more I like her. Smart lady. Good head on those pretty shoulders."

"Are you going to let me talk?" I asked.

Nana frowned and gave me her serious look. "You always get to say what you want, just not at the exact moment you want to say it. Do you love this woman?"

"From the first time I saw her, I felt something extraordinary. Heart leads head. I know that sounds crazy."

She shook her head and still managed to sip steaming hot tea. "Alex, as smart as you are, you sometimes seem to get everything backwards. You don't sound crazy at all. You sound like you're better for the first time since Maria died. Will you look at the evidence that we have here? You have a spring back in your step again. Your eyes are bright and smiling. You're even being nice to me lately. Put it all together—your heart is working again."

"She's afraid that I could die on the job. Her husband was murdered, remember?"

Nana rose from her chair at the kitchen table. She shuffled around to my side, and she stood very close to me. She was so much smaller than she used to be, and that worried me. I couldn't imagine my life without her in it.

"I love you, Alex," she said. "Whatever you do, I'll still love you. *Marry her.* At least live with Christine." She laughed to herself. "I can't believe I said that."

Nana gave me a kiss, and then headed back to bed.

"I *do too* have suitors," she called from the hall.

"Marry one," I called back at her.

"I'm not in love, lemon meringue man. You are."

CHAPTER 24

FIRST THING in the morning, 6:35 to be exact, Sampson and I took the Metroliner to New York's Penn Station. It was almost as fast as driving to the airport, parking, finagling with the airlines—and besides, I wanted to do some thinking about *trains*.

A theory that Soneji was the Penn Station slasher had been advanced by the NYPD. I'd have to know more about the killings in New York, but it was the kind of high-profile situation that Soneji had been drawn to in the past.

The train ride was quiet and comfortable, and I had the opportunity to think about Soneji for much of the trip. What I couldn't reconcile was why Soneji was committing crimes that appeared to be acts of desperation. They seemed suicidal to me.

I had interviewed Soneji dozens of times after I had apprehended him a few years ago. That was the Dunne-Goldberg case. I certainly didn't believe he was suicidal then. He was too much of an egomaniac, even a megalomaniac.

Maybe these were copycat crimes. *Whatever* he was doing now didn't track. *What had changed? Was it Soneji who was doing the killings? Was he pulling some kind of trick or stunt? Could this be a clever trap? How in hell had he gotten my blood on the sniper's rifle in Union Station?*

*What kind of trap? For what reason? Soneji obsessed
on his crimes. Everything had a purpose with him.*

*So why kill strangers in Union and Penn Stations?
Why choose railroad stations?*

"Oh ho, smoke's curling out of your forehead,
Sugar. You aware of that?" Sampson looked over at me
and made an announcement to the nice folks seated
around us in the train car.

"Little wisps of white smoke! See? Right *here*. And
here."

He leaned in close and started hitting me with his
newspaper as if he were trying to put out a small fire.

Sampson usually favors a cool deadpan delivery to
slapstick. The change of pace was effective. We both
started to laugh. Even the people sitting around us
smiled, looking up from their newspapers, coffees,
laptop computers.

"Phew. Fire seems to be out," Sampson said and
chuckled deeply. "Man, your head is *hot* as Hades to
the touch. You must have been brainstorming some
powerful ideas. Am I right about that?"

"No, I was thinking about Christine," I told Sampson.

"You lying sack. You *should* have been thinking
about Christine Johnson. Then I would have had to
beat the fire out someplace else. How you two doing?
If I might be so bold as to ask."

"She's great, she's the best, John. Really something
else. She's smart and she's funny. Ho ho, ha ha."

"And she's almost as good-looking as Whitney

Houston, and she's sexy as hell. But none of that answers my question. What's happening with you two? You trying to hide your love on me? My spy, Ms. Jannie, told me you had a date the other night. Did you have a big date and not tell me about it?"

"We went to Kinkead's for dinner. Had a good time. Good food, great company. One little minor problem, though: She's afraid I'm going to get myself killed, so she doesn't want to see me anymore. Christine's still mourning her husband."

Sampson nodded, slid down his shades to check me out sans light filtration. "That's interesting. Still mourning, huh? Proves she's a good lady. By the by, since you brought up the forbidden topic, something I should tell you, all-star. You ever get capped in action, your family will mourn you for an indecent length of time. Myself, I would carry the torch of grief up to and through the funeral services. That's it, though. Thought you should know. So, are you two star-crossed lovers going to have another date?"

Sampson liked to talk as if we were girlfriends in a Terry McMillan novel. We could be like that sometimes, which is unusual for men, especially two tough guys like us. He was on a roll now. "I think you two are so cute together. Everybody does. Whole town is talking. The kids, Nana, your aunties."

"They are, are they?"

I got up and sat down across the aisle from him. Both seats were empty. I spread out my notes on Gary Soneji and started to read them again.

"Thought you would never get the hint," Sampson said as he stretched his wide body across both seats.

As always, there was nothing like working a job with him. Christine was wrong about my getting hurt. Sampson and I were going to live forever. We wouldn't even need DHEA or melatonin to help.

"We're going to get Gary Soneji's ass in a sling. Christine's going to fall hard for you, like you obviously already fell for her. Everything will be beautiful, Sugar. Way it has to be."

I don't know why, but I couldn't quite make myself believe that.

"I know you're thinking negative shit already," Sampson said without even looking over at me, "but just watch. Nothing but happy endings this time."

CHAPTER 25

S AMPSON AND I arrived in New York City around nine o'clock in the morning. I vividly remembered an old Stevie Wonder tune about getting off the bus in New York for the first time. The mixture of hopes and fears and expectations most people associate with the city seems a universal reaction.

As we climbed the steep stone steps from the underground tracks in Penn Station, I had an insight about the case. If it was right, it would definitely tie Soneji to both train-station massacres.

"I might have something on Soneji," I told Sampson as we approached the bright lights gleaming at the top of the stairs. He turned his head toward me but kept on climbing.

"I'm not going to guess, Alex, because my mind doesn't ever go where yours does." Then he mumbled, "Thank the Lord and Savior Jesus for that. Addlehead brother."

"You trying to keep me amused?" I asked him. I could hear music coming from the main terminal now—it sounded like Vivaldi's *The Four Seasons*.

"Actually, I'm trying not to let the fact that Gary Soneji is on this current mad-ass rampage upset my equilibrium or otherwise depress the hell out of me. Tell me what you're thinking."

"When Soneji was at Lorton Prison, and I inter-

viewed him, he always talked about how his stepmother kept him in the cellar of their house. He was
obsessed about it."

Sampson's head bobbed. "Knowing Gary as we do,
I can't completely blame the poor woman."

"She would keep him down there for hours at a time,
sometimes a whole day, if his father happened to be
away from home. She kept the lights off, but he
learned to hide candles. He would read by candlelight
about kidnappers, rapists, mass murderers, all the other
bad boys."

"And so, Dr. Freud? These mass killers were his
boyhood role models?"

"Something like that. Gary told me that when he
was in the cellar, he would fantasize about committing
murders and other atrocities—*as soon as he was let
out.* His idée fixe was that release from the cellar
would give him back his freedom and power. He'd sit
in the cellar obsessing on what he was going to do as
soon as he got out. You happen to notice any cellarlike
locations around here? Or maybe at Union Station?"

Sampson showed his teeth, which are large and very
white, and can give you the impression that he likes
you maybe more than he does. "The train tunnels represent the cellar of Gary's childhood house, right?
When he gets out of the tunnels, all hell breaks loose.
He finally takes his revenge on the world."

"I think that's part of what's going on," I said. "But
it's never that simple with Gary. It's a start anyway."

We had reached the main level of Penn Station. This

was probably how it had been when Soneji arrived here the night before. More and more I was thinking that the NYPD had it right. Soneji could definitely be the Penn Station killer, too.

I saw a mob of travelers lingering beneath the flipping numbers of the Train Departures board. I could almost see Gary Soneji standing where I was now, taking it all in—*released from the cellar to be the Bad Boy again! Still wanting to do famous crimes and succeeding beyond his craziest dreams.*

"Dr. Cross, I presume."

I heard my name as Sampson and I wandered into the brightly lit waiting area of the station. A bearded man with a gold ear stud was smiling at his small joke. He extended his hand.

"I'm Detective Manning Goldman. Good of you to come. Gary Soneji was here yesterday." He said it with absolute certainty. The fact that he couldn't prove it to me didn't seem to bother him.

"We have no proof of that. He wasn't fingerprinted by us," said his partner, who had just joined us. This other detective was dressed in a blue pin-striped suit, white shirt, tightly knotted rep tie. He looked like a successful Wall Street stockbroker. He definitely didn't look like any New York City cop I had ever met before.

"Detective John Moody," he said and also shook my hand. "We appreciate your coming up here, Dr. Cross."

"We don't actually have a positive ID," Goldman continued. His bearded partner never said a word. "And yet, we don't have a good ID of him—each witness gives a different description—so, hell, it just makes sense to me. You have any ideas, Dr. Cross?"

Detective Goldman was good at making up his mind. He annoys people, especially the police, Dr. Cross.

CHAPTER 26

SAMPSON AND I shook hands with Goldman and also his partner, a younger detective who appeared to defer to Goldman. Manning Goldman wore a bright blue sport shirt with three of the buttons undone. He had on a ribbed undershirt that exposed silver and reddish gold chest hairs sprouting toward his chin. His partner was dressed from head to toe in black. Talk about your odd couples, but I still preferred Oscar and Felix.

Goldman started in on what he knew about the Penn Station stabbings. The New York detective was high-energy, a rapid-fire talker. He used his hands constantly, and appeared confident about his abilities and opinions. The fact that he'd called us in on his case was proof of that. He wasn't threatened by us.

"We know that the killer came up the stairs at track ten here, just like the two of you just did. We've talked to three witnesses who may have seen him on the Metroliner from Washington," Goldman explained. His swarthy, dark-haired partner never said a word. "And yet, we don't have a good ID of him—each witness gave a different description—which doesn't make any sense to me. You have any ideas on that one?"

"If it's Soneji, he's good with makeup and disguises. He enjoys fooling people, especially the police. Do you know where he got on the train?" I asked.

Goldman consulted a black leather notebook. "The stops for that particular train were D.C., Baltimore, Philadelphia, Wilmington, Princeton Junction, and New York. We assumed he got on in D.C."

I glanced at Sampson, then back at the NYPD detectives. "Soneji used to live in Wilmington with his wife and little girl. He was originally from the Princeton area."

"That's information we didn't have," Goldman said. I couldn't help noticing that he was talking only to me, as if Sampson and Groza weren't even there. It was peculiar, and made it uncomfortable for the rest of us.

"Get me a schedule for yesterday's Metroliner, the one that arrived at five-ten. I want to double-check the stops," he barked at Groza. The younger detective skulked off to do Goldman's bidding.

"We heard there were three stabbings, three deaths?" Sampson finally spoke. I knew that he'd been sizing up Goldman. He'd probably come to the conclusion that the detective was a New York asshole of the first order.

"That's what it says on the front pages of all the daily newspapers," Goldman cracked out of the side of his mouth. It was a nasty remark, delivered curtly.

"The reason I was asking—" Sampson started to say, still keeping his cool.

Goldman cut him off with a rude swipe of the hand. "Let me show you the sites of the stabbings." He turned his attention back to me. "Maybe it will jog something else you know about Soneji."

"Detective Sampson asked you a question," I said.

"Yeah, but it was a pointless question. I don't have time for PC crap or pointless questions. Like I said, let's move on. Soneji is on the loose in my town."

"You know much about knives? You cover a lot of stabbings?" Sampson asked. I could tell that he was starting to lose it. He towered over Manning Goldman. Actually, both of us did.

"Yeah, I've covered quite a few stabbings," Goldman said. "I also know where you're going. It's extremely unlikely for Soneji to kill three out of three with a knife. Well, the knife he used had a double serpentine blade, extremely sharp. He cut each victim like some surgeon from NYU Medical Center. Oh yeah, he tipped the knife with potassium cyanide. Kill you in under a minute. I was getting to that."

Sampson backed off. The mention of poison on the knife was news to us. John knew we needed to hear what Goldman had to say. We couldn't let this get personal here in New York. Not yet anyway.

"Soneji have any history with knives?" Goldman asked. He was talking to me again. "Poisons?"

I understood that he wanted to pump me, to use me. I didn't have a problem with it. Give and take is as good as it gets on most multijurisdictional cases.

"Knives? He once killed an FBI agent with a knife. Poisons? I don't know. I wouldn't be surprised. He also shot an assortment of handguns and rifles while he was growing up. Soneji likes to kill, Detective Goldman. He's a quick study, so he could have picked it up. Guns and knives, and poisons, too."

"Believe me, he did pick it up. He was in and out of here in a couple of minutes. Left three dead bodies just like *that*." Goldman snapped his fingers.

"Was there much blood at the scene?" I asked Goldman. It was the question I'd had on my mind all the way from Washington.

"There was a *helluva* lot of blood. He cut each victim deep. Slashed two of their throats. Why?"

"There could be an angle connected with all the blood." I told Goldman one of my findings at Union Station. "The sniper in D.C. made a mess. I'm pretty sure Soneji did it on purpose. He used hollow-points. He also left traces of my blood on his weapon," I revealed to Goldman.

He probably even knows I'm here in New York, I thought. *And I'm not completely sure who is tracking whom.*

CHAPTER 27

F OR THE next hour, Goldman, with his partner practically walking up his heels, showed us around Penn Station, particularly the three stabbing sites. The body markings were still on the floor, and the cordoned-off areas were causing more than the usual congestion in the terminal.

After we finished with a survey of the station, the NYPD detectives took us up to the street level, where it was believed Soneji had caught a cab headed uptown.

I studied Goldman, watched him work. He was actually pretty good. The way he walked around was interesting. His nose was poised just a little higher than those belonging to the rest of the general population. His posture made him look haughty, in spite of the odd way he was dressed.

"I would have guessed he'd use the subway to escape," I offered as we stood out on noisy Eighth Avenue. Above our heads, a sign announced that Kiss was appearing at Madison Square Garden. Shame I'd have to miss it.

Goldman smiled broadly. "I had the same thought. Witnesses are split on which way he went. I was curious whether you'd have an opinion. I think Soneji used the subway, too."

"Trains have a special significance for him. I think

trains are part of his ritual. He wanted a set of trains as a kid, but never got it."

"Ah, *quod erat demonstrandum*," Goldman said and smirked. "So now he kills people in train stations. Makes perfect sense to me. Wonder he didn't blow up the whole fucking train."

Even Sampson laughed at Goldman's delivery on that one.

After we had finished the tour of Penn Station and the surrounding streets, we made a trip downtown to One Police Plaza. By four o'clock I knew what the NYPD had going—at least everything that Manning Goldman was prepared to tell me at this time.

I was almost sure that Gary Soneji was the Penn Station killer. I personally contacted Boston, Philly, and Baltimore and suggested tactfully that they pay attention to the train terminals. I passed on the same advice to Kyle Craig and the FBI.

"We're going to head back to Washington," I finally told Goldman and Groza. "Thanks for calling us in on this. This helps a lot."

"I'll call if there's anything. You do the same, hey?" Manning Goldman put out his hand, and we shook. "I'm pretty sure we haven't heard the last of Gary Soneji."

I nodded. I was sure of it, too.

CHAPTER 28

I N HIS mind, Gary Soneji lay down beside Charles Joseph Whitman on the roof of the University of Texas tower, circa 1966.

All in his goddamn incredible mind!!

He had been up there with Charlie Whitman *many, many times before*—ever since 1966, when the spree killer had become one of his boyhood idols. Over the years, other killers had captured his imagination, but none were like Charlie Whitman. Whitman was an American original, and there weren't many of those left.

Let's see now, Soneji ran down the names of his favorites: James Herberty, who had opened fire without warning inside the McDonald's in San Ysidro, California. He had killed twenty-one, killed them at an even faster clip than they could dish out greasy hamburgers. Soneji had actually copycatted the McDonald's shootings a few years earlier. That was when he'd first met Cross face to face.

Another of his personal favorites was postman Patrick Sherill, who'd blown away fourteen coworkers in Edmond, Oklahoma, and also probably started the postman-as-madman paranoia. More recently, he had admired the handiwork of Martin Bryant at the Port Arthur penal colony in Tasmania. Then there was Thomas Watt Hamilton, who invaded the mind space of virtually everyone on the planet after his shooting spree at a primary school in Dunblane, Scotland.

Gary Soneji desperately wanted to invade everybody's mind space, to become a large, disturbing icon on the world's Internet. He was going to do it, too. He had everything figured out.

Charlie Whitman was still his sentimental favorite, though. Whitman was the original, the "madman in the tower." A Bad Boy down there in Texas.

God, how many times had he lain on that same tower, in the blazing August sun, along with Bad Boy Charlie?

All in his incredible mind!

Whitman had been a twenty-five-year-old student of architectural engineering at the University of Texas when he'd gone tapioca pudding. He'd brought an arsenal up onto the observation deck of the limestone tower that soared three hundred feet above the campus, and where he must have felt like God.

Just before he'd gone up in the clock tower, he had murdered his wife and mother. Whitman had made Charlie Starkweather look like a piker and a real chump that afternoon in Texas. The same could be said for Dickie Hickock and Perry Smith, the white-trash punks Truman Capote immortalized in his book *In Cold Blood*. Charles Whitman made those two look like crap, too.

Soneji never forgot the actual passage from the *Time* magazine story on the Texas tower shootings. He knew it word for word: *"Like many mass murderers, Charles*

Whitman had been an exemplary boy, the kind that neighborhood mothers hold up as a model to their own recalcitrant youngsters. He was a Roman Catholic altar boy, and a newspaper delivery boy."

Cool goddamn beans.

Another master of disguise, right. Nobody had known what Charlie was thinking, or what he was ultimately going to pull off.

He had carefully positioned himself under the "VI" numeral of the tower's clock. Then Charles Whitman opened fire at 11:48 in the morning. Beside him on the six-foot runway that went around the tower were a machete, a Bowie knife, a 6mm Remington bolt-action rifle, a 35mm Remington, a Luger pistol, and a .357 Smith & Wesson revolver.

The local and state police fired thousands of rounds up onto the tower, almost shooting out the entire face of the clock—but it took over an hour and a half to bring an end to Charlie Whitman. The whole world marveled at his audacity, his unique outlook and perspective. The whole goddamn world took notice.

Someone was pounding on the door of Soneji's hotel room! The sound brought him back to the here and now. He suddenly remembered where he was.

He was in New York City, in Room 419 of the Plaza, which he always used to read about as a kid. He had always fantasized about coming by train to New York and staying at the Plaza. *Well, here he was.*

"Who's out there?" he called from the bed. He

pulled a semi-automatic from under the covers. Aimed it at the peephole in the door.

"Maid service," an accented Spanish female voice said. "Would you like your bed turned down?"

"No, I'm comfortable as is," Soneji said and smiled to himself. *Well actually, senorita, I'm preparing to make the NYPD look like the amateurs that cops usually are. You can forget the bed turndown and keep your chocolate mints, too. It's too late to try and make up to me now.*

On second thought—"Hey! You can bring me some of those chocolate mints. I like those little mints. I need a little sweet treat."

Gary Soneji sat back against the headboard and continued to smile as the maid unlocked the door and entered. He thought about doing her, boffing the scaggy hotel maid, but he figured that wasn't such a good idea. He wanted to spend one night at the Plaza. He'd been looking forward to it for years. It was worth the risk.

The thing that he loved the most, what made it so perfect, was that nobody had any idea where this was going.

Nobody would guess the end to this one.

Not Alex Cross, not anybody.

CHAPTER 29

I VOWED I would not let Soneji wear me down this time. I wouldn't let Soneji take possession of my soul again.

I managed to get home from New York in time for a late dinner with Nana and the kids. Damon, Jannie, and I cleaned up downstairs and then we set the table in the dining room. Keith Jarrett was playing ever so sweetly in the background. This was nice. This was the way it was supposed to be and there was a message in that for me.

"I'm so impressed, Daddy," Jannie commented as we circled the table, putting out the "good" silverware, and also glasses and dinner plates I'd picked out years ago with my wife, Maria. "You went all the way to New York. You came all the way back again. You're here for dinner. Very good, Daddy."

She beamed and giggled and patted me on my arm as we worked. I was a good father tonight. Jannie approved. She bought my act completely.

I took a small formal bow. "Thank you, my darling daughter. Now this trip to New York I was on, about how far would you say that might be?"

"Kilometers or miles?" Damon broke in from the other side of the table, where he was folding napkins like fans, the way they do in fancy restaurants. Damon can be quite the little scene stealer.

"Either measurement would be fine," I told him.

"Approximately two hundred forty-eight miles, one way," Jannie answered. "Howzat?"

I opened my eyes as wide as I could, made a funny face, and let my eyes roll up into my forehead. I can still steal a scene or two myself. "Now, *I'm* impressed. Very good, Jannie."

She took a little bow and then did a mock curtsy. "I asked Nana how far it was this morning," she confessed. "Is that okay?"

"That's cool," Damon offered his thought on his sister's moral code. "It's call research, Velcro."

"Yeah, that's cool, Baby," I said and we all laughed at her cleverness and sense of fun.

"Round-trip, it's four hundred ninety-six miles," Damon said.

"You two are . . . smart!" I exclaimed in a loud, playful voice. "You're both smarty-pants, smart-alecks, smarties of the highest order!"

"What's going on in there? What am I missing out on?" Nana finally called from the kitchen, which was overflowing with good smells from her cooking. She doesn't like to miss anything. Ever. To my knowledge, she just about never has.

"G.E. College Bowl," I called out to her.

"You will lose your shirt, Alex, if you play against those two young scholars," she warned. "Their hunger for knowledge knows no bounds. Their knowledge is fast becoming encyclopedic."

"En-cy-clo-pedic!" Jannie grinned.

"Cakewalk!" she said then, and did the lively old dance that had originated back in plantation times. I'd taught it to her one day at the piano. The cakewalk music form was actually a forerunner of modern jazz. It had fused polyrhythms from West Africa with classical melodies and also marches from Europe.

Back in plantation days, whoever did the dance best on a given night won a cake. Thus the phrase "that takes the cake."

All of this Jannie knew, and also how to actually do the damn dance in high style, and with a contemporary twist or two. She can also do James Brown's famous Elephant Walk and Michael Jackson's Moonwalk.

After dinner, we did the dishes and then we had our biweekly boxing lesson in the basement. Damon and Jannie are not only smart, they're tough little weasels. Nobody in school picks on those two. "Brains and a wicked left hook!" Jannie brags to me sometimes. "Hard combination to beat."

We finally retired to the living room after the Wednesday-night fights. Rosie the cat was curled up on Jannie's lap. We were watching a little of the Orioles baseball game on television when Soneji slid into my head again.

Of all the killers I had ever gone up against, he was the scariest. Soneji was single-minded, obsessive, but he was also completely whacked-out, and that's the proper medical term I learned years ago at Johns Hopkins. He had a powerful imagination fueled by anger, and he acted on his fantasies.

Months back, Soneji had called to tell me that he'd left a cat at our house, a little present. He knew that we had adopted her, and loved little Rosie very much. He said that every time I saw Rosie the cat, I should think: *Gary's in the house, Gary is right there.*

I had figured that Gary had seen the stray cat at our house, and just made up a nasty story. Gary loved to lie, especially when his lies hurt people. That night, though, with Soneji running out of control again, I had a bad thought about Rosie. It frightened the hell out of me.

Gary is in the house. Gary is right here.

I nearly threw the cat out of the house, but that wasn't an option, so I waited until morning to do what had to be done with Rosie. *Goddamn Soneji. What in hell did he want from me? What did he want from my family?*

What could he have done to Rosie before he left her at our house?

CHAPTER 30

I FELT like a traitor to my kids and also to poor little Rosie. I was feeling subhuman as I drove thirty-six miles to Quantico the next morning. I was betraying the kids' trust and possibly doing a terrible thing, but I didn't see that I had any other choice.

At the start of our trip, I had Rosie trapped in one of those despicable, metal-wire pet carriers. The poor thing cried and meowed and scratched so hard at the cage and at me that I finally had to let her out.

"You be good now," I gave her a mild warning. Then I said, "Oh, go ahead and raise hell if you want to."

Rosie proceeded to lay a huge guilt trip on me, to make me feel miserable. Obviously, she'd learned this lesson well from Damon and Jannie. Of course, she had no idea how angry she ought to be at me. But maybe she did. Cats are intuitive.

I was fearful that the beautiful red-and-brown Abyssinian would have to be destroyed, possibly this morning. I didn't know how I could ever explain it to the kids.

"Don't scratch up the car seats. And don't you dare jump on top of my head!" I warned Rosie, but in a pleasant, conciliatory voice.

She meowed a few times, and we had a more or less peaceful and pleasant ride to the FBI quarters in Quantico. I had already spoken to Chet Elliott in the Bureau's SAS, or Scientific Analysis Section. He was waiting for Rosie and me. I was carrying the cat in one arm, with her cage dangling from the other.

Now things were going to get very hard. To make things worse, Rosie got up on her hind legs and nuzzled my face. I looked into her beautiful green eyes and I could hardly stand it.

Chet was outfitted in protective gear: a white lab coat, white plastic gloves, even gold-tinted goggles. He looked like the king of the geeks. He peered at Rosie, then at me and said, "Weird science."

"Now what happens?" I asked Chet. My heart had sunk to the floorboards when I'd spotted him in his protective gear. He was taking this seriously.

"You go over to Admin," he said. "Kyle Craig wants to see you. Says it's important. Of course, everything with Kyle is important as hell and can't wait another second. I know he's crazed about Mr. Smith. We all are. Smith is the craziest fucker yet, Alex."

"What happens to Rosie?" I asked.

"First step, some X rays. Hopefully, little Red here isn't a walking bomb, compliments of our friend Soneji. If she isn't, we'll pursue toxicology. Examine her for the presence of drugs or poison in the tissues and fluids. You run along. Go see Uncle Kyle. Red and I will be just fine. I'll try to do right by her, Alex. We're all cat people in my family. I'm a cat person, can't you tell? I understand about these things."

He nodded his head and then flipped down his swimmer-style goggles. Rosie rubbed up against him, so I figured she knew he was okay. So far, anyway.

It was later that worried me, and almost brought tears to my eyes.

CHAPTER 31

I WENT to see what Kyle had on his mind, though I thought I knew what it was. I dreaded the confrontation, the war of the wills that the two of us sometimes get into. Kyle wanted to talk about his Mr. Smith case. Smith was a violent killer who had murdered more than a dozen people in America and Europe. Kyle said it was the ugliest, most chilling spree he had ever seen, and Kyle isn't known for hyperbole.

His office was on the top floor of the Academy Building, but he was working out of a crisis room in the basement of Admin. From what he'd told me, Kyle was practically camping out inside the war room, with its huge Big Board, state-of-the-art computers, phones, and a whole lot of FBI personnel, none of whom looked too happy on the morning of my visit.

The Big Board read: MR. SMITH 19—GOOD GUYS 0, in bright red letters.

"Looks like you're in your glory again. Nowhere to go but up," I said. Kyle was sitting at a big walnut desk, lost in study of the evidence board, at least he seemed to be.

I already knew about the case—more than I wanted to. "Smith" had started his string of gory murders in Cambridge, Massachusetts. He had then moved on to Europe, where he was currently blazing a bewildering trail. The latest victim was a policeman in London, a well-known inspector who had just been assigned to the Mr. Smith case.

Smith's work was so strange and kinky and *unhinged* that it was seriously discussed in the media that he might be an alien, as in a visitor from outer space. At any rate, "Smith" definitely seemed inhuman. No human could have committed the monstrosities that he had. That was the working theory.

"I thought you'd never get here," Kyle said when he saw me.

I raised my hands defensively. "Can't help. Won't do it, Kyle. First, because I'm already overloaded with Soneji. Second, because I'm losing my family on account of my work habits."

Kyle nodded. "All right, all right. I hear you. I see the larger picture. I even understand and sympathize, to a degree. But since you're here, with a little time on your hands, I do need to talk to you about Mr. Smith. Believe me, Alex, you've never seen anything like this. You've got to be a little curious."

"I'm not. In fact, I'm going to leave now. Walk right out that door I came in."

"We've got an unbelievably ugly problem on our hands, Alex. Just let me talk, and you listen. Just *listen*," Kyle pleaded.

I relented, but just a little. "I'll listen. That's all. I'm not getting involved with this."

Kyle made a small, ceremonial bow in my direction. "Just listen," Kyle said. "Listen and keep an open mind, Alex. This is going to blow your mind, I guarantee it. It's blown mine."

Then Kyle proceeded to tell me about an agent named Thomas Pierce. Pierce was in charge of the Mr. Smith case. What *was* intriguing was that Smith had brutally murdered Pierce's fiancée some years back.

"Thomas Pierce is the most thorough investigator and the most brilliant person I've ever met," Kyle told me. "At first, we wouldn't let him anywhere near the Smith case, for obvious reasons. He worked it on his own. He made progress where we hadn't. Finally, he made it clear that if he couldn't work on Smith, he'd leave the Bureau. He even threatened to try and solve the case on his own."

"You put him on the case?" I asked Kyle.

"He's very persuasive. In the end, he made his case to the Director. He sold Burns. Pierce is logical, and he's creative. He can analyze a problem like nobody I've ever seen. He's been fanatical on Mr. Smith. Works eighteen- and twenty-hour days."

"But even Pierce can't crack this case," I said and pointed at the Big Board.

Kyle nodded. "We're finally getting close, Alex. I desperately need your input. And I want you to meet Thomas Pierce. You have to meet Pierce."

"I said I'd listen," I told Kyle. "But I don't have to meet anyone."

Nearly four hours later, Kyle finally let me out of his clutches. He *had* blown my mind, all right—about Mr.

Smith *and* about Thomas Pierce—but I wasn't getting involved. I couldn't.

I finally made my way back to SAS to check on Rosie. Chet Elliott was able to see me right away. He was still wearing his lab coat, gloves, and the gold-tinted goggles. His slow-gaited walk toward me said *bad* news. I didn't want to hear it.

Then he surprised me and grinned. "We don't see anything wrong with her, Alex. I don't think Soneji did anything to her. He was just mind-humping you. We checked her for volatile compounds—nada. Then for nonvolatile organic compounds that would be unusual in her system—also negative. Forensic serology took some blood. You ought to leave Red with us for a couple of days, but I doubt we'll find anything. You can leave her here, period, if you like. She's a really cool cat."

"I know." I nodded and breathed a sigh of relief. "Can I see her?" I asked Chet.

"Sure can. She's been asking for you all morning. I don't know why, but she seems to like you."

"She knows I'm a cool cat, too." I smiled.

He took me back to see Rosie. She was being kept in a small cage, and she looked pissed as hell. I'd brought her here, hadn't I? I might as well have administered the lab tests myself.

"Not my fault," I explained as best I could. "Blame that nutcase Gary Soneji, not me. Don't look at me like that."

She finally let me pick her up and she even nuzzled

my cheek. "You're being a very brave good girl," I whispered. "I owe you one, and I always pay my debts."

She purred and finally licked my cheek with her sandpaper tongue. *Sweet lady, Rosie O'Grady.*

CHAPTER 32

London, England

MR. SMITH was dressed like an anonymous street person in a ripped and soiled black anorak. The killer was walking quickly along Lower Regent Street in the direction of Piccadilly Circus.

Going to the Circus, oh boy, oh boy! he was thinking. His cynicism was as thick and heavy as the air in London.

No one seemed to notice him in the late-afternoon crowds. No one paid much attention to the poor in any of the large, "civilized" capitals. Mr. Smith had noticed that, and used it to his advantage.

He hurried along with his duffel bag until he finally reached Piccadilly, where the crowds were even denser.

His attentive eyes took in the usual traffic snarl, which could be expected at the hub of five major streets. He also saw Tower Records, McDonald's, the Trocadero, far too many neon ads. Backpackers and camera hounds were everywhere on the street and sidewalks.

And a single alien creature—himself.

One being who didn't fit in any way with the others.

Mr. Smith suddenly felt so alone, incredibly lonely in the middle of all these people in London town.

He set down the long, heavy duffel bag directly under the famous statue in the Circus—*Eros*. Still, no one was paying attention to him.

He left the bag sitting there, and he walked along Piccadilly and then onto Haymarket.

When he was a few blocks away, he called the police, as he always did. The message was simple, clear, to the point. *Their time was up.*

"Inspector Drew Cabot is in Piccadilly Circus. He's in a gray duffel bag. What's left of him. You blew it. Cheers."

CHAPTER 33

SONDRA GREENBERG of Interpol spotted Thomas Pierce as he walked toward the crime scene at the center of Piccadilly Circus. Pierce stood out in a crowd, even one like this.

Thomas Pierce was tall; his long blond hair was pulled back in a ponytail; and he usually wore dark glasses. He did not look like your typical FBI agent, and, in fact, Pierce was nothing like any agent Greenberg had ever met or worked with.

"What's all the excitement about?" he asked as he got up close. "Mr. Smith out for his weekly kill. Nothing so unusual." His habitual sarcasm was at work.

Sondra looked around at the packed crowd at the homicide scene and shook her head. There were press reporters and television news trucks everywhere.

"What's being done by the local geniuses? The police?" said Pierce.

"They're canvassing. *Obviously*, Smith has been here."

"The bobbies want to know if anyone saw a little green man? Blood dripping from his little green teeth?"

"Exactly, Thomas. Have a look?"

Pierce smiled and it was entirely captivating. Definitely not the American FBI's usual style. "You said that like, *spot of tea? . . . Have a look?*"

Greenberg shook her head of dark curls. She was nearly as tall as Pierce, and pretty in a tough sort of way. She always tried to be nice to Pierce. Actually, it wasn't hard.

"I guess I'm finally becoming jaded," she said. "I wonder why."

They walked toward the crime scene, which was almost directly under the towering, waxed aluminum figure of Eros. One of London's favorite landmarks, Eros was also the symbol for the *Evening Standard* newspaper. Although people believed the statue was a representation of erotic love, it had actually been commissioned as a symbol for Christian charity.

Thomas Pierce flashed his ID and walked up to the "body bag" that Mr. Smith had used to transport the remains of Chief Inspector Cabot.

"It's as if he's *living* a Gothic novel," Sondra Greenberg said. She was kneeling beside Pierce. Actually, they looked like a team, even like a couple.

"Smith called you here, too—to London? Left a voice mail?" Pierce asked her.

Greenberg nodded. "What do you think of the body? The latest kill? Smith packed the bag with body parts in the most careful and concise way. Like you would if you had to get everything into a suitcase."

Thomas Pierce frowned. "Freak, goddamn butcher."

"Why Piccadilly? A hub of London. Why under Eros?"

"He's leaving clues for us, obvious clues. We just

don't understand," Thomas Pierce said and continued to shake his head.

"Right you are, Thomas. Because we don't speak Martian."

CHAPTER 34

*C*RIME MARCHES *on and on.*

Sampson and I drove to Wilmington, Delaware, the following morning. We had visited the city made famous by the Du Ponts during the original manhunt for Gary Soneji a few years before. I had the Porsche floored the entire ride, which took a couple of hours.

I had already received some very good news that morning. We'd solved one of the case's nagging mysteries. I had checked with the blood bank at St. Anthony's. A pint of my blood was missing from our family's supply. Someone had taken the trouble to break in and take my blood. *Gary Soneji? Who else? He continued to show me that nothing was safe in my life.*

"Soneji" was actually a pseudonym Gary had used as part of a plan to kidnap two children in Washington. The strange name had stuck in news stories, and that was the name the FBI and media used now. His real name was Gary Murphy. He had lived in Wilmington with his wife, Meredith, who was called Missy. They had one daughter, Roni.

Actually, Soneji was the name Gary had appropriated when he fantasized about his crimes as a young boy locked in the cellar of his house. He claimed to have been sexually abused by a neighbor in Princeton, a grade-school teacher named Martin Soneji. I suspected serious problems with a relative, possibly his paternal grandfather.

We arrived at the house on Central Avenue at a little past ten in the morning. The pretty street was deserted, except for a small boy with Rollerblades. He was trying them out on his front lawn. There should have been local police surveillance here, but, for some reason, there wasn't. At least I didn't see any sign of it yet.

"Man, this perfect little street kills me," Sampson said. "I still keep looking for Jimmy Stewart to pop out of one of these houses."

"Just as long as Soneji doesn't," I muttered.

The cars parked up and down Central Avenue were almost all American makes, which seemed quaint nowadays: Chevys, Olds, Fords, some Dodge Ram pickup trucks.

Meredith Murphy wasn't answering her phone that morning, which didn't surprise me.

"I feel sorry for Mrs. Murphy and especially the little girl," I told Sampson as we pulled up in front of the house. "Missy Murphy had no idea who Gary really was."

Sampson nodded. "I remember they seemed nice enough. Maybe too nice. Gary fooled them. Ole Gary the Fooler."

There were lights burning in the house. A white Chevy Lumina was parked in the driveway. The street was as quiet and peaceful as I remembered it from our last visit, when the peacefulness had been short-lived.

We got out of the Porsche and headed toward the front door of the house. I touched the butt of my Glock as we walked. I couldn't help thinking that Soneji could be waiting, setting some kind of trap for Sampson and me.

The neighborhood, the entire town, still reminded me of the 1950s. The house was well kept and looked as if it had recently been painted. That had been part of Gary's careful facade. It was the perfect hiding place: a sweet little house on Central Avenue, with a white picket fence and a stone walkway bisecting the front lawn.

"So what do you figure is going on with Soneji?" Sampson asked as we came up to the front door. "He's changed some, don't you think? He's not the careful planner I remember. More impulsive."

It seemed that way. "Not everything's changed. He's still playing parts, acting. But he's on a rampage like nothing I've seen before. He doesn't seem to care if he's caught. Yet everything he does is planned. He *escapes*."

"And why is that, Dr. Freud?"

"That's what we're here to find out. And that's why we're going to Lorton Prison tomorrow. Something weird is going on, even for Gary Soneji."

I rang the front doorbell. Sampson and I waited for Missy Murphy on the porch. We didn't fit into the small-town-America neighborhood, but that wasn't so unusual. We didn't exactly fit into our own neighborhood back in D.C. either. That morning we were both wearing dark clothes and dark glasses, looking like musicians in somebody's blues band.

"Hmm, no answer," I muttered.

"Lights blazing inside," Sampson said. "Somebody must be here. Maybe they just don't want to talk to Men In Black."

"Ms. Murphy," I called out in a loud voice, in case someone was inside but not answering the door. "Ms. Murphy, open the door. It's Alex Cross from Washington. We're not leaving without talking to you."

"Nobody home at the Bates Motel," Sampson grunted.

He wandered around the side of the house, and I followed close behind. The lawn had been cut recently and the hedges trimmed. Everything looked so neat and clean and so harmless.

I went to the back door, the kitchen, if I remembered. I wondered if he could be hiding inside. Anything was possible with Soneji—the more twisted and unlikely the better for his ego.

Things about my last visit were flashing back. Nasty memories. It was Roni's birthday party. She was seven. Gary Soneji had been inside the house that time, but he had managed to escape. A regular Houdini. A very smart, very creepy creep.

Soneji could be inside now. Why did I have the unsettling feeling that I was walking into a trap?

I waited on the back porch, not sure what to do next. I rang the bell. Something was definitely wrong about the case, everything about it was wrong. Soneji here in

Wilmington? Why here? Why kill people in Union and Penn Stations?

"Alex!" Sampson shouted. "Alex! Over here! Come quick. Alex, *now!*"

I hurried across the yard with my heart in my throat. Sampson was down on all fours. He was crouched in front of a doghouse that was painted white and shingled to look like the main residence. What in hell was inside the doghouse?

As I got closer, I could see a thick black cloud of flies.

Then I heard the buzzing.

CHAPTER 35

"OH, GODDAMN it, Alex, look at what that mad-man did. Look at what he did to her!"

I wanted to avert my eyes, but I had to look. I crouched down low beside Sampson. Both of us were batting away horse-flies and other unpleasant swarming insects. White larvae were all over everything—the doghouse, the lawn. I held a handkerchief bunched over my nose and mouth, but it wasn't enough to stifle the putrid smell. My eyes began to water.

"What the hell is wrong with him?" Sampson said. "Where does he get his insane ideas?"

Propped up inside the doghouse was the body of a golden retriever, or what remained of it. Blood was spattered everywhere on the wooden walls. The dog had been decapitated.

Firmly attached to the dog's neck was the head of Meredith Murphy. Her head was propped perfectly, even though it was too large proportionately for the re-triever's body. The effect was beyond grotesque. It re-minded me of the old Mr. Potato Head toys. Meredith Murphy's open eyes stared out at me.

I had met Meredith Murphy only once, and that had been almost four years before. I wondered what she could have done to enrage Soneji like this. He had never talked much about his wife during our sessions. He had despised her, though. I remembered his nicknames for her: "Simple Cipher," "The Headless Haus-frau," "Blonde Cow."

"What the hell is going on inside that sick, sorry son of a bitch's head? You understand this?" Sampson muttered through his handkerchief-covered mouth.

I thought that I understood psychotic rage states, and I had seen a few of Soneji's, but nothing had pre-pared me for the past few days. The current murders were extreme, and bloody. They were also clustered, happening much too frequently.

I had the grim feeling Soneji couldn't turn off his rage, not even after a new kill. None of the murders satisfied his need anymore.

"Oh, God." I rose to my feet. "John, his little girl," I said. "His daughter, Roni. What has he done with her?"

The two of us searched the wooded half lot, includ-ing a copse of bent, wind-battered evergreens on the northeast side of the house. No Roni. No other bodies, or grossly severed parts, or other grisly surprises.

We looked for the girl in the two-car garage. Then in the tight, musty crawl space under the back porch. We checked the trio of metal garbage cans neatly lined alongside the garage. Nothing anywhere. Where was Roni Murphy? Had he taken her with him? Had Soneji kidnapped his daughter?

I headed back toward the house, with Sampson a step or two behind me. I broke the window in the kitchen door, unlocked it, and rushed inside. I feared the worst. Another murdered child?

"Go easy, man. Take it slow in here," Sampson whispered from behind. He knew how I got when children were involved. He also sensed this could be a trap Soneji had set. It was a perfect place for one.

"Roni!" I called out. "Roni, are you in here? Roni, can you hear me?"

I remembered her face from the last time I'd been in this house. I could have drawn her picture if I had to.

Gary had told me once that Roni was the only thing that mattered in his life, the only good thing he'd ever done. At the time, I believed him. I was probably projecting my feelings for my own kids. Maybe I was fooled into thinking that Soneji had some kind of conscience and feelings because that was what I wanted to believe.

"Roni! It's the police. You can come out now, honey. Roni Murphy, are you in here? Roni?"

"Roni!" Sampson joined in, his deep voice just as loud as mine, maybe louder.

Sampson and I covered the downstairs, throwing open every door and closet as we went. Calling out her name. Dear God, I was praying now. It was sort of a prayer anyway. *Gary—not your own little girl. You don't have to kill her to show us how bad you are, how angry. We get the message. We understand.*

I ran upstairs, taking the creaking wooden steps two at a time. Sampson was close behind me, a shadow. It usually doesn't show on his face, but he gets as upset as I do. Neither of us is jaded yet.

I could hear it in his voice, in the shallow way he

was breathing. "Roni! Are you up here? Are you hiding somewhere?" he called out.

"Roni! It's the police. You're safe now, Roni! You can come out."

Someone had ransacked the master bedroom. Someone had invaded this space, desecrated it, broken every piece of furniture, overturned beds and bureaus.

"You remember her, John?" I asked as we checked the rest of the bedrooms.

"I remember her pretty good," Sampson said in a soft voice. "Cute little girl."

"Oh, no—*nooo*—"

Suddenly I was running down the hallway, back down the stairs. I raced through the kitchen and pulled open a hollow-core door between the refrigerator and a four-burner stove.

We both hurried down into the basement, into the *cellar* of the house.

My heart was out of control, *beating, banging, thudding* loudly inside my chest. I didn't want to be here, to see any more of Soneji's handiwork, his nasty surprises.

The cellar of his house.

The symbolic place of all Gary's childhood nightmares.

The cellar.

Blood.

Trains.

The cellar in the Murphy house was small and neat. I looked around. *The trains were gone!* There had been a train set down here the first time we came to the house.

I didn't see any signs of the girl, though. Nothing looked out of place. We threw open work cabinets. Sampson yanked open the washer, then the clothes dryer.

There was an unpainted wooden door to one side of the water heater and a fiberglass laundry sink. There was no sign of blood in the sink, no bloodstained clothes. Was there a way outside? Had the little girl run away when her father came to the house?

The closet! I yanked open the door.

Roni Murphy was bound with rope and gagged with old rags. Her blue eyes were large with fear. She was alive!

She was shaking badly. He didn't kill her, but he had killed her childhood, just as his had been killed. A few years before, he had done the same thing with a girl called Maggie Rose.

"Oh, sweet girl," I whispered as I untied her and took out the cloth gag her father had stuffed into her mouth. "Everything is all right now. Everything is okay, Roni. You're okay now."

What I didn't say was, *Your father loved you enough not to kill you—but he wants to kill everything and everyone else.*

"You're okay, you're okay, baby. Everything is okay," I lied to the poor little girl. "Everything is okay now."

Sure it is.

CHAPTER 36

ONCE UPON a long time ago, Nana Mama had been the one who had taught me to play the piano.

In those days, the old upright sat like a constant invitation to make music in our family room. One afternoon after school, she heard me trying to play a little boogie-woogie. I was eleven years old at the time. I remember it well, as if it were yesterday. Nana swept in like a soft breeze and sat next to me on the piano bench, just the way I do now with Jannie and Damon.

"I think you're a little ahead of yourself with that cool jazz stuff, Alex. Let me show you something beautiful. Let me show you where you might start your music career."

She made me practice my Czerny finger exercises every day until I was ready to play and appreciate Mozart, Beethoven, Handel, Haydn—all from Nana Mama. She taught me to play from age eleven until I was eighteen, when I left for school at Georgetown and then Johns Hopkins. By that time, I was ready to play that cool jazz stuff, and to know what I was playing, and even know why I liked what I liked.

When I came home from Delaware, very late, I found Nana on the porch and she was playing the piano. I hadn't heard her play like that in many years.

She didn't hear me come in, so I stood in the door-

way and watched her for several minutes. She was
playing Mozart and she still had a feeling for the music
that she loved. She'd once told me how sad it was that
no one knew where Mozart was buried.

When she finished, I whispered, "Bravo. Bravo.
That's just beautiful."

Nana turned to me. "Silly old woman," she said and
wiped away a tear I hadn't been able to see from where
I was standing.

"Not silly at all," I said. I sat down and held her in
my arms on the piano bench. "Old yes, really old and
cranky, but never silly."

"I was just thinking," she said, "about that third
movement in Mozart's Concerto No. 21, and then I had
a memory of how I used to be able to play it, a long,
long time ago." She sighed. "So I had myself a nice
cry. Felt real good, too."

"Sorry to intrude," I said as I continued to hold her
close.

"I love you, Alex," my grandmother whispered.
"Can you still play 'Clair de Lune'? Play Debussy for
me."

And so with Nana Mama close beside me, I played.

CHAPTER 37

THE GROAN-and-grunt work continued the following morning.

First thing, Kyle faxed me several stories about his agent, Thomas Pierce. The stories came from cities where Mr. Smith had committed murders: Atlanta, St. Louis, Seattle, San Francisco, London, Hamburg, Frankfurt, Rome. Pierce had helped to capture a murderer in Fort Lauderdale in the spring, unrelated to Smith.

Other headlines:

FOR THOMAS PIERCE, THE CRIME SCENE IS IN THE MIND
MURDER EXPERT HERE IN ST. LOUIS
THOMAS PIERCE—GETTING INTO KILLERS' HEADS
NOT ALL PATTERN KILLERS ARE BRILLIANT—BUT AGENT
THOMAS PIERCE IS
MURDERS OF THE MIND, THE MOST CHILLING
MURDERS OF ALL

If I didn't know better, I'd have thought Kyle was trying to make me jealous of Pierce. I wasn't jealous. I didn't have the time for it right now.

A little before noon, I drove out to Lorton Prison, one of my least favorite places in the charted universe.

Everything moves slowly inside a high-security federal prison. It is like being held underwater, like being drowned by unseen human hands. It happens over days, over years, sometimes over decades.

At an administrative max facility, prisoners are kept in their cells twenty-two to twenty-three hours a day. The boredom is incomprehensible to anyone who hasn't served time. *It is not imaginable.* Gary Soneji told me that, created the drowning metaphor when I interviewed him years back at Lorton.

He also thanked me for giving him the experience of being in prison, and he said that one day he would reciprocate if he possibly could. More and more, I had the sense that my time had come, and I had to guess what the excruciating payback might be.

It was not imaginable.

I could almost feel myself drowning as I paced inside a small administrative room near the warden's office on the fifth floor at Lorton.

I was waiting for a double murderer named Jamal Autry. Autry claimed to have important information about Soneji. He was known inside Lorton as the Real Deal. He was a predator, a three-hundred-pound pimp who had murdered two teenage prostitutes in Baltimore.

The Real Deal was brought to me in restraints. He was escorted into the small, tidy office by two armed guards with billy clubs.

"You Alex Cross? Gah-damn. Now ain't that somethin'," Jamal Autry said with a middle-South twang.

He smiled crookedly when he spoke. The lower half of his face sagged like the mouth and jaw of a bottom feeder. He had strange, uneven piggy eyes that were hard to look at. He continued to smile as if he were about to be paroled today, or had just won the inmates' lottery.

I told the two guards that I wanted to talk to Autry alone. Even though he was in restraints, they departed reluctantly. I wasn't afraid of this big load, though. I wasn't a helpless teenage girl he could beat up on.

"Sorry, I missed the joke," I finally said to Autry. "Don't quite know why it is that you're smiling."

"Awhh, don't worry 'bout it, man. You get the joke okay. Eventually," he said with his slow drawl. "You'll get the joke, Dr. Cross. See, *it's on you.*"

I shrugged. "You asked to see me, Autry. You want something out of this and so do I. I'm not here for your jokes or your private amusement. You want to go back to your cell, just turn the hell around."

Jamal Autry continued to smile, but he sat down on one of two chairs left for us. "We boff want some-thin'," he said. He began to make serious eye contact with me. He had the don't-mess-with-me look now. His smile evaporated.

"Tell me what you've got to trade. We'll see where it goes," I said. "Best I can do for you."

"Soneji said you a hard-ass. Smart for a cop. We'll see what we see," he drawled.

I ignored the bullshit that flowed so easily from his overlarge mouth. I couldn't help thinking about the two sixteen-year-old girls he'd murdered. I imagined him smiling at them, too. Giving them the look. "The two of you talked sometimes? Soneji was a friend of yours?" I asked him.

Autry shook his head. The look stayed fixed. His piggy eyes never left mine. "Naw, man. Only talked when he needed somethin'. Soneji rather sit in his cell, stare out into far space, like Mars or someplace. Soneji got no friends in here. Not me, not anybody else."

Autry leaned forward in his chair. He had something to tell me. Obviously, he thought it was worth a lot. He lowered his voice as if there were someone in the room besides the two of us.

Someone like Gary Soneji, I couldn't help thinking.

CHAPTER 38

"LOOKIT, SONEJI didn't have no friends in here. He didn't need nobody. Man had a guest in his attic. Know what I mean? Only talked to me when he wanted something."

"What kind of things did you do for Soneji?" I asked.

"Soneji had simple needs. Cigars, fuck-books, mustard for his Froot Loops. He paid to keep certain individuals away. Soneji always had money."

I thought about that. Who gave Gary Soneji money while he was in Lorton? It wouldn't have come from his wife—at least I didn't think so. His grandfather was still alive in New Jersey. Maybe the money had come from his grandfather. He had only one friend that I knew of, but that had been way back when he was a teenager.

Jamal Autry continued his bigmouthed spiel. "Check it out, man. Protection Gary bought from me was good—the best. Best anybody could do in here."

"I'm not sure I follow you," I said. "Spell it out for me, Jamal. I want all the details."

"You can protect *some* of the people *some* of the time. That's all it is. There was another prisoner here, name of Shareef Thomas. Real crazy nigger, originally from New York City. Ran with two other crazy niggers—Goofy and Coco Loco. Shareef's out now, but when he inside, Shareef did whatever the hell he wanted. Only way you control Shareef, you cap him. *Twice*, just to make sure."

Autry was getting interesting. He definitely had something to trade. "What was Gary Soneji's connection with Shareef?" I asked.

"Soneji tried to cap Shareef. Paid the money. But Shareef was smart. Shareef was lucky, too."

"Why did Soneji want to kill Shareef Thomas?"

Autry stared at me with his cold eyes. "We have a deal, right? I get privileges for this?"

"You have my full attention, Jamal. I'm here, I'm listening to you. Tell me what happened between Shareef Thomas and Soneji."

"Soneji wanted to kill Shareef 'cause Shareef was fuckin' him. Not just one time either. He wanted Gary to know he was *the man*. He was the one man even crazier than Soneji in here."

I shook my head and leaned forward to listen. He had my attention, but something wasn't tracking for me. "Gary was separated from the prison population. Maximum security. How the hell did Thomas get to him?"

"Gah-damn, I told you, things get done in here. Things always get done. Don't be fooled what you hear on the outside, man. That's the way it is, way it's always been."

I stared into Autry's eyes. "So you took Soneji's money for protection, and Shareef Thomas got to him anyway? There's more, isn't there?"

I sensed that Autry was relishing his own punch line, or maybe he just liked having the power over me.

"There's more, yeah. Shareef gave Gary Soneji the Fever. Soneji has the bug, man. He's dying. Your old friend Gary Soneji is dying. He got *the message* from God."

The news hit me like a sucker punch. I didn't let it show, didn't give away any advantage, but Jamal Autry had just made some sense of everything Soneji had done so far. He had also shaken me to the quick. *Soneji has the Fever. He has AIDS. Gary Soneji is dying. He has nothing to lose anymore.*

Was Autry telling the truth or not? Big question, important question.

I shook my head. "I don't believe you, Autry. Why the hell should I?" I said.

He looked offended, which was part of his act. "Believe what you want. But you *ought* to believe. Gary got the message to me in here. Gary *contacted* me this week, two days ago. Gary let me know he has the Fever."

We had come full circle. Autry knew that he had me from the minute he walked into the room. Now I got to hear the punch line of his joke—the one he'd promised at the start. First, though, I had to be his straight man for a little while longer.

"Why? Why would he tell you he's dying?" I played my part.

"Soneji said you'd come here asking questions. He knew you were coming. He knows you, man—better

140 / James Patterson

than you know him. Soneji wanted me to give you the
message personally. He gave me the message, just for
you. *He said to tell you that.*"

Jamal Autry smiled his crooked smile again. "What
do you say now, Dr. Cross? You get what you come
here for?"

I had what I needed all right. Gary Soneji was dying.
He wanted me to follow him into hell. He was on a
rampage with nothing to lose, nothing to fear from
anyone.

CHAPTER 39

WHEN I got home from Lorton Prison I called Christine Johnson. I needed to see her. I needed to get away from the case. I held my breath as I asked her to dinner at Georgia Brown's on McPherson Square. She surprised me—she said yes.

Still on pins and needles, but kind of liking the feeling, I showed up at her place with a single red rose. Christine smiled beautifully, took the rose and put it in water as if it were an expensive arrangement.

She was wearing a gray calf-length skirt and a matching soft gray V-necked blouse. She looked stunning again. We talked about our respective days on the drive to the restaurant. I liked her day a lot better than mine.

We were hungry, and started with hot buttermilk biscuits slathered with peach butter. The day was definitely improving. Christine ordered Carolina shrimp and grits. I got the Carolina Perlau—red rice, thick chunks of duck, shrimp, and sausage.

"No one has given me a rose in a long time," she told me. "I love that you thought to do that."

"You're being too nice to me tonight," I said as we started to eat.

She tilted her head to one side and looked at me from an odd angle. She did that now and again. "Why do you say that I'm being too nice?"

"Well, you can tell I'm not exactly the best company tonight. It's what you're afraid of, isn't it? That I can't turn off my job."

She took a sip of wine. Shook her head. Finally she smiled, and the smile was so down-to-earth. "You're *so* honest. But you have a good sense of humor about it. Actually, I hadn't noticed that you weren't operating at one hundred and ten percent."

"I've been distant and into myself all night," I said. "The kids say I get twilight zoned."

She laughed and rolled her eyes. "Stop it, stop it. You are the least into-yourself man I think I've ever met. I'm having a very nice time here. I was planning on a bowl of Sugar Puffs for my dinner at home."

"Sugar Puffs and milk are good. Curl up in bed with a movie or book. Nothing wrong with that."

"That was my plan. I finally gave in and started *The Horse Whisperer*. I'm glad you called and spoiled it for me, took me out of my own twilight zone."

"You must really think I'm crazy," Christine said and smiled a little later during dinner. "Lawdy, Miss Clawdy, I believe I *am* crazy."

I laughed. "For going out with me? Absolutely crazy."

"No, for telling you I didn't think we should see each other, and now late dinner at Georgia Brown's. Forsaking my Sugar Puffs and *Horse Whisperer*."

I looked into her eyes, and I wanted to stay right there for a very long time, at least until Georgia

Brown's asked us to leave. "What happened? What changed?" I asked.

"I stopped being afraid," she said, "Well, almost stopped. But I'm getting there."

"Yeah, maybe we both are. I was afraid, too."

"That's nice to hear. I'm glad you told me. I couldn't imagine that you get afraid."

I drove Christine home from Georgia Brown's around midnight. As we rode on the John Hansen Highway, all I could think about was touching her hair, stroking the side of her cheek, maybe a few other things. Yes, definitely a few other things.

I walked Christine to her front door and I could hardly breathe. Again. My hand was lightly on her elbow. She had her house key clasped in her hand.

I could smell her perfume. She told me it was called Gardenia Passion, and I liked it a lot. Our shoes softly scraped the cement.

Suddenly, Christine turned and put her arms around me. The movement was graceful, but she took me by surprise.

"I have to find something out," she said.

Christine kissed me, just as we had a few days before. We kissed sweetly at first, then harder. Her lips were soft and moist against mine, then firmer, more urgent. I could feel her breasts press against me; then her stomach, her strong legs.

She opened her eyes, looked at me, and she smiled. I loved that natural smile—loved it. *That smile—no other one.*

She gently pulled herself away from me. I felt the separation and I didn't want her to go. I sensed, I knew, I should leave it at that.

Christine opened her front door and slowly backed inside. I didn't want her to go in just yet. I wanted to know what she was thinking, all her thoughts.

"The first kiss wasn't an accident," she whispered.

"No, it wasn't an accident," I said.

CHAPTER 40

GARY SONEJI *was in the cellar again.*
Whose dank, dark cellar was it, though?
That was the $64,000 question.

He didn't know what time it was, but it had to be very early in the morning. The house upstairs was as quiet as death. He liked that image, the rub of it inside his mind.

He loved it in the dark. He went back to being a small boy. He could still feel it, as if it had happened only yesterday. His stepmother's name was Fiona Morrison, and she was pretty, and everybody believed she was a good person, a good friend and neighbor, a good mother. It was all a lie! She had locked him away like a hateful animal—*no,* worse than an animal! He remembered shivering in the cellar, and peeing in his pants in the beginning, and sitting in his own urine as it turned from warm to icy cold. He remembered the feeling that he wasn't like the rest of his family. He wasn't like anybody else. There was nothing about him that anybody could love. There was nothing good about him. He had no inner core.

He sat in the dark cellar now and wondered if he was where he thought he was.

Which reality was he living in?
Which fantasy?
Which horror story?

He reached around on the floor in the dark. *Hmmm.* He wasn't in the cellar in the old Princeton house. He could tell he wasn't. Here the cold cement floor was smooth. And the smell was different. Dusty and musty. Where was he?

He turned on his flashlight. Ahhh!

No one was going to believe this one! No one would guess whose house this was, whose cellar he was hiding in now.

Soneji pushed himself up off the floor. He felt slightly nauseated and achy, but he ignored the feeling. The pain was incidental. He was ready to go upstairs now.

No one would believe what he was going to do next. How outrageous.

He was several steps ahead of everybody else.

He was way ahead.

As always.

CHAPTER 41

SONEJI ENTERED the living room and saw the correct time on the Sony television's digital clock. It was 3:24 in the morning. Another witching hour.

Once he reached the upstairs part of the house, he decided to crawl on his hands and knees.

The plan was good. Damn it, he *wasn't* worthless and useless. He hadn't deserved to be locked in the cellar. Tears welled in his eyes and they felt hot and all too familiar. His stepmother always called him a crybaby, a little pansy, a fairy. She never stopped calling him names, until he fried her mouth open in a scream.

The tears burned his cheeks as they ran down under his shirt collar. He was dying, and he didn't deserve to die. He didn't deserve any of this. So now someone had to pay.

He was silent and careful as he threaded his way through the house, slithering on his belly like a snake. The floorboards underneath him didn't even creak as he moved forward. The darkness felt charged with electricity and infinite possibilities.

He thought about how frightened people were of intruders inside their houses and apartments. They ought to be afraid, too. There were monsters preying just outside their locked doors, often watching their windows at night. There were Peeping Garys in every town, small and large. And there were thousands more, twisted perverts, just waiting to come inside and feast. The people in their so-called safe houses were monster fodder.

He noticed that the upstairs part of the house had green walls. *Green walls. What luck!* Soneji had read somewhere that hospital operating walls were often painted green. If the walls were white, doctors and nurses sometimes saw ghost images of the ongoing operation, the blood and gore. It was called the "ghosting effect," and green walls masked the blood.

No more intruding thoughts, no matter how relevant, Soneji told himself. No more interruptions. Be perfectly calm, be careful. The next few minutes were the dangerous ones.

This particular house was dangerous—which was why the game was so much fun, such a mind trip.

The bedroom door was slightly ajar. Soneji slowly, patiently, inched it open.

He heard a man softly snoring. He saw another digital clock on a bedside table. *Three-twenty-three.* He had *lost* time.

He rose to his full height. He was finally out of the cellar, and he felt an incredible surge of anger now. He felt rage, and it was justified.

Gary Soneji angrily sprang forward at the figure in bed. He clasped a metal pipe tightly in both his hands. He raised it like an ax. He swung the pipe down as hard as he could.

"Detective Goldman, so nice to meet you," he whispered.

CHAPTER 42

THE JOB was always there, waiting for me to catch up, demanding everything I could give it, and then demanding some more.

The next morning I found myself hurrying back to New York. The FBI had provided me with a helicopter. Kyle Craig was a good friend, but he was also working his tricks on me. I knew it, and he knew I did. Kyle was hoping that I would eventually get involved in the Mr. Smith case, that I would meet agent Thomas Pierce. I knew that I wouldn't. Not for now anyway, maybe not ever. I had to meet Gary Soneji again first.

I arrived before 8:30 A.M. at the busy New York City heliport in the East Twenties. Some people call it "the New York Hellport." The Bureau's black Bell Jet floated in low over the congested FDR Drive and the East River. The craft dropped down as if it owned the city, but that was just FBI arrogance. No one could own New York—except maybe Gary Soneji.

Detective Carmine Groza was there to meet me and we got into his unmarked Mercury Marquis. We sped up the FDR Drive to the exit for the Major Deegan. As we crossed over into the Bronx, I remembered a funny line from the poet Ogden Nash: "The Bronx, no thonx." I needed some more funny lines in my life.

I still had the irritating noise of the helicopter's propellers roaring inside my head. It made me think of the nasty *buzzing* in the doghouse in Wilmington. Everything was happening too fast again. Gary Soneji had us off balance, the way he liked it, the way he always worked his nastiness.

Soneji got in your face, applied intense pressure, and then waited for you to make a crucial mistake. I was trying not to make one right now, not to end up like Manning Goldman.

The latest homicide scene was up in Riverdale. Detective Groza talked nervously as he drove the Deegan. His chattering reminded me of an old line I try to live by—*never miss a good chance to shut up.*

Logically, the Riverdale area should be part of Manhattan, he said, but it was actually part of the Bronx. To confuse matters further, Riverdale was the site of Manhattan College, a small private school having no affiliation with either Manhattan or the Bronx. New York's mayor, Rudy Giuliani, had attended Manhattan, Groza said.

I listened to the detective's idle chitchat until I felt he had talked himself out. He seemed a different man from the one I'd met earlier in the week at Penn Station when he was partnered with Manning Goldman.

"Are you okay?" I finally asked him. I had never lost a partner, but I had come close with Sampson. He had been stabbed in the back. That happened in North Carolina, of all places. My niece, Naomi, had been kidnapped. I have counseled detectives who have lost partners, and it's never an easy thing.

"I didn't really like Manning Goldman," Groza admitted, "but I respected things he did as a detective. No one should die the way he did."

"No, no one should die like that," I agreed. *No one was safe.* Not the wealthy, certainly not the poor, and not even the police. It was a continuing refrain in my life, the scariest truth of our age.

We finally turned off the crowded Deegan Expressway and got onto an even busier, much noisier Broadway. Detective Groza was clearly shook up that morning. I didn't show it, but so was I.

Gary Soneji was showing us how easy it was for him to get into a cop's home.

CHAPTER 43

MANNING GOLDMAN'S house was located in an upscale part of Riverdale known as Fieldston. The area was surprisingly attractive—for the Bronx. Police cruisers and a flock of television vans and trucks were parked on the narrow and pretty residential streets. A FOX-TV helicopter hovered over the trees, peeking through the branches and leaves.

The Goldman house was more modest than the Tudors around it. Still, it seemed a nice place to live. Not a typical cop's neighborhood, but Manning Goldman hadn't been a typical cop.

"Goldman's father was a big doctor in Mamaroneck," Groza continued to chatter. "When he passed away, Manning came into some money. He was the black sheep in his family, the rebel—a cop. Both of his brothers are dentists in Florida."

I didn't like the look and feel of the crime scene, and I was still two blocks away. There were too many blue-and-whites and official-looking city cars. Too much help, too much interference.

"The mayor was up here early. He's a pisser. He's all right, though," Groza said. "A cop gets killed in New York, it's a huge thing. Big news, lots of media."

"Especially when a detective gets killed right in his own home," I said.

Groza finally parked on the tree-lined street, about a

block from the Goldman house. Birds chattered away, oblivious to death.

As I walked toward the crime scene, I enjoyed one aspect of the day, at least: the anonymity I felt in New York. In Washington, many reporters know who I am. If I'm at a homicide scene, it's usually a particularly nasty one, a big case, a violent crime.

Detective Carmine Groza and I were ignored as we walked through the crowd of looky-loos up to the Goldman house. Groza introduced me around inside and I was allowed to see the bedroom where Manning Goldman had been brutally murdered. The NYPD cops all seemed to know who I was and why I was there. I heard Soneji's name muttered a couple of times. Bad news travels fast.

The detective's body had already been removed from the house, and I didn't like arriving at the murder scene so late. Several NYPD techies were working the room. *Goldman's blood was everywhere.* It was splattered on the bed, the walls, the beige-carpeted floor, the desk and bookcases, and even on a gold menorah. I already knew why Soneji was so interested in spilling blood now—his blood was deadly.

I could feel Gary Soneji here in Goldman's room, *I could see him,* and it stunned me that I could imagine his presence so strongly, physically and emotionally. I remembered a time when Soneji had entered my home in the night and with a knife. *Why would he come here?* I wondered. *Was he warning me, playing with my head?*

"He definitely wanted to make a high-profile statement," I muttered, more to myself than to Carmine Groza. "He knew that Goldman was running the case in New York. He's showing us that he's in complete control."

There was something else, though. There had to be more to this than I was seeing so far. I paced around the bedroom. I noticed that the computer on the desk was turned on.

I spoke to one of the techies, a thin man with a small, grim mouth. Perfect for homicide scenes. "The computer was on when they found Detective Goldman?" I asked.

"Yeah. The Mac was on. It's been dusted."

I glanced at Groza. "We know he's looking for Shareef Thomas, and that Thomas was originally from New York. He's supposed to be back here now. Maybe he made Goldman pull up Thomas's file before he killed him."

For once Detective Groza didn't answer. He was quiet and unresponsive. I wasn't completely certain myself. Still, I trusted my instincts, especially when it came to Soneji. I was following in his bloody footsteps and I didn't think I was too far behind.

CHAPTER 44

THE SURPRISINGLY hospitable New York police had gotten me a room for the night at the Marriott Hotel on Forty-second Street. They were already checking on Shareef Thomas for me. What could be done was being taken care of, but Soneji was on the loose for another night on the town.

Shareef Thomas had lived in D.C., but he was originally from Brooklyn. I was fairly certain Soneji had followed him here. Hadn't he told me as much through Jamal Autry at Lorton Prison? He had a score to settle with Thomas, and Soneji settled his old scores. I ought to know.

At eight-thirty I finally left Police Plaza, and I was physically whipped. I was driven uptown in a squad car. I'd packed a duffel bag, so I was set for a couple of days, if it came to that. I hoped that it wouldn't. I like New York City under the right circumstances, but this was hardly Fifth Avenue Christmas shopping in December, or a Yankee World Series game in the fall.

Around nine, I called home and got our automatic answering machine—Jannie. She said, "Is this E.T.? You calling *home?*"

She's cute like that. She must have known the phone call would be from me. I always call, no matter what.

"How are you, my sweet one? Light of my life?" Just the sound of her voice made me miss her, miss being home with my family.

"Sampson came by. He was checking on us. We were supposed to do boxing tonight. Remember, Daddy?" Jannie played her part with a heavy hand, but it worked. "Bip, bip, bam. Bam, bam, bip," she said, creating a vivid picture out of sound.

"Did you and Damon practice anyway?" I asked. I was imagining her face as we talked. Damon's face. Nana's, too. The kitchen where Jannie was talking. I missed having supper with my family.

"We sure did. I knocked his block right off. I put out his lights for the night. But it's not the same without you. Nobody to show off for."

"You just have to show off for yourself," I told her.

"I know, Daddy. That's what I did. I showed off for myself, and myself said, 'Good show.'"

I laughed out loud into the phone receiver. "I'm sorry about missing the boxing lesson with you two pit bulls. Sorry, sorry, sorry," I said in a bluesy, singsong voice. "Sorry, sorry, sorry, sorry."

"That's what you *always* say," Jannie whispered, and I could hear the crackle of hurt in her voice. "Someday, it's not going to work anymore. Mark my words. Remember where you heard it first. Remember, remember, remember."

I took her counsel to heart in the lonely New York City hotel room as I ate a room-service burger and looked out over Times Square. I remembered an old joke among shrinks: "*Schizophrenia beats eating alone.*" I thought about my kids, and about Christine Johnson, and then about Soneji and Manning Goldman, murdered in his own house. I tried to read a few pages of *Angela's Ashes*, which I'd packed in my bag. I couldn't handle the beautifully described Limerick ghetto that night.

I called Christine when I thought I had my head screwed on straight. We talked for almost an hour. Easy, effortless talk. Something was changing between us. I asked her if she wanted to spend some time together that weekend, maybe in New York if I still had to be here. It took some nerve for me to ask. I wondered if she could hear it in my voice.

Christine surprised me again. She wanted to come to New York. She laughed and said she could do some early Christmas shopping in July, but I had to *promise* to make time for her.

I promised.

I must have slept some finally, because I woke in a strange bed, in a stranger town, wrapped in my bedsheets as if I were trapped in a straitjacket.

I had a strange, discomforting thought. Gary Soneji is tracking *me*. It's not the other way round.

CHAPTER 45

*H*E WAS *the Angel of Death.* He had known that since he was eleven or twelve years old. He had killed someone back then, just to see if he could do it. The police had never found the body. Not to this day. Only he knew where all the bodies were buried, and he wasn't telling.

Suddenly, Gary Soneji drifted back to reality, to the present moment in New York City.

Christ, I'm snickering and laughing to myself inside this bar on the East Side. I might have even been talking to myself.

The bartender at Dowd & McGoey's had already spotted him, talking to himself, nearly in a trance. The sneaky, red-haired Irish prick was pretending to polish beer glasses, but all the time he was watching out of the corner of his eye. *When Irish eyes are spying.*

Soneji immediately beckoned the barman over with a wave and a shy smile. "Don't worry, I'm cutting myself off. Starting to get a little out of control here. What do I owe you, Michael?" The name was emblazoned on the barman's shirt tag.

The phony, apologetic act seemed to work okay, so he settled his bill and left. He walked south for several blocks on First Avenue, then west on East Fiftieth Street.

He saw a crowded spot called Tatou. It looked

promising. He remembered his mission: He needed a place to stay the night in New York, someplace safe. The Plaza hadn't really been such a good idea.

Tatou was filled to the rafters with a lively crowd come to talk, rubberneck, eat and drink. The first floor was a supper club; the second floor was set up for dancing. *What was the scene here about?* he wondered. He needed to understand. Attitude was the answer he came up with. Stylish businessmen and professional women in their thirties and forties came to Tatou, probably straight from work in midtown. It was a Thursday night. Most of them were trying to set up something interesting for the weekend.

Soneji ordered a white wine and he began to eye the men and women lined up along the bar. They looked so perfectly in tune with the times, so desperately cool. *Pick me, choose me, somebody please notice me*, they seemed to plead.

He chatted up a pair of lady lawyers who, unfortunately, were joined at the hip. They reminded him of the strange girls in the French movie *La Cérémonie*. He learned that Theresa and Jessie had been roommates for the past eleven years. Jesus! They were both thirty-six. Their clocks were ticking very loudly. They worked out religiously at the Vertical Club on Sixty-first Street. Summered in Bridgehampton, a mile from the water. They were all wrong for him and, apparently, for everyone else at the bar.

Soneji moved on. He was starting to feel a little pressure. The police knew he was using disguises.

Only not what he might look like on a given day. Yesterday, he was a dark-haired Spanish-looking man in his mid-forties. Today, he was blond, bearded, and fit right in at Tatou. Tomorrow, who knew? He could make a dumb mistake, though. He could be picked up and everything would end.

He met an advertising art director, a creative director in a large ad factory on Lexington Avenue. Jean Summerhill was originally from Atlanta, she told him. She was small and very slim, with blond hair, lots of it. She wore a single trendy braid down one side, and he could tell she was full of herself. In an odd way, she reminded him of his Meredith, his Missy. Jean Summerhill had her own place, a condo. She lived alone, in the Seventies.

She was too pretty to be in here alone, looking for company in all the wrong places, but Soneji understood why once they'd talked: Jean Summerhill was too smart, too strong and individualistic for most men. She scared men off without meaning to, or even knowing that she had.

She didn't scare him, though. They talked easily, the way strangers sometimes do at a bar. Nothing to lose, nothing to risk. She was very down-to-earth. A woman with a need to be seen as "nice"; unlucky in love, though. He told her that and, since it was what she wanted to hear, Jean Summerhill seemed to believe him.

"You're easy to talk to," she said over their third or fourth drink. "You're very calm. Centered, right?"

"Yeah, I am a little boring," Soneji said. He knew he was anything but that. "Maybe that's why my wife left me. Missy fell for a rich man, her boss on Wall Street. We both cried the night that she told me. Now she lives in a big apartment over on Beekman Place. Real fancy digs." He smiled. "We're still friends. I just saw Missy recently."

Jean looked into his eyes. There was something sad about the look. "You know what I like about you," she said, "it's that you're not afraid of me."

Gary Soneji smiled. "No, I guess I'm not."

"And I'm not afraid of you either," Jean Summerhill whispered.

"That's the way it should be," Soneji said. "Just don't lose your head over me. Promise?"

"I'll do my best."

The two of them left Tatou and went to her condo together.

CHAPTER 46

I STOOD all alone on Forty-second Street in Manhattan, anxiously waiting for Carmine Groza to show. The homicide detective finally picked me up at the front entrance of the Marriott. I jumped into his car and we headed to Brooklyn. Something good had finally happened on the case, something promising.

Shareef Thomas had been spotted at a crackhouse in the Bedford-Stuyvesant section of Brooklyn. Did Gary Soneji know where Thomas was, too? How much, if anything, had he learned from Manning Goldman's computer files?

At seven on Saturday morning, traffic in the city was a joy to behold. We raced west to east across Manhattan in less than ten minutes. We crossed the East River on the Brooklyn Bridge. The sun was just coming up over a group of tall apartment buildings. It was a blinding yellow fireball that gave me an instant headache.

We arrived in Bed-Stuy a little before seven-thirty. I'd heard of the Brooklyn neighborhood and its tough reputation. It was mostly deserted at that time of the morning. Racist cops in D.C. have a nasty way of describing this kind of inner-city area. They call them "self-cleaning ovens." You just close the door and let it clean itself. Let it burn. Nana Mama has another word for America's mostly neglectful social programs for the inner cities: genocide.

The local bodega had a handpainted sign scrawled in red letters on yellow: FIRST STREET DELI AND TOBACCO, OPEN 24 HOURS. The store was closed. So much for the sign.

Parked in front of the deserted deli was a maroon-and-tan van. The vehicle had silver-tinted windows and a "moonlight over Miami" scene painted on the side panels. A lone female addict slogged along in a knock-kneed swaying walk. She was the only person on the street when we arrived.

The building that Shareef Thomas was in turned out to be two-storied, with faded gray shingles and some broken windows. It looked as if it had been condemned a long time ago. Thomas was still inside the crackhouse. Groza and I settled in to wait. We were hoping Gary Soneji might show up.

I slid down into a corner of the front seat. In the distance, I could see a peeling billboard high above a red-brick building: COP SHOT $10,000 REWARD. Not a good omen, but a fair warning.

The neighborhood began to wake up and show its character around nine or so. A couple of elderly women in blousy white dresses walked hand in hand toward the Pentecostal church up the street. They made me think of Nana and her buddies back in D.C. Made me miss being home for the weekend, too.

A girl of six or seven was playing jump rope down the street. I noticed she was using salvaged electrical wire. She moved in a kind of listless trance.

It made me sad to watch the little sweetheart play. I wondered what would become of her? What chance did she have to make it out of here? I thought of Jannie and Damon and how they were probably "disappointed" in me for being away on Saturday morning. *Saturday is our day off, Daddy. We only have Saturdays and Sundays to be together.*

Time passed slowly. It almost always does on surveillance. I had a thought about the neighborhood—*tragedy can be addictive, too.* A couple of suspicious-looking guys in sleeveless T-shirts and cutoff shorts pulled up in an unmarked black truck around ten-thirty. They set up shop, selling watermelons, corn on the cob, tomatoes, and collard greens on the street. The melons were piled high in the scummy gutter.

It was almost eleven o'clock now and I was worried. Our information might be wrong. Paranoia was starting to run a little wild in my head. Maybe Gary Soneji had already visited the crackhouse. He was good at disguises. He might even be in there now.

I opened the car door and got out. The heat rushed at me and I felt as if I were stepping into a blast oven. Still, it was good to be out of the car, the cramped quarters.

"What are you doing?" Groza asked. He seemed prepared to sit in the car all day, playing everything by the book, waiting for Soneji to show.

"Trust me," I said.

CHAPTER 47

I TOOK OFF my white shirt and tied it loosely around my waist. I narrowed my eyes, let them go in and out of focus.

Groza called out: "Alex." I ignored him and I began to shuffle toward the dilapidated crackhouse. I figured I looked the street-junkie part okay. It wasn't too hard. God knows I'd seen it played enough times in my own neighborhood. My older brother was a junkie before he died.

The crackhouse was being operated out of an abandoned building on a dead-end corner. It was pretty much standard operating procedure in all big cities I have visited: D.C., Baltimore, Philly, Miami, New York. Makes you wonder.

As I opened the graffiti-painted front door, I saw that the place was definitely bottom of the barrel, even for crackhouses. This was end-of-the-line time. Shareef Thomas had the Virus, too.

Debris was scattered everywhere across the grimy, stained floor. Empty soda cans and beer bottles. Fast-food wrappers from Wendy's and Roy's and Kentucky Fried. Crack vials. Hanger wires used to clean out crack pipes. Hot time, summer in the city.

I figured that a down-and-out dump like this would be run by a single "clerk." You pay the guy two or three dollars for a space on the floor. You can also buy syringes, pipes, papers, butane lighters, and maybe even a soda pop or cerveza.

"Fuck it" and "AIDS" and "Junkies of the World" were scrawled across the walls. There was also a thick, smoky fog that seemed allergic to the sunlight. The stink was fetid, worse than walking around in a city dump.

It was incredibly quiet, strangely serene, though. I noticed everything at a glance, but no Shareef Thomas. No Gary Soneji either. At least I didn't see him yet.

A Latino-looking man with a shoulder holster over a soiled Bacardi T-shirt was in charge of the early-morning shift. He was barely awake, but still managed to look in control of the place. He had an ageless face and a thick mustache.

It looked as if Shareef Thomas had definitely fallen down a few notches. If he was here, he was hanging with the low end of the low. Was Shareef dying? Or just hiding? Did he know Soneji might be looking for him?

"What do you want, chief?" the Latino man asked in a low grumble. His eyes were thin slits.

"Little peace and quiet," I said. I kept it respectful. As if this were church, which it was for some people.

I handed him two crumpled bills and he turned away with the money. "In there," he said.

I looked past him into the main room, and I felt as if a hand were clutching my heart and squeezing it tight.

About ten or twelve men and a couple of women were sitting or sprawled on the floor and on a few soiled, incredibly thin mattresses. The pipeheads were mostly staring into space, doing nothing, and doing it well. It was as if they were slowly fading or evaporating into the smoke and dust.

No one noticed me, which was okay, which was good. Nobody much cared who came or left this hell-hole. I still hadn't spotted Shareef. Or Soneji.

It was as dark as a moonless night in the main room of the crackhouse. No lights except for an occasional match being struck. The sound of the match-head strike, then a long, extended hiss.

I was looking for Thomas, but I was also carefully playing my part. Just another strung-out junkie pipehead. Looking for a spot to smoke, to nod out in peace, not here to bother anyone.

I spotted Shareef Thomas on one of the mattresses, near the rear of the dark, dingy room. I recognized him from pictures I'd studied at Lorton. *I forced my eyes away from him.*

My heart started to pump like crazy. Could Soneji be here, too? Sometimes he seemed like a phantom or ghost to me. I wondered if there was a door back out. I had to find a place to sit down before Thomas became suspicious.

I made it to a wall and started to slide down to the floor. I watched Shareef Thomas out of the corner of my eye. Then all kinds of unexpected madness and chaos broke out inside the crackhouse.

The front door was thrown open and Groza and two uniforms burst in. So much for trust. "Muhfucker," a man near me woke up and moaned in the smoky shadows.

"Police! Don't move!" Carmine Groza yelled. "Nobody move. Everybody stay cool!" He sounded like a street cop anyway.

My eyes stayed glued to Shareef Thomas. He was already getting up off the mattress, where he'd been content as a cat just a few seconds ago. Maybe he wasn't stoned at all. Maybe he *was* hiding.

I grabbed for the Glock under my rolled-up shirt, tucked at the small of my back. I brought it around in front of me. I hoped against hope I wouldn't have to use it in these close quarters.

Thomas raised a shotgun that must have been hidden alongside his mattress. The other pipeheads seemed unable to move and get out of the way. Every red-rimmed eye in the room was opened wide with fear.

Thomas's Street Sweeper exploded! Groza and the uniformed cops hit the floor, all three of them. I couldn't tell if anyone had been hit up front.

The Latino at the door yelled, "Cut this shit out! Cut the shit!" He was down low on the floor himself, screaming without raising his head into the line of fire.

"Thomas!" I yelled at the top of my voice.

Shareef Thomas was moving with surprising speed and alertness. Quick, sure reflexes, even under the influence. He turned the shotgun on me. His dark eyes glared.

There is nothing to compare with the sight of a shotgun pointed right at you. I had no choice now. I squeezed the trigger of the Glock.

Shareef Thomas took a thunderbolt in his right shoulder. He spun hard left, but he didn't go down. He pivoted smoothly. He'd been here before. So had I.

I fired a second time, hit him in the throat or lower jaw. Thomas flew back and crashed into the paper-thin walls. The whole building shook. His eyeballs flipped back and his mouth sagged open wide. He was gone before he hit the crackhouse floor.

I had killed our only connection to Gary Soneji.

CHAPTER 48

I HEARD CARMINE Groza shouting into his radio. The words chilled me. "Officer down at 412 Macon. *Officer down!*"

I had never been on the scene when another officer was killed. As I got to the front of the crackhouse, though, I was certain one of the uniforms was going to die. Why had Groza come in here like that? Why had he brought in patrolmen with him? Well, it didn't matter much now.

The uniformed man lay on his back on the littered floor near the front door. His eyes were already glazed and I thought he was in shock. Blood was trickling from the corner of his mouth.

The shotgun had done its horrifying work, just as it would have done me. Blood was splashed on the walls and across the scarred wooden floor. A scorched pattern of bullet holes was tattooed in the wall above the patrolman's body. There was nothing any of us could do for him.

I stood near Groza, still holding my Glock. I was clenching and unclenching my teeth. I was trying not to be angry with Groza for overreacting and causing this to happen. I had to get myself under control before I spoke.

A uniformed cop to my left was muttering, "Christ, Christ," over and over again. I could see how traumatized he was. The uniformed man kept wiping his hand across his forehead and over his eyes, as if to wipe out the bloody scene.

EMS arrived in a matter of minutes. We watched while two medics tried desperately to save the patrolman's life. He was young and looked to be only in his mid-twenties. His reddish hair was in a short brush cut. The front of his blue shirt was soaked with blood.

In the rear of the crackhouse another medic was trying to save Shareef Thomas, but I already knew that Thomas was gone.

I finally spoke to Groza, low and serious. "*We* know that Thomas is dead, but there's no reason Soneji has to know. This could be how we get to him. If Soneji *thought* Thomas was alive at a New York hospital."

Groza nodded. "Let me talk to somebody downtown. Maybe we could take Thomas to a hospital. Maybe we could get the word to the press. It's worth a shot."

Detective Groza didn't sound very good and he didn't look too good. I was sure I didn't either. I could still see the ominous billboard in the distance: COP SHOT $10,000 REWARD.

CHAPTER 49

NO ONE in the police manhunt would ever guess the beginning, the middle, but especially the end. None of them could imagine where this was heading, where it had been going from the first moment inside Union Station.

Gary Soneji had all the information, all the power. He was getting famous again. He was somebody. He was on the news at ten-minute intervals.

It didn't much matter that they were showing pictures of him. Nobody knew what he looked like today, or yesterday, or tomorrow. They couldn't go around and arrest everyone in New York, could they?

He left the late Jean Summerhill's apartment around noon. The pretty lady had definitely lost her head over him. Just like Missy in Wilmington. He used her key and locked up tight. He walked west on Seventy-third Street until he got to Fifth, then he turned south. The train was back on the track again.

He bought a cup of black coffee in a cardboard container with Greek gods all over the sides. The coffee was absolute New York City swill, but he slowly sipped it anyway. He wanted to go on another rampage right here on Fifth Avenue. He really wanted to go for it. He imagined a massacre, and he could already see the *live* news stories on CBS, ABC, CNN, FOX.

Speaking of news stories, Alex Cross had been on

TV that morning. Cross and the NYPD had nabbed Shareef Thomas. Well hooray for them. It proved they could follow instructions at least.

As he passed chic, well-dressed New Yorkers, Soneji couldn't help thinking how smart he was, how much brighter than any of these uptight assholes. If any of these snooty bastards could get inside his head, just for a minute, then they'd know.

No one could, though, no one had ever been able to. No one could guess.

Not the beginning, the middle, or the end.

He was getting very angry now, almost uncontrollably so. He could feel the rage surging as he walked the overcrowded streets. He almost couldn't see straight. Bile rose in his throat.

He flung his coffee, almost a full cup of the steamy liquid, at a passing businessman. He laughed right in the shocked, outraged face. He howled at the sight of coffee dripping from the New Yorker's aquiline nose, his squarish chin. Dark coffee stained the expensive shirt and tie.

Gary Soneji could do anything he wanted to, and most often, he did.

Just you watch.

CHAPTER 50

A T SEVEN that night, I was back in Penn Station. It wasn't the usual commuter crowd, so it wasn't too bad on Saturdays. The murders that had taken place at Union Station in Washington, and here, were spinning around in my mind. The dark train tunnels were the "cellar" to Soneji, symbols of his tortured boyhood. I had figured out that much of the delusionary puzzle. When Soneji came up out of the cellar, he exploded at the world in a murderous rage. . . .

I saw Christine coming up the stairs from the train tunnels.

I began to smile in spite of the locale. I smiled, and shifted my weight from foot to foot, almost dancing. I felt light-headed and excited, filled with a hope and desire that I hadn't felt in a long time. She had really come.

Christine was carrying a small black bag with "Sojourner Truth School" printed on it. She was traveling light. She looked beautiful, proud, more desirable than ever, if that was possible. She was wearing a white short-sleeved dress with a jewel neckline and her usual flats in black patent leather. I noticed people looking at her. They always did.

We kissed in a corner of the train station, keeping our privacy as best we could. Our bodies pressed together and I could feel her warmth, her bones, her flesh. I heard the bag she was carrying drop at her feet.

Her brown eyes looked into mine and they were wide and questioning at first, but then became very soft and light. "I was a little afraid you wouldn't be here," she said. "I had visions of you off on some police emergency, and me standing here alone in the middle of Penn Station."

"There's no way I would let that happen," I said to her. "I'm so glad you're here."

We kissed again, pressing even harder together. I didn't want to stop kissing Christine, holding her tightly. I wanted to take her where we could be alone. My body nearly convulsed. It was that bad, that good.

"I tried," she said and grinned, "but I couldn't stay away from you. New York scares me a little, but here I am."

"We're going to have a great time. You'll see."

"You promise? Will it be unforgettable?" she teased me.

"Unforgettable, I promise," I said.

I held her tightly in my arms. I couldn't let her go.

CHAPTER 51

THE BEGINNING of "unforgettable" felt like this, looked like this, sounded like this.

The Rainbow Room at eight-thirty on a Saturday night. Christine and I waltzed off the glitzy elevator, arm in arm. We were immediately swept into another era, another lifestyle, maybe another life. A fancy silver-on-black placard near the elevator door read: "The Rainbow Room, Step into an MGM Musical." Hundreds of minispotlights kicked off from the dazzling chrome and crystal. It was over the top, and just about perfect.

"I'm not sure if I'm dressed right for an MGM musical, but I don't particularly care. What a wonderful idea," Christine said as we made our way past overdone, outrageous-looking ushers and usherettes. We were directed to a desk that looked down onto the deco ballroom but also had panoramic views of New York. The room was jam-packed on a Saturday night; every table and the dance floor was filled.

Christine was dressed in a simple black sheath. She wore the same necklace, made from an old-fashioned brooch, that she wore at Kinkead's. It had belonged to her grandmother. Because I'm six three, she wasn't afraid to wear dressier shoes with high heels, rather than her comfortable flats. I had never realized it before, but I liked being with a woman who was nearly as tall as I am.

I had dressed up, too. I'd chosen a charcoal gray, summerweight suit, crisp white shirt, blue silk tie. For tonight anyway, I was definitely not a police detective from D.C. I didn't look like Dr. Alex Cross from Southeast. Maybe more like Denzel Washington playing the part of Jay Gatsby. I liked the feeling, for a night on the town anyway. Maybe even for a whole weekend.

We were escorted to a table in front of a large window that overlooked the glittering East Side of Manhattan. A five-piece Latin band was onstage, and they were cooking pretty good. The slowly revolving dance floor was still full. People were having a fine time, lots of people dancing the night away.

"It's funny, beautiful, and ridiculous, and I think it's as special as anywhere I've been," Christine said once we were seated. "That's about all the superlatives you're going to hear from me tonight."

"You haven't even seen me dance," I said.

"I already know that you can dance." Christine laughed and told me, "Women always know which men can dance, and which men can't."

We ordered drinks, straight Scotch for me, Harvey's sherry for Christine. We picked out a bottle of sauvignon blanc, and then spent a few delicious minutes just taking in the spectacle of the Rainbow Room.

The Latin combo was replaced by a "big band combo," which played swing and even took a swipe at the blues. A whole lot of people still knew how to jitterbug and waltz and even tango, and some of them were pretty good.

"You ever been here before?" I asked Christine as the waiter came with our drinks.

"Only while I was watching *The Prince of Tides* alone in my bedroom at home," she said, and smiled again. "How about you? Come here often, sailor?"

"Just the one time I was chasing down this split-personality ax murderer in New York. He went right out that picture window over there. Third from the left."

Christine laughed. "I wouldn't be surprised if it was true, Alex. I wouldn't be a bit surprised."

The band started to play "Moonglow," which is a pretty song, and we had to get up and dance. Gravity just pulled us. At that moment, I couldn't think of too many things in the world I wanted to do more than hold Christine in my arms. Actually, I couldn't think of anything at all.

At some point in time, Christine and I had agreed to take a risk and see what would happen. We'd both lost people we loved. We knew what it meant to be hurt, and yet here we were, ready to go out on the dance floor of life again. I think I'd wanted to slow-dance with Christine from the very first time I saw her at the Sojourner Truth School.

Now, I tucked her in close and my left arm encircled her waist. My right hand clasped hers. I felt her soft intake of breath. I could tell she was a little nervous, too.

I started to hum softly. I might have been floating a little, too. My lips touched hers and my eyes closed. I could feel the silk of her dress under my fingers. And yes, I could dance pretty well, but so could she.

"Look at me," she whispered, and I opened my eyes. She was right. It was much better that way.

"What's going on here? What *is* this? I don't think I've ever felt like this, Alex."

"Neither have I. But I could get used to it. I know that I like it."

I lightly brushed her cheek with my fingers. The music was working and Christine seemed to flow with me. Graceful, moonlit choreography. All my body parts were moving. I was finding it hard to breathe.

Christine and I were in harmony together. We both could dance well enough, but together it was something special. I moved slowly and smoothly with her. The palm of her hand felt magnetized to mine. I spun her slowly, a playful half turn underneath my arm.

We came back together and our lips were inches apart. I could feel the warmth of her body right through my clothes. Our lips met again, just for an instant, and the music stopped. Another song began.

"Now *that* is a hard act to follow," she said as we sashayed back to our table after the slow dance. "I knew you could dance. Never a doubt in my mind. But I didn't know you could *dance*."

"You haven't seen anything. Wait until they play a samba," I told her. I was still holding her hand, couldn't let go. Didn't want to.

"I *think* I can samba," she said.

We danced a lot, we held hands constantly, and I think we even ate dinner. We definitely danced some more, and I could not let go of Christine's hand. She couldn't let go of mine. We talked nonstop, and later, I couldn't remember most of what had been said. I think that happens high above New York City in the Rainbow Room.

The first time I looked at my watch all night it was nearly one o'clock and I couldn't believe it. That same mysterious time-loss thing had happened a couple of times when I'd been with Christine. I paid our bill, our *big* bill, and I noticed that the Rainbow Room was nearly empty. Where had everybody gone?

"Can you keep a secret?" Christine whispered as we were going down to the lobby in the walnut-paneled elevator. We were alone in the car with its soft yellow light. I was holding her in my arms.

"I keep lots of secrets," I said.

"Well, here it is," Christine said as we reached the bottom floor with just the lightest *bump*. She held me inside after the door had opened. She wasn't going to let me out of the softly lit elevator until she finished saying what she had to say.

"I really like that you got me my own room at the Astor," she said. "But Alex, I don't think I'll be needing it. Is that okay?"

We stood very still in the elevator and began to kiss again. The doors shut, and the elevator slowly climbed back up to the roof. So we kissed going up, and we kissed on the way back down to the lobby, and it wasn't nearly a long enough round-trip.

"You know what, though?" she finally said as we reached the ground floor of Rockefeller Center a second time.

"What, though?" I asked her.

"That's what's *supposed* to happen when you go to the Rainbow Room."

CHAPTER 52

IT WAS unforgettable. Just like the magical Nat King Cole song, and the more recent version with Natalie Cole.

We were standing at the door to my hotel room, and I was completely lost in the moment. I had let go of Christine's hand to open the door—and I was *lost*. I fumbled the key slightly and missed the lock. She gently placed her hand on mine and we glided the key into the lock, turned the tumblers together.

An eternity of seconds passed, at least it seemed that way. I knew that I would never forget any of this. I wouldn't let skepticism or cynicism diminish it either.

I knew what was happening to me. I was feeling the dizzying effect of a return to intimacy. I hadn't realized how much I'd missed it. I had let myself be numb, let myself live numb for the past few years. It's easy enough to do, so easy that you don't even realize your life has become a deep rut.

The hotel door slowly opened, and I had the thought that the two of us were giving up something of our past now. Christine turned to me at the threshold. I heard the faint swish of her silk dress.

Her beautiful face tilted toward mine. I reached for her and balanced her chin with my fingertips. I felt as if I hadn't been able to breathe properly all night, not from the moment she'd arrived at Penn Station.

"Musician's hands. Piano player fingers," she said. "I love the way you touch me. I always knew I would. I'm not afraid anymore, Alex."

"I'm glad. Neither am I."

The heavy wooden door of the hotel room seemed to close all by itself.

It didn't really matter where we were right now, I was thinking. The twinkling lights outside, or maybe a boat gliding by on the river, gave the impression that the floor was gently moving, much as the dance floor at the Rainbow Room had moved under our feet.

I had switched hotels for the weekend, moving to the Astor on Manhattan's East Side. I'd wanted someplace special. The room was on the twelfth floor, facing out on the river.

We were drawn to the picture window, attracted by the strobing lights of the New York skyline to the southeast. We watched the silent, strangely beautiful movement of traffic passing the United Nations, moving toward the Brooklyn Bridge.

I remembered taking the bridge earlier today on our way to a crackhouse in Brooklyn. It seemed so long ago. I saw the face of Shareef Thomas, then the dead policeman's, then Soneji's, but I shut down those images immediately. I wasn't a police detective here. Christine's lips were on my skin, lightly bussing my throat.

"Where did you go just now? You went away, didn't you?" she whispered. "You were in a dark place."

"Just for a few seconds." I confessed the truth, my flaw. "A flashback from work. It's gone." I was holding her hand again.

She kissed me lightly on the cheek, a paper-thin kiss, then very lightly on the lips. "You can't lie, can you, Alex? Not even tiny white lies."

"I try not to. I don't like lies. If I lie to you, then who am I?" I said and smiled. "What's the point?"

"I love that about you," she whispered. "Lots of other things, too. I find something else every time I'm with you."

I nuzzled the top of her head, then I kissed Christine's forehead, her cheek, her lips, and finally the sweet hollow of her throat. She was trembling a little. So was I. Thank God that neither of us was afraid, right. I could feel the pulse tripping under her skin.

"You're so beautiful," I whispered. "Do you know that?"

"I'm way too tall, too thin. *You're* the beautiful one. You are, you know. Everybody says so."

Everything felt electric and so right. It seemed a miracle that we had found each other, and now we were here together. I was so glad, felt so lucky, that she had decided to take a chance with me, that I had taken a chance, too.

"Look in the mirror there. See how beautiful you are," she said. "You have the sweetest face. You *are* trouble, though, aren't you, Alex?"

"I won't give you too much trouble tonight," I said. I wanted to undress her, to do everything for and to

Christine. A funny word, strange word was in my head, *rapture*. She slid her hand over the front of my pants and felt how hard I was.

"Hmmm," she whispered and smiled.

I began to unzip her dress. I couldn't remember wanting to be with someone like this, not for a long time anyway. I ran my hand over her face, memorizing every part, every feature. Christine's skin was so soft and silky underneath my fingers.

We started to dance again, right there in the hotel room. There wasn't any music, but we had our own. My hand pressed just below her waist, folding her in close to me.

Moonlit choreography again. We slowly rocked back and forth, back and forth, a sensuous cha-cha-cha next to the broad picture window. I held her buttocks in the palms of my hands. She wiggled into a position she liked. I liked it, too. A whole lot.

"You dance real good, Alex. I just knew you would."

Christine reached down and tugged at my belt until the prong came free. She unzipped me, lightly fondled me. I loved her touch, anywhere, everywhere. Her lips were on my skin again. Everything about her was erotic, irresistible, unforgettable.

We both knew to do this slowly, no need to hurry anything tonight. Rushing would spoil this, and it mustn't be spoiled in any way.

I held the thought that we'd both been here before, but never like this. We were in this very special place for the first time. This would only happen one time.

My kisses slowly swept over her shoulders and I could feel her breasts rising and falling against me. I felt the flatness of her stomach, and her legs pressing. I cupped Christine's breasts in my hands. Suddenly I wanted everything, all of her at once.

I sank to my knees. I ran my hands up and down her soft legs, along her waist.

I rose to my feet. I unzipped her black sheath the rest of the way, and it trailed down her long arms to the floor. It made a shimmering black puddle surrounding her ankles, her slender feet.

Finally, when there were no more clothes, we looked at each other. Christine watched my eyes and I watched hers. Her eyes shamelessly traveled down my chest, past my waist. I was still highly aroused. I wanted to be inside her so much.

She took a half step back. I couldn't breathe. I could hardly bear this. But I didn't want to stop. I was feeling again, remembering how to feel, remembering how good it could be.

She pulled her hair to one side, behind one ear. Such a simple, graceful movement.

"Do that again." I smiled.

She laughed and repeated the movement with her hair. "Anything that you want."

"Stay there," she whispered. "Don't move, Alex. Don't come closer—we might both catch fire. I mean it."

"This could take the rest of the weekend," I said and started to laugh.

"I hope it does."

I heard the tiniest *click*.

Was that the door to our room?

Had I closed it?

Was someone out there?

Jesus, no.

CHAPTER 53

SUDDENLY NERVOUS and paranoid, I peered back at the door to the hotel room. It was closed and locked tight. Nobody there, nothing to worry about. Christine and I were safe here. Nothing bad was going to happen to either of us tonight.

Still, the moment of fear and doubt had raised the hairs on my neck. Soneji has a habit of doing that to me. *Damn it, what did he want from me?*

"What's wrong, Alex? You just left me." Christine touched me, brought me back. Her fingers were like feathers on the side of my cheek. "Just be here with me, Alex."

"I'm here. I just thought I heard something."

"I know you did. No one is there. You locked the door behind us. We're fine. It's okay, it's okay."

I pulled Christine close against my body again and she felt electric and incredibly warm. I drew her down onto the bed and rolled over her, holding my weight on the palms of my hands. I dipped and kissed her sweet face again, then each of her breasts; I pulled at the nipples with my lips, licked them with my tongue. I kissed between her legs, down her long legs, her slender ankles, her toes. *Just be here with me, Alex.*

She arched herself toward me and she gasped, but she was smiling radiantly. She was moving her body against me and we had already found a nice rhythm. We were both breathing faster and faster.

"Please, do it now," she whispered, her teeth biting into my shoulder near the clavicle. "Please now, *right now*. I want you inside." She rubbed my sides with the palms of her hands. She rubbed me like kindling sticks.

A fire ignited. I could feel it spreading through my body. I entered her for the first time. I slid inside slowly, but I went as deep as I could go. My heart was pounding, my legs felt weak. My stomach was taut and I was so hard it hurt.

I was all the way inside Christine. I knew I'd wanted to be here for a long time. I had the thought that I was made for this, for being in this bed with this woman.

Gracefully and athletically, she rolled on top of me and sat up proud and tall. We began to rock slowly like that. I felt our bodies surge and peak, surge and peak, surge.

I heard my own voice crying yes, yes, yes. Then I realized it was both our voices.

Then Christine said something so magical. She whispered, *"You're the one."*

Part Three
The Cellar of Cellars

CHAPTER 54

Paris, France

DR. ABEL Sante was thirty-five years old, with longish black hair, boyish good looks, and a beautiful girlfriend named Regina Becker, who was a painter, and a very good one, he thought. He had just left Regina's apartment, and was winding his way home on the back streets of the sixth arrondissement at around midnight.

The narrow streets were quiet and empty and he loved this time of day for collecting his thoughts, or sometimes for not thinking at all. Abel Sante was musing on the death of a young woman earlier today, a patient of his, twenty-six years old. She had a loving husband and two beautiful daughters. He had a perspective about death that he thought was a good one: Why should leaving the world, and rejoining the cosmos, be any scarier than entering the world, which wasn't very scary at all.

Dr. Sante didn't know where the man, a street person in a soiled gray jacket and torn, baggy jeans had come from. Suddenly the man was at his side, nearly attached to his left elbow.

"Beautiful," the man said.

"I'm sorry, excuse me?" Abel Sante said, startled, coming out of his inner thoughts in a hurry.

"It's a beautiful night and our city is so perfect for a late walk."

"Yes, well it's been nice meeting you," Sante said to the street person. He'd noticed that the man's French was slightly accented. Perhaps he was English, or even American.

"You shouldn't have left her apartment. Should have stayed the night. A gentleman always stays the night—unless of course he's asked to leave."

Dr. Abel Sante's back and neck stiffened. He took his hands from his trouser pockets. Suddenly he was afraid, very much so.

He shoved the street person away with his left elbow.

"What are you talking about? Why don't you just get out of here?"

"I'm talking about you and Regina. Regina Becker, the painter. Her work's not bad, but not good enough, I'm afraid."

"Get the hell away from me."

Abel Sante quickened his pace. He was only a block from his home. The other man, the street person, kept up with him easily. He was larger, more athletic than Sante had noticed at first.

"You should have given her babies. That's my opinion."

"Get away. Go!"

Suddenly, Sante had both fists raised and clasped tightly. This was insane! He was ready to fight, if he had to. He hadn't fought in twenty years, but he was strong and in good shape.

The street person swung out and knocked him down. He did it easily, as if it were nothing at all.

Dr. Sante's pulse was racing rapidly. He couldn't see very well out of his left eye, where he'd been struck.

"Are you a complete maniac? Are you out of your mind?" he screamed at the man, who suddenly looked powerful and impressive, even in the soiled clothes.

"Yes, of course," the man answered. "Of course I'm out of my mind. *I'm Mr. Smith*—and you're next."

CHAPTER 55

GARY SONEJI hurried like a truly horrifying city rat through the low dark tunnels that wind like intestines beneath New York's Bellevue Hospital. The fetid odor of dried blood and disinfectants made him feel sick. He didn't like the reminders of sickness and death surrounding him.

No matter, though, he was properly revved for today. He was wired, flying high. *He was Death. And Death was not taking a holiday in New York.*

He had outfitted himself for his big morning: crisply pressed white pants, white lab coat, white sneakers; a laminated hospital photo ID around his neck on a beaded silver chain.

He was here on morning rounds. Bellevue. *This was his idea of rounds anyway!*

There was no way to stop any of this: his train from hell, his destiny, his last hurrah. No one could stop it because no one would ever figure out where the last train was headed. Only he knew that, only Soneji himself could call it off.

He wondered how much of the puzzle Cross had already pieced together. Cross wasn't in his class as a thinker, but the psychologist and detective wasn't without crude instincts in certain specialized areas. Maybe he was underestimating Dr. Cross, as he had once before. Could he be caught now? Perhaps, but it really didn't matter. The game would continue to its end without him. That was the beauty of it, the evil of what he had done.

Gary Soneji stepped into a stainless-steel elevator in the basement of the well-known Manhattan hospital. A pair of porters shared the narrow car with him, and Soneji had a moment of paranoia. They might be New York cops working undercover.

The NYPD actually had an office on the main floor of the hospital. It was there under "normal" circumstances. *Bellevue. Jesus, what a sensational madhouse this was. A hospital with a police station inside.*

He eyed the porters with a casual and disinterested city-cool look. *They can't be policemen,* he thought. *Nobody could look that dumb.* They were what they looked like—slow-moving, slow-thinking hospital morons.

One of them was pushing around a stainless-steel cart with *two* bum wheels. It was a wonder that any patient ever made it out of a New York City hospital alive. Hospitals here were run with about the same personnel standards as a McDonald's restaurant, probably less.

He knew one patient who wasn't going to leave Bellevue alive. The news reports said that Shareef Thomas was being kept here by the police. Well, Thomas was going to suffer before he left this so-called "vale of tears." Shareef was about to undergo a world of suffering.

Gary Soneji stepped out of the elevator onto the first floor. He sighed with relief. The two porters went about their business. They weren't cops. No, they were dumber and dumbest.

Canes, wheelchairs, and metal walkers were everywhere. The hospital artifacts reminded him of his own mortality. The halls on the first floor were painted off-white, the doors and radiators were a shade of pink like "old gum." Up ahead was a strange coffee shop, dimly lit like a subway passageway. *If you ate in that place,* he thought to himself, *they ought to lock you up in Bellevue!*

As he walked from the elevator, Soneji caught his own reflection in a stainless-steel pillar. *The master of a thousand faces,* he couldn't help thinking. It was true. His own stepmother wouldn't recognize him now, and if she did, she would scream her bloody lungs out. She'd know he'd come all the way to hell to get her.

He walked down the corridor, singing very softly in a reggae lilt, "I shot the Shareef, but I did not shoot the dep-u-tee."

No one paid him any mind. Gary Soneji fit right in at Bellevue.

CHAPTER 56

SONEJI HAD a perfect memory, so he would recall everything about this morning. He would be able to play it back for himself with incredible detail. This was true for all of his murders. He scanned the narrow, high-ceilinged hallways as if he had a surveillance camera mounted where his head was. His powers of concentration gave him a huge advantage. He was almost supernaturally aware of everything going on around him.

A security guard was riffing with young black males outside the coffee shop. They were all mental defectives for sure, the toy cops especially.

No threat there.

Silly baseball caps were bobbing everywhere. New Jork Janquis. San Francisco Jints. San Jose Sharks. None of the ballcap wearers looked as if they could play ball worth spit. Or harm, or stop him.

The Hospital Police Office was up ahead. The lights were out, though. Nobody home right now. So where were the hospital patrol cops? Were they waiting for him someplace? Why didn't he see any of them? Was that the first sign of trouble?

At the inpatient elevator, a sign read: ID REQUIRED. Soneji had his ready. For today's masquerade, he was Francis Michael Nicolo, R.N.

A framed poster was on the wall: PATIENTS' RIGHTS AND RESPONSIBILITIES. Signs stared out from behind fuzzy Plexiglas everywhere he looked. It was worse than a New York highway: RADIOLOGY, UROLOGY, HEMATOLOGY. *I'm sick, too,* Soneji wanted to yell out to the powers that be. *I'm as sick as anybody in here. I'm dying. Nobody cares. Nobody has ever cared.*

He took the central elevator to four. No problems so far, no hassles. No police. He got off at his stop, pumped to see Shareef Thomas again, to see the look of shock and fear on his face.

The hallway on four had a hollowed-out basement feel to it. Nothing seemed to absorb sound. The whole building felt as if it were made entirely of concrete.

Soneji peered down the corridor to where he knew Shareef was being kept. His room was at the far end of the building. Isolated for safety, right? So this was the high-and-mighty NYPD in action. What a joke. Everything was a joke, if you thought about it long and hard enough.

Soneji lowered his head and started to walk toward Shareef Thomas's hospital room.

CHAPTER 57

CARMINE GROZA and I were inside the private hospital room waiting for Soneji, hoping that he would show. We had been here for hours. How would I know what Soneji looked like now? That was a problem, but we would take them one at a time.

We never heard a noise at the door. Suddenly it was swinging open. Soneji exploded into the room, expecting to find Shareef Thomas. He stared at Groza and me.

His hair was dyed silver-gray and combed straight back. He looked like a man in his fifties or early sixties—but the height was about right. His light blue eyes widened as he looked at me. It was the eyes that I recognized first.

He smiled the same disdainful dismissive smirk I'd seen so many times, sometimes in my nightmares. He thought he was so damn superior to the rest of us. He *knew* it.

Soneji said only two words: "Even better."

"New York police! Freeze," Groza barked a warning in an authoritative tone.

Soneji continued to smirk as if this surprise reception pleased him no end, as if he'd planned it himself. His confidence, his arrogance, was incredible to behold.

He's wearing a bulletproof vest, my mind registered a bulge around his upper body. *He's protected. He's ready for whatever we do.*

There was something clasped tightly in his left hand. I couldn't tell what. He'd entered the room with the arm half-raised.

He flipped a small green bottle in his hand toward Groza and me. Just the *flip* of his hand. The bottle clinked as it hit the wooden floor. It bounced a second time. Suddenly I understood . . . but too late, seconds too late.

"Bomb!" I yelled at Groza. "Hit the floor! Get down!"

Groza and I dove away from the bed and the caroming green bottle. We managed to put up sitting chairs as shields. The flash inside the room was incredibly bright, a splintered shock of white light with an afterglow of the brightest yellow. Then everything around us seemed to catch fire.

For a second or two, I was blinded. Then I felt as if I were burning up. My trousers and shoes were engulfed in flames. I covered my face, mouth, and eyes with my hands. "Jesus, God," Groza screamed.

I could hear a sizzle, like bacon on a grill. I prayed it wasn't me that was cooking. Then I was choking and gurgling and so was Groza. Flames burst and danced across my shirt, and through it all I could hear Soneji. He was laughing at us.

"Welcome to hell, Cross," he said. "Burn, baby, burn."

CHAPTER 58

GROZA AND I stripped the bed of blankets and sheets and beat out our burning trousers. We were lucky, at least I hoped we were. We smothered the flames. The ones on our legs and shoes.

"He wanted to burn Thomas alive," I told Groza. "He's got *another* firebomb. I saw another green bottle, at least one."

We hobbled as best we could down the hospital corridor, chasing after Soneji. Two other detectives were already down outside, wounded. Soneji *was* a phantom.

We followed him down several twisting flights of back stairs. The sound of the footrace echoed loudly on the stairway. My eyes were watering, but I could see okay.

Groza alerted and clued in other detectives on his two-way. "Suspect has a firebomb! Soneji has a bomb. Use extreme care."

"What the hell does he want?" the detective yelled at me as we kept moving. "What the hell's he going to do now?"

"I think he wants to die," I gasped. "And he wants to be famous. Go out with a bang. That's his way. Maybe right here at Bellevue."

Attention was what Gary Soneji had always craved. From his boyhood years, he'd been obsessed with stories of "crimes of the century." I was sure that Soneji wanted to die now, but he had to do it with a huge noise. He wanted to control his own death.

I was wheezing and out of breath when we finally got to the lobby floor. Smoke had seared my throat, but otherwise I was doing okay. My brain was fuzzy and unclear about what to do next.

I saw a blur of hectic movement ahead, maybe thirty yards across the front lobby.

I pushed through the nervous crowd trying to exit the building. Word had spread about the fire upstairs. The flow of people in and out of Bellevue was always as steady as at a subway turnstile, and that was *before* a bomb went off inside.

I made it onto the stoop in front of the hospital. It was raining hard, gray and awful outside. I looked everywhere for Soneji.

A cluster of hospital staff and visitors were under the front awning, smoking cigarettes. They seemed unaware of the emergency situation, or maybe these workers were just used to them. The brick path leading away from the building was crowded with more pedestrians coming and going in the downpour. The umbrellas were blocking my vision.

Where the hell had Gary Soneji gone? Where could he have disappeared to? I had the sinking feeling that I'd lost him again. I couldn't stand any more of this.

Out on First Avenue, food vendors under colorful umbrellas stained with dirt were peddling gyros, hot dogs, and New York–style pretzels.

No Soneji anywhere.

I kept searching, frantically looking up and down the busy, noisy street. I couldn't let him get away. I would never get another chance as good as this. There was an opening in the crowd. I could see for maybe half a block.

There he was!

Soneji was moving with a small clique of pedestrians headed north on the sidewalk. I started to go after him. Groza was still with me. We both had our weapons out. We couldn't risk a shot in the crowds, though. Lots of mothers and children and elderly people, patients coming and going from the hospital.

Soneji peered to the left, the right, and then behind. He saw us coming. I was sure he'd seen me.

He was improvising his escape, a way out of the extreme and dangerous mess. The sequence of recent events showed deterioration in his thinking. He was losing his sharpness and clarity. *That's why he's ready to die now. He's tired of dying slowly. He's losing his mind. He can't bear it*

A Con Ed crew had blocked off half the intersection. Hard hats bobbed in the rain. Traffic was trying to maneuver around the roadwork, nonstop honkers everywhere.

I saw Soneji make a sudden break from the crowd. What the hell? He was running toward First Avenue, racing down the slippery street. He was weaving, running in a full sprint.

I watched as Gary Soneji spun quickly to his right.

Do us all a favor. Go down! He ran along the side of a white and blue city bus that had stopped for passengers.

He was still slipping, sliding. He almost fell. Then he was inside the goddamn bus.

The bus was standing-room only. I could see Soneji frantically waving his arms, screaming orders at the other passengers. *Jesus, God, he's got a bomb on that city bus.*

CHAPTER 59

DETECTIVE GROZA staggered up beside me. His face was smudged with soot and his flowing black hair was singed. He signaled wildly for a car, waving both arms. A police sedan pulled up beside us and we jumped inside.

"You all right?" I asked him.

"I guess so. I'm here. Let's go get him."

We followed the bus up First Avenue, weaving in and out of traffic, siren full blast. We almost hit a cab, missed by inches, if that.

"You sure he's got another bomb?"

I nodded. "At least one. Remember the Mad Bomber in New York? Soneji probably does. The Mad Bomber was famous."

Everything was crazy and surreal. The rain was coming down harder, making loud bangs on the sedan's roof.

"He has hostages," Groza spoke into the two-way on the dash. "He's on a city bus heading up First Avenue. He appears to have a bomb. The bus is an M-15. All cars stay on the bus. Do not intercept at this point. He has a goddamn bomb on the M-15 bus."

I counted a half a dozen blue-and-whites already in pursuit. The city bus was stopping for red lights, but it was no longer picking up passengers. People standing in the rain, bypassed at stops, waved their arms angrily at the M-15. None of them understood how lucky they were that the bus doors didn't open for them.

"Try to get close," I told the driver. "I want to talk to him. Want to see if he'll talk anyway. It's worth a try."

The police sedan accelerated, then weaved on the wet streets. We were getting closer. We were inching alongside the bright blue bus. A poster advertised the musical *Phantom of the Opera* in bold type. *A real live phantom was on board the bus.* Gary Soneji was back in the spotlight that he loved. He was playing New York now.

I had the side window of the car rolled down. Rain and wind attacked my face, but I could see Soneji inside the bus. *Jesus, he was still improvising*—he had somebody's child, a bundle of pink and blue, cradled in his arm. He was screaming orders, his free arm swinging in angry circles.

I leaned as far as I could outside the car. "Gary!" I yelled. "What do you want?" I called out again, fighting the traffic noise, the loud roar of the bus. *"Gary! It's Alex Cross!"*

Passengers inside the bus were looking out at me. They were terrified, beyond terror, actually.

At Forty-second Street and First, the bus made a sudden, sweeping left turn!

I looked at Groza. "This the regular route?"

"No way," he said. "He's making his own route up as he goes."

"What's on Forty-second Street? What's up ahead? Where the hell could he be going?"

Groza threw up his hands in desperation. "Times Square is across town, home of the skells, the city's worst derelicts and losers. Theater district's there, too. Port Authority Bus Terminal. We're coming up on Grand Central Station."

"Then he's going to Grand Central," I told Groza. "I'm sure of it. This is the way he wants it. In a train station!" Another cellar, a glorious one that went on for city blocks. *The cellar of cellars.*

Gary Soneji was already out of the bus and running on Forty-second Street. He was headed toward Grand Central Station, headed toward home. He was still carrying the baby in one arm, swinging it loosely, showing us how little he cared about the child's life.

Goddamn him to hell. He was on the homestretch, and only he knew what that meant.

CHAPTER 60

I MADE MY way down the crowded stone-and-mortar passageway from Forty-second Street. It emptied into an even busier Grand Central Station. Thousands of already harried commuters were arriving for work in the midtown area. They had no idea how truly bad their day was about to become.

Grand Central is the New York end for the New York Central, the New York, New Haven, and Hartford trains, and a few others. And for three IRT subway lines. Lexington Avenue, Times Square–Grand Central Shuttle, and Queens. The terminal covers three blocks between Forty-second and Forty-fifth Streets. Forty-one tracks are on the upper level and twenty-six on the lower, which narrows to a single four-track line to Ninety-sixth Street.

The lower level is a huge labyrinth, one of the largest anywhere in the world.

Gary's cellar.

I continued to push against the densely packed rush-hour crowd. I made it through a waiting room, then emerged into the cavernous and spectacular main concourse. Construction work was in progress everywhere. Giant cloth posters for Pan Am Airlines and American Express and Nike sneakers hung down over the walls. The gates to dozens of tracks were visible from where I stood.

Detective Groza caught up with me in the concourse. We were both running on adrenaline. "He's still got the baby," he huffed. "Somebody spotted him running down to the next level."

Leading a merry chase, right? Gary Soneji was heading to the cellar. That wouldn't be good for the thousands of people crowding inside the building. He had a bomb, and maybe more than one.

I led Groza down more steep stairs, under a lit sign that said OYSTER BAR ON THIS LEVEL. The entire station was still under massive construction and renovation, which only added to the confusion. We pushed past crowded bakeries and delis. Plenty to eat here while you waited for your train, or possibly to be blown up. I spotted a Hoffritz cutlery shop up ahead. Maybe Hoffritz was where Soneji had purchased the knife he'd used in Penn Station.

Detective Groza and I reached the next level. We entered a spacious arcade, surrounded by more railway-track doorways. Signs pointed the way to the subways, to the Times Square Shuttle.

Groza had a two-way cupped near his ear. He was getting up-to-the-second reports from around the station. "He's down in the tunnels. We're close," he told me.

Groza and I raced down another steep deck of stone steps. We ran side by side. It was unbearably hot down below and we were sweating. The building was vibrating. The gray stone walls and the floor shook beneath

our feet. We were in hell now, the only question was,
which circle?

I finally saw Gary Soneji up ahead. Then he disappeared again. He still had the baby, or maybe it was
just the pink-and-blue blanket puffed in his arms.

He was back in sight. Then he *stopped* suddenly.
Soneji turned and stared down the tunnel. He wasn't
afraid of anything anymore. I could see it in his eyes.

"Dr. Cross," he yelled. "You follow directions beautifully."

CHAPTER 61

SONEJI'S DARK secret still worked, still held true for him: Whatever would make people intensely angry, whatever would make them inconsolably sad, whatever would hurt them—*that's what he did.*

Soneji watched Alex Cross approaching. *Tall and arrogant black bastard. Are you ready to die, too, Cross?*

Right when your life seems so promising. Your young children growing up. And your beautiful new lover.

Because that's what's going to happen. You're going to die for what you did to me. You can't stop it from happening.

Alex Cross kept walking toward him, parading across the concrete train platform. He didn't look afraid. Cross definitely walked the walk. That was his strength, but it was also his folly.

Soneji felt as if he were floating in space right now. He felt so free, as if nothing could hurt him anywhere. He could be exactly who he wanted to be, act as he wished. He'd spent his life trying to get here.

Alex Cross was getting closer and closer. He called out a question across the train platform. It was always a question with Cross.

"What do you want, Gary? What the hell do you want from us?"

"Shut your hole! What do you think I want?" Soneji shouted back. "You! I finally caught *you*."

CHAPTER 62

I HEARD WHAT Soneji said, but it didn't matter anymore. This thing between us was going down now. I kept coming toward him. One way or the other, this was the end.

I walked down a flight of three or four stone steps. I couldn't take my eyes off Soneji. I couldn't. I refused to give up now.

Smoke from the hospital fire was in my lungs. The air in the train tunnel didn't help. I began to cough.

Could this be the end of Soneji? I almost couldn't believe it. What the hell did he mean *he finally caught me?*

"Don't anybody move. Stop! Not another step!" Soneji yelled. He had a gun. The baby. "I'll tell you who moves, and who doesn't. That includes you, Cross. *So just stop walking.*"

I stopped. No one else moved. It was incredibly quiet on the train platform, deep in the bowels of Grand Central. There were probably twenty people close enough to Soneji to be injured by a bomb.

He held the baby from the bus up high, and that had everybody's attention. Detectives and uniformed police stood paralyzed in the wide doorways around the train tunnel. We were all helpless, powerless to do anything to stop Soneji. We had to listen to him.

He began to turn in a small, tight, frenzied circle. His body twirled around and around. A strange whirling dervish. He was clutching the infant in one arm, holding her like a doll. I had no idea what had become of the child's mother.

Soneji almost seemed in a trance. He looked crazy now—maybe he was. "The good Doctor Cross is here," he yelled down the platform. "How much do you know? How much do you *think* you know? Let *me* ask the questions for a change."

"I don't know enough, Gary," I said, keeping my answer as low-key as possible. Not playing to the crowd, *his* crowd. "I guess you still like an audience."

"Why yes, I do, Dr. Cross. I love an appreciative crowd. What's the point of a great performance with no one to see it? I crave the look in all of your eyes, your fear, your hatred." He continued to turn, to spin as if he were playing a theater-in-the-round. "You'd all like to kill me. You're all killers, too!" he screeched.

Soneji did another slow spin around, his gun pointed out, the baby cradled in his left arm. The infant wasn't crying, and that worried me sick. The bomb could be in a pocket of his trousers. It was somewhere. I hoped it wasn't in the baby's blanket.

"You're back there in the cellar? Aren't you?" I said. At one time I had believed Gary Soneji was schizophrenic. Then I was certain that he wasn't. Right now, I wasn't sure of anything.

He gestured with his free arm at the underground caverns. He continued to walk slowly toward the rear of the platform. We couldn't stop him. "As a kid, this is where I always dreamed I would escape to. Take a big, fast train to Grand Central Station in New York City. Get away clean and free. *Escape* from everything."

"You've done it. You finally won. Isn't that why you led us here? To catch you?" I said.

"I'm *not* done. Not even close. I'm not finished with you yet, Cross," he sneered.

There was his threat again. It made my stomach drop to hear him talk like that. "What about me?" I called. "You keep making threats. I don't see any action."

Soneji stopped moving. He stopped backing toward the rear of the platform. Everyone was watching him now, probably thinking none of this was real. I wasn't even sure if I did.

"This doesn't end here, Cross. *I'm coming for you*, even from the grave if I have to. There's no way you can stop this. You remember that! Don't you forget now! I'm sure you won't."

Then Soneji did something I would never understand. His left arm shot up. He threw the baby high in the air. The people watching gasped as the child tumbled forward.

They sighed audibly as a man fifteen feet down the platform caught the baby perfectly.

Then, the infant started to cry.

"Gary, no!" I shouted at Soneji. He was running again.

"Are you ready to die, Dr. Cross?" he screamed back at me. *"Are you ready?"*

CHAPTER 63

SONEJI DISAPPEARED through a silver, metallic door at the rear of the platform. He was quick, and he had surprise on his side. Gunshots rang out—Groza fired—but I didn't think Soneji had been hit.

"There's more tunnels back there, lots of train tracks down here," Groza told me. "We're walking into a dark, dirty maze."

"Yeah, well let's go anyway," I said. "Gary loves it down here. We'll make the best of it."

I noticed a maintenance worker and grabbed his flashlight. I pulled out my Glock. Seventeen shots. Groza had a .357 Magnum. Six more rounds. How many shots would it take to kill Soneji? Would he ever die?

"He's wearing a goddamn vest," Groza said.

"Yeah, I saw that." I clicked the safety off the Glock. "He's a Boy Scout—*always prepared*."

I opened the door through which Soneji had disappeared, and it was suddenly as dark as a tomb. I leveled the barrel of the Glock in front of me and continued forward. This was the cellar, all right, his private hell on a very large scale.

Are you ready to die, Dr. Cross?

There's no way you can stop it from happening.

I bobbed and weaved as best I could and the flashlight beam shook all over the walls. I could see dim light, dusty lamps up ahead, so I turned off the flash. My lungs hurt. I couldn't breathe very well, but maybe some of the physical distress was claustrophobia and terror.

I didn't like it in his cellar. This is how Gary must have felt when he was just a boy. Was he telling us that? Letting us experience it?

"Jesus," Groza muttered at my back. I figured that he felt what I felt, disoriented and afraid. The wind howled from somewhere inside the tunnel. We couldn't see much of anything up ahead.

You had to use your imagination in the dark, I was thinking as I proceeded forward. Soneji had learned how to do that as a boy. There were voices behind us now, but they were distant. The ghostly voices echoed off the walls. Nobody was hurrying to catch up with Soneji in the dark, dingy tunnel.

The brakes of a train screeched on the other side of the blackened stone walls. The subway was down here, just parallel to us. There was a stench of garbage and waste that kept getting worse the farther we walked.

I knew that street people lived in some of these tunnels. The NYPD had a Homeless Unit to deal with them.

"Anything there?" Groza muttered, fear and uncertainty in his voice. "You see anything?"

"Nothing." I whispered. I didn't want to make any more noise than we had to. I sucked in another harsh breath. I heard a train whistle on the other side of the stone walls.

There was dim light in parts of the tunnel. A scrim of garbage was underfoot, discarded fast-food wrappers, torn and grossly soiled clothing. I had already seen a couple of oversized rats scurrying alongside my feet, out food shopping in the Big Apple.

Then I heard a scream right on top of me. My neck and back stiffened. It was Groza! He went down. I had no idea what had hit him. He didn't make another sound, didn't move on the tunnel floor.

I whirled around. Couldn't see anyone at first. The darkness seemed to swirl.

I caught a flash of Soneji's face. One eye and half his mouth in dark profile. He hit me before I could get the Glock up. Soneji screamed—a brutal, primal yell. No recognizable words.

He hit me with tremendous power. A punch to the left temple. I remembered how incredibly strong he was, and how crazy he had become. My ears rang, and my head was spinning. My legs were wobbly. He'd almost taken me out with the first punch. Maybe he could have. But he wanted to punish me, wanted his revenge, his payback.

He screamed again—this time inches from my face.

Hurt him back, I told myself. *Hurt him now, or you won't get another chance.*

Soneji's strength was as brutal as it had been the last time we met, especially fighting in close like this. He had me wrapped in his arms and I could smell his breath. He tried to crush me with his arms. White lights flickered and danced before my eyes. I was nearly out on my feet.

He screamed again. I butted with my head. It took him by surprise. His grip loosened, and I broke away for a second.

I threw the hardest punch of my life and heard the crunch of his jaw. Soneji didn't go down! What did it take to hurt him?

He came at me again, and I struck his left cheek. I felt bone crush under my fist. He screamed, then moaned, but he didn't fall, didn't stop coming after me.

"You can't hurt me," he gasped, growled. "You're going to die. You can't stop it from happening. You can't stop this now."

Gary Soneji came at me again. I finally raised the Glock, got it out. *Hurt him, hurt him, kill him right now.*

I fired! And although it happened fast, it seemed like slow motion. I thought I could *feel* the gunshot travel through Soneji's body. The shot bulldozed through his lower jaw. It must have blown his tongue away, his teeth.

What remained of Soneji reached out to me, tried to hold on, to claw at my face and throat. I pushed him away. *Hurt him, hurt him, kill him.*

He staggered several steps down the darkened tunnel. I don't know where he got the strength. I was too tired to chase him, but I knew I didn't have to.

He fell toward the stone floor. He dropped like a deadweight. As he hit the ground, the bomb in his pocket ignited. Gary Soneji exploded in flames. The tunnel behind him was illuminated for at least a hundred feet.

Soneji screamed for a few seconds, then he burned in silence—a human torch in his cellar. He had gone straight to hell.

It was finally over.

CHAPTER 64

THE JAPANESE have a saying—after victory, tighten your helmet cord. I tried to keep that in mind.

I was back in Washington early on Tuesday, and I spent the whole day at home with Nana and the kids and with Rosie the cat. The morning started when the kids prepared what they called a "bubba-bath" for me. It got better from there. Not only didn't I tighten my helmet cord, I took the damn thing off.

I tried not to be upset by Soneji's horrible death, or his threat against me. I'd lived with worse from him in the past. Much worse. Soneji was dead and gone from all of our lives. I had seen him blown to hell with my own eyes. I'd helped blow him there.

Still, I could hear his voice, his warning, his threat at different times during my day at home.

You're going to die. You can't stop it from happening.

I'm coming for you, from the grave if I have to.

Kyle Craig called from Quantico to congratulate me and ask how I was doing. Kyle still had an ulterior motive. He tried to suck me into his Mr. Smith case, but I told him no. Definitely no way. I didn't have the heart for Mr. Smith right now. He wanted me to meet his superagent Thomas Pierce. He asked if I'd read his faxes on Pierce. *No.*

That night I went to Christine's house, and I knew I had made the right decision about Mr. Smith and the FBI's continuing problems with the case. I didn't spend the night because of the kids, but I could have. I wanted to. "You promised you'd be around until we were both at least in our eighties. This is a pretty good start," she said when I was leaving for the night.

On Wednesday, I had to go to the office to start closing down the Soneji case. I wasn't thrilled that I had killed him, but I was glad it was over. Everything but the blasted paperwork.

I got home from work around six. I was in the mood for another "bubba-bath," maybe some boxing lessons, a night with Christine.

I walked in the front door of my house—and all hell broke loose.

CHAPTER 65

NANA AND the kids were standing before me in the living room. So was Sampson, several detective friends, neighbors, my aunties, a few uncles, and all of their kids. Jannie and Damon started the group yell on cue, "Surprise, Daddy! Surprise party!" Then everybody else in kingdom come joined in. "Surprise, Alex, surprise!"

"Who's Alex? Who's Daddy?" I played dumb at the door. "What the hell is going on here?"

Toward the back of the room I could see Christine, at least her smiling face. I waved at her, even as I was being hugged and pounded on the back and shoulders by all my best friends in the world.

I thought Damon was acting a little too respectful, so I swooped him up in my arms (this was probably the last year I would be able to do it) and we hollered assorted sports and war cries, which seemed to fit the party scene.

It's not usually a very charitable idea to celebrate the death of another human being but, in this case, I thought a party was a terrific idea. It was an appropriate and fitting way to end what had been a sad and scary time for all of us. Somebody had hung a droopy, badly hand-painted banner over the doorway between the living room and dining area. The banner read: *Congratulations, Alex! Better luck next lifetime, Gary S.!*

Sampson led me into the backyard, where even more friends were waiting in ambush. Sampson had on baggy black shorts, a pair of combat boots, and his shades. He wore a beat-up Homicide cap and had a silver loop in one ear. He was definitely ready to party, and so was I.

Detectives from all around D.C. had come to offer their hearty congratulations, but also to eat my food and drink my liquor.

Succulent kabobs and racks of baby-back ribs were arranged beside homemade breads, rolls, and an impressive array of hotsauce bottles. It made my eyes water just to look at the feast. Aluminum tubs overflowed with beer and ale and soda pop on ice. There was fresh corn on the cob, colorful fruit salads, and summer pastas by the bowlful.

Sampson grabbed my arm tight, and hollered so I could hear him over the noise of joyful voices and also Toni Braxton wailing her heart out on the CD player. "You party on, Sugar. Say hello to all your other guests, all your peeps. I plan to be here until closing time."

"I'll catch you later," I told him. "Nice boots, nice shorts, nice legs."

"Thank you, thank you, thank you. You got that son of a bitch, Alex! You did the right thing. May his evil, hair-bag ass burn and rot in hell. I'm just sorry I wasn't there with you."

Christine had taken a quiet spot in the corner of the yard under our shade tree. She was talking with my favorite aunt, Tia, and my sister-in-law, Cilla. It was like her to put herself last on the greeting line.

I kissed Tia and Cilla, and then reached out and gave Christine a hug. I held her and didn't want to let go. "Thank you for coming here for all this madness," I said. "You're the best surprise of all."

She kissed me, and then we pulled apart. I think we were overly conscious that Damon and Jannie had never seen us together. Not like this anyway.

"Oh shit," I muttered. "Look there."

The two little devil-demons *were* watching us. Damon winked outrageously, and Jannie made an okay sign with her busy and quick little fingers.

"They're way, way ahead of us," Christine said and laughed. "Figures, Alex. We should have known."

"Why don't you two head on up to bed?" I kidded the kids.

"It's only six o'clock, Daddy!" Jannie yelped, but she was grinning and laughing and so was everybody else.

It was a wild, let-loose party and everybody quickly got into the spirit. The monkey of Gary Soneji was finally off my back. I spotted Nana talking to some of my police friends

I heard what she was saying as I passed. It was pure Nana Mama. "There is *no* history that I know of that has led from slavery to freedom, but there is sure a history from the slingshot to the Uzi," she said to her audience of homicide detectives. My friends were grinning and nodding their heads as if they understood what she was saying, where she was coming from. I did. For better or for worse, Nana Mama had taught me how to think.

On the lighter side there was dancing to everything, from Marsalis to hip-hop. Nana even danced some. Sampson ran the barbecue in the backyard, featuring hot-and-spicy sausages, barbecued chicken, and more ribs than you would need for a Redskins tailgate party.

I was called upon to play a few tunes, so I banged out " 'S Wonderful," and then a jazzy version of "Ja Da"—"Ja da, Ja da, Ja da, jing, jing, jing!"

"Here's a stupid little melody," Jannie hammed it up at my side, "but it's so *soo-thing* and *appealing* to me."

I grabbed some slow dances with Christine as the sun set and the night progressed. The fit of our bodies was still magical and right. Just as I remembered it from the Rainbow Room. She seemed amazingly comfortable with my family and friends. I could tell that they *approved* of her big time.

I sang along with a Seal tune as we danced in the moonlight. "No, we're never going to survive—Unless—We get a little cra-azy."

"Seal would be sooo proud," she whispered in my ear.

"Mmm. Sure he would."

"You are such a good, smooth dancer," she said against my cheek.

"For a gumshoe and a flatfoot," I said. "I only dance with you, though."

She laughed, and then punched my side. "Don't you lie! I *saw* you dancing with John Sampson."

"Yes, but it didn't mean anything. It was only for the cheap sex."

Christine laughed and I could feel a small quiver in her stomach. It reminded me of how much life she had in her. It reminded me that she wanted kids, and that she ought to have them. I remembered everything about our night at the Rainbow Room, and afterward at the Astor. I felt as if I had known her forever. *She's the one, Alex.*

"I have summer school in the morning," Christine finally told me. It was already past midnight. "I brought my car. I'm okay. I've been drinking kiddie cocktails mostly. You enjoy your party, Alex."

"You sure?"

Her voice was firm. "Absolutely. I'm fine. I'm cool. And I'm outta here."

We kissed for a long time, and when we had to come up for air, we both laughed. I walked her out to her car. "Let me drive you home at least," I protested as I stood with my arms around her. "I want to. I insist."

"No, then my car would still be here. *Please* enjoy your party. Be with your friends. You can see me tomorrow, if you like. I'd like that. I won't take no for an answer."

We kissed again, and then Christine got in her car and drove away to Mitchellville.

I missed her already.

CHAPTER 66

I COULD STILL feel Christine's body against me, smell her new Donna Karan perfume, hear the special music of her voice. Sometimes you just get lucky in life. Sometimes the universe takes care of you pretty good. I wandered back to the party taking place in my house.

Several of my detective friends were still hanging out, including Sampson. There was a joke going around about Soneji having "angel lust." "Angel lust" was what they called cadavers at the morgue with an erection. The party was going *there*.

Sampson and I drank way too much beer, and then some B&B on the back porch steps—after everyone else was long gone.

"Now *that* was a hell of a party," Two-John said. "The all-singing, all-dancing model."

"It was pretty damn good. Of course, we are still *standing*. Sitting up anyway. I feel real good, but I'm going to feel pretty bad."

Sampson was grinning and his shades were placed slightly crooked on his face. His huge elbows rested on his knees. You could strike a match on his arms or legs, probably even on his head.

"I'm proud of you, man. We all are. You definitely got the twenty-thousand-pound gorilla off your back. I haven't see you smiling so much in a long, long while.

More I see of Ms. Christine Johnson, the more I like her, and I liked her to begin with."

We were on the porch steps, looking over Nana's garden of wildflowers, her roses that bloomed so abundantly, and garden lilies, looking over the remains of the party, all that food and booze.

It was late. It was already tomorrow. The wildflower garden had been there since we were little kids. The smell of bonemeal and fresh dirt seemed particularly ageless and reassuring that night.

"You remember the first summer we met?" I asked John. "You called me watermelon-ass, which burned me, because it was complete bullshit. I had a tight butt, even then."

"We tangled good in Nana's garden, right in the brier patch over yonder. I couldn't believe you would tangle with me. Nobody else would do that, still don't. Even back then you didn't know your limitations."

I smiled at Sampson. He finally had taken off his shades. It always surprises me how sensitive and warm his eyes are. "You call me watermelon-ass, we'll tangle again."

Sampson continued to nod and grin. Come to think of it, I hadn't seen him smiling so much in a long while. Life was good tonight. The best it had been in a while.

"You really like Ms. Christine. I think you've found yourself another special person. I'm sure of it. You're down for the count, champ."

"You jealous?" I asked him.

"Yeah, of course I am. Damn straight. Christine is all that and a bag of chips. But I would just fuck it up if I ever found somebody sweet and nice like that. You're easy to be with, Sugar. Always have been, even when you had your little watermelon-ass. Tough when you have to be, but you can show your feelings, too. Whatever it is, Christine likes you a lot. Almost as much as you like her."

Sampson pushed himself up off the sagging back porch step, which I needed to replace soon.

"God willing, I'm going to walk on home. Actually, I'm going to Cee Walker's house. The beautiful diva left the party a little early, but she was kind enough to give me a key. I'll be back, pick up my car in the morning. Best not to drive when you can hardly walk."

"Best not to," I agreed. "Thanks for the party."

Sampson waved good-bye, saluted, and then he went around the corner of the house, which he bumped on the way out.

I was alone on the back porch steps, staring out over Nana's moonlit garden, smiling like the fool I can be sometimes, but maybe not often enough.

I heard Sampson call out. Then his deep laugh came from the front of the house.

"Good night, watermelon-ass."

CHAPTER 67

I CAME FULLY awake, and I wondered what I was afraid of, what the hell was happening here. My first conscious fear was that *I was having a heart attack in my own bed.*

I was spacey and woozy, still flying high from the party. My heart was beating loudly, thundering in my chest.

I thought that I had heard a deep, low, pounding noise from somewhere inside the house. The noise was *close*. It sounded as if a heavy weight, maybe a club, had been striking something down the hallway.

My eyes weren't adjusted to the darkness yet. I listened for another noise.

I was frightened. I couldn't remember where I left my Glock last night. What could possibly make that heavy *pounding* sound inside the house?

I listened with all the concentration I could command.

The refrigerator purred down in the kitchen.

A distant truck changed gears on the mean streets.

Still, something about that sound, the pounding noise, bothered me a lot. *Had there even been a sound?* I wondered. *Was it just the first warnings of a powerful headache coming on?*

Before I realized what was happening, a shadowy figure rose from the other side of the bed.

Soneji! He's kept his promise. He's here in the house!

"Aaagghhgghh!" the attacker screamed and swung at me with a large club of some sort.

I tried to roll, but my body and mind weren't cooperating. I'd had too much to drink, too much party, too much fun.

I felt a powerful blow to my shoulder! My whole body went numb. I tried to scream, but suddenly I had no voice. I couldn't scream. I could barely move.

The club descended swiftly again—this time it struck my lower back.

Someone was trying to beat me to death. Jesus, God. I thought of the loud pounding sounds. *Had he gone to Nana's room first? Damon and Jannie's? What was happening in our house?*

I reached for him and managed to grab his arm. I yanked hard and he shrieked again, a high-pitched sound, but definitely a man's voice.

Soneji? How could it be? I'd seen him die in the tunnels of Grand Central Station.

What was happening to me? Who was in my bedroom? Who was upstairs in our house?

"Jannie? Damon?—" I finally mumbled, tried to call to them. *"Nana? Nana?"*

I began scratching at his chest, his arms, felt something sticky, probably drawing blood. I was fighting with only one arm, and barely able to do that.

"Who are you? What are you doing? *Damon! Damon!*" I called out again. Much louder this time.

He broke loose and I fell out of the bed, face first. The floor came at me hard, *struck,* and my face went numb.

My whole body was on fire. I began to throw up on the carpet.

The bat, the sledgehammer, the crowbar, whatever in hell it was—came down again and seemed to split me in two. I was burning up with pain. *Ax! Has to be ax!*

I could feel and smell blood everywhere around me on the floor. My blood?

"I told you there was no way to stop me!" he screamed. "I told you."

I looked up and thought I recognized the face looming above me. *Gary Soneji? Could it possibly be Soneji? How could that possibly be? It couldn't!*

I understood that I was dying, and I didn't want to die. I wanted to run, to see my kids one more time. Just one more look at them.

I knew I couldn't stop the attack. Knew there was nothing I could do to stop this horror from happening.

I thought of Nana and Jannie, Damon, Christine. My heart ached for them.

Then I let God do His will.

Part Four
Thomas Pierce

CHAPTER 68

MATTHEW LEWIS happily drove the graveyard shift on the city bus line that traveled along East Capitol Street in D.C. He was absently whistling a Marvin Gaye song, "What's Going On," as he piloted his bus through the night.

He had driven this same route for nineteen years and was mostly glad to have the work. He also enjoyed the solitude. Lewis had always been a fairly deep thinker, according to his friends and Alva, his wife of twenty years. He was a history buff, and interested in government, sometimes a little sociology, too. He had developed the interests in his native Jamaica and had kept up with them.

For the past few months, he had been listening to self-improvement tapes from an outfit called the Teaching Company, in Virginia. As he rode along East Capitol at five in the morning, he was really getting into an excellent lecture called "The Good King—the American Presidency Since the Depression." Sometimes he'd knock off two or three lectures in a single night, or maybe he'd listen to a particularly good tape a couple of times in a night.

He saw the sudden movement out of the corner of his eye. He swerved the steering wheel. The brakes screeched. His bus skidded hard right and wound up diagonally across East Capitol.

The bus emitted a loud hiss. There wasn't any traffic coming, thank goodness, just a string of green lights as far as he could see.

Matthew Lewis threw open the bus doors and climbed out. He hoped he'd missed whoever, or whatever, had run into the street.

He wasn't sure, though, and he was afraid of what he might find. Except for the drone of his tape inside the bus, it was quiet. This was so weird, and as bad as can be, he thought to himself.

Then he saw an elderly black woman lying in the street. She was wearing a long, blue-striped bathrobe. Her robe was open and he could see her red nightgown. Her feet were bare. His heart bucked dangerously.

He ran across the street to help her, and thought he was going to be sick. In his headlights he saw that her nightgown wasn't red. It was bright red blood, all over her. The sight was gruesome and awful. It wasn't the worst thing he'd encountered in his years on the night route, but it was right up there.

The woman's eyes were open and she was still conscious. She reached out a frail, thin arm toward him. *Must be domestic violence,* he thought. *Or maybe a robbery at her home.*

"Please help us," Nana Mama whispered. "Please help us."

CHAPTER 69

FIFTH STREET was blocked off and completely barricaded to traffic! John Sampson abandoned his black Nissan and ran the rest of the way to Alex's house. Police cruiser and ambulance sirens were wailing everywhere on the familiar street that he almost thought of as his own.

Sampson ran as he never had before, in the grip of the coldest fear of his life. His feet pounded heavily on the sidewalk stones. His heart felt heavy, ready to break. He couldn't catch a breath, and he was certain he would throw up if he didn't stop running this second. The hangover from the night before had dulled his senses, but not nearly enough.

Metro police personnel were still arriving at the confused, noisy, throbbing scene. Sampson pushed his way past the neighborhood looky-loos. His contempt for them had never been more obvious or more intense. People were crying everywhere Sampson looked—people he knew, neighbors and friends of Alex. He heard Alex's name being spoken in whispers.

As he reached the familiar wooden picket fence that surrounded the Cross property, he heard something that turned his stomach inside out. He had to steady himself against the whitewashed fence.

"They're all dead inside. The whole Cross family gone," a pock-faced woman in the crowd was shooting off her mouth. She looked like a character from the TV show *Cops*, had the same crude lack of sensitivity.

He spun round toward the source of the words, toward the hurt. Sampson gave the woman a glazed look and pushed forward into the yard, past collapsible sawhorses and yellow crime-scene tape.

He took the front porch steps in two long, athletic strides, and nearly collided with EMS medics hurrying a litter out of the living room.

Sampson stopped cold on the Cross's front porch. He couldn't believe any of this. Little Jannie was on the litter and she looked so small. He bent over, and then collapsed hard on his knees. The porch shook beneath his weight.

A low moan escaped his mouth. He was no longer strong, no longer brave. His heart was breaking and he choked back a sob.

When she saw him, Jannie started to cry. "Uncle John, Uncle John." She said his name in the tiniest, saddest, hurt voice.

Jannie isn't dead, Jannie is alive, Sampson thought, and the words almost tumbled out of his mouth. He wanted to shout the truth to the looky-loos. *Stop your damn rumors and lies!* He wanted to know everything, all at once, but that just wasn't possible.

Sampson leaned in close to Jannie, his goddaughter, whom he loved as if she were his own child. Her nightgown was smeared with blood. The coppery smell of blood was strong and he was almost sick again.

More blood ribboned through Jannie's tight, carefully braided hair. She was so proud of her braids, her beautiful hair. *Oh, dear God. How could this happen? How could it be?* He remembered her singing "Ja Da," just the night before.

"You're okay, baby," Sampson whispered, the words catching like barbed wire in his throat. "I'm going to be back here with you in a minute. You're okay, Jannie. I need to run upstairs. I'll be right back, baby. Be right back, Promise you."

"What about Damon? What about my daddy?" Jannie whimpered as she softly cried.

Her eyes were wide with fear, with a terror that made Sampson's heart break all over again. She was just a little girl. How could anyone do this?

"Everybody's okay, baby. They're okay," Sampson whispered again. His tongue was thick, his mouth as dry as sandpaper. He could barely get out the words. *Everybody's okay, baby.* He prayed that was true.

The EMS medics did their best to wave Sampson away, and they carried Jannie down to a waiting ambulance. More ambulances were still arriving in front, and more police cruisers as well.

He pushed his way into the house, which was crowded with police—both street officers and detectives. When the first alarm came, half of the precinct must have rushed over to the Cross house. He had never seen so many cops in one place.

He was late as usual—the *late* John Sampson, Alex liked to call him. He'd slept at a woman's house, Cee Walker's, and couldn't be reached right away. His

beeper was off, taking a night off after Alex's party—
after the big celebration.

Someone knew Alex would have his guard down,
Sampson thought, being a homicide detective already.
Who knew? Who did this terrible thing?

What in the name of God happened here?

CHAPTER 70

SAMPSON BOLTED up the narrow, twisting stairs to the second floor of the house. He wanted to shout above the blaring noise, the buzz of the incipient police investigation, to yell Alex's name, to see him appear out of one of the bedrooms.

He'd had way too much to drink the night before and he was reeling, feeling shaky, rubbery all over. He rushed into Damon's room and let out a deep moan. The boy was being transferred from his bed to a litter. Damon looked so much like his father, so much like Alex when he was Damon's age.

He looked worse than Jannie. The side of his face was beaten raw. One of Damon's eyes was closed, swollen to twice its size. Deep purple and scarlet bruises were around the eye. There were contusions and lacerations.

Gary Soneji was dead—he'd gone down in Grand Central Station. He couldn't have done this horrible thing at Alex's house.

And yet, he had promised that he would!

Nothing made sense to Sampson yet. He wished he were dreaming this nightmare, but knew he wasn't.

A detective named Rakeem Powell grabbed him by the shoulder, grabbed him hard and shook him. "Damon's all right, John. Somebody came in here, beat the living hell out of the kids. Looks like he just used fists. Hard punches. Didn't mean to kill them, though, or maybe the cowardly fuck couldn't finish the job. Who the hell knows at this point. Damon's all right. *John?* Are you all right?"

Sampson pushed Rakeem away, threw him off impatiently. "What about Alex? Nana?"

"Nana was beaten bad. Bus driver found her on the street, took her to St. Tony's. She's conscious, but she's an old woman. Skin rips when they're old. Alex got shot in his bedroom, John. They're up there with him."

"Who's in there?" Sampson groaned. He was close to tears, and he never cried. He couldn't help himself now, couldn't hide his feelings.

"Christ, who isn't?" Rakeem said and shook his head. "EMS, us, FBI. Kyle Craig is here."

Sampson broke away from Rakeem Powell and lunged toward the bedroom. *Everybody wasn't dead inside the house—but Alex had been shot. Somebody came here to get him! Who could it have been?*

Sampson tried to go into Alex's bedroom, but he was held back by men he didn't know—probably FBI from the look of them.

Kyle Craig was in the room. He knew that much. The FBI was here already. "Tell Kyle I'm here," he told the men at the door. "Tell Kyle Craig it's Sampson."

One of the FBI agents ducked inside. Kyle came out immediately, pushed his way into the hall to Sampson.

"Kyle, what the hell?" Sampson tried to talk. "*Kyle,* what happened?"

"He's been shot twice. Shot and beaten," Kyle said. "I need to talk to you, John. Listen to me, just *listen* to me, will you."

CHAPTER 71

S AMPSON TRIED to hold back his fears, his true
feelings, tried to control the chaos in his mind. Detectives and police personnel were clustered at the
bedroom door in the narrow hallway. A couple of them
were crying. Others were trying not to.

None of this could be happening!

Sampson turned away from the bedroom. He was
afraid he was going to lose it, something he never did.
Kyle hadn't stopped talking, but he couldn't really follow what Kyle was saying. He couldn't concentrate on
the FBI man's words.

He inhaled deeply, trying to fight off the reverbera-
tions of shock. It *was* shock, wasn't it? Then hot tears
started to stream down his cheeks. He didn't care if
Kyle saw. The pain in his heart cut so deep, cut right to
the bone. His nerve endings were already rubbed raw.
Never anything like this before.

"Listen to me, John," Kyle said, but Sampson wasn't
listening.

Sampson's body slumped heavily against the wall.
He asked Kyle how he'd gotten here so fast. Kyle had
an answer, always an answer for everything. Still—
nothing was really making sense to Sampson, not a
word of it.

He was looking at something over the FBI man's
shoulder. Sampson couldn't believe it. Through the

window, he could see an FBI helicopter. It was landing in the vacant lot just across Fifth Street. Things were getting stranger and stranger.

A figure lurched out of the helicopter, crouched under the rotor blades, then started toward the Cross house. It almost seemed as if he were levitating above the blowing grass in the yard.

The man was tall and slender, with dark sunglasses, the kind with small round lenses. His long blond hair was bound in a ponytail. He didn't look like FBI.

There was definitely something different about him, something radical for the Bureau. He almost looked angry as he pushed the looky-loos away. He also looked as if he were in charge, at least in charge of himself.

Now . . . what was this? Sampson thought. *What's going on here?*

"Who the hell is that?" he asked Kyle Craig. "Who is that, Kyle? Who is that goddamn ponytailed asshole?"

CHAPTER 72

MY NAME is Thomas Pierce, but the press usually call me "Doc." I was once a medical student at Harvard. I graduated, but never worked a day in a hospital, never practiced medicine. Now I'm part of the Behavioral Science Unit of the FBI. I'm thirty-three years old. Truthfully, the only place I might look like a "Doc" is in an episode of the TV show *ER*.

I was rushed from the training compound at Quantico to Washington early that morning. I had been ordered to help investigate the attack on Dr. Alex Cross and members of his immediate family. To be candid, I didn't want to be involved in the case for a number of reasons. Most important, I was already part of a difficult investigation, one that had drained nearly all of my energy—the Mr. Smith case.

Instinctively, I knew that some people would be angry with me because of the shooting of Alex Cross and my being at the crime scene so quickly. I knew with absolute certainty I would be seen as opportunistic, when that couldn't be farther from the truth.

There was nothing I could do about it now. The Bureau wanted me there. So I put it out of my mind. I tried to anyway. I was performing my job, the same as Dr. Cross would have done for me under comparably unfortunate circumstances.

I was certain of one thing, though, from the moment

I arrived. I knew I looked as shocked and outraged as anyone else standing sentinel in the crowd gathered at the house on Fifth Street. I probably looked angry to some of them. I *was* angry. My mind was full of chaos, fear of the unknown, fear of failure, too. I was close to the state of mind described as "toast." Too many days, weeks, months in a row with Mr. Smith. Now this new bit of blasphemy.

I had listened to Alex Cross speak once at a profiler seminar at the University of Chicago. He had made an impression. I hoped that he would live, but the reports were all bad. Nothing I'd heard so far left room for hope.

I figured that was why they'd brought me in on the case right away. The vicious attack on Cross would mean major headlines, and put intense pressure on both the Washington police and the Bureau. I was there on Fifth Street for the simplest of reasons—to relieve the pressure.

I felt an unpleasant aura, residue from the recent violence, as I approached the tidy, white-shingled Cross house. Some policemen I passed were red-eyed and a few seemed almost to be in shock. It was all very strange and disquieting.

I wondered if Alex Cross had died since I had left Quantico. I already had a sixth sense for the terrible and unexpected violence that had taken place inside the modest, peaceful-looking house. I wished that none of the others were at the crime scene, so I could absorb everything without all these distractions.

That was what I had been brought here to do. Observe the scene of unbelievable mayhem. Get a gut feeling for what might have happened in the early hours of the morning. Figure everything out quickly and efficiently.

Out of the corner of my eye, I saw Kyle Craig coming out of the house. He was in a hurry, as he always is. I sighed. *Now it begins, now it begins.*

Kyle crossed Fifth Street in a quick jog. He came up to me and we shook hands. I was glad to see him. Kyle is smart and very organized, and also supportive of those he works with. He's famous for getting things done.

"They just moved Alex," he said. "He's hanging on."

"What's the prognosis? Tell me, Kyle." I needed to know everything. I was there to collect facts. This was the start of it.

Kyle averted his eyes. "Not good. They say he won't live. They're sure he won't live."

CHAPTER 73

THE PRESS CORPS intercepted Kyle and me as we headed toward the Cross house. There were already a couple dozen reporters and cameramen at the scene. The vultures effectively blocked our way, wouldn't let us pass. They knew who Kyle was and possibly they knew about me, too.

"Why is the FBI already involved?" one of them shouted above the street noise and general commotion. Two news helicopters fluttered overhead. They loved this sort of disaster. "We hear this is connected to the Soneji case. Is that true?"

"Let me talk to them," Kyle whispered close to my ear.

I shook my head. "They'll want to talk to me about it anyway. They'll find out who I am. Let's get the silly shit over with."

Kyle frowned, but then he nodded slowly. I tried to control my impatience as I walked toward the horde of reporters.

I waved my hands over my head and that quieted some of them. The media is extremely visual, I've learned the hard way, even the print journalists, the so-called wordsmiths. They all watch far too many movies. Visual signals work best with them.

"I'll answer your questions," I volunteered and served up a thin smile, "as best I can anyway."

"First question, who are you?" a man with a scraggly red beard and Salvation Army store taste in clothes hollered from the front of the pack. He looked like the reclusive novelist Thomas Harris, and maybe he was.

"That's an easy one," I answered, "I'm Thomas Pierce. I'm with BSU."

That quieted the reporters for a moment. Those who didn't recognize my face knew the name. The fact that I'd been brought in on the Cross case was news in itself. Camera flashes exploded in front of me, but I was used to them by now.

"Is Alex Cross still alive?" someone called out. I had expected that to be the *first* question, but there's no way to predict with the press corps.

"Dr. Cross is alive. As you can see, I just got here, so I don't know much. So far, we have no suspects, no theories, no leads, nothing particularly interesting to talk about," I said.

"What about the Mr. Smith case," a woman reporter shouted at me. She was a dark-haired anchorperson type, perky as a chipmunk. "Are you putting Mr. Smith on hold now? How can you work two big cases? What's up, Doc?" the reporter said and smiled. She was obviously smarter and wittier than she looked.

I winced, rolled my eyes, and smiled back at her. "No suspects, no theories, no leads, nothing interesting to talk about," I repeated. "I have to go inside. The interview's over. Thanks for your concern. I know it's genuine in this god-awful case. I admire Alex Cross, too."

"Did you say admire or admired?" another reporter shouted at me from the back.

"Why did they bring you in on this, Mr. Pierce? Is Mr. Smith involved?"

I couldn't help arching my eyebrows at the question. I felt an unpleasant itch in my brain. "I'm here because I get lucky sometimes, all right? Maybe I'll get lucky again. I have to go into the trenches now. I promise that I'll tell you if and when we have anything. I sincerely doubt that Mr. Smith attacked Alex Cross last night. And I said *admire*, present tense."

I pulled Kyle Craig out of there with me, holding on to his arm for support as much as anything. He grinned as soon as we had our backs to the horde.

"That was pretty goddamn good," he said. "I think you managed to confuse the hell out of them, even beyond the usual blank stares."

"Mad dogs of the Fourth Estate," I shrugged. "Smears of blood on their lips and cheeks. They couldn't care less about Cross or his family. Not one question about the kids. Edison said, 'We don't know a millionth of one per cent about *anything!*' The press doesn't get that. They want everything in black-and-white. They mistake simplicity, and simplemindedness, for the truth."

"Make nice with the D.C. police," Kyle cajoled, or maybe he was giving me a friendly warning. "This is an emotional time for them. That's Detective John Sampson on the porch. He's a friend of Alex. Alex's closest friend, in fact."

"Great," I muttered. "Just who I don't want to see right now."

I glanced at Detective Sampson. He looked like a bad storm about to happen. *I didn't want to be here. Didn't want or need any of this.*

Kyle patted my shoulder. "We need you on this one. Soneji promised this would happen," he suddenly told me. "He *predicted* it."

I stared at Kyle Craig. He'd delivered his stunning thunderbolt of news in his usual deadpan, understated way, sort of like Sam Shepard on Quaalude.

"Say again? What was that last bit?"

"Gary Soneji warned Alex that he'd get him, even if he died. Soneji said he couldn't be stopped. It looks like he made good on his promise. I want you to tell me how. Tell me how Soneji did it. *That's* why you're here, Thomas."

CHAPTER 74

M Y NERVES were already on edge. My awareness was heightened to a level I found almost
painful. I couldn't believe I was here in Washington, involved in this case. *Tell me how Gary Soneji
did this?* Tell me how it could have happened. That's
all I had to do.

The press had one thing right. It's fair to say that I
am the FBI's current hotshot profiler. I should be used
to graphic, violent crime scenes, but I'm not. It stirs up
too much white noise, too many memories of Isabella.
*Of Isabella and myself. Of another time and place, an-
other life.*

I have a sixth sense, which is nothing paranormal,
nothing like that at all. It's just that I can process raw
information and data better than most people, better
than most policemen anyway. I feel things very pow-
erfully, and sometimes my "felt" hunches have been
useful not only to the FBI but also to Interpol and Scotland Yard.

My methods differ radically from the Federal Bureau's famed investigative process, however. In spite
of what they say, the Bureau's Behavioral Science Unit
believes in formalistic investigation with much less
room for surprising hunches. I subscribe to a belief in
the widest possible array of hunches and instincts, followed by the most exacting science.

The FBI and I are polar opposites, yet to their credit they continue to use me. Until I screw up badly, which I could do at any moment. Like right now.

I had been working hard at Quantico, reporting in on the gruesome and complex "Mr. Smith" investigation, when the news arrived about the attack on Cross. Actually, I had been in Quantico for less than a day, having just returned from England, where "Smith" was blazing his killer trail and I was in lukewarm pursuit.

Now I was in Washington, at the center of a raging storm over the Cross family attack. I looked at my watch, a TAG Heuer 6000 given to me by Isabella, the only material possession I really care about. It was a few minutes past eight when I entered the Cross front yard. I noted the time. Something about it bothered me, but I wasn't sure what it was yet.

I stopped beside a battered and rusting EMS truck. The roof lights were flashing, the rear doors thrown open. I looked inside and saw a boy—it had to be Damon Cross.

The boy had been badly beaten. His face and arms were bloody, but he was alert and talking in a soft voice to the medics, who tried to be gentle and comforting.

"Why wouldn't he have killed the children? Why just thrash out at them?" Kyle said. We had the same mind-set on that question.

"His heart wasn't in it." I said the first thing that came into my head, the first *feeling* I had. "He was compelled to make a symbolic gesture toward the Cross children, but no more than that."

I turned to look at Kyle. "I don't know, Kyle. Maybe he was frightened. Or in a hurry. Maybe he was afraid of waking Cross." All of those thoughts invaded my mind, almost in an instant. *I felt as if I had briefly met the attacker.*

I looked up at the old house, the Cross house. "Okay, let's go to the bedroom, if you don't mind. I want to see it before the techies do their number in there. I need to see Alex Cross's room. I don't know, but I think something is seriously fucked up here. This certainly wasn't done by Gary Soneji *or* his ghost."

"How do you know that?" Kyle grabbed his arm and made eye contact. "How can you know for sure?"

"Soneji would have killed the two kids and the grandmother."

CHAPTER 75

ALEX CROSS'S blood was spattered everywhere in the corner bedroom. I could see where a bullet had exited through the window directly behind Cross's bed. The glass fracture was clean and the radial lines even: The shooter had fired from a standing position, directly across the bed. I made my first notes, and also a quick sketch of the small, unadorned bedroom.

There was other "evidence." A shoe print had been discovered near the cellar. The Metro police were working on a "walking picture" of the assailant. A white male had been spotted around midnight in the mostly black neighborhood. For a moment, I was almost glad I'd been rushed up here from Virginia. There was so much raw data to take in and process, almost too much. The mussed bed, where Cross had apparently slept on top of a hand-sewn quilt. Photos of his children on the walls.

Alex Cross had been moved to St. Anthony's Hospital, but his bedroom was intact, just the way the mysterious assailant had left it.

Had he left the room like this on purpose? Was this his first message to us?

Of course it was.

I looked at the papers still out on Cross's small work desk. They were notes on Gary Soneji. They had been left undisturbed by the assailant. Was that important?

Someone had taped a short poem to the wall over the desk. *Wealth covers sins—the poor/Are naked as a pin.*

Cross had been reading a book called *Push*, a novel. A piece of lined yellow paper was stuck inside, so I read it: *Write the talented author about her wonderful book!*

The time I spent in the room passed like a snap of the fingers, almost a mind fugue. I drank several cups of coffee. I remembered a line from the offbeat TV show *Twin Peaks*, "Damn fine cup of coffee, and hot!"

I had been inside Cross's bedroom for almost an hour and a half, lost in forensic detail, hooked on the case in spite of myself. It was a nasty and disturbing puzzle, but a very intriguing one. Everything about the case was intense, and highly unusual.

I heard footsteps thumping outside in the hallway and looked up, my concentration interrupted. The bedroom door suddenly swung open and thudded against the wall.

Kyle Craig popped his head inside. He looked concerned. His face was white as chalk. Something had happened. "I have to go right now. Alex has gone into cardiac arrest!"

CHAPTER 76

"I'LL GO with you," I said to Kyle. I could tell that Kyle badly needed company. I wanted to see Alex Cross before he died, if that was what it had come to, and it sounded like it, felt like it to me.

On the ride over to St. Anthony's I gently questioned Kyle about the extent of Dr. Cross's injuries and the tenor of concern at the hospital. I also made a guess about the cause of the cardiac arrest.

"It sounds like it's due to blood loss. There's a lot of blood in the bedroom. It's all over the sheets, the floor, the walls. Soneji was obsessed with blood, right? I heard that at Quantico before I left this morning."

Kyle was quiet for a moment in the car, and then he asked the question I expected. I'm sometimes a step or two ahead in conversations.

"Do you ever miss it, not being a doctor anymore?"

I shook my head, frowned a little. "I really don't. Something delicate and essential broke inside me when Isabella died. It will never be repaired, Kyle, at least I don't think so. I couldn't be a doctor now. I find it hard to believe in healing anymore."

"I'm sorry," he whispered solemnly.

"And I'm sorry about your friend. I'm sorry about Alex Cross," I said to him.

In the spring of 1993, I had just graduated from Harvard Medical School. My life seemed to be spiraling upward at dizzying speed, when the woman I loved more than life itself was murdered in our apartment in Cambridge. Isabella Calais was my lover, and she was my best friend. She was one of the first victims of "Mr. Smith."

After the murder, I never showed up at Massachusetts General, where I'd been accepted as an intern. I didn't even contact them. I knew I would never practice medicine. In an odd way, my life had ended with Isabella's, at least that was how I saw it.

Eighteen months after the murder, I was accepted into the FBI's Behavioral Science Unit, what some wags call the "b.s. group." It was what I wanted to do, what I needed to do. Once I had proven myself in the BSU, I asked to be put on the Mr. Smith case. My superiors fought the move at first, but finally they gave in.

"Maybe you'll change your mind one day," Kyle said. I had a feeling that he personally believed I would. Kyle likes to believe that everyone thinks as he does: with perfectly clear logic and a minimum of emotional baggage.

"I don't think so," I told him, without sounding argumentative, or even too firm on the point. "Who knows, though?"

"Maybe after you finally catch Smith," he persisted with his point.

"Yes, maybe then," I said.

"You don't think Smith—" he started to say, but then backed off from the absurd notion that Mr. Smith could be involved with the attack here in Washington.

"No," I said, "I do not. Smith couldn't have made this attack. They would all be dead and mutilated if he had."

CHAPTER 77

A T ST. Anthony's Hospital, I left Kyle and roamed about playing "Doc." It didn't feel too bad to be working in a hospital, contemplating what it might have been like. I tried to find out as much as I could about Alex Cross's condition, and his chances of surviving his wounds.

The staff nurses and doctors were surprised that I understood so much about trauma and gunshot wounds, but no one pressed me as to how or why. They were too busy trying to save Alex Cross's life. He had done pro bono work at the hospital for years and no one there could bear to let him die. Even the porters liked and respected Cross, calling him a "regular brother."

I learned that the cardiac arrest had been caused by the loss of blood, as I had guessed. According to the doctor in charge, Alex Cross had gone into massive arrest minutes after he arrived at the ER. His blood pressure had dipped dangerously low: 60 over 0.

The staff's prognosis was that he could probably die during the surgery necessary to repair his massive internal injuries, but that he would definitely die without the surgery. The more I heard, the more I was certain they were right. An old saying of my mother's ran through my head, "May his body rise to heaven, before the devil finds out he's dead."

266 / James Patterson

Kyle caught up with me in the busy and chaotic hallway on the fourth floor at St. Anthony's. A lot of people working there knew Cross personally. They were all visibly upset and helpless to do anything about it. The hospital scene was raw and emotional, and I couldn't help being swept up in the tragedy, even more so than I had been at the Cross house.

Kyle was still pale, his brow furrowed and punctuated by blisters of sweat. His eyes had a distant look as he gazed down the hospital corridor. "What did you find out? I know you've been poking around," he said. He rightly suspected that I would have already conducted my own mini-investigation. He knew my style, even my motto: Assume nothing, question everything.

"He's in surgery now. He's not expected to make it," I gave him the bad news. Unsentimentally, the way I knew he wanted it. "That's what the doctors believe. But what the hell do doctors know?" I added.

"Is that what you think?" Kyle asked.

The pupils of his eyes were the tiniest, darkest points. He was taking this as badly as I'd seen him react to anything since I'd known him. He was being very emotional for Kyle. I understood how close he and Cross had been.

I sighed and shut my eyes. I wondered if I should tell him what I really thought. Finally, I opened them. I said, "It might be better if he doesn't make it, Kyle."

CHAPTER 78

"**C**'MON WITH me," he said, pulling me along. "I want you to meet someone. C'mon."

I followed Kyle down one floor to a room on three. The patient in the room was an elderly black woman.

Her head was swathed in Webril, a stretchy woven bandage. The head bandage resembled a turban. A few wisps of gray hair hung loose from the dressing. Telfa bandages covered the abrasions on her face.

There were two IV lines, "cut downs," one for blood and one for fluids and antibiotics. She was hooked to a cardiac monitor.

She looked up at us as if we were intruders, but then she recognized Kyle.

"How is Alex? Tell me the truth," she said in a hoarse, nearly whispering voice that still managed to be firm. "No one here will tell me the truth. Will you, Kyle?"

"He's in surgery now, Nana. We won't know anything until he comes out," Kyle said, "and maybe not even then."

The elderly woman's eyes narrowed. She shook her head sadly.

"I asked you for the truth. I deserve at least that much. *Now, how is Alex?* Kyle, is Alex still alive?"

Kyle sighed loudly. It was weary sound, and a sad one. He and Alex Cross had been working together for years.

"Alex's condition is extremely grave," I said, as gently as I could. "That means—"

"I know what grave means," she said. "I taught school for forty-seven years. English, History, Boolean algebra."

"I'm sorry," I said, "I didn't mean to sound over-bearing." I paused for a second or two, then continued to answer her question.

"The internal injuries involve a kind of 'ripping,' probably with a high degree of contamination to the wounds. The most serious wound is to his abdomen. The shot passed through the liver and apparently nicked the common hepatic artery. That's what I was told. The bullet lodged in the rear of the stomach, where it's now pressing onto the spinal column."

She winced, but she was listening intently, waiting for me to finish. I was thinking that if Alex Cross was anything near as strong as this woman, as willful, then he must be something special as a detective.

I went on.

"Because of the nick to the artery there was consid-erable blood loss. The contents of the stomach itself and the small bowel can be sources of *E. coli* infection. There's a danger of inflammation of the abdominal cavity—peritonitis, and possibly pancreatitis, all of which can be fatal. The gunshot wound is the *injury*, the infection is the *complication*. The second shot went through his left wrist, without shattering bone, but missed the radial artery. That's what we know so far. That's the truth."

I stopped at that point. My eyes never left those of the elderly woman, and hers never left mine.

"Thank you," she said in a resigned whisper. "I appreciate that you didn't condescend to me. Are you a doctor here at the hospital? You speak as if you were."

I shook my head. "No, I'm not. I'm with the FBI. I studied to be a doctor."

Her eyes widened and seemed even more alert than when we had come in. I sensed that she had tremendous reserves of strength. "Alex is a doctor *and* a detective."

"I'm a detective, too," I said.

"I'm Nana Mama. I'm Alex's grandmother. What's your name?"

"Thomas," I told her. "My name is Thomas Pierce."

"Well, thank you for speaking the truth."

CHAPTER 79

Paris, France

THE POLICE would never admit it, but *Mr. Smith had control of Paris now. He had taken the city by storm and only he knew why.* The news of his fearsome presence spread along boulevard Saint-Michel, and then rue de Vaugirard. This sort of thing wasn't supposed to happen in the "*très luxe*" sixth arrondissement.

The seductively chic shops along boulevard Saint-Michel lured tourists and Parisians alike. The Panthéon and beautiful Jardins du Luxembourg were nearby. Lurid murders weren't supposed to happen here.

Clerks from the expensive shops were the first to leave their posts and hurriedly walk or run toward No. 11 rue de Vaugirard. They wanted to *see* Smith, or at least his handiwork. They wanted to see the so-called Alien with their own eyes.

Shoppers and even owners left the fashionable clothing shops and cafés. If they didn't walk up rue de Vaugirard, they at least looked down to where several police black-and-whites and also an army bus were parked. High above the eerie scene, pigeons fluttered and squawked. They seemed to want to see the famous criminal as well.

Across Saint-Michel stood the Sorbonne, with its foreboding chapel, its huge clock, its open cobblestone terrace. A second bus filled with soldiers was parked in the plaza. Students tentatively wandered up rue Champollion to have a look-see. The tiny street had been named after Jean-François Champollion, the French Egyptologist who had discovered the key to Egyptian hieroglyphics while deciphering the Rosetta stone.

A police inspector named Rene Faulks shook his head as he pulled onto rue Champollion and saw the crowd. Faulks understood the common man's sick fascination with "Mr. Smith." It was the fear of the unknown, especially fear of sudden, horrible death, that drew people's interest to these bizarre murders. Mr. Smith had gained a reputation because his actions were so completely incomprehensible. He actually did seem to be an "alien." Few people could conceive of another human acting as Smith routinely did.

The inspector let his eyes wander. He took in the electronic sign hanging at the Lycée St. Louis corner. Today it advertised "Tour de France Femina" and also something called "Formation d'artistes." More madness, he thought. He coughed out a cynical laugh.

He noticed a sidewalk artist contemplating his sidewalk chalk masterpiece. The man was oblivious to the police emergency. The same could be said of a homeless woman blithely washing her breakfast dishes in the public fountain.

Good for both of them. They passed Faulks's test for sanity in the modern age.

272 / James Patterson

As he climbed the gray stone stairway leading to a blue painted door, he was tempted to turn toward the crowd of onlookers massed on rue de Vaugirard, and to scream, "Go back to your little chores and your even smaller lives. Go see an art movie at Cinéma Champollion. This has nothing whatsoever to do with you. Smith takes only interesting and deserving specimens—so you people have absolutely nothing to worry about."

That morning, one of the finest young surgeons at L'Ecole Pratique de Médecine had been reported missing. If Mr. Smith's pattern held, within a couple of days, the surgeon would be found dead and mutilated. That was the way it had been with all the other victims. It was the only strand that represented anything like a repeating pattern. *Death by mutilation.*

Faulks nodded and said hello to two flics and another low-ranking inspector inside the surgeon's expensively furnished apartment. The place was magnificent, filled with antique furniture, expensive art, with a view of the Sorbonne.

Well, the golden boy of L'Ecole Pratique de Médecine had finally gotten a bad break. Yes, things had suddenly gotten very bleak for Dr. Abel Sante.

"Nothing, no sign of a struggle?" Faulks asked the closest flic as he entered the apartment.

"Not a trace, just like the others. The poor rich bastard is gone, though. He's disappeared, and Mr. Smith has him."

"He's probably in Smith's space capsule," another

flic said, a youngish man with longish red hair and trendy sunglasses.

Faulks turned brusquely. "*You!* Get the hell out of here! Go out on the street with the rest of the madmen and the goddamned pigeons! I would hope Mr. Smith might take *you* for his *space capsule* but, unfortunately, I suspect his standards are too high."

Having said his piece and banished the offending police officer, the inspector went to examine the handiwork of Mr. Smith. He had a *procès-verbal* to write up. He had to make some sense out of the madness somehow. All of France, all of Europe, waited to hear the latest news.

CHAPTER 80

FBI HEADQUARTERS in Washington is located on Pennsylvania Avenue between Ninth and Tenth Streets. I spent from four until almost seven in a BOGSAAT with a half dozen special agents, including Kyle Craig. BOGSAAT is a *bunch of guys sitting around a table*. Inside a Strategic Ops Center conference room, we vigorously discussed the Cross attack.

At seven that night, we learned that Alex Cross had made it through the first round of surgery. A cheer went up around the table. I told Kyle that I wanted to go back to St. Anthony's Hospital.

"I need to see Alex Cross," I told him. "I really do need to see him, even if he can't talk. No matter what condition he's in."

Twenty minutes later, I was in an elevator headed to the sixth floor of St. Anthony's. It was quieter there than the rest of the building. The high floor was a little spooky, especially under the circumstances.

I entered a private recovery room near the center of the semidarkened floor. I was too late. Someone was already in there with Cross.

Detective John Sampson was standing vigil by the bed of his friend. Sampson was tall and powerful, at least six foot six, but he looked incredibly weary, as if he were ready to fall over from exhaustion and the long day's stress.

Sampson finally looked at me, nodded slightly, then turned his attention back to Dr. Cross. His eyes were a strange mixture of anger and sadness. I sensed that he knew what was going to happen here.

Alex Cross was hooked up to so many machines it was a visceral shock to see him. I knew that he was in his early forties. He looked younger than his age. That was the only good news.

I studied the charts at the base of the bed. He had suffered severe-to-moderate blood loss secondary to the tearing of the radial artery. He had a collapsed lung, numerous contusions, hematomas, and lacerations. The left wrist had been injured. There was blood poisoning, and the morbidity of the injuries put him on the "could be about to check out" list.

Alex Cross was conscious, and I stared into his brown eyes for a long time. What secrets were hidden there? What did he know? Had he actually seen the face of his assailant? *Who did this to you? Not Soneji. Who dared to go into your bedroom?*

He couldn't talk and I could see nothing in his eyes. No awareness that I was there with Detective Sampson. He didn't seem to recognize Sampson either. Sad.

Dr. Cross was getting excellent care at St. Anthony's. The hospital bed had a Stryker frame attached to it. The injured wrist was encased in an elastoplast cast and the arm was anchored to a trapeze bar. He was receiving oxygen through a clear tube that ran into an outlet in the wall. A fancy monitor called a Slave scope was providing pulse, temp, blood pressure, and EKG readings.

"Why don't you leave him alone?" Sampson finally spoke after a few minutes. "Why don't you leave both of us. You can't help here. Please, go."

I nodded, but continued to look into the eyes of Alex Cross for a few more seconds. Unfortunately, he had nothing to tell me.

I finally left Cross and Sampson alone. I wondered if I would ever see Alex Cross again. I doubted that I would. I didn't believe in miracles anymore.

CHAPTER 81

THAT NIGHT, I couldn't get Mr. Smith out of my head, as usual, and now Alex Cross and his family were residing there as well. I kept revisiting different scenes from the hospital, and from the Cross house. Who had entered the house? Who had Gary Soneji gotten to? That had to be it.

The crisscrossing flashbacks were maddening and running out of control. I didn't like the feeling, and I didn't know if I could conduct an investigation, much less two, under these stressful, almost claustrophobic, conditions.

It had been twenty-four hours from hell. I had flown to the United States from London. I'd landed at National Airport, in D.C., and gone to Quantico, Virginia. Then I had been rushed back to Washington, where I worked until ten in the evening on the Cross puzzle.

To make things worse, if they could get any worse, I found I couldn't sleep when I finally got to my room at the Washington Hilton & Towers. My mind was in a chaotic state that steadfastly refused sleep.

I didn't like the working hypothesis on Cross that I had heard from the FBI investigators at headquarters that night. They were stuck in their usual rut: They were like slow students who scan classroom ceilings for answers. Actually, most police investigators reminded me of Einstein's incisive definition of insanity.

I had first heard it at Harvard: *"Endlessly repeating the same process, hoping for a different result."*

I kept flashing back to the upstairs bedroom where Alex Cross had been brutally attacked. I was looking for something—but what was it? I could see his blood spattered on the walls, on the curtains, the sheets, the throw rug. *What was I missing? Something?*

I couldn't sleep, goddamn it.

I tried work as a sedative. It was my usual antidote. I had already begun extensive notes and sketches on the scene of the attack. I got up and wrote some more. My PowerBook was beside me, always at the ready. My stomach wouldn't stop rolling and my head throbbed in a maddening way.

I typed: *Could Gary Soneji possibly still be alive? Don't rule anything out yet, not even the most absurd possibility.*

Exhume Soneji's body if necessary.

Read Cross's book—Along Came a Spider.

Visit Lorton Prison, where Soneji was held.

I pushed aside my computer after an hour's work. It was nearly two in the morning. My head felt stuffed, as if I had a terrible, nagging cold. I still couldn't sleep. I was thirty-three years old; I was already beginning to feel like an old man.

I kept seeing the bloody bedroom at the Cross house. No one can imagine what it's like to live with such imagery day and night. I saw Alex Cross—the way he looked at St. Anthony's Hospital. Then I was remembering victims of Mr. Smith, his "studies," as he called them.

The terrifying scenes play on and on and on in my head. Always leading to the same place, the same conclusion.

I can see another bedroom. It is the apartment Isabella and I shared in Cambridge, Massachusetts.

With total clarity, I remembered running down the narrow hallway that terrible night. I remember my heart pushing into my throat, its feeling larger than a clenched fist. I remember every pounding step that I took, everything I saw along the way.

I finally saw Isabella, and I thought it must be a dream, a terrible nightmare.

Isabella was in our bed, and I knew that she was dead. No one could have survived the butchery I witnessed there. No one did survive—neither of us.

Isabella had been savagely murdered at twenty-three, in the prime of her life, before she could be a mother, a wife, the anthropologist she'd dreamed of becoming. I couldn't help myself, couldn't stop. I bent and held what was left of Isabella, *what was left.*

How can I ever forget any of it? How can I turn that sight off in my mind?

The simple answer is, I cannot.

CHAPTER 82

I WAS ON the hunt again, the loneliest road on this earth. Truthfully, there wasn't much else that had sustained me during the past four years, not since Isabella's death.

The moment I awoke in the morning, I called St. Anthony's Hospital. Alex Cross was alive, but in a coma. His condition was listed as grave. I wondered if John Sampson had remained at his bedside. I suspected he had.

By nine in the morning, I was back at the Cross house. I needed to study the scene in much greater depth, to gather every fact, every splinter and fragment. I tried to organize everything I knew, or thought I knew at this early stage of the investigation. I was reminded of a maxim that was frequently used at Quantico—All truths are half-truths and possibly not even that.

A fiendish "ghoul" had supposedly struck back from the grave and attacked a well-known policeman and his family in their home. The ghoul had warned Dr. Cross that he would come. There was no way to stop it from happening. It was the ultimate in cruel and effective revenge.

For some reason, though, the assailant had failed to execute. None of the family members, or even Alex Cross, had been killed. That was the perplexing and most baffling part of the puzzle for me. That was the key!

I arrived at the cellar in the Cross house just before eleven in the morning. I had asked the Metro police and FBI technicians not to mess around down there until I was finished with my survey of the other floors. My data gathering, my science, was a methodical, step-by-step process.

The attacker had hidden himself (herself?) in the basement while a party had been in progress upstairs and in the backyard. There was a partial footprint near the entryway to the cellar. It was a size nine. It wasn't much to go on, not unless the perpetrator had wanted us to find the print.

One thing struck me right away. *Gary Soneji had been locked in a cellar as a child. He'd been excluded from family activities in the rest of the house. He'd been physically abused in the cellar. Just like the one in the Cross house.*

The attacker had definitely hidden in the cellar. That couldn't be a coincidence.

Had he known about Gary Soneji's explicit warning to Cross? That possibility was disturbing as hell. I didn't want to settle on any theories or premature conclusions yet. I just needed to collect as much raw data and information as I could. Possibly because I'd been to medical school, I approached cases as a clinical scientist would.

Collect all the data first. Always the data.

It was quiet in the cellar, and I could focus and concentrate all my attention on my surroundings. I tried to imagine the attacker lurking here during the party, and then afterward, as the house grew quiet, until Alex Cross finally went to bed.

The attacker was a coward.

He wasn't in a rage state. He was methodical.

It was not a crime of passion.

The intruder had struck out at each of the children first, but not fatally. He had beaten Alex Cross's grandmother, but had spared her. *Why?* Only Alex Cross was meant to die, and so far even that hadn't happened.

Had the attacker failed? Where was the intruder now?

Was he still in Washington? Checking out the Cross house right now? Or at St. Anthony's Hospital, where the Metro police were guarding Alex Cross?

As I passed an ancient coal stove, I noticed the metal door was slightly ajar. I poked it open with my handkerchief and peered inside. I couldn't see very well and took out a penlight. There were inches of ash that were light gray in color. Someone had burned a flammable substance recently, possibly newspapers or magazines.

Why start a fire in the middle of summer? I wondered.

A small hand shovel was on a worktable near the stove. I used the shovel to sift through the ashes.

I carefully scraped along the stove's bottom.

I heard a *clink*. A metal-against-metal noise.

I scooped out a shovelful of ash. Something came with the ash. It was hard, heavier. My expectations weren't high. I was still just collecting data, anything and everything, even the contents of an old stove. I emptied the ashes onto the worktable in a pile, then smoothed it out.

I saw what the small shovel had struck. I flipped over the new evidence with the tip of the shovel. *Yes,* I said to myself. I finally had something, the first bit of evidence.

It was Alex Cross's detective shield, and it was burned and charred.

Someone wanted us to find the shield.

The intruder wants to play! I thought. *This is cat and mouse.*

CHAPTER 83

Ile-de-France

DR. ABEL SANTE was normally a calm and collected man. He was widely known in the medical community to be erudite, but surprisingly down-to-earth. He was a nice man, too, a gentle physician.

Now he desperately tried to put his mind somewhere other than where his body was. Just about anywhere else in the universe would do just fine.

He had already spent several hours remembering minute details from his pleasant, almost idyllic, boyhood in Rennes; then his university years at the Sorbonne and L'Ecole Pratique de Médecine; he had replayed tennis and golf sporting events; he had relived his seven-year love affair with Regina Becker—dear, sweet Regina.

He needed to be somewhere else, to exist anywhere else but where he actually was. He needed to exist in the past, or even in the future, but not in the present. He was reminded of *The English Patient*—both the book and the movie. He was Count Almasy now, wasn't he? Only his torture was even worse than Almasy's horribly burned flesh. He was in the grasp of Mr. Smith.

He thought about Regina constantly now, and he realized that he loved her fiercely, and what a fool he'd been not to marry her years ago. What an arrogant bastard, and what a huge fool!

How dearly he wanted to live now, and to see Regina again. Life seemed so damned precious to him at this moment, in this terrible place, under these monstrous conditions.

No, this wasn't a good way to be thinking. It brought him down—it brought him back to reality, to the present. *No, no no! Go somewhere else in your mind. Anywhere but here.*

The present line of thought brought him to this tiny compartment, this infinitesimal x on the globe where he was now a prisoner, and where no one could possibly find him. Not the flics, not Interpol, not the entire French Army, or the English, or the Americans, or the Israelis!

Dr. Sante could easily imagine the furor and outrage, the panic continuing in Paris and throughout France. NOTED PHYSICIAN AND TEACHER ABDUCTED! The headline in *Le Monde* would read something like that. Or, NEW MR. SMITH HORROR IN PARIS.

He was the horror! He was certain that tens of thousands of police, as well as the army, were searching for him now. Of course, every hour he was missing, his chances for survival grew dimmer. He knew that from reading past articles about Mr. Smith's unearthly abductions, and what happened to the victims.

Why me? God Almighty, he couldn't stand this infernal monologue anymore.

He couldn't stand this nearly upside-down position, this terribly cramped space, for one more second.

He just couldn't bear it. Not one more second!

Not one more second!

Not one more second!

He couldn't breathe!

He was going to die in here.

Right here, in a goddamn dumbwaiter. Stuck between floors, in a godforsaken house in Ile-de-France somewhere on the outskirts of Paris.

Mr. Smith had put him in the dumbwaiter, stuffed him inside like a bundle of dirty laundry, and then left him there—for God only knew how long. It seemed like hours, at least several hours, but Abel Sante really wasn't sure anymore.

The excruciating pain came and went, but mostly it rushed through his body in powerful waves. His neck, his shoulders, and his chest ached so badly, beyond belief, beyond his tolerance for pain. The feeling was as if he'd been slowly crushed into a squarish heap. If he hadn't been claustrophobic before, he was now.

But that wasn't the worst part of this. No, it wasn't the worst. The most terrifying thing was that he knew what all of France wanted to know, what the whole world wanted to know.

He knew certain things about Mr. Smith's identity. He knew precisely how he talked. He believed that Mr. Smith might be a philosopher, perhaps a university professor or student.

He had even *seen* Mr. Smith.

He had looked out from the dumbwaiter—upside down, no less—and stared into Smith's hard, cold eyes, seen his nose, his lips.

Mr. Smith saw that.

Now there was no hope for him.

"Damn you, Smith. Damn you to hell. I know your shitty secret. I know everything now. You *are* a fucking alien! *You aren't human.*"

CHAPTER 84

"YOU REALLY think we're going to track down this son of a bitch? You think this guy is dumb?" John Sampson asked me point-blank, challenging me. He was dressed all in black, and he wore Ray-Ban sunglasses. He looked as if he were already in mourning. The two of us were flying in an FBI Bell Jet helicopter from Washington to Princeton, New Jersey. We were supposed to work together for a while.

"You think Gary Soneji did this somehow? Think he's Houdini? You think maybe he's still alive?" Sampson went on. "What the hell do you think?"

"I don't know yet." I sighed. "I'm still collecting data. It's the only way I know how to work. No, I don't *think* Soneji did it. He's always worked alone before this. Always."

I knew that Gary Soneji had grown up in New Jersey, then gone on to become one of the most savage murderers of the times. It didn't seem as if his run were over yet. Soneji was part of the ongoing mystery.

Alex Cross's notes on Soneji were extensive. I was finding useful and interesting insights all through the notes, and I was less than a third of the way through. I had already decided that Cross was a sharp police detective but an even better psychologist. His hypotheses and hunches weren't merely clever and imaginative; they were often right. There's an important difference in that, which many people fail to see, especially people in medium-high places.

I looked up from my reading.

"I've had some luck with difficult killers before. All except the one I really want to catch," I told Sampson.

He nodded, but his eyes stayed locked onto mine. "This Mr. Smith something of a cult hero now? Over in Europe, especially, the Continent, London, Paris, Frankfurt."

I wasn't surprised that Sampson was aware of the ongoing case. The tabloids had made Mr. Smith their latest icon. The stories were certainly compelling reading. They played up the angle that Smith might be an alien. Even newspapers like the *New York Times* and the *Times* of London had run stories stating that police authorities believed Smith might be an extraterrestrial being who had come here to study humans. To *grok*, as it were.

"Smith has become the evil E.T. Something for *X-Files* fans to contemplate between TV episodes. Who knows, perhaps Mr. Smith *is* a visitor from outer space, at least from some other parallel world. He doesn't have anything in common with human beings, I can vouch for that. I've visited the murder scenes."

Sampson nodded. "Gary Soneji didn't have much in common with the human race," he said in his deep, strangely quiet voice. "Soneji was from another planet, too. He's an ALF, alien life-form."

"I'm not sure he fits the same psychological profile as Smith."

"Why is that?" he asked. His eyes narrowed. "You think your mass killer is smarter than our mass killer?"

"I'm not saying that. Gary Soneji was very bright, but he made mistakes. So far, Mr. Smith hasn't made any."

"And that's why you're going to solve this hinky mystery? Because Gary Soneji makes mistakes?"

"I'm not making predictions," I told Sampson. "I know better than that. So do you."

"Did Gary Soneji make a mistake at Alex's house?" he suddenly asked, his dark eyes penetrating.

I sighed out loud. "I think someone did."

The helicopter was settling down to land outside Princeton. A thin line of cars silently streamed past the airfield on a state highway. People watched us from the cars. It could safely be assumed that everything had started here. The house where Gary Soneji had been raised was less than six miles away. This was the monster's original lair.

"You're sure Soneji's not still alive?" John Sampson asked one more time. "Are you absolutely sure about that?"

"No," I finally said. "I'm not sure of anything yet."

CHAPTER 85

*A*SSUME NOTHING, *question everything.*

As we set down in the small private airfield, I could feel the hair on the back of my neck standing on end. *What was wrong here? What was I feeling about the Cross case?*

Beyond the thin ribbons of landing strip were acre upon acre of pine forests and hills. The beauty of the countryside, the incredible shades of green, reminded me of something Cézanne had once said: "When color is at its richest, form is at its fullest." I never looked at the world in quite the same way after hearing that.

Gary Soneji was brought up near here, I thought to myself. *Was it possible that he could still be alive? No, I didn't believe that. But could there be connections?*

We were met in New Jersey by two field agents who brought a blue Lincoln sedan for our use. Sampson and I proceeded from Princeton to Rocky Hill and then over to Lambertville, to see his grandfather. I knew that Sampson and Alex Cross had been to Princeton less than a week ago. Still, I had questions of my own, theories that needed field-testing.

I also wanted to see the entire area where Gary Soneji had grown up, where his madness had been inflicted and nurtured. Mostly I wanted to talk with someone neither Cross nor Sampson had spent much time investigating, a brand-new suspect.

Assume nothing, question everything . . . and everyone.

Seventy-five-year-old Walter Murphy, Gary's grandfather, was waiting for us on a long, whitewashed porch. He didn't ask us inside his house.

The porch had a nice view out from the farmhouse. I saw multiflora rose everywhere, an impenetrable bramble. The nearby barn was also overrun by sumac and poison ivy. I guessed that the grandfather was letting this happen.

I could feel Gary Soneji at his grandfather's farm, I felt him everywhere.

According to Walter Murphy, he'd had no inkling that Gary was capable of murder. Not at any time. Not a clue.

"Some days I think I've gotten used to what's happened, but then suddenly it's fresh and incomprehensible to me all over again," he told us as the midday breeze ruffled his longish white hair.

"Did you stay close to Gary as he got older?" I asked cautiously. I was studying his build, which was large. His arms were thick and looked as if they could still do physical damage.

"I remember long talks with Gary from the time he was a boy right up until it was alleged he'd kidnapped those two children in Washington." *Alleged.*

"And you were taken by surprise?" I said. "You had no idea?"

Walter Murphy looked directly at me—for the first time. I knew that he resented my tone, the irony in it.

How angry could I make him? How much of a temper did the old man have?

I leaned in and listened more closely. I watched every gesture, every tic. *Collected the data.*

"Gary always wanted to fit in, just like everybody else does," he said abruptly. "He trusted me because he knew I accepted him for what he was."

"What was it about Gary that needed to be accepted?"

The old man shifted his eyes to the peaceful-looking pine woods surrounding the farm. *I could feel Soneji in those woods. It was as if he were watching us.*

"He could be hostile at times, I'll admit. His tongue was sharp, double-barbed. Gary had an air of superiority that ruffled some tail feathers."

I kept at Walter Murphy, didn't give him space to breathe. "But not when he was around you?" I asked. "He didn't ruffle your feathers?"

The old man's clear blue eyes returned from their trip into the woods. "No, we were always close. I know we were, even if the expensive shrinks say it wasn't possible for Gary to feel love, to feel anything for anybody. I was never the target for any of his temper explosions."

That was a fascinating revelation, but I sensed it was a lie. I glanced at Sampson. He was looking at me in a new way.

"These explosions at other people, were they ever premeditated?" I asked.

"Well, you know damn well he burned down his father and stepmother's house. They were in it. So were his stepbrother and stepsister. He was supposed to be away at school. He was an honor student at the Peddie School in Hightstown. He was making friends there."

"Did you ever meet any of the friends from Peddie?" The quickening tempo of my questions made Walter Murphy uneasy. Did he have his grandson's temper?

A spark flared in the old man's eyes. Unmistakable anger was there now. Maybe the real Walter Murphy was appearing.

"No, he never brought his friends from school around here. I suppose you're suggesting that he didn't have friends, that he just wanted to seem more normal than he was. Is that your two-bit analysis? Are you a forensic psychologist, by the way? Is that your game?"

"Trains?" I said.

I wanted to see where Walter Murphy would go with it. This was important, a test, a moment of truth and reckoning.

C'mon, old man. Trains?

He looked off into the woods again, still serene and beautiful. "Mmm. I'd forgotten, hadn't thought of the trains in a while. Fiona's son, her real son, had an expensive set of Lionel trains. Gary wasn't allowed to even be in the same room with them. When he was ten or eleven, the train set disappeared. The whole damn set, gone."

"What happened to the train set?"

Walter Murphy almost smiled. "They all knew Gary had taken it. Destroyed it, or maybe buried it somewhere. They spent an entire summer questioning him as to the train set's whereabouts, but he never told them squat. They grounded him for the summer and he still never told."

"It was his secret, his power over them," I said, offering a little more "two-bit analysis."

I was beginning to feel certain disturbing things about Gary and his grandfather. I was starting to know Soneji and, maybe in the process, getting closer to whoever had attacked the Cross house in Washington. Quantico was researching possible copycat theories. I liked the partner angle—except for the fact that Soneji had never had one before.

Who had crept into Cross's house? And how?

"I was reading some of Dr. Cross's detective logs on the way here," I told the grandfather. "Gary had a recurring nightmare. It took place here on your farm. Are you aware of it? Gary's nightmare at your farm?"

Walter Murphy shook his head. He was blinking his eyes, twitching. He knew something.

"I'd like your permission to do something here," I finally said. "I'll need two shovels. Picks, if you have them."

"And if I say no?" he raised his voice suddenly. It was the first time he'd been openly uncooperative.

And then it struck me. The old man is acting, too. That's why he understood so much about Gary. He looks off into the trees to set his mind and gain control for the next few lines he has to deliver. *The grandfather is an actor! Just not as good as Gary.*

"Then we'll get a search warrant," I told him. "Make no mistake. We will do the search anyway."

CHAPTER 86

"WHAT THE hell is this all about?" Sampson asked as we trudged from the ramshackle barn to a gray fieldstone fireplace that stood in an open clearing. "You think this is how we catch the Bug-Eyed Monster? Beating up on this old man?"

Both of us carried old metal shovels, and I had a rusted pickax also.

"I told you—*data*. I'm a scientist by training. Trust me for about half an hour. The old man is tougher than he looks."

The stone fireplace had been built for family cookouts a long time ago, but apparently had not been used in recent years. Sumac and other vines were creeping over the fireplace, as if to make it disappear.

Just beyond the fireplace was a rotting, wooden-plank picnic table with splintered benches on either side. Pines, oaks, and sugar maples were everywhere.

"Gary had a recurring dream. That's what brought me here. This is where the dream takes place. Near the fireplace and the picnic table at Grandpa Walter's farm. It's quite horrible. The dream comes up several times in the notes Alex made on Soneji when he was inside Lorton Prison."

"Where Gary should have been *cooked*, until he was crispy on the outside, slightly pink toward the center," Sampson said.

I laughed at his dark humor. It was the first light moment I'd had in a long time and it felt good to share it with someone.

I picked out a spot midway between the old fireplace and a towering oak tree that canted toward the farmhouse. I drove the pickax into the ground, drove it hard and deep. *Gary Soneji. His aura, his profound evil. His paternal granddaddy. More data.*

"In his bizarre dreams," I told Sampson, "Gary committed a gruesome murder when he was a young boy. He *may* have buried the victim out here. He wasn't sure himself. He felt he couldn't separate dreams from reality sometimes. Let's spend a little time searching for Soneji's ancient burial ground. Maybe we're about to enter Gary's earliest nightmare."

"Maybe I don't want to enter Gary Soneji's earliest nightmare," Sampson said laughing again. The tension between us was definitely breaking some. This was better.

I lifted the pickax high and swung down with great force. I repeated the action again and again, until I found a smooth, comfortable, working rhythm.

Sampson looked surprised as he watched me handle the pick. "You've done this kind of fieldwork before, boy," he said, and began to dig at my side.

"Yes, I lived on a farm in El Toro, California. My father, his father, and my grandfather's father were all small-town doctors. But they continued to live on our family horse farm. I was supposed to go back there to set up practice, but then I never finished my medical training."

The two of us were hard at work now. Good, honest work: looking for old bodies, searching for ghosts from Gary Soneji's past. Trying to goad Grandfather Murphy.

We took off our shirts, and soon both of us were covered with sweat and dust.

"This was like a *gentleman's* farm? Back in California? The one you lived on as a boy?"

I snorted out a laugh as I pictured the *gentleman's* farm. "It was a very small farm. We had to struggle to keep it going. My family didn't believe a doctor should get rich taking care of other people. 'You shouldn't take a profit from other people's misery,' my father said. He still believes that."

"Huh. So your whole family's weird?"

"That's a reasonably accurate portrait."

CHAPTER 87

AS I continued to dig in Walter Murphy's yard, I thought back to our farm in Southern California. I could still vividly see the large red barn and two small corrals.

When I lived there we owned six horses. Two were breeding stallions, Fadl and Rithsar. Every morning I took rake, pitchfork, and wheelbarrow, and I cleared the stalls; and then made my trip to the manure pile. I put down lime and straw, washed out and refilled the water buckets, made minor repairs. Every single morning of my youth. So yes, I knew how to handle a shovel and pickax.

It took Sampson and me half an hour before we had a shallow ditch stretching toward the ancient oak tree in the Murphy yard. The sprawling tree had been mentioned several times in Gary's recounting of his dreams.

I had almost expected Walter Murphy to call the local police on us, but it didn't happen. I half expected Soneji to suddenly appear. That didn't happen either.

"Too bad old Gary didn't just leave us a map." Sampson grunted and groaned under the hot, beating sun.

"He was very specific about his dream. I think he wanted Alex to come out here. Alex, or somebody else."

"Somebody else did. The two of us. Hot shit, there's something down here. Something under my feet," Sampson said.

I moved around toward his spot in the trench. The two of us continued to dig, picking up the pace. We worked side by side, sweating profusely. *Data*, I reminded myself. *It's all just data on the way to an answer. The beginning of a solution.*

And then I recognized the fragments we had uncovered in the shallow grave, in Gary's hiding place near the fireplace.

"Jesus Christ, I don't believe it. Oh God, Jesus!" Sampson said.

"Animal bones. Looks like the skull and upper thigh bone of a medium-sized dog," I said to Sampson.

"Lots of bones!" he added.

We continued to dig even faster. Our breathing was harsh and labored. We had been digging in the summer heat for nearly an hour. It was in the nineties, sticky-hot, and claustrophobic. We were in a hole up to our waists.

"Shit! Here we go again. You recognize this from any of your med-school anatomy classes?" Sampson asked.

We were looking down at fragments from a human skeleton. "It's the scapula and mandible. It could be a young boy or girl," I told him.

"So this is the handiwork of young Gary? This Gary's first kill? Another kid?"

"I don't know for sure. Let's not forget about

Grandpa Walter. Let's keep looking. If it is Gary, maybe he left a sign. These would be his earliest souvenirs. They would have been precious to him."

We kept on digging and, minutes later, we found another cache. Only the sound of our labored breathing broke the silence.

There were more bones, possibly from a large animal, possibly a deer, but probably human.

And there was something else, a definite sign from young Gary. It had been wrapped in tinfoil, which I now carefully removed.

It was a Lionel locomotive, undoubtedly the one he had stolen from his stepbrother.

The toy train that launched a hundred deaths.

CHAPTER 88

CHRISTINE JOHNSON knew she had to go to the Sojourner Truth School, but once she got there, she wasn't sure she was ready for work yet. She was nervous, distracted, and not herself. Maybe school would help to get her mind off Alex, though.

She stopped at Laura Dixon's first-grade class on her morning walk. Laura was one of her best friends in the world, and her classes were stimulating and fun. Besides, first graders were so damn cute to be around. "Laura's babies," she called them. Or, "Laura's cuddly kittens and perky puppies."

"Oh, *look* who it is, look who's come to visit. Aren't we the luckiest first-grade class in the whole world!" the teacher cried when she spotted Christine at the door.

Laura was just a smidgen over five foot tall, but she was still a very *big* girl, large at the hips and breasts. Christine couldn't keep from smiling at her friend's greeting. Trouble was, she was also incredibly close to tears. She realized she *wasn't* ready for school.

"Good morning, Ms. Johnson!" the first graders chorused like a practiced glee club. God, they were wonderful! So bright and enthusiastic, sweet and good.

"Good morning back at you." Christine beamed. There, she felt a little better. A big letter *B* was scrawled on the blackboard, as well as Laura's sketches of a *B*umblebee *B*uzzing around *B*atman and a *B*ig *B*lue *B*oat.

"Don't let me interrupt progress," she said. "I'm just here for a little refresher course. *B* is for *B*eautiful *B*eginnings, *B*abies."

The class laughed, and she felt *connected* with them, thank God. It was at times like this when she dearly wished she had kids of her own. She loved the first graders, loved kids, and, at thirty-two, it was definitely time.

Then, out of nowhere, an image flashed from the terrible scene a few days earlier. Alex being moved from his house on Fifth Street to one of the ambulances! She had been called to the scene by neighbors, friends of hers. Alex was conscious. He said, "Christine, you look so beautiful. Always." And then they took him away from her.

The image from that morning and his final words made her shiver to remember. The Chinese had a saying that had been in her mind for a while, troubling her: *Society prepares the crime; the criminal only commits it.*

"Are you all right?" Laura Dixon was at her side, had seen Christine falter at the door.

"Excuse us, ladies and gentlemen," she said to her class. "Ms. Johnson and I have to chat for a minute right outside the door. You may chat as well. Quietly. Like the ladies and gentlemen that you are, I trust."

Then Laura took Christine's arm and walked her out into the deserted hallway.

"Do I look *that* bad?" Christine asked. "Does it show all over my face, Laura?"

Laura hugged her tightly and the heat from her friend's ample body felt good. Laura *was* good.

"Don't you try to be so *goddamn* strong, don't try to be so brave," Laura said. "Have you heard anything more, sweetheart? Tell Laura. Talk to me."

Christine mumbled into Laura's hair. It felt so good to hold her, to hold on to someone. "Still listed as critical. Still no visitors. Unless you happen to be high up in the Metro police or the FBI."

"Christine, Christine," Laura whispered softly. "What am I going to do with you?"

"What, Laura? I'm okay now. I really am."

"You are so strong, girl. You are about the best person I have ever met. I love you dearly. That's all I'll say for right now."

"That's enough. Thank you," Christine said. She felt a little better, not quite so hollowed out and empty, but the feeling didn't last very long.

She started to walk back to her office.

As she turned down the east corridor, she spotted the FBI's Kyle Craig waiting for her near her office. She hurried down the hallway toward him. *This is not good,* she told herself. *Oh dear God, no. Why is Kyle here? What does he have to tell me?*

"Kyle, what is it?" Her voice trembled and nearly went out of control.

"I have to talk to you," he said, taking her hand. "Please, just listen. Come inside your office, Christine."

CHAPTER 89

THAT NIGHT, back in my room at the Marriott in Princeton, I couldn't sleep again. It was two cases, both running concurrently in my mind. I skimmed several chapters from a rather pedestrian book about trains, just to gather *data*.

I was starting to familiarize myself with the vocabulary of trains: vestibules, step boxes, roomettes, annunciators, the deadman control. I knew that trains were a key part to the mystery I had been asked to solve.

What part had Gary Soneji played in the attack at Alex Cross's house?

Who was his partner?

I went to work at my PowerBook, which I'd had set up on the hotel room desk. As I would later relate to Kyle Craig, I no sooner sat down than the specially designed alarm in the computer started to *beep*. A fax was waiting for me.

I knew instantly what it was—Smith was calling. He had been contacting me for over a year, on a regular basis. Who was tracking whom? I sometimes asked myself.

The fax message was classic Smith. I read it line by line.

Paris—Wednesday.

In Foucault's Discipline & Punish, the philosopher suggests that in the modern age we are moving from individual punishment to a paradigm of generalized punishment. I, for one, believe that is an unfortunate happenstance. Do you see where I might be going with this line of thinking, and what my ultimate mission might be?

I'm missing you over here on the Continent, missing you terribly. Alex Cross isn't worth your valuable time and energy.

I've taken one here in Paris in your honor—a doctor! A doctor, a surgeon, just like you wanted to be once upon a time.

Always,
Mr. Smith

CHAPTER 90

THIS WAS THE WAY the killer communicated with me for more than a year. E-mail messages arrived on the PowerBook at any time of day or night. I would then transmit them to the FBI. Mr. Smith was so contemporary, a creature of the nineties.

I relayed the message to the Behavioral Science Unit at Quantico. Several of the profilers were still working. I could visualize the scene of consternation and frustration. My trip to France was approved.

Kyle Craig telephoned my room at the Marriott a few minutes after the message had been relayed to Quantico. Mr. Smith was giving me another window of opportunity to catch him, usually only a day or so, but sometimes only hours. Smith was challenging me to save the kidnapped doctor in Paris.

And yes, I did believe Mr. Smith was far superior to Gary Soneji. Both his mind and his methodology outstripped Soneji's more primitive approach.

I was carrying my travel bag and computer when I saw John Sampson. He was outside in the parking lot of the hotel. It was a little past midnight. I wondered what he'd been up to in Princeton that night.

"What the hell is this, Pierce? Where do you think you're going?" he said in a loud, angry voice. He towered over me in the parking lot. His shadow stretched out thirty or forty feet from the lights of the building.

"Smith contacted me about thirty minutes ago. He does this just before he makes a kill. He gives me a location and challenges me to stop the murder."

Sampson's nostrils flared. He was shaking his head from side to side. There was only one case in his mind.

"So you're just dropping what we're working on here? You weren't even going to tell me, were you? Just leave Princeton in the dead of night." His eyes were cold and unfriendly. I had lost his trust.

"John, I left a message explaining everything to you. It's at the front desk. I already spoke to Kyle. I'll surely be back in a few days. Smith never takes long. He knows it's too dangerous. I need time to think about this case anyway."

Sampson frowned and he continued to shake his head. "You said it was important to visit Lorton Prison. You said Lorton is the one place where Soneji could have gotten somebody to do his dirty work. His partner probably came from Lorton."

"I still plan to visit Lorton Prison. Right now, I have to try and prevent a murder. Smith abducted a doctor in Paris. He's dedicating the kill to me."

John Sampson wasn't impressed with anything I'd said.

I didn't get a chance to tell him the other thing, the part that bothered me the most. I hadn't told Kyle Craig either.

Isabella had come from Paris. Paris was her home. I hadn't been there since her murder.

Mr. Smith knew that.

CHAPTER 91

IT WAS a beautiful spot, and Mr. Smith wanted to spoil it, to ruin it forever inside his mind. The small stone house with its earth-grouted walls and white-shuttered windows and country-lace curtains was peaceful and idyllic. The garden was surrounded by twig fencing. Under a lone apple tree sat a long wooden table, where friends, family, and neighbors might gather to eat and talk.

Smith carefully spread out pages from *Le Monde* across the linoleum floor of the spacious farmhouse kitchen. Patti Smith—not a relation—was screeching from his CD player. She sang "Summer Cannibals," and the blatant irony wasn't lost on him.

The newspaper front page screamed as well—*Mr. Smith Takes Surgeon Captive in Paris!*

And so he had, so he had.

The idée fixe that had captured the public's fancy and fear was that Mr. Smith might be an alien visitor roaming and ravaging the earth for dark, unknown, perhaps *unknowable* reasons. He didn't share any traits with humans, the lurid news stories reasoned. He was described as "not of the earth," "incapable of any human emotion."

His name—Mr. Smith—came from "Valentine Michael Smith," a visitor from Mars in Robert Heinlein's science fiction novel *Stranger in a Strange Land*. The book had always been a cult favorite. *Stranger* was the single book in Charles Manson's backpack when he was captured in California.

He studied the French surgeon lying nearly unconscious on the kitchen floor. One FBI report stated that "Mr. Smith seems to appreciate beauty. He has a human artist's eye for composition. Observe the studied way in which he arranges the corpses."

A human artist's eye for beauty and composition. Yes, that was true enough. He had loved beauty once, lived for it, actually. The artful arrangements were one of the clues he left for . . . *his followers.*

Patti Smith finished her song, and the Doors immediately came on. "People Are Strange." The moldy oldie was wonderful mood music as well.

Smith let his gaze wander around the country kitchen. One entire wall was a stone fireplace. Another wall was white tile, with antique shelves that held copper pots, white café au lait bowls, antique jam jars, or *confitures fines,* as they were called here. He knew that, knew just about everything about everything. There was an antique black cast-iron stove with brass knobs. And a large white porcelain sink. Adjacent to the sink, just above a butcher-block worktable, hung an impressive array of kitchen knives. The knives were beautiful, absolutely perfect in every way.

He was avoiding looking at the victim, wasn't he?

He knew that he was. He always did.

Finally, he lowered his eyes and looked into the victim's.

So this was Abel Sante.

This was lucky number nineteen.

CHAPTER 92

THE VICTIM was a very successful thirty-five-year-old surgeon. He was good-looking in a Gallic sort of way, in excellent shape even without very much meat left on his bones. He seemed a nice person, an "honorable" man, a "good" doctor.

What was human? What exactly was human-ness? Mr. Smith wondered. That was the fundamental question he still had, after physical exams like this, in nearly a dozen countries around the world.

What was human? What, exactly, did the word mean?

Could he finally find an answer here in this French country kitchen? The philosopher Heidegger believed the *self is revealed* by what we truly care about. Was Heidegger onto something? What was it that Mr. Smith truly cared about? That was a fair question to ask.

The French surgeon's hands were tightly tied behind his back. The ankles were bound to the hands; the knees were bent back toward the head. The remaining length of rope was attached to the neck in a noose.

Abel Sante had already realized that any struggling, any thrashing about, created intense strangulation pressure. As the legs eventually tired, they would become numb and painful. The urge to straighten them would be overpowering. If he did this, it would induce self-strangulation.

Mr. Smith was ready. He was on a schedule. The autopsy would start at the top of the body, then work its way down. The correct order: neck, spine, chest. Then abdomen, pelvic organs, genitalia. The head and brain would be examined last, in order to allow the blood to drain as much as possible—*for maximum viewing.*

Dr. Sante screamed, but no one could hear him out here. It was an ungodly sound and almost made Smith scream, too.

He entered the chest via a classic "Y" incision. The first cut went across the chest from shoulder to shoulder, continued over the breasts, then traveled from the tip of the sternum. He cut down the entire length of the abdomen to the pubic area.

The brutal murder of an innocent surgeon named Abel Sante.

Absolutely inhuman, he thought to himself.

Abel Sante—he was the key to everything, and none of the police masterminds could figure it out. None of them were worth shit as detectives, as investigators, as anything. It was so simple, if only they would use their minds.

Abel Sante.

Abel Sante.

Abel Sante.

The autopsy finished, Mr. Smith lay down on the kitchen floor with what was left of poor Dr. Sante. He did this with every victim. Mr. Smith hugged the bleeding corpse against his own body. He whispered and sighed, whispered and sighed. It was always like this.

And then, Smith sobbed loudly. "I'm so sorry. I'm so sorry. Please forgive me. Somebody forgive me," he moaned in the deserted farmhouse.

Abel Sante.

Abel Sante.

Abel Sante.

Didn't anyone get it?

CHAPTER 93

O N THE American Airlines flight to Europe, I noticed that mine was the only overhead lamp glaring as the flight droned over the Atlantic.

Occasionally, one of the stewardesses stopped to offer coffee or liquor. But for the most part, I just stared into the blackness of the night.

There had never been a mass killer to match Mr. Smith's unique approach to violence, not from a scientific vantage point anyway. That was one thing the Behavioral Science Unit at Quantico and I agreed on. Even the contrarians at Interpol, the international clearinghouse for police information, agreed with us.

In point of fact, the community of forensic psychologists is, or at least had been, in relative agreement about the different repeat- or pattern-murderer types; and also the chief characteristics of their disorders. I found myself reviewing the data as I flew.

Schizoid personality disorder types, as they are currently called, tend to be introverted and indifferent to social relationships. This freak is a classic loner. He tends to have no close friends or close relationships, except possibly family. He exhibits an inability to show affection in acceptable ways. He usually chooses solitary activities for his free time. He has little or no interest in sex.

Narcissists are different. They exhibit little or no

concern for anyone but themselves, though they some-times pretend to care about others. True narcissists can't empathize. They have an inflated sense of self, can become highly unstable if criticized, and feel they are entitled to special treatment. They are preoccupied with grandiose feelings of success, power, beauty, and love.

Avoidant personality disorder types usually won't get involved with other people unless they're com-pletely sure of acceptance. These types avoid jobs and situations involving social contact. They are usually quiet and embarrass easily. They're considered "sneaky dangerous."

Sadistic personality disorder types are the ultimate in badness, as destructive individuals go. They habitu-ally use violence and cruelty to establish control. They enjoy inflicting physical and psychological pain. They like to tell lies, simply for the purpose of inflicting pain. They are obsessed with involving violence, tor-ture, and especially the death of others.

As I said, all of this ran through my mind as I sat in my airplane seat high over the Atlantic. What inter-ested me mostly, though, was the conclusion I'd reached about Mr. Smith, and which I had recently shared with Kyle Craig at Quantico.

At different times during the long and complex in-vestigation, Mr. Smith *had fit all four of these classic murderer types.* He would seem to fit one personality disorder type almost perfectly—then change into an-other—back and forth at whim. He might even be a fifth type of psychopathic killer, a whole new breed of disorder type.

Perhaps the tabloids were right about Mr. Smith, and he *was* an alien. He wasn't like any other human. I knew that. *He had murdered Isabella.*

This was really why I couldn't sleep on the flight to Paris. It was why I could never sleep anymore.

CHAPTER 94

WHO COULD ever begin to forget the cold-blooded murder of a loved one? I couldn't. Nothing has diminished its vividness or unreality in four years. It goes like this, exactly the way I told it to the Cambridge police.

It is around two in the morning, and I use my key to open the front door of our two-bedroom apartment on Inman Street in Cambridge. Suddenly, I stop. I have the sense that something is wrong in the apartment.

Details inside are particularly memorable. I will never forget any of it. A poster in our foyer: *Language is more than speech.* Isabella is a closet linguist, a lover of words and word games. So am I. It's an important connection between us.

A favorite Noguchi rice paper lamp of Isabella's.

Her treasured paperbacks from home, most of them Folio. White uniformed spines with black lettering, so perfect and neat.

I'd had a few glasses of wine at Jillian's with some other medical students, recent graduates like myself. We were letting off steam after too many days and nights and weeks and years in the Harvard pressure cooker. We were comparing notes about the hospitals each of us would be working at in the fall. We were promising to stay in touch, knowing that we probably wouldn't.

The group included three of my best friends through medical school. Maria Jane Ruocco, who would be working at Children's Hospital in Boston; Chris Sharp, who was soon off to Beth Israel; Michael Fescoe, who had landed a prize internship at NYU. I had been fortunate, too. I was headed to Massachusetts General, one of the best teaching hospitals in the world. My future was assured.

I was high from the wine, but not close to being drunk, when I got home. I was in a good mood, unusually carefree. Odd, guilty detail—I was horny for Isabella. *Free.* I remember singing "With or Without You" on the way back in my car, a ten-year-old Volvo befitting my economic status as a med student.

I vividly remember standing in the foyer, seconds after I flicked on the hall lights. Isabella's Coach purse is on the floor. The contents are scattered about in a three- or four-foot radius. Very, very strange.

Loose change, her favorite Georg Jensen earrings, lipstick, assorted makeup containers, compact, cinnamon gum—all there on the floor.

Why didn't Isabella pick up her purse? Is she pissed at me for going out with my med-school chums?

That wouldn't be like Isabella. She is an open woman, liberal-minded to a fault.

I start back through the narrow, long apartment, looking for her everywhere. The apartment is laid out railroad-style, small rooms on a tight track leading to a single window that looks onto Inman Street.

Some of our secondhand scuba equipment is sitting

in the hall. We had been planning a trip to California. Two air tanks, weight belts, wet suits, two sets of rubber fins clutter the hallway.

I grab a speargun—just in case. *In case of what?* I have no idea. How could I?

I become more and more frantic, and then afraid. "Isabella!" I call at the top of my voice. "*Isabella? Where are you?*"

Then I stop, everything in the world seems to stop. I let go of the speargun, let it fall, crash and clatter against the bare hardwood floor.

What I see in our bedroom will never leave me. I can still *see, smell,* even *taste,* every obscene detail. Maybe this is when my sixth sense is born, the strange feeling that is so much a part of my life now.

"Oh God! Oh Jesus, no!" I scream loud enough for the couple who live above us to hear. *This isn't Isabella,* I remember thinking. Those words of total disbelief. I may have actually spoken them aloud. *Not Isabella. It couldn't be Isabella. Not like this.*

And yet—I recognize the flowing auburn hair that I so love to stroke, to brush; the pouting lips that can make me smile, make me laugh out loud, or sometimes duck for cover; a fan-shaped, mother-of-pearl barrette Isabella wears when she wants to look particularly coquettish.

Everything in my life has changed in a heartbeat, or lack of one. I check for signs of breathing, a sign of life. I can feel no pulse in the femoral or carotid arteries. Not a beat. Nothing at all. *Not Isabella. This can't be happening.*

Cyanosis, a bluish coloration of the lips, nail beds, and skin is already taking place. Blood is pooled on the underside of her body. The bowels and bladder have relaxed, but these bodily secretions are nothing to me. They are nothing under the circumstances.

Isabella's beautiful skin looks waxy, almost translucent, as if it isn't her after all. Her pale green eyes have already lost their liquid and are flattening out. They can no longer see me, can they? I realize they will never look at me again.

The Cambridge police arrive at the apartment somehow. They are everywhere all at once, looking as shocked as I know I look. My neighbors from the building are there, trying to comfort me, trying to calm me, trying not to be sick themselves.

Isabella is gone. We never even got to say good-bye. Isabella is dead, and I can't bring myself to believe it. An old James Taylor lyric, one of our favorites, weaves through my head. "But I always thought that I'd see you, one more time again." The song was "Fire and Rain." It was our song. It still is.

A terrible fiend was loose in Cambridge. He had struck less than a dozen blocks from Harvard University. He would soon receive a name: *Mr. Smith,* a literary allusion that could have happened only in a university town like Cambridge.

The worst thing, what I would never forget or forgive—the final thing—*Mr. Smith had cut out Isabella's heart.*

My reverie ended. My plane was landing at Charles de Gaulle Airport. I was in Paris.

So was Smith.

CHAPTER 95

I CHECKED INTO the Hôtel de la Seine. Up in my room, I called St. Anthony's Hospital in Washington. Alex Cross was still in grave condition. I purposely avoided meeting with the French police or the crisis team. The local police are never any help anyway. I preferred to work alone, and did so for half a day.

Meanwhile, Mr. Smith contacted the Sûreté. He always did it this way; plus a call to the local police, a personal affront to everyone involved in chasing him. Bad news, always terrible news. *All of you have failed to catch me. You've failed, Pierce.*

He had revealed where the body of Dr. Abel Sante could be found. He taunted us, called us pathetic losers and incompetents. He always mocked us after a kill.

The French police, as well as members of Interpol, were gathered in large numbers at the entrance to the Parc de Montsouris. It was ten after one in the morning when I arrived there.

Because of the possibility of crowds of onlookers and the press, the CRS, a special force of the Paris police, had been called in to secure the scene.

I spotted an inspector from Interpol whom I knew and waved in her direction. Sondra Greenberg was nearly as obsessed about catching Mr. Smith as I was.

She was stubborn, excellent at her job. She had as good a chance as anyone of catching Mr. Smith.

Sondra looked particularly tense and uneasy as she walked toward to me. "I don't think we need all these people, all this *help*," I said, smiling thinly. "It shouldn't be too damn hard to find the body, Sandy. He told us where to look."

"I agree with you," she said, "but you know the French. This was the way they decided it should be done. *Le grand* search party for *le grand* alien space criminal." A cynical smile twisted along the side of her mouth. "Good to see you, Thomas. Shall we begin our little hunt? How is your French, by the way?"

"Il n'y a rien a voir, Madame, rentrez chez vous!"

Sandy laughed out of the side of her mouth. Some of the French policemen were looking at us as if we were both crazy. "I will *like hell* go home. Fine, though. *You* can tell the flics what we'd like them to do. And then they'll do the exact opposite, I'm quite sure."

"Of course they will. They're French."

Sondra was a tall brunette, willowy on top but with heavy legs, almost as if two body types had been fused. She was British, witty and bright, yet tolerant, even of Americans. She was devoutly Jewish and militantly gay. I enjoyed working with her, even at times like this.

I walked into the Parc de Montsouris with Sandy Greenberg, arm in arm. Once more into the fray.

"Why do you think he sends us *both* messages? Why does he want us *both* here?" she mused as we tramped across damp lawns that glistened under streetlights.

324 / James Patterson

"We're the stars in his weird galaxy. That's my theory anyway. We're also authority figures. Perhaps he likes to taunt authority. He might even have a modicum of respect for us."

"I sincerely doubt that," Sandy said.

"Then perhaps he likes showing us up, making himself feel superior. How about that theory?"

"I rather like it, actually. He could be watching us right now. I know he's an egomaniac of the highest order. *Hello there, Mr. Smith from planet Mars. Are you watching? Enjoying the hell out of this?* God, I hate that creepy bastard!"

I peered around at the dark elm trees. There was plenty of cover here if someone wanted to observe us.

"Perhaps he's here. He might be able to change shapes, you know. He could be that *balayeur des rues,* or that gendarme, or even that *fille de trottoir* in disguise," I said.

We began the search at quarter past one. At two in the morning, we still hadn't located the body of Dr. Abel Sante. It was strange and worrisome to everyone in the search party. It was obvious to me that Smith wanted to make it hard for us to locate the body. He had never done that before. He usually discarded bodies the way people throw away gum wrappers. *What was Smith up to?*

The Paris newspapers had evidently gotten a tip that we were searching the small park. They wanted a hearty serving of blood and guts for their breakfast editions. TV helicopters hovered like vultures overhead.

Police barricades had been set up out on the street. We had everything except a victim.

The crowd of onlookers already numbered in the hundreds—and it was two o'clock in the morning. Sandy peered out at them. "Mr. Smith's sodding fan club," she sneered. "What a time! What a civilization! Cicero said that, you know."

My beeper went off at half past two. The noise startled Sandy and me. Then hers went off. *Dueling beepers. What a world, indeed.*

I was certain it was Smith. I looked at Sandy.

"What the hell is he pulling this time?" she said. She looked frightened. "Or maybe it's a *she*—what is *she* pulling?"

We removed our laptops from our shoulder bags. Sandy began to check her machine for messages. I got to mine first.

Pierce, the e-mail read,

welcome back to the real work, to the real chase. I lied to you. That was your punishment for unfaithfulness. I wanted to embarrass you, whatever that means. I wanted to remind you that you can't trust me, or anyone else—not even your friend, Ms. Greenberg. Besides, I really don't like the French. I've thoroughly enjoyed torturing them here tonight.

Poor Dr. Abel Sante is at the Buttes-Chaumont

*Park. He's up near the temple. I swear it. I
promise you.*

*Trust me. Ha, ha! Isn't that the quaint sound
you humans make when you laugh? I can't quite
make the sound myself. You see, I've never actually laughed.*

*Always,
Mr. Smith*

Sandy Greenberg was shaking her head, muttering
curses in the night air. She had gotten a message, too.

"Buttes-Chaumont Park," she repeated the location.
Then she added, "He says that I shouldn't trust you.
Ha, ha! Isn't that the quaint sound we humans make
when we laugh?"

CHAPTER 96

THE HUGE, unwieldy search team swept across Paris to the northeast, heading toward the Buttes-Chaumont Park. The syncopated wail of police sirens was a disturbing, fearsome noise. Mr. Smith still had Paris in an uproar in the early-morning hours.

"He's in control now," I said to Sandy Greenberg as we sped along dark Parisian streets in the blue Citroën I had rented. The car tires made a ripping sound on the smooth road surface. The noise fit with everything else that was happening. "Smith is in his glory, however ephemeral it may turn out to be. This is his time, his moment," I rattled on.

The English investigator frowned. "Thomas, you continue to ascribe human emotions to Smith. When are you going to get it through your skull that we're looking for a *little green man*."

"I'm an empirical investigator. I'll believe it only when I *see* a little green man with blood dripping from his little green mouth."

Neither of us had ever given a millisecond's credence to the "alien" theories, but space-visitor jokes were definitely a part of the dark humor of this man-hunt. It helped to keep us going, knowing that we would soon be at a particularly monstrous and disturbing murder scene.

It was nearly three in the morning when we arrived at the Buttes-Chaumont. What difference did the late hour make to me. I never slept anymore.

The park was deserted, but brightly lit with streetlamps and police and army searchlights. A low, bluish gray fog had settled in, but there was still enough visibility for our search. The Buttes-Chaumont is an enormous area, not unlike Central Park in New York. Back in the mid-1800s, a manmade lake was dug there and fed by the St. Martin's Canal. A mountain of rocks was then constructed, and it is full of caves and waterfalls now. The foliage is dense almost anywhere you choose to roam, or perhaps to hide a body.

It took only a few minutes before a police radio message came for us. Dr. Sante had been located not far from where we had entered the park. Mr. Smith was finished playing with us. For now.

Sandy and I got out of the patrol car at the gardener's house near the temple, and we began to climb the steep stone steps. The flics and French soldiers around us weren't just tired and shell-shocked, they looked afraid. The body-recovery scene would stay with all of them for the rest of their lives. I had read John Webster's *The White Devil* while I was an undergrad at Harvard. Webster's weird seventeenth-century creation was filled with devils, demons, and werewolves—*all of them human*. I believed Mr. Smith was a human demon. The worst kind.

We pushed our way forward through thick bushes and brush. I could hear the low, pitiful whine of search dogs nearby. Then I saw four high-strung, shivering animals leading the way.

Predictably, the new crime scene was a unique one. It was quite beautiful, with an expansive view of Montmartre and Saint-Denis. During the day, people came here to stroll, climb, walk pets, live life as it should be lived. The park closed at 11:00 P.M. for safety reasons.

"Up ahead," Sandy whispered. "There's something."

I could see soldiers and police loitering in small groups. Mr. Smith had definitely been here. A dozen or more "packets," each wrapped in newspaper, were carefully laid out on a sloping patch of grass.

"Are we sure this is it?" one of the inspectors asked me in French. His name was Faulks. "What the hell is this? Is he making a joke?"

"It is not a joke, I can promise you that. Unwrap one of the bundles. Any one will do," I instructed the French policeman. He just looked at me as if I were mad.

"As they say in America," Faulks said in French, "this is your show."

"Do you speak English?" I spit out the words.

"Yes, I do," he answered brusquely.

"Good. Go fuck yourself," I said.

I walked over to the eerie pile of "packages," or perhaps "gifts" was the better word. There were a variety of shapes, each packet meticulously wrapped in newspaper. Mr. Smith the artiste. A large round packet looked as if it might be a head.

"French butcher shop. That's his motif for tonight. It's all just meat to him," I muttered to Sandy Greenberg. "He's mocking the French police."

I carefully unwrapped the newspaper with plastic gloves. "Christ Jesus, Sandy."

It wasn't quite a head—*only half a head.*

Dr. Abel Sante's head had been cleanly separated from the rest of the body, like an expensive cut of meat. It was sliced in half. The face was washed, the skin carefully pulled away. Only half of Sante's mouth screamed at us—a single eye reflected a moment of ultimate terror.

"You're right. It *is* just meat to him," Sandy said. "How can you stand being right about him all the time?"

"I can't," I whispered. "I can't stand it at all."

CHAPTER 97

OUTSIDE WASHINGTON, an FBI sedan stopped to pick up Christine Johnson at her apartment. She was ready and waiting, standing vigil just inside the front door. She was hugging herself, always hugging herself lately, always on the edge of fear. She'd had two glasses of red wine and had to force herself to stop at two.

As she hurried to the car she kept glancing around to see if a reporter was staking out her apartment. They were like hounds on a fresh trail. Persistent, sometimes unbelievably insensitive and rude.

A black agent whom she knew, a smart, nice man named Charles Dampier, hopped out and held the car's back door open for her. "Good evening, Ms. Johnson," he said as politely as one of her students at school. She thought that he had a little crush on her. She was used to men acting like that, but tried to be kind.

"Thank you," she said as she got into the gray-leather backseat. "Good evening, guys," she said to Charles and the driver, a man named Joseph Denjeau.

During the ride, no one spoke. The agents had obviously been instructed not to make small talk unless she initiated it. *Strange, cold world they live in*, Christine thought to herself. *And now I guess I live there, too. I don't think I like it at all.*

She had taken a bath before the agents arrived. She sat in the tub with her red wine and reviewed her life. She understood the good, bad, and ugly about herself pretty well. She knew she had always been a little afraid to jump off the deep end in the past, but she'd wanted to, and she'd gotten oh-so-close. There was definitely a streak of wildness inside her, *good* wildness, too. She had actually left George for six months during the early years of their marriage. She'd flown to San Francisco and studied photography at Berkeley, lived in a tiny apartment in the hills. She had loved the solitude for a while, the time for thinking, the simple act of recording the beauty of life with her camera every day.

She had come back to George, taught, and eventually got the job at the Sojourner Truth School. Maybe it was being around the children, but she absolutely loved it at the school. God, she loved kids, and she was good with them, too. She wanted children of her own so badly.

Her mind was all over the place tonight. Probably the late hour, and the second glass of merlot. The dark Ford sedan cruised along deserted streets at midnight. It was the usual route, almost always the same trail from Mitchellville to D.C. She wondered if that was wise, but figured they knew how to do their jobs.

Occasionally Christine glanced around, to see if they were being followed. She felt a little silly doing it. Couldn't help it, though.

She was part of a case that was important to the press now. And dangerous, too. They had absolutely no respect for her privacy or feelings. Reporters would show up at the school and try to question other teachers. They called her at home so frequently that she finally changed her number to an unlisted one.

She heard the *whoop* of nearby police or ambulance sirens and the unpleasant sound brought her out of her reverie. She sighed. She was almost there now.

She shut her eyes and took deep, slow breaths. She dropped her head down near her chest. She was tired and thought she needed a good cry.

"Are you all right, Ms. Johnson?" agent Dampier inquired. *He's got eyes in the back of his head. He's been watching me,* Christine thought. *He's watching everything that happens, but I guess that's good.*

"I'm fine." She opened her eyes and offered a smile. "Just a little tired is all. Too many early mornings and late nights."

Agent Dampier hesitated, then he said, "I'm sorry it has to be this way."

"Thank you," she whispered. "You make it a lot easier for me with your kindness. And *you're* a real good driver," she kidded agent Denjeau, who mostly kept quiet, but laughed now.

The FBI sedan hurtled down a steep concrete ramp and entered the building from the rear. This was a delivery entrance, she knew by now. She noticed that she was hugging herself again. Everything about the nightly trip seemed so unreal to her.

Both agents escorted her upstairs, right to the door, at which point they stepped back and she entered alone.

334 / James Patterson

She gently closed the door and leaned against it. Her heart was pounding—it was always this way.

"Hello, Christine," Alex said, and she went and held him so tight, *so tight,* and everything was suddenly so much better. Everything made sense again.

CHAPTER 98

MY FIRST morning back in Washington, I decided to visit the Cross house on Fifth Street again. I needed to look over Cross's notes on Gary Soneji one more time. I had a deepening sense that Alex Cross knew his assailant, had met the person at some time before the vicious attack.

As I drove to the house through the crowded D.C. streets I went over the physical evidence again. The first really significant clue was that the bedroom where Cross was attacked had been tightly controlled. There was little or no evidence of chaos, of someone being out of his mind. There was ample evidence that the assailant was in what is called a cold rage.

The other significant factor was the evidence of "overkill" in the bedroom. Cross had been struck half a dozen times before he was shot. That would seem to conflict with the tight control at the crime scene, but I didn't think so: Whoever came to the house had a deep hatred for Cross.

Once inside the house, the attacker operated as Soneji would have. The assailant had hidden in the cellar. Then he copycatted an earlier attack Soneji had made at the house. No weapons had been found, so the attacker was definitely clearheaded. No souvenirs had been taken from Cross's room.

Alex Cross's detective shield had been left behind. The attacker wanted it found. What did that tell me— that the killer was proud of what he had accomplished?

Finally, I kept returning to the single most striking and meaningful clue so far. It had jumped at me from the first moment I arrived on Fifth Street and began to collect data.

The attacker had left Alex Cross and his family alive. Even if Cross died, the assailant had departed from the house with the knowledge that Cross was still breathing.

Why would the intruder do that? He could have killed Cross. Or was it always part of a plan to leave Cross alive? If so, why?

Solve that mystery, answer that question—case solved.

CHAPTER 99

THE HOUSE was quiet, and it had a sad and empty feeling, as houses do when a big, important piece of the family is missing.

I could see Nana Mama working feverishly in her kitchen. The smell of baking bread, roast chicken, and baked sweet potatoes flowed through the house, and it was soothing and reassuring. She was lost in her cooking, and I didn't want to disturb her.

"Is she okay?" I asked Sampson. He had agreed to meet me at the house, though I could tell he was still angry about my leaving the case for a few days.

He shrugged his shoulders. "She won't accept that Alex isn't coming back, if that's what you mean," he said. "If he dies, I don't know what will happen to her."

Sampson and I climbed the stairs in silence. We were in the hallway when the Cross children appeared out of a side bedroom.

I hadn't formally met Damon and Jannie, but I had heard about them. Both children were beautiful, though still showing bruises from the attack. They had inherited Alex's good looks. They had bright eyes and their intelligence showed.

"This is Mr. Pierce," Sampson said, "he's a friend of ours. He's one of the good guys."

"I'm working with Sampson," I told them. "Trying to help him."

"Is he, Uncle John?" the little girl asked. The boy just stared at me—not angry, but wary of strangers. I could see his father in Damon's wide brown eyes.

"Yes, he is working with me, and he's very good at it," Sampson said. He surprised me with the compliment.

Jannie stepped up close to me. She was the most beautiful little girl, even with the lacerations and a bruise the size of a baseball on her cheek and neck. Her mother must have been a beautiful woman.

She reached out and shook my hand. "Well, you can't be as good as my daddy, but you can use my daddy's bedroom," she said, "but only until he comes back home."

I thanked Jannie, and nodded respectfully at Damon. Then I spent the next hour and a half going over Cross's extensive notes and files on Gary Soneji. *I was looking for Soneji's partner.* The files dated back over four years. I was convinced that whoever attacked Alex Cross didn't do it randomly. There had to be a powerful connection with Soneji, *who claimed to always work alone.* It was a knotty problem and the profilers at Quantico weren't making headway with it either.

When I finally trudged back downstairs, Sampson and Nana were both in the kitchen. The uncluttered and practical-looking room was cozy and warm. It brought back memories of Isabella, who had loved to

cook and was good at it, too, memories of our home
and life together.

Nana looked up at me, her eyes as incisive as I remembered. "I remember you," she said. "You were the
one who told me the truth. Are you close to anything
yet? Will you solve this terrible thing?" she asked.

"No, I haven't solved it, Nana," I told her the truth
again. "But I think Alex might have. Gary Soneji
might have had a partner all along."

CHAPTER 100

A RECURRING THOUGHT was playing constantly inside my head: *Who can you trust? Who can you really believe? I used to have somebody—Isabella.*

John Sampson and I boarded an FBI Bell Jet Ranger around eleven the following morning. We had packed for a couple of days' stay.

"So who is this partner of Soneji's? When do I get to meet him?" Sampson asked during the flight.

"You already have," I told him.

We arrived in Princeton before noon and went to see a man named Simon Conklin. Sampson and Cross had questioned him before. Alex Cross had written several pages of notes on Conklin during the investigation of the sensational kidnapping of two young children a few years back: Maggie Rose Dunne and Michael "Shrimpie" Goldberg. The FBI had never really followed up on the extensive reports at the time. They wanted the high-profile kidnapping case closed.

I'd read the notes through a couple of times now. Simon Conklin and Gary had grown up on the same country road, a few miles outside the town of Princeton. The two friends thought of themselves as "superior" to other kids, and even to most adults. Gary had called himself and Conklin the "great ones." They were reminiscent of Leopold and Loeb, two highly intelligent teens who had committed a famous thrill killing in Chicago one year.

As boys, Simon Conklin and Gary had decided that life was nothing more than a cock-and-bull "story" conveniently cooked up by the people in charge. Either you followed the "story" written by the society you lived in, or you set out to write your own.

Cross double-underscored in the notes that *Gary had been in the bottom fifth of his class at Princeton High School, before he transferred to The Peddie School. Simon Conklin had been number one, and gone on to Princeton University.*

A few minutes past noon, Sampson and I stepped out into the dirt-and-gravel parking lot of a dreary little strip mall between Princeton and Trenton, New Jersey. It was hot and humid and everything looked bleached out by the sun.

"Princeton education sure worked out well for Conklin," Sampson said with sarcasm in his voice. "I'm really impressed."

For the past two years, Simon Conklin had managed an adult bookstore in the dilapidated strip mall. The store was located in a single-story, red-brick building. The front door was painted black and so were the padlocks. The sign read ADULT.

"What's your feeling about Simon Conklin? Do you remember much about him?" I asked as we walked toward the front door. I suspected there was a back way out, but I didn't think he would run on us.

"Oh, Simon Says is definitely a world-class freaka-zoid. He was high on my Unabomber list at one time. Has an alibi for the night Alex was attacked."

"He would," I muttered. "Of course he would. He's a clever boy. Don't ever forget that."

We walked inside the seedy, grungy store and flashed our badges. Conklin stepped out from behind a raised counter. He was tall and gangly and painfully thin. His milky brown eyes were distant, as if he were someplace else. He was instantly unlikable.

He had on faded black jeans and a studded black leather vest, no shirt under the vest. If I hadn't known a few Harvard flameouts myself, I wouldn't have imagined he had graduated from Princeton and ended up like this. All around him were pleasure kits, mas-turbators, dildos, pumps, restraints. Simon Conklin seemed right in his element.

"I'm starting to enjoy these unexpected visits from you assholes. I didn't at first, but now I'm getting into them," he said. "I remember you, Detective Sampson. But *you're* new to the traveling team. You must be Alex Cross's unworthy replacement."

"Not really," I said. "Just haven't felt like coming around to this shithole until now."

Conklin snorted, a phlegmy sound that wasn't quite a laugh. "You haven't felt like it. That means you have feelings that you occasionally act on. How quaint. Then you *must* be with the FBI's Criminal Investiga-tive Analysis Program. Am I right?"

I looked away from him and checked out the rest of the store.

"Hi," I said to a man perusing a rack with Spanish Fly Powder, Sta-Hard, and the like. "Find anything you like today? Are you from the Princeton area? I'm Thomas Pierce with the FBI."

The man mumbled something unintelligible into his chin and then he scurried out, letting a blast of sunlight inside.

"Ouch. That's not nice," Conklin said. He snorted again, not quite a laugh.

"I'm not very nice sometimes," I said to him.

Conklin responded with a jaw-cracking yawn. "When Alex Cross got shot, I was with a friend all night. Your very thorough cohorts already spoke to my squeeze, Dana. We were at a party in Hopewell till around midnight. Lots and lots of witnesses."

I nodded, looked as bored as he did. "On another, more promising subject, tell me what happened to Gary's trains? The ones he stole from his stepbrother?"

Conklin wasn't smiling anymore. "Look, actually I'm getting a little tired of the bullshit. The repetition bores me and I'm not into ancient history. Gary and I were friends until we were around twelve years old. After that, we never spent time together. He had his friends, and so did I. *The end.* Now get the hell out of here."

I shook my head. "No, no, Gary never had any other friends. He only had time for the 'great ones.' He believed you were one of them. He told that to Alex

Cross. I think you were Gary's friend until he died. That's why you hated Dr. Cross. You had a reason to attack his house. You had a motive, Conklin, and you're the *only* one who did."

Conklin snorted out of his nose and the side of his mouth again. "And if you can prove that, then I go directly to jail. I do not pass Go. But you can't prove it. *Dana. Hopewell. Several witnesses.* Bye-bye, assholes."

I walked out the front door of the adult bookstore. I stood in the blazing heat of the parking lot and waited for Sampson to catch up with me.

"What the hell is going on? Why did you just walk out like that?" he asked.

"Conklin is the leader," I said. "Soneji was *the follower.*"

CHAPTER 101

SOONER OR later almost every police investigation becomes a game of cat and mouse. The difficult, long-running ones always do. First you have to decide, though: *Who is the cat? Who is the mouse?*

For the next few days, Sampson and I kept Simon Conklin under surveillance. We let him know we were there, waiting and watching, always just around the next corner, and the corner after that. I wanted to see if we could pressure Conklin into a telling action, or even a mistake.

Conklin's reply was an occasional jaunty salute with his middle finger. That was fine. We were registering on his radar. He knew we were there, always there, watching. I could tell we were unnerving him, and I was just beginning to play the game.

John Sampson had to return to Washington after a few days. I had expected that. The D.C. police department couldn't let him work the case indefinitely. Besides, Alex Cross and his family needed Sampson in Washington.

I was alone in Princeton, the way I liked it, actually.

Simon Conklin left his house on Tuesday night. After some maneuvering of my own, I followed in my Ford Escort. I let him see me early on. Then I dropped back in the heavy traffic out near the malls, and I let him go free!

I drove straight back to his house and parked off the main road, which was hidden from sight by thick scrub pines and brambles. I walked through the dense woods as quickly as I could. I knew I might not have a lot of time.

No flashlight, no lights of any kind. I knew where I was going now. I was pumped up and ready. I had figured it all out. I understood the game now, and my part in it. My sixth sense was active.

The house was brick and wood and it had a quirky hexagonal window in the front. Loose, chipped, aqua-colored shutters occasionally banged against the house. It was more than a mile from the closest neighbor. No one would see me break in through the kitchen door.

I was aware that Simon Conklin might circle back behind me—if he was as bright as he thought he was. I wasn't worried about that. I had a working theory about Conklin and his visit to Cross's house. I needed to test it out.

I suddenly thought about Mr. Smith as I was picking the lock. *Smith was obsessed with studying people, with breaking and entering into their lives.*

The inside of the house was absolutely unbearable: Simon Conklin's place smelled like Salvation Army furniture laced with BO and immersed in a McDonald's deep fryer. No, it was actually worse than that. I held a handkerchief over my nose and mouth as I began to search the filthy lair. I was afraid that I might find a body in here. Anything was possible.

Every room and every object was coated with dust and grime. The best that could be said for Simon Conklin was that he was an avid reader. Volumes were spread open in every room, half a dozen on his bed alone.

He seemed to favor sociology, philosophy, and psychology: Marx, Jung, Bruno Bettelheim, Malraux, Jean Baudrillard. Three unpainted floor-to-ceiling bookcases were crammed with books piled horizontally. My initial impression of the place was that it had already been ransacked by someone.

All of this fit with what had really happened at Alex Cross's house.

Over Conklin's rumpled, unmade bed was a framed Vargas girl, signed by the model, with a lipstick kiss next to the butt.

A rifle was stashed under the bed. It was a BAR— the same model Browning Gary Soneji had used in Washington. A smile slowly broke across my face.

Simon Conklin knew the rifle was circumstantial evidence, that it proved nothing about his guilt or innocence. *He wanted it found. He wanted Cross's badge found. He liked to play games. Of course he did.*

I climbed down creaking wooden stairs to the basement. I kept the house lights off and used only my penlight.

There were no windows in the cellar. There were dust and cobwebs, and a loudly dripping sink. Curled photographic prints were clipped to strings dangling from the ceiling.

My heart was beating in double time. I examined the dangling pictures. They were photos of Simon Conklin himself, different pics of the auteur cavorting in the buff. They appeared to have been taken inside the house.

I shined the light haphazardly around the basement, glancing everywhere. The floor was dirt and there were large rocks on which the old house was built. Ancient medical equipment was stored: a walker, an aluminum-framed potty, an oxygen tank with hoses and gauges still attached, a glucose monitor.

My eyes trailed over to the far side, the southern wall of the house. *Gary Soneji's train set!*

I was in the house of Gary's best friend, his only friend in the world, the man who had attacked Alex Cross and his family in Washington. I was certain of it. I was certain I had solved the case.

I was better than Alex Cross.

There, I've said it.

The truth begins.

Who is the cat? Who is the mouse?

Part Five
Cat & Mouse

CHAPTER 102

A DOZEN OF the best FBI agents available stood in an informal grouping on the airfield in Quantico, Virginia. Directly behind them, two jet black helicopters were waiting for takeoff. The agents couldn't have looked more solemn or attentive, but also puzzled.

As I stood before them, my legs were shaking and my knees were hitting together. I had never been more nervous, more unsure of myself. I had also never been more focused on a murder case.

"For those of you who don't know me," I said, pausing not for effect, but because of nerves, "I'm Alex Cross."

I tried to let them see that physically I was fine. I wore loosefitting khaki trousers and a long-sleeved navy blue cotton knit shirt open at the collar. I was doing my best to disguise a mess of bruises and lacerations.

A lot of troubling mysteries had to unfold now. Mysteries about the savage, cowardly attack at my house in Washington—and who had done it; dizzying mysteries about the mass murderer Mr. Smith; and about Thomas Pierce of the FBI.

I could see by their faces that some of the agents remained confused. They clearly looked as if they'd been blindsided by my appearance.

I couldn't blame them, but I also knew that what had happened was necessary. It seemed like the only way to catch a terrifying and diabolical killer. That was the plan, and the plan was all-consuming.

"As you can all see, rumors of my imminent demise have been greatly exaggerated. I'm just fine, actually," I said and cracked a smile. That seemed to break the ice a little with the agents.

"The official statements out of St. Anthony's Hospital—'not expected to live,' 'grave condition,' 'highly unusual for someone in Dr. Cross's condition to pull through'—were overstatements, and sometimes outright lies. The releases were manufactured for Thomas Pierce's benefit. The releases were a hoax. If you want to blame someone, blame Kyle Craig," I said.

"Yes, definitely blame me," Kyle said. He was standing at my side, along with John Sampson and Sondra Greenberg from Interpol. "Alex didn't want to go this way. Actually, he didn't want any involvement at all, if my memory serves me."

"That's right, but now I am involved. I'm in this up to my eyebrows. Soon you will be, too. Kyle and I are going to tell you everything."

I took a breath, then I continued. My nervousness was mostly gone.

"Four years ago, a recent Harvard Medical School grad named Thomas Pierce discovered his girlfriend murdered in their apartment in Cambridge. That was the police finding at the time. It was later corroborated by the Bureau. Let me tell you about the actual murder. Now let me tell you what Kyle and I believe really happened. This is how it went down that night in Cambridge."

CHAPTER 103

THOMAS PIERCE had spent the early part of the night out drinking with friends at a bar called Jillian's in Cambridge. The friends were recent med-school graduates and they'd been drinking hard since about two in the afternoon.

Pierce had invited Isabella to the bar, but she'd turned him down and told him to have fun, let off some steam. He deserved it. That night, as he had been doing for the past six months, a doctor named Martin Straw came over to the apartment Isabella and Pierce shared. Straw and Isabella were having an affair. He had promised he would leave his wife and children for her.

Isabella was asleep when Pierce got to the apartment on Inman Street. He knew that Dr. Martin Straw had been there earlier. He had seen Straw and Isabella together at other times. He'd followed them on several occasions around Cambridge and also on day trips out into the countryside.

As he opened the front door of his apartment, he could feel, in every inch of his body, that Martin Straw had been there. Straw's scent was unmistakable, and Thomas Pierce wanted to scream. He had never cheated on Isabella, never even come close.

She was fast asleep in their bed. He stood over her for several moments and she never stirred. He had always loved the way she slept, loved watching her like this. He had always mistaken her sleeping pose for innocence.

He could tell that Isabella had been drinking wine. He smelled the sweet odor from where he stood.

She had on perfume that night. For Martin Straw.

It was Jean Patou's Joy—very expensive. He had bought it for her the previous Christmas.

Thomas Pierce began to cry, to sob into his hands.

Isabella's long auburn hair was loose and strands and bunches flowed free on the pillows. For Martin Straw.

Martin Straw always lay on the left side of the bed. He had a deviated septum that he should have tended to, but doctors put off operations, too. He couldn't breathe very well out of the right nostril.

Thomas Pierce knew this. He had *studied* Straw, tried to understand him, his so-called humanity.

Pierce knew he had to act now, knew that he couldn' take too much time.

He fell on Isabella with all his weight, his force, his power. His tools were ready. She struggled, but he held her down. He clutched her long swanlike throat with his strong hands. He wedged his feet under the mattress for leverage.

The struggle exposed her bare breasts and he was reminded of how "sexy" and "absolutely beautiful" Isabella was; how they were "perfect together"; "Cambridge's very own Romeo and Juliet." What bullshit it was. A sorry myth. The perception of people who couldn't see straight. She didn't really love him, but how he had loved her. Isabella made him *feel* for the one and only time in his life.

Thomas Pierce looked down at her. Isabella's eyes were like sandblasted mirrors. Her small, beautiful mouth fell open to one side. Her skin still felt satin soft to his touch.

She was helpless now, but she could see what was happening. Isabella was aware of her crimes and the punishment to come.

"I don't know what I'm doing," he finally said. "It's as if I'm outside myself, watching. And yet . . . I can't tell you how alive I feel right now."

Every newspaper, the news magazines, TV, and radio reported what happened in gruesome detail, but nothing like what really happened, what it was like in the bedroom, staring into Isabella's eyes as he murdered her.

He cut out Isabella's heart.

He held her heart in his hands, still pumping, still alive, and watched it die.

Then he impaled her heart on a spear from his scuba equipment.

He *"pierced"* her heart. That was the clue he left. The very first clue.

He had the feeling, the sixth sense, that he actually watched Isabella's spirit leave her body. Then he thought he felt his own soul depart. He believed that he died that night, too.

Smith was born from death that night in Cambridge. *Thomas Pierce was Mr. Smith.*

CHAPTER 104

"THOMAS PIERCE *is* Mr. Smith," I said to the agents gathered at Quantico. "If any of you still doubt that, even a little bit, please don't. It could be dangerous to you and everyone else on this team. Pierce is Smith, and he's murdered nineteen people so far. He will murder again."

I had been speaking for several moments, but now I stopped. There was a question from the group. Actually, there were several questions. I couldn't blame them—I was full of questions myself.

"Can I backtrack for just a second here? Your family *was* attacked?" A young crew-cut agent asked. "You *did* sustain injuries?"

"There *was* an attack at my house. For reasons that we don't understand yet, the intruder stopped short of murder. My family is all right. Believe me, I want to understand about the attack, and the intruder, more than anyone does. I want that bastard, whoever he is."

I held up my cast for all of them to see. "One bullet clipped my wrist. A second entered my abdomen, but passed through. The hepatic artery was not nicked, as was reported. I was definitely banged up, but my EKG never showed 'a pattern of decreased activity.' That was for Pierce's benefit. Kyle? You want to fill in some more of the holes you helped create?"

This was Kyle Craig's master plan, and he spoke to the agents.

"Alex is right about Pierce. He is a cold-blooded killer and what we hope to do tonight is dangerous. It's unusual, but this situation warrants it. For the past several weeks, Interpol and the Bureau have been trying to set a foolproof trap for the elusive Mr. Smith, who we believe to be Thomas Pierce," Kyle repeated. "We haven't been able to catch him at anything conclusive, and we don't want to do something that might spook him, make him run."

"He's one scary, spooky son of a bitch, I'll tell you that much," John Sampson said from his place alongside me. I could tell he was holding back, keeping his anger inside. "And the bastard is *very careful*. I never caught him in anything close to a slipup while I was working with him. Pierce played his part perfectly."

"So did you, John." Kyle offered a compliment. "Detective Sampson has been in on the ruse, too," he explained.

A few hours earlier, Sampson had been with Pierce in New Jersey. He knew him better than I did, though not as well as Kyle or Sondra Greenberg of Interpol, who had originally profiled Pierce, and was with us now at Quantico.

"How is he acting, Sondra?" Kyle asked Greenberg. "What have you noticed?"

The Interpol inspector was a tall, impressive-looking woman. She'd been working the case for nearly two years in Europe. "Thomas Pierce is an arrogant bastard. Believe me, he's laughing at all of us. He's one hundred percent sure of himself. He's also high-strung. He never stops looking over his shoulder. Sometimes, I don't think he's human either. I do believe he's going to blow soon. The pressure we've applied is working."

"That's becoming more evident," said Kyle, picking up the thread. "Pierce was very cool in the beginning. He had everyone fooled. He was as professional as any agent we've ever had. Early on, no one in the Cambridge police believed he had murdered Isabella Calais. He never made a mistake. His grief over her death was astonishing."

"He's for real, ladies and gents." Sampson spoke up again. "He's smart as hell. Pretty good investigator, too. His instincts are sharp and he's disciplined. He did his homework, and he went right to Simon Conklin. I think he's competing with Alex."

"So do I," said Kyle, nodding at Sampson. "He's very complex. We probably don't know the half of it yet. That's what scares me."

Kyle had come to me about Mr. Smith before the Soneji shooting spree had started. We had talked again when I'd taken Rosie to Quantico for tests. I worked with him on an unofficial basis. I helped with the profile on Thomas Pierce, along with Sondra Greenberg. When I was shot at my house, Kyle rushed to Washington out of concern. But the attack was nowhere near as bad as everyone thought, or as we led them to believe.

It was Kyle who decided to take a big chance. So

far, Pierce was running free. Maybe if he brought him in on the case, on *my* case? It would be a way to watch him, to put pressure on Pierce. Kyle believed that Pierce wouldn't be able to resist. Big ego, tremendous confidence. Kyle was right.

"Pierce is going to blow," Sondra Greenberg said again. "I'm telling you. I don't know everything that's going on in his head, but he's close to the limit."

I agreed with Greenberg. "I'll tell you what could happen next. The two personas are starting to fuse. Mr. Smith and Thomas Pierce could merge soon. Actually, it's the Thomas Pierce part of his personality that seems to be diminishing. I think he just might have *Mr. Smith take out Simon Conklin.*"

Sampson leaned into me and whispered, "I think it's time that you met Mr. Pierce *and* Mr. Smith."

CHAPTER 105

THIS WAS it. The end. It had to be.

Everything we could think of was tightly in place by seven o'clock that night in Princeton. Thomas Pierce had proven to be elusive in the past, almost illusory. He kept mysteriously slipping in and out of his role as "Mr. Smith." But he was clearly about to blow.

How he accomplished his black magic, no one knew. There were never any witnesses. No one was left alive.

Kyle Craig's fear was that we would never catch Pierce in the act, never be able to hold him for more than forty-eight hours. Kyle was convinced that Pierce was smarter than Gary Soneji, cleverer than any of us.

Kyle had objected to Thomas Pierce's assignment to the Mr. Smith case, but he'd been overruled. He had watched Pierce, listened to him, and became more and more convinced that Pierce was involved—at least with the death of Isabella Calais.

Pierce never seemed to make a mistake, though. He covered all of his tracks. Then a break came. Pierce was seen in Frankfurt, Germany, on the same day a victim disappeared there. Pierce was supposed to be in Rome.

It was enough for Kyle to approve a search of Pierce's apartment in Cambridge. Nothing was found.

Kyle brought in computer experts. They *suspected* that Pierce might be sending himself messages, supposedly from Smith, but there was no proof. Then Pierce was seen in Paris on the day Dr. Abel Sante disappeared. His logs stated that he was in London all day. It was circumstantial, but Kyle knew he had his killer.

So did I.

Now we needed concrete proof.

Nearly fifty FBI agents were in the Princeton area, which seemed like the last place in the world where a shocking crime ought to occur, or a notorious murder spree end.

Sampson and I waited in the front seat of a dark sedan parked on an anonymous-looking street. We weren't part of the main surveillance team, but we stayed close. We were never more than a mile, or at most two, from Pierce. Sampson was restless and irritable through the early night. It had gotten excruciatingly personal between him and Pierce.

I had a very personal reason to be in Princeton myself. I wanted a crack at Simon Conklin. Unfortunately, Pierce was between me and Conklin for now.

We were a few blocks from the Marriott in town where Pierce was staying.

"Quite a plan," Sampson mumbled as we sat and waited.

"The FBI tried just about everything else. Kyle thinks this will work. He feels Pierce couldn't resist solving the attack on my house. It's the ultimate competition for him. Who knows?"

Sampson's eyes narrowed. I knew the look—sharp, comprehending. "Yeah, and you had no part in any of the hinky shit, right?"

"Maybe I did offer a suggestion about why the setup might be attractive to Thomas Pierce, to his huge ego. Or why he might be cocky enough to get caught."

Sampson rolled his eyes back into his forehead, the way he'd been doing since we were about ten years old. "Yeah, maybe you did. By the way, he's an even bigger pain in the ass than you are to work with. Anal as shit, to coin a phrase."

We waited on the side street in Princeton as night blanketed the university town. It was déjà vu all over again. John Sampson and Alex Cross on stakeout duty.

"You still love me," Sampson said and grinned. He doesn't get giddy too often, but when he does—watch out. "You do love me, Sugar?"

I put my hand high on his thigh. "Sure do, big fellow."

He punched me in the shoulder—*hard*. My arm went numb. My fingers tingled. The man can *hit*.

"I want to put the hurt on Thomas Pierce! I'm going to put the hurt on Pierce!" Sampson yelled out in the car.

"Put the hurt on Thomas Pierce," I yelled with him. "And Mr. Smith, too!"

"Put the hurt on Mr. Smith and Mr. Pierce," we sang in unison, doing our imitation of the *Bad Boys* movie. *Yeah!*

We were back. Same as it ever was.

CHAPTER 106

THOMAS PIERCE felt that he was invincible, that he couldn't be stopped.

He waited in the dark, trancelike, without moving. He was thinking about Isabella, seeing her beautiful face, seeing her smile, hearing her voice. He stayed like that until the living room light was switched on and he saw Simon Conklin.

"Intruder in the house," Pierce whispered. "Sound familiar? Ring any bells for you, Conklin?"

He held a .357 Magnum pointed directly at Conklin's forehead. He could blow him right out the front door and down the porch stairs.

"What the—?" Conklin was blinky-eyed in the bright light. Then his dark eyes grew beady and hard. "This is unlawful entry!" Conklin screamed. "You have no right to be here in my house. Get the hell out!"

Pierce couldn't hold back a smile. He definitely *got* the humor in life, but sometimes he didn't take enough pleasure in it. He got up out of the chair, holding the gun perfectly still in front of him.

There wasn't much space to move in the living room, which was filled with tall stacks of newspapers, books, clippings, and magazines. Everything was categorized by date and subject. He was pretty sure that not-so-Simple Simon had an obsessive-compulsive disorder.

"Downstairs. We're going to your basement," he said. "Down to *the cellar*."

The light was already on downstairs. Thomas Pierce had gotten everything ready. An old cot was set up in the center of the crowded basement room. He had cleared away stacks of survivalist and sci-fi books to make room for the cot.

He wasn't sure, but he thought Conklin's obsession had to do with the end of the human race. He hoarded books, journals, and newspaper stories that supported his pathological idea. The cover of a science journal was taped to the cellar wall. It read: "Sex Changes in Fish—A Look at Simultaneous and Sequential Hermaphrodites."

"What the hell?" Simon Conklin yelled when he saw what Pierce had done.

"That's what they all say," Thomas Pierce said and shoved him. Conklin stumbled down a couple of stairs.

"You think I'm afraid of you?" Conklin whirled and snarled. "I'm not afraid of you."

Pierce nodded his head once and cocked an eyebrow. "I hear you, and I'm gong to straighten that out right now."

He shoved Conklin hard again and watched him tumble down the rest of the stairs. Pierce walked slowly down toward the heap. "You *starting* to get afraid of me now?" he asked.

He whacked Conklin with the side of the Magnum and watched as blood spit from Simon Conklin's head. "You starting to get afraid now?"

He bent down and put his mouth close to Conklin's hairy ear.

"You don't understand very much about pain. I know that about you," he whispered. "You don't have much in the way of guts either. You were the one in the Cross house, but you *couldn't* kill Alex Cross, could you? You *couldn't* kill his family. You punked out at his house. You blew it. That's what I *already know*."

Thomas Pierce was enjoying the confrontation, the satisfaction of it. He was curious about what made Simon Conklin tick. He wanted to "study" Conklin, to understand his humanity. To know Simon Conklin was to know something about himself.

He stayed in Conklin's face. "First, I want you to *tell* me that you're the one who snuck into Alex Cross's house. *You did it!* Now just tell me you did it. What you say here will *not* be held against you, and will *not* be used in a court of law. It's just between us."

Simon Conklin looked at him as if he were a complete madman. *How perceptive.*

"You're crazy. You can't do this. This won't matter in court," Conklin squealed.

Pierce's eyes widened in disbelief. He looked at Conklin as if *he* were the madman. "Didn't I just say precisely that? Weren't you listening? Am I talking to myself here? No, it won't matter in *their* court. This is *my* court. So far, you're losing your case, Simple Simon. You're smart, though. I'm confident you can do a much better job over the next few hours."

Simon Conklin gasped. A shiny, stainless-steel scalpel was pointed at his chest.

CHAPTER 107

"*LOOK AT ME!* Would you focus on what I'm saying, Simon. I'm not another gray suit from the FBI—I have important questions to ask. I want you to answer them truthfully. You *were* the one at Cross's house! You attacked Cross. Let's proceed from there."

With a swift move of his left arm, Pierce pulled Conklin roughly up off the cellar floor. His physical strength was a shock to Conklin.

Pierce put his scalpel down and hog-tied Conklin to the cot with rope.

Pierce leaned in close to Simon Conklin once he was tied down and helpless. "Here's a news flash—I don't like your superior attitude. Believe me, *you aren't superior.* Somehow, and this amazes me, I don't think I've made myself clear yet. You're a *specimen,* Simon. Let me show you something creepy."

"Don't!" Conklin screeched. He was helpless as Pierce made a sudden incision in the upper chest. He couldn't believe what was happening. Simon Conklin screamed.

"Can you concentrate better now, Simon? See what's on the table here? It's your tape recorder. I just want you to confess. Tell me what happened inside Dr. Cross's house. I want to hear everything."

"Leave me alone," Conklin whispered weakly.

"No! That's not going to happen. You will never be alone again. All right, forget the scalpel and the tape recorder. I want you to focus on *this*. Ordinary can of Coca-Cola. *Your Coke,* Simon."

He shook the bright red can, shook it up good, and popped it open. Then he pulled Conklin's head back. Grabbed a handful of long, greasy hair. Pierce pushed the harmless-looking can under Conklin's nostrils.

The soda exploded upward, fizz, bubbles, sugary-brown water. It shot up Conklin's nose and toward the brain. It was an army interrogator's trick. Excruciatingly painful, and it always worked.

Simon Conklin choked horribly. He couldn't stop coughing, gagging.

"I hope you appreciate the kind of resourcefulness I'm showing. I can work with any household object. Are you ready to confess? Or would you like some more Coke?"

Simon Conklin's eyes were wider than they had ever been before. "I'll *say* whatever you want! Just please stop."

Thomas Pierce shook his head back and forth. "I just want the truth. I want the facts. I want to know I solved the case that Alex Cross couldn't."

He turned on the tape recorder and held it under Conklin's bearded chin. "Tell me what happened."

"I was the one who attacked Cross and his family. Yes, yes, it was me," Simon Conklin said in a choked voice that made each word sound even more emotional. "Gary made me. He said if I didn't, somebody would come for me. They'd torture and kill me. Somebody he knew from Lorton Prison. That's the truth, I swear it is. Gary was the leader, not me!"

Thomas Pierce was suddenly almost tender, his voice soft and soothing. "I knew that, Simon. I'm not stupid. I knew that Gary made you do it. Now, when you got to the Cross house, you couldn't kill him, could you? You'd fantasized about it, but then you couldn't do it."

Simon Conklin nodded. He was exhausted and frightened. He wondered if Gary had sent this madman and thought that maybe he had.

Pierce motioned with the Coke can for him to keep going. He took a hit of the Coke as he listened. "Go on, Simon. Tell me all about you and Gary."

Conklin was crying, bawling like a child, but he was talking. "We got beat up a lot when we were kids. We were inseparable. I was there when Gary burned down his own house. His stepmother was inside with her two kids. So was his father. I watched over the two kids he kidnapped in D.C. I was the one at Cross's house. You were right! It might as well have been Gary. He planned everything."

Pierce finally took away the tape player and shut it off. "That's much better, Simon. I do believe you."

What Simon Conklin had just said seemed like a good break point—somewhere to end. The investigation was over. He'd proved he was better than Alex Cross.

"I'm going to tell you something. Something amazing, Simon. You'll appreciate this, I think."

He raised the scalpel and Simon Conklin tried to squirm away. He knew what was coming.

"Gary Soneji was a pussycat compared to me," Thomas Pierce said. "*I'm Mr. Smith.*"

CHAPTER 108

SAMPSON AND I rushed through Princeton, breaking just about every speed limit. The agents trailing Thomas Pierce had temporarily lost him. The elusive Pierce, or was it Mr. Smith—was on the loose. They thought they had him again, at Simon Conklin's. Everything was chaos.

Moments after we arrived, Kyle gave the signal to move in on the house. Sampson and I were supposed to be Jafos at the scene—*just a fucking observer.* Sondra Greenberg was there. She was a Jafo, too.

A half dozen FBI agents, Sampson, myself, and Sondra hurried through the yard. We split up. Some went in the front and others through the back of the ramshackle house. We were moving quickly and efficiently, handguns and rifles out. Everybody wore windbreakers with "FBI" printed large on the back.

"I think he's here," I told Sampson. "I think we're about to meet Mr. Smith!"

The living room was darker and gloomier than I remembered from an earlier visit. We didn't see anyone yet, neither Pierce nor Simon Conklin nor Mr. Smith. The house looked as if it had been ransacked and it smelled terrible.

Kyle gave a hand signal and we fanned out, hurrying through the house. Everything was tense and unsettling.

"See no evil, hear no evil," Sampson muttered at my side, "but it's here all the same."

I wanted Pierce to go down, but I wanted to get Simon Conklin even more. I figured it was Conklin who had come into my house and attacked my family. I needed five minutes alone with Conklin. Therapy time—for me. Maybe we could talk about Gary Soneji, about the "great ones," as they called themselves.

An agent called out—*"The basement! Down here! Hurry!"*

I was out of breath and hurting already. My right side burned like hell. I followed the others down the narrow, twisting stairs. "Awhh Jesus," I heard Kyle say from his position up ahead.

I saw Simon Conklin lying spread-eagled across an old striped-blue mattress on the floor. The man who had attacked me and my family had been mutilated. Thanks to countless anatomy classes at John Hopkins, I was better prepared than the others for the gruesome murder scene. Simon Conklin's chest, stomach, and pelvic area had been cut open, as if a crackerjack medical examiner had just performed an on-the-scene autopsy.

"He's been gutted," an FBI agent muttered, and turned away from the body. "Why in the name of God?"

Simon Conklin had no face. A bold incision had been made at the top of his skull. The cut went through the scalp and clear down to the bone. Then the scalp had been pulled down over the front of the face.

Conklin's long black hair hung from his scalp to where the chin should have been. It looked like a beard. I suspected that this meant something to Pierce. *What did obliterating a face mean to him, if anything.*

There was an unpainted wooden door in the cellar, another way out, but none of the agents stationed outside had seen him leave. Several agents were trying to chase down Pierce. I stayed inside with the mutilated corpse. I couldn't have run down Nana Mama right then. For the first time in my life, I understood what it would be like to be physically old.

"He did this in just a couple of minutes?" Kyle Craig asked. "Alex, could he work this fast?"

"If he's crazy as I think he is, yeah, he could have. Don't forget he did this in med school, not to mention his other victims. He has to be incredibly strong, Kyle. He didn't have morgue tools, no electric saws. He used a knife, and his hands."

I was standing close to the mattress, staring down at what remained of Simon Conklin. I thought of the cowardly attack on me, on my family. I'd wanted him caught, but not like this. Nobody deserved this. Only in Dante were such fierce punishments imposed on the damned.

I leaned in closer and peered at the remains of Simon Conklin. *Why was Thomas Pierce so angry at Conklin? Why had he punished Conklin like this?*

The basement of the house was eerily quiet. Sondra Greenberg looked pale, and was leaning against a cellar wall. I would have thought she'd be used to the

murder scenes, but maybe that wasn't possible for anybody.

I had to clear my throat before I could speak again.
"He cut away the front quadrant of the skull," I said.
"He performed a frontal craniotomy. It looks like
Thomas Pierce is practicing medicine again."

CHAPTER 109

I HAD KNOWN Kyle Craig for ten years, and been his friend for nearly that long. I had never seen him so troubled and disconsolate about a case before, no matter how difficult or gruesome. The Thomas Pierce investigation had ruined his career, or at least he thought so, and maybe he was right.

"How the hell does he keep slipping away?" I said. We were still in Princeton the next morning, having breakfast at PJ's Pancake House. The food was excellent, but I just wasn't hungry.

"That's the worst part of it—he knows everything we would do. He anticipates our actions and procedures. He was one of us."

"Maybe he *is* an alien," I said to Kyle, who nodded wearily.

Kyle ate the remainder of his soft, runny eggs in silence. His face was bent low over his plate. He wasn't aware of how comically depressed he looked.

"Those eggs must be real good." I finally broke the silence with something other than the scraping sound of Kyle's fork on the plate.

He looked up at me with his usual deadpan look. "I really messed this up, Alex. I should have taken Pierce in when I had the chance. We talked about it down in Quantico."

"You would have had to let him go, release him in a

few hours. Then what would you do? You couldn't keep Pierce under surveillance forever."

"Director Burns wanted to sanction Pierce, take him out, but I strongly disagreed. I thought I could get him. I told Burns I would."

I shook my head. I couldn't believe what I'd just heard. "The director of the FBI approved a sanction on Pierce? Jesus."

Kyle ran his tongue back and forth over his teeth. "Yes, and not just Burns. This went all the way to the attorney general's office. God knows where else. I had them convinced Pierce was Mr. Smith. Somehow the idea of an FBI field agent who's also a multiple killer didn't sit very well with them. We'll never catch him now. There's no real pattern, Alex, at least nothing to follow. No way to trace him. He's laughing at us."

"Yeah, he probably is," I agreed. "He's definitely competitive on some level. He likes to feel superior. There's a whole lot more to this, though."

I had been thinking about the possibility of some kind of abstract or artistic pattern since I'd first heard about the complicated case. I was well aware of the theory that each of the murders was different, and worse, seemed arbitrary. That would make Pierce almost impossible to catch. The more I thought about the series of murders, though, and especially about Thomas Pierce's history, the more I suspected that there had to be a pattern, a mission behind all of this. The FBI had simply missed it. Now I was missing it, too.

"What do you want to do, Alex?" Kyle finally asked. "I understand if you're not going to work this one, if you're not up to it."

I thought about my family back home, about Christine Johnson and the things we'd talked over, but I didn't see how I could step away from this awful case right now. I was also somewhat afraid of retribution from Pierce. There was no way to predict how he might react now.

"I'll stay with you for a few days. I'll be around, Kyle. No promises beyond that. Shit, I *hate* that I said that. Damn it!" I pounded the table and the plates and flatware jumped.

For the first time that morning, Kyle offered up half a smile. "So, what's your plan? Tell me what you're going to do."

I shook my head back and forth. I still couldn't believe I was doing this. "My plan is as follows. I'm going home to Washington, and that's nonnegotiable. Tomorrow or the next day, I'll fly up to Boston. I want to see Pierce's apartment. He wanted to see my house, didn't he? Then, we'll see, Kyle. Please keep your evidence gatherers on a leash before I get to his apartment. *Look, photograph,* but don't move anything around. Mr. Smith is a very orderly man. I want to see how Pierce's place looks, how he arranged it for us."

Kyle was back to the deadpan look, superserious, which I actually prefer. "We're not going to get him, Alex. He's been given a warning. He'll be more careful from now on. Maybe he'll disappear like some killers do, just vanish off the face of the earth."

"That would be nice," I said, "but I don't think it's going to happen. There *is* a pattern, Kyle. We just haven't found it."

CHAPTER 110

A S THEY say in the wild, Wild West, you have to get right back on the horse that threw you. I spent two days back in Washington, but it seemed more like a couple of hours. Everybody was mad at me for getting into the hunt. Nana, the kids, Christine. So be it.

I took the first flight into Boston and was at Thomas Pierce's apartment in Cambridge by nine in the morning. Reluctantly, the dragon slayer was back in play.

Kyle Craig's original plan to catch Pierce was one of the most audacious ever to come out of the usually conservative Bureau, but it probably had to be. The question now—had Thomas Pierce been able to get out of the Princeton area somehow? Or was he still down there?

Had he circled back to Boston? Fled to Europe? Nobody knew for sure. It was also possible that we might not hear from Pierce, or from Mr. Smith, for a long time.

There was a pattern. We just had to find it.

Pierce and Isabella Calais had lived together for three years in the second-floor apartment of a building in Cambridge. The front door of the place opened onto the foyer and kitchen. Then came a long railroad-style hallway. The apartment was a revelation. *There were memories and reminders of Isabella Calais everywhere.*

It was strange and overwhelming, as if she still lived here and might suddenly appear from one of the rooms.

There were photographs of her in every single room. I counted more than twenty pictures of Isabella on my first pass, a quick sight-seeing tour of the apartment.

How could Pierce bear to have this woman's face everywhere, looking at him, staring silently, accusing him of the most unspeakable murder?

In the pictures, Isabella Calais has the most beautiful auburn hair, worn long and perfectly shaped. She has a lovely face and the sweetest, natural smile. It was easy to see how he could have loved her. But her eyes had a far-off look in some of the pictures, as if she weren't quite there.

Everything about their apartment made my head spin, my insides, too. Was Pierce trying to tell us, or maybe tell himself, that he felt absolutely nothing—no guilt, no sadness, no love in his heart?

As I thought about it, I was overwhelmed with sadness myself. I could imagine the torture that must be his life every day—never to experience real love or deep feelings. In his crazed mind did Pierce think that by dissecting each of his victims he would find the answer to himself?

Maybe the opposite was true.

Was it possible that Pierce needed to feel her presence, to *feel* everything with the greatest intensity imaginable? Had Thomas Pierce loved Isabella Calais more than he'd thought he was capable of loving any-

one? Had Pierce felt redeemed by their love? When
he'd learned of her affair with a doctor named Martin
Straw, had it driven him to madness and the most unspeakable of acts: the murder of the only person he had
ever loved?

Why were her pictures still looming everywhere in
the apartment? Why had Thomas Pierce been torturing
himself with this constant reminder?

Isabella Calais was watching me as I moved through
every room in the apartment. What was she trying to
say?

"Who is he, Isabella?" I whispered. "What is he up
to?"

CHAPTER 111

I BEGAN a more detailed search of the apartment. I paid careful attention not just to Isabella's things, but to Pierce's, too. Since both had been students, I wasn't surprised by the academic texts and papers lying about.

I found a curious test-tube rack of corked vials of sand. Each vial was labeled with the name of a different beach: Laguna, Montauk, Normandy, Parma, Virgin Gorda, Oahu. I thought about the curious notion that Pierce had bottled something so vast, infinite, and random to give it order and substance.

So what was his organizing principle for Mr. Smith's murders? What would explain them?

There were GT Zaskar mountain bikes stored inside the apartment and two GT Machete helmets. Isabella and Thomas biked together through New Hampshire and across into Vermont. More and more, I was sure that he had loved her deeply. Then his love had turned to a hatred so intense few of us could imagine it.

I recalled that the first Cambridge police reports had convincingly described Pierce's grief at the murder scene as "impossible to fake." One of the detectives had written, "He is shocked, surprised, utterly heartbroken. Thomas Pierce not considered a suspect at this time."

What else, what else? There had to be a clue here. There had to be a pattern.

A framed quote was hung in the hallway. *Without God, We Are Condemned to Be Free.* Was it Sartre? I thought so. I wondered whose thinking it really represented. Did Pierce take it seriously himself or was he making a joke? *Condemned* was a word that interested me. Was Thomas Pierce a condemned man?

In the master bedroom there was a bookcase with a well-preserved, three-volume set of H. L. Mencken's *The American Language.* It rested on the top shelf. Obviously, this was a prized possession. Maybe it had been a gift? I remembered that Pierce had been a dual major as an undergraduate: biology and philosophy. Philosophy texts were everywhere in the apartment. I read the spines: Jacques Derrida, Foucault, Jean Baudrillard, Heidegger, Habermas, Sartre.

There were several dictionaries as well: French, German, English, Italian, and Spanish. A compact, two-volume set of the *Oxford English Dictionary* had type so small it came with a magnifying glass.

There was a framed diagram of the human voice mechanism directly over Pierce's work desk. And a quote: *"Language is more than speech."* Several books by the linguist and activist Noam Chomsky were on his desk. What I remembered about Chomsky was that he had suggested a complex biological component of language acquisition. He had a view of the mind as a set of mental organs. I *think* that was Chomsky.

I wondered what, if anything, Noam Chomsky or the diagram of the human voice mechanism had to do with Smith, or the death of Isabella Calais.

I was lost in my thoughts, when I was startled by a loud *buzzing* noise. It came from the kitchen at the other end of the hall.

I thought I was alone in the apartment, and the buzzing spooked me. I took my Glock from its shoulder holster and started down the long narrow hallway. Then I began to run.

I entered the kitchen with my gun in position and then understood what the buzzing was. I had brought along a PowerBook that Pierce had left in his hotel room in Princeton. *Left on purpose? Left as another clue?* A special alarm on the laptop personal computer was the source of the noise.

Had he sent a message to us? A fax or voice mail? Or perhaps someone was sending a message to Pierce? Who would be sending him messages?

I checked voice mail first.

It was Pierce.

His voice was strong and steady and almost soothing. It was the voice of someone in control of himself and the situation. It was eerie under the circumstances, to be hearing it alone in his apartment.

Dr. Cross—at least I suspect it's you I've reached. This is the kind of message I used to receive when I was tracking Smith.

Of course, I was using the messages for misdirection, sending them myself. I wanted to mislead the police, the FBI. Who knows, maybe I still do.

*At any rate, here's your very first message—
Anthony Bruno, Brielle, New Jersey.*

*Why don't you come to the seashore and join
me for a swim? Have you arrived at any conclusions about Isabella yet? She is important to all of
this. You're right to be in Cambridge.*

Smith/Pierce

CHAPTER 112

THE FBI provided me with a helicopter out of Logan International Airport to fly me to Brielle, New Jersey. I was on board the Disorient Express and there was no getting off.

I spent the flight obsessing about Pierce, his apartment, Isabella Calais, *their* apartment, his studies in biology and modern philosophy, Noam Chomsky. I wouldn't have thought it possible, wouldn't have dreamed it possible, but Pierce was already eclipsing Gary Soneji and Simon Conklin. I despised everything about Pierce. Seeing the pictures of Isabella Calais had done it for me.

Alien? I wrote on the foolscap pad lying across my lap. *He identifies with descriptor.*

Alienated? Alienated from what? Idyllic upbringing in California. Doesn't fit any of the psychopathic profiles we used before. He's an original. He secretly enjoys that, doesn't he?

No discernible pattern to murders that link with a psychological motive.

Murders seem haphazard and arbitrary! He revels in his own originality.

Dr. Sante, Simon Conklin, now Anthony Bruno. Why them? Does Conklin count?

Seems impossible to predict Thomas Pierce's next move. His next kill.

Why go south toward the New Jersey Shore?

It had occurred to me that he was originally from a shore town. Pierce had grown up near Laguna Beach in Southern California. Was he going home, in a manner of speaking? Was the New Jersey Shore as close to home as he could get—as close as he dared go?

I now had a reasonable amount of information about his background in California before he came east. He had lived on a working farm not far from the famous Irvine Ranch properties. Three generations of doctors in the family. Good, hardworking people. His siblings were all doing well, and not one of them believed that Thomas was capable of any of this mayhem and murder he was accused of committing.

FBI says Mr. Smith is disorganized, chaotic, unpredictable, I scribbled in my pad.

What if they're wrong? Pierce is responsible for much of their data about Smith. Pierce created Mr. Smith, then did the profile on him.

I kept revisiting his and Isabella's apartment in my mind. The place was so very neat and organized. The home had a definite *organizing principle*. It revolved around Isabella—her pictures, clothes, even her perfume bottles had been left in place. The smell of L'Air du Temps and Je Reviens permeated their bedroom to this day.

Thomas Pierce had loved her. *Pierce had loved.* Pierce had felt passion and emotion. That was another thing the FBI was wrong about. He'd killed because he thought he was losing her, and he couldn't bear it. Was Isabella the only person who had ever loved Pierce?

Another small piece of the puzzle suddenly fell into place! I was so struck by it that I said it aloud in the helicopter. *"Her heart on a spear!"*

He had "pierced" her heart! Jesus Christ! He had confessed to the very first murder! He had confessed!

He'd left a clue, but the police missed it. What else were we missing? What was he up to now? What did "Mr. Smith" represent inside his mind? Was everything representational for him? Symbolic? Artistic? Was he creating a kind of language for us to follow? Or was it even simpler? He had "pierced" her heart. Pierce wanted to be caught. Caught and punished.

Crime and punishment.

Why couldn't we catch him?

I landed in New Jersey around five at night. Kyle Craig was waiting for me. Kyle was sitting on the hood of a dark blue Town Car. He was drinking Samuel Adams beer out of a bottle.

"You find Anthony Bruno yet?" I called out as I walked toward him. "You find the body?"

CHAPTER 113

*M*R. SMITH *goes to the seashore*. Sounded like an unimaginative children's story.

There was enough moonlight for Thomas Pierce to make his way along the long stretch of glowing white sand at Point Pleasant Beach. He was carrying a corpse, what was left of it. He had Anthony Bruno loaded on his back and shoulders.

He walked just south of popular Jenkinson's Pier and the much newer Seaquarium. The boarded-up arcades of the amusement park were tightly packed along the beach shoulder. The small, grayish buildings looked forlorn and mute in their shuttered state.

As usual, music ran through his head—first Elvis Costello's "Clubland," then Beethoven's Piano Sonata No. 21, then "Mother Mother" by Tracy Bonham. The savage beast inside him wasn't calmed, not even close, but at least he could feel a beat.

It was quarter to four in the morning and even the surfcasting fishermen weren't out yet. He'd seen only one police patrol car so far. The police in the tiny beach town were a joke anyway.

Mr. Smith against the Keystone Kops.

This whole funky seashore area reminded him of Laguna Beach, at least the *tourista* parts of Laguna. He could still picture the surf shops that dotted the Pacific Coast Highway back home—the Southern California artifacts: Flogo sandals, Stussy T's, neoprene gloves and wet suits, beach boots, the unmistakable smell of board wax.

He was physically strong—had a workingman's build. He carried Anthony Bruno over one shoulder without much effort. He had cut out all the vital parts, so there wasn't much of Anthony anymore. Anthony was a shell. No heart, liver, intestines, lungs, or brain.

Thomas Pierce thought about the FBI's continuing search. The Bureau's fabled "manhunts" were over-rated—a holdover from the glory days of John Dillinger and Bonnie and Clyde. He knew this to be so after years of observing the Bureau chase Mr. Smith. They would never have caught Smith, not in a hundred years.

The FBI was looking for him in all the wrong places. They would surely have "numbers," meaning excessive force, their trademark maneuver. They would be all over the airports, probably expecting him to head back to Europe. And what about the wild cards in the search, people like Alex Cross? Cross had made his bones, no doubt about that. Maybe Cross was more than he seemed to be. At any rate, he relished the thought of Dr. Cross being in on this, too. He liked the competition.

The dead weight on his back and shoulder was starting to get heavy. It was almost morning, close to daybreak. It wouldn't do to be found lugging a disemboweled corpse across Point Pleasant Beach.

He carried Anthony Bruno another fifty yards to a glistening white lifeguard's chair. He climbed the creaking rungs of the chair, and propped the body in the seat.

The remains of the corpse were naked and exposed for the world to see. Quite a sight. *Anthony was a clue.* If anybody on the search team had half a brain and was using it properly.

"I'm not an alien. Do any of you follow that?" Pierce shouted above the ocean's steady roar.

"I'm human. I'm perfectly normal. I'm just like you."

CHAPTER 114

IT WAS all a mind game, wasn't it—Pierce against the rest of us.

While I had been at his apartment in Cambridge, a team of FBI agents went out to Southern California to meet with Thomas Pierce's family. The mother and father still lived on the same farm, between Laguna and El Toro, where Thomas Pierce had grown up.

Henry Pierce practiced medicine, mostly among the indigent farmworkers in the area. His lifestyle was modest and the reputation of the family impeccable. Pierce had an older brother and sister, doctors in Northern California, who were also well regarded and worked with the poor.

Not a person the profilers spoke to could imagine Thomas a murderer. He'd always been a good son and brother, a gifted student who seemed to have close friends and no enemies.

Thomas Pierce fit no brief for a pattern killer that I was familiar with. He was an original.

"Impeccable" was a word that jumped out of the FBI profiler reports. Maybe Pierce didn't want to be impeccable.

I re-reviewed the news articles and clippings about Pierce from the time of Isabella Calais's gruesome murder. I was keeping track of the more perplexing no-tions on three-by-five index cards. The packet was growing rapidly.

Laguna Beach—commercial shore town. Parts similar to Point Pleasant and Bay Head. Had Pierce killed in Laguna in the past? Had the disease now spread to the Northeast?

Pierce's father was a doctor. Pierce didn't "make it" to Dr. Pierce, but as a med student he had performed autopsies.

Looking for his humanity when he kills? Studying humans because he fears he has no human qualities himself?

He had a dual major as an undergrad: biology and philosophy. Fan of the linguist Noam Chomsky. Or is it Chomsky's political writings that turn Pierce on? Plays word and math games on his PowerBook.

What were we all missing so far?

What was I missing?

Why was Thomas Pierce killing all of these people?

He was "impeccable," wasn't he.

CHAPTER 115

PIERCE STOLE a forest green BMW convertible in the expensive, quaint, quite lovely shore town of Bay Head, New Jersey. On the corner of East Avenue and Harris Street, a prime location, he hot-wired and grabbed the vehicle as slickly as a pickpocket working the boardwalks down at Point Pleasant Beach. He was so good at this, overqualified for the scut work.

He drove west through Brick Town at moderate speeds, to the Garden State Parkway. He played music all the way—Talking Heads, Alanis Morissette, Melissa Etheridge, Blind Faith. Music helped him to *feel something*. It always had, from the time he'd been a boy. An hour and a quarter later he entered Atlantic City.

He sighed with pleasure. He loved it instantly—the shameless tawdriness, the grubbiness, the tattered sinfulness, the soullessness of the place. He felt as if he were "home," and he wondered if the FBI geniuses had linked the Jersey Shore to Laguna Beach yet?

Entering Atlantic City, he had half expected to see a beautifully maintained expanse of lawn sloping down to the ocean. Surfers with peroxided, gnarly hair; volleyball played around the clock.

But no, no, this was New Jersey. Southern California, his real home, was thousands of miles away. He mustn't get confused now.

He checked into Bally's Park Place. Up in his room, he started to make phone calls. He wanted to "order in." He stood at a picture window and watched the ghostly waves of the Atlantic punish the beach again and again. Far down the beach he could see Trump Plaza. The audacious and ridiculous penthouse apartments were perched on the main building, like a space shuttle ready to take off.

Yes, ladies and gentlemen, of course there was a pattern. Why couldn't anyone figure it out? Why did he always have to be misunderstood?

At two in the morning, Thomas Pierce sent the trackers another voice-mail message: *Inez in Atlantic City.*

CHAPTER 116

*G*ODDAMN HIM! Half a day after we recovered the body of Anthony Bruno, we got the next message from Pierce. He had taken another one already.

We were on the move immediately. Two dozen of us rushed to Atlantic City and prayed he was still there, that someone named Inez hadn't already been butchered and "studied" by Mr. Smith and discarded like the evening trash.

Giant billboards screamed all along the Atlantic City Expressway. Caesars Atlantic City, Harrah's, Merv Griffin's Resorts Casino Hotel, Trump's Castle, Trump Taj Mahal. Call 1-800-GAMBLER. Now *that* was funny.

Inez, Atlantic City, I kept hearing inside my head. *Sounds like Isabella.*

We set up shop in the FBI field office, which was only a few blocks from the old Steel Pier and the so-called "Great Wooden Way." There were usually only four agents in the small office. Their expertise was organized crime and gambling, and they weren't considered movers and shakers inside the Bureau. They weren't prepared for a savage, unpredictable killer who had once been a very good agent.

Someone had bought a stack of newspapers and they were piled high on the conference table. The New

York, Philly, and Jersey headline writers were having a field day with this one.

ALIEN KILLER VISITS JERSEY SHORE . . .

FBI KILLER-DILLER IN ATLANTIC CITY . . .

MR. SMITH MANHUNT: Hundreds of Federal agents
flock to New Jersey Shore . . .

MONSTER ON THE LOOSE IN NEW JERSEY!

Sampson came up to the beach from Washington. He wanted Pierce as badly as any of us. He, Kyle, and I worked together, brainstorming over what Pierce-Mr. Smith might do next. Sondra Greenberg from Interpol worked with us, too. She was seriously jet-lagged, and had deep circles under her eyes, but she knew Pierce and had been at most of the European murder sites.

"He's not a goddamn split personality?" Sampson asked. "Smith and Pierce?"

I shook my head. "He seems to be in control of his faculties at all times. He created 'Smith' to serve some other purpose."

"I agree with Alex," Sondra Greenberg said from across the table, "but *what* is the sodding purpose?"

"Whatever it was, it worked," Kyle joined in. "He had us chasing Mr. Smith halfway around the world. We're still chasing. No one has ever jerked around the Bureau like this."

"Not even the great J. Edgar Hoover?" Sondra said and winked.

"Well," Kyle softened, "as a pure psychopath, Hoover was in a class by himself."

I was up and pacing again. My side was hurting, but I didn't want anyone to know about it. They would try to send me home, make me miss the fun. I let myself ramble—sometimes it works.

"He's trying to tell us something. He's communicating in some strange way. *Inez?* The name reminds us of Isabella. He's obsessed with Isabella. You should see the apartment in Cambridge. Is Inez a substitute for Isabella? Is Atlantic City a substitute for Laguna Beach? Has he brought Isabella home? Why bring Isabella home?"

It went on and on like that: wild hunches, free association, insecurity, fear, unbearable frustration. As far as I could tell nothing worthwhile was said all day and late into the night, but who could really tell.

Pierce didn't try to make further contact. There were no more voice-mail messages. That surprised us a little. Kyle was afraid he'd moved on, and that he would keep moving until he drove us completely insane. Six of us stayed in the field office throughout the night and into the early morning. We slept in our clothes, on chairs, tables, and the floor.

I paced inside the office, and occasionally outside on the glittery, fog-laden boardwalk. As a last desperate resort, I bought a bag of Fralinger's salt water taffy and tried to get sick to my stomach.

What kind of logic system is he using? Mr. Smith is his creation, his Mr. Hyde. What is Smith's mission?

Why is he here? I wondered, occasionally talking to myself as I strolled the mostly deserted boardwalk.

Inez is Isabella?

It couldn't be that simple. Pierce wouldn't make it simple for us.

Inez is not Isabella. There was only one Isabella. So why does Pierce keep killing again and again?

I found myself at the corner of Park Place and Boardwalk, and that finally brought a smile. *Monopoly. Another kind of game? Is that it?*

I wandered back to the FBI field office and got some sleep. But not nearly enough. A few hours at most.

Pierce was here.

So was Mr. Smith.

CHAPTER 117

A FLAT, *still sandy, still meadowy region . . . a superb range of ocean beach—miles and miles of it. The bright sun, the sparkling waves, the foam, the view—a sail here and there in the distance.* Walt Whitman had written that about Atlantic City a hundred years before. His words were inscribed on the wall of a pizza and hot-dog stand now. Whitman would have been stricken to see his words on such a backdrop.

I went by myself for another stroll on the Atlantic City boardwalk around ten o'clock. It was Saturday, and so hot and sunny that the eroding beach was already dotted with swimmers and sunbathers.

We still hadn't found Inez. We didn't have a single clue. We didn't even know who she was.

I had the uncomfortable feeling that Thomas Pierce was watching us, or that I might suddenly come upon him in the dense, sweltering crowds. I had my pager just in case he tried to contact us at the field office.

There was nothing else to be done right now. Pierce–Mr. Smith was in control of the situation and our lives. A madman was in control of the planet. It seemed like it anyway.

I stopped near Steeplechase Pier and the Resorts Casino Hotel. People were playing under a hot sun in the high, rolling surf. They seemed to be enjoying themselves and didn't appear to have a care in the world. How nice for them.

This was the way it should be, and it reminded me of Jannie and Damon, my own family, and of Christine. She desperately wanted me to leave this job and I couldn't blame her. I didn't know if I could walk away from police work, though. I wondered why that was so. *Physician, heal thyself.* Maybe I would someday soon.

As I continued my walk along the boardwalk, I tried to convince myself that everything that could be done to catch Pierce was being done. I passed a Fralinger's, and a James Candy store. And the old Peanut Shoppe, where a costumed Mr. Peanut was stumbling about in the mid-ninety-degree heat.

I had to smile as I saw the Ripley's Believe It or Not Museum up ahead, where you could see a lock of George Washington's hair, and a roulette table made of jelly beans. No, *I could not believe it.* I didn't think anyone on the crisis team could, but here we were.

I was jolted out of my thoughts by the beeper vibrating against my leg. I ran to a nearby phone and called in.

Pierce had left another message. Kyle and Sampson were already out on the boardwalk. Pierce was near the Steel Pier. He claimed that Inez was with him! *He said we could still save them!*

Pierce specifically said *them.*

I shouldn't have been running around like this. My side began to throb and hurt like hell. I'd never been out of shape like this, not in my life, and I didn't like the feeling. I hadn't felt so vulnerable and relatively helpless before.

Finally, I realized: *I'm actually afraid of Pierce, and of Mr. Smith.*

By the time I got near the Steel Pier, my clothes were dripping wet and I was breathing hard. I pulled off my sport shirt and waded out into the crowd barechested. I pushed my way past old-style jitneys and newer step vans, past tandem bikes and joggers.

I was taped and bandage and I must have looked like an escapee from a local ER. Even so, it was hard to stand out on a beach like the one at Atlantic City. An ice-cream man hauling a box on his shoulder cried out, "Hitch your tongue to a sleigh ride! Get your Fudgie Wudgies here!"

Was Thomas Pierce watching us and laughing? He could be the ice-cream man, or anyone else in this frenetic mob scene.

I cupped my hands over my eyes and looked up and down the beach. I spotted policemen and FBI agents moving into the crowd. There must have been at least fifty thousand sunbathers on the beach. I could faintly hear electronic bells from the slot machines in one of the nearby hotels.

Inez. Atlantic City. Jesus!

A madman on the loose near the famous Steel Pier.

I looked for Sampson or Kyle, but I didn't see either of them. I searched for Pierce, and for Inez, and for Mr. Smith.

I heard a loud voice, and it stopped me in my tracks. *"This is the FBI."*

CHAPTER 118

THE VOICE boomed over a loudspeaker. Probably from one of the hotels, or maybe a police hookup. "This is the FBI," Kyle Craig announced.

"Some of our agents are on the beach now. Cooperate with them and also with the Atlantic City police. Do whatever they ask. There's no reason for undue concern. Please cooperate with police officers."

The huge crowd became strangely quiet. Everyone was staring around, looking for the FBI. No, there was no reason for *undue concern*—not unless we actually found Pierce. Not unless we discovered Mr. Smith operating on somebody in the middle of this beach crowd.

I made my way toward the famous amusement pier, where as a young boy I had actually seen the famous diving horse. People were standing out in the low surf, just looking in toward shore. It reminded me of the movie *Jaws*.

Thomas Pierce was in control here.

A black Bell Jet Ranger hovered less than seventy yards from shore. A second helicopter came into view from the northeast. It swept in close to the first, then fluttered away in the direction of the Taj Mahal Hotel complex. I could make out sharpshooters positioned in the helicopters.

So could Pierce, and so could the people on the

beach. I knew there were FBI marksmen in the nearby hotels. Pierce would know that. Pierce was FBI. He knew everything we did. That was his edge and he was using it against us. He was winning.

There was a disturbance up closer to the pier. People were pushing forward to see, while others were moving away as fast as they could. I moved forward.

The beach crowd's noise level was building again. En Vogue played from somebody's blaster. The smell of cotton candy and beer and hot dogs was thick in the air. I began to run toward the Steel Pier, remembering the diving horse and Lucy the Elephant from Margate, better times a long time ago.

I saw Sampson and Kyle up ahead.

They were bending over something. *Oh God, Oh God, no. Inez, Atlantic City!* My pulse raced out of control.

This was not good.

A dark-haired teenage girl was sobbing against an older man's chest. Others gawked at the dead body, which had been clumsily wrapped in beach blankets. I couldn't imagine how it had gotten here—but there it was.

Inez, Atlantic City. It had to be her.

The murdered woman had long bleach blond hair and looked to be in her early twenties. It was hard to tell now. Her skin was purplish and waxy. The eyes had flattened because of a loss of fluid. Her lips and nail beds were pale. He had operated on Inez: The ribs and cartilage had been cut away, exposing her lungs, esophagus, trachea, and heart.

Inez sounds like Isabella.

Pierce knew that.

He hadn't taken out Inez's heart.

The ovaries and fallopian tubes were neatly laid out beside the body. The tubes looked like a set of earrings and a necklace.

Suddenly, sunbathers were pointing to something out over the ocean.

I turned and I looked up, shading my eyes with one hand.

A prop plane was lazily making its way down the shoreline from the north. It was the kind of plane you rented for commercial messages. Most of the messages on forty-foot banners hyped the hotels, local bars, area restaurants, and casinos.

A banner waved behind the sputtering plane, which was getting closer and closer. I couldn't believe what I was reading. It was another message.

Mr. Smith is gone for now! Wave good-bye.

CHAPTER 119

EARLY THE next morning, I headed home to Washington. I needed to see the kids, needed to sleep in my own bed, to be far, far away from Thomas Pierce and his monstrous creation—*Mr. Smith.*

Inez had turned out to be an escort from a local service. Pierce had called her to his room at Bally's Park Place. I was starting to believe that Pierce could *find intimacy only with his victims now,* but what else was driving him to commit these horrifying murders? Why Inez? Why the Jersey Shore?

I had to escape for a couple of days, or even a few hours, if that was all I could get. At least we hadn't already gotten another name, another location to rush off to.

I called Christine from Atlantic City and asked her if she wanted to have dinner with my family that night. She said yes, she'd like that a lot. She said she'd "be there with bells on." That sounded unbelievably good to me. The best medicine I could imagine for what ailed me.

I kept the sound of her voice in my head all the way home to Washington. She would be there with bells on.

Damon, Jannie, and I spent a hectic morning getting ready for the party. We shopped for groceries at Citronella, and then at the Giant. *Veni, vidi, Visa.*

I had *almost* put Pierce–Mr. Smith out of my mind, but I still had my Glock in an ankle holster to go grocery shopping.

At the Giant, Damon scouted on ahead to find some RC Cola and tortilla chips. Jannie and I had a chance to talk the talk. I knew she was dying to *bzzz-bzzz-bzzz*. I can always tell. She has a fine, overactive imagination, and I couldn't wait to hear what was on her little mind.

Jannie was in charge of pushing the shopping cart, and the metal handle of the cart was just above her eye level. She stared at the immense array of cereals in our aisle, looking for the best deals. Nana Mama had taught her the fine art of grocery shopping, and she can do most of the math in her head.

"Talk to me," I said. "My time is your time. Daddy's home."

"For today." She sent a hummer right past my ear, brushed me right back from home plate with a high, hard one.

"It's not easy being green," I said. It was an old favorite line between us, compliments of Kermit the Frog. She shrugged it off today. No sale. No easy deals.

"You and Damon mad at me?" I asked in my most soothing tones. "Tell me the truth, girlfriend."

She softened a little. "Oh, it's not so much that, Daddy. You're doing the best you can," she said, and finally looked my way. "You're trying, right? It's just hard when you go away from home. I get lonely for you. It's not the same when you're away."

I shook my head, smiled, and wondered where she got much of her thinking from. Nana Mama swears that Jannie has a mind of her own.

"You okay with our dinner plans?" I asked, treading carefully.

"Oh *ab*-solutely." She suddenly beamed. "That's not a problem at all. I *love* dinner parties."

"Damon? Is he okay with Christine coming over tonight?" I asked my confidante.

"He's a little scared 'cause she's the principal of our school. But he's cool, too. You know Damon. He's the man."

I nodded. "He *is* cool. So dinner's not a problem? You're not even a little scared?"

Jannie shook her head. "Nope. Not because of that. Dinners can't scare me. Dinner is dinner."

Man, she was smart, and so subtle for her age. It was like talking to a very wise adult. She was already a poet, and a philosopher, too. She was going to be competition for Maya Angelou and Toni Morrison one day. I loved that about her.

"Do you have to keep going after him? After this bum Mr. Smith?" Jannie finally asked me. "I guess you do." She answered her own question.

I echoed her earlier line. "I'm doing the best I can."

Jannie stood up on her tippy-toes. I bent low to her, but not as far as I used to. She kissed me on the cheek, a nice *smacker,* as she calls the kisses.

"You're the bee's knees," she said. It was one of Nana's favorite things to say and she'd adopted it.

"Boo!" Damon peeked around the soda-pop aisle at the two of us. His head was framed against a red, white, and blue sea of Pepsi bottles and cans. I pulled Damon close, and I kissed him on the cheek, too. I kissed the top of his head, held him in a way I would have liked my father to have held me a long time ago. We made a little spectacle of ourselves in the grocery-store aisle. Nice spectacle.

God, I loved the two of them, and what a continued dilemma it presented. The Glock on my ankle weighed a ton and felt as hot as a poker from a fire. I wanted to take it off and never put the weapon on again.

I knew I wouldn't, though. Thomas Pierce was still out there somewhere, and Mr. Smith, and all the rest of them. For some reason I felt it was my responsibility to make them all go away, to make things a little safer for everyone.

"Earth to Daddy," Jannie said. She had a small frown on her face. "See? You went away again. You were with Mr. Smith, weren't you?"

CHAPTER 120

*C*HRISTINE *can save you. If anyone can, if it's possible for you to be salvaged at this point in your life.*

I got to her place around six-thirty that night. I'd told her I would pick her up out in Mitchellville. My side was hurting again, and I definitely felt like damaged goods, but I wouldn't have missed this for anything.

She came to the front door in a bright tangerine sundress and heeled espadrilles. She looked slightly beyond great. She wore a bar pin with tiny silver bells. She *did* have bells on.

"Bells." I smiled.

"You bet. You thought I was kidding."

I took her in my arms right there on the red-brick front stoop, with blooming red and white impatiens and climbing roses all around us. I hugged Christine tightly against my chest and we started to kiss.

I was lost in her sweet, soft mouth, in her arms. My hands flew up to her face, lightly tracing her cheekbones, her nose, her eyelids.

The shock of intimacy was rare and overwhelming. So good, so fine, and missing for such a long time.

I opened my eyes and saw that she was looking at me. She had the most expressive eyes I'd ever seen. "I love the way you hold me, Alex," she whispered, but her eyes said much more. "I love your touch."

We backed into the house, kissing again.

"Do we have time?" She laughed.

"Shhh. Only a crazy person wouldn't. We're not crazy."

"Of course we are."

The bright tangerine sundress fell away to the floor. I liked the feel of shantung, but Christine's bare skin felt even better. She was wearing Shalimar and I liked that, too. I had the feeling that I had been here before with her, maybe in a dream. It was as if I had been imagining this moment for a long time and now it was here.

She helped me with her white-lace demibra. We slid down the matching panties, two pairs of hands working together. Then we were naked, except for the fine rope necklace with a fire opal around her neck. I remembered a poem, something magical about the nakedness of lovers, but with just a touch of jewelry to set it off. Baudelaire? I bit gently into her shoulder. She bit back.

I was so hard it hurt, but the pain was exquisite, the pain had its own raw power. I loved this woman completely, and I was also turned on by her, every inch of her being.

"You know," I whispered, "you're driving me a little crazy."

"Oh. Just a little?"

I let my lips trail down along her breasts, her stomach. She was lightly scented with perfume. I kissed between her legs and she began to gently call my name, then not so gently. I entered Christine as we stood against the cream living room wall, as we seemed to push our bodies *into* the wall.

"I love you," I whispered.

"I love you, Alex."

She was strong and gentle and graceful, all at the same time. We danced, but not in the metaphorical sense. We really *danced*.

I loved the sound of her voice, the softest cry, the song she sang when she was with me like this.

Then I was singing, too. I had found my voice again, for the first time in many years. I don't know how long we were like that. Time wasn't part of this. Something in it was eternal, and something was so very real and right now in the present.

Christine and I were soaking wet. Even the wall behind me was slippery and wet. The wild ride at the beginning, the rocking and rolling, had transformed itself into a slower rhythm that was even stronger. I knew that no life was right without this kind of passion.

I was barely moving inside her. She tightened around me and I thought I could feel the edges of her. I surged deeper and Christine seemed to swell around me. We began to move into each other, trying to get closer. We shuddered, and got closer still.

Christine climaxed, and then the two of us came together. We danced and we sang. I felt myself melting into Christine and we were both whispering *yes, yes, yes, yes, yes, yes*. No one could touch us here, not Thomas Pierce, no one.

"Hey, did I tell you I loved you?"

"Yes, but tell me again."

CHAPTER 121

KIDS ARE so damn much smarter than we usually give them credit for. Kids know just about everything, and they often know it before we do.

"You two are *late*! You have a flat tire—or were you just smooching?" Jannie wanted to know as we came in the front door. She can say some outrageous things and get away with them. She knows it, and pushes the envelope every chance she gets.

"We were smooching," I said. "Satisfied?"

"Yes I am," Jannie smiled. "Actually, you're not even late. You're right on time. Perfect timing."

Dinner with Nana and the children wasn't an anticlimax. It was such a sweet, funny time. It was what being home is all about. We all pitched in and set the table, served the food, then ate with reckless abandon. The meal was swordfish steaks, scalloped potatoes, summer peas, buttermilk biscuits. Everything was served piping hot, expertly prepared by Nana, Jannie, and Damon. Dessert was Nana's world-famous lemon meringue pie. She made it specially for Christine.

I believe the simple yet complex word that I'm searching for is *joy*.

It was so obvious around the dinner table. I could see it in the bright and lively eyes of Nana and Damon and Jannie. I had already seen it in Christine's eyes. I watched her at dinner and I had the thought that she could have been somebody famous in Washington, anything she wanted to be. She chose to be a teacher, and I loved that about her.

We repeated stories that had been in the family for years, and are always repeated at such occasions. Nana was lively and funny all through the night. She gave us her best advice on aging: "If you can't recall it, forget it."

Later on, I played the piano and sang rhythm-and-blues songs. Jannie showed off and did the cakewalk to a jazzy version of "Blueberry Hill." Even Nana did a minute of jitterbugging, protesting, "I really can't dance, I never could dance," as she did just beautifully.

One moment, one picture, sticks out in my mind, and I'm sure it will be there until the day I die. It was just after we'd finished dinner and were cleaning up the kitchen.

I was washing dishes in the sink, and as I reached to get another plate I stopped in midturn, frozen in the moment.

Jannie was in Christine's arms, and the two of them looked just beautiful together. I had no idea how she had gotten there, but they were both laughing and it was so natural and real. As I never had before, I knew and understood that Jannie and Damon were missing so much without a mother.

Joy—that's the word. So easy to say, so hard to find in life sometimes.

In the morning, I had to go back to work.

I was still the dragonslayer.

CHAPTER 122

I SHUT MYSELF AWAY to think, to quietly obsess about Thomas Pierce and Mr. Smith.

I made suggestions to Kyle Craig about moves that Pierce might make and precautions he should think about taking. Agents were dispatched to watch Pierce's apartment in Cambridge. Agents camped out at his parents' house outside Laguna Beach, and even at the gravesite of Isabella Calais.

Pierce had been passionately in love with Isabella Calais! She had been the only one for him! Isabella and Thomas Pierce! That was the key—Pierce's obsessive love for her.

He's suffering from unbearable guilt, I wrote in my notepad.

If my hypothesis is right, then what clues are missing?

Back at Quantico, a team of FBI profilers was trying to solve the problem on paper. They had all worked closely with Pierce in the BSU. Absolutely nothing in Pierce's background was consistent with the psychopathic killers they had dealt with before. Pierce had never been abused, either physically or sexually. There was no violence of any kind in his background. At least not as far as anyone knew. There was no warning, no hint of madness, no sign until he blew sky-high. *He*

*was an original. There had never been a monster any-
thing like him. There were no precedents.*

I wrote: *Thomas Pierce was deeply in love. You are
in love, too.*

*What would it mean to murder the only person in the
world whom you loved?*

CHAPTER 123

I COULDN'T MANAGE any sympathy, or even a modicum of clinical empathy, for Pierce. I despised him, and his cruel, coldblooded murders, more than any of the other killers I had taken down—even Soneji. Kyle Craig and Sampson felt the same, and so did most of the Bureau, especially the good folks in Behavioral Science. We were the ones in a rage state now. We were obsessed with stopping Pierce. Was he using that to beat our brains in?

The following day, I worked at home again. I locked myself away with my computer, several books, and my crime-scene notepads. The only time I took off was to walk Damon and Jannie to school, and then have a quick breakfast with Nana.

My mouth was full of poached egg and toast when she leaned across the kitchen table and launched one of her famous sneak attacks on me.

"Am I correct in saying that you don't want to discuss your murder case with me?" she asked.

"I'd rather talk about the weather or just about anything else. Your garden looks beautiful. Your hair looks nice."

"We all like Christine very much, Alex. She's knocked our socks off. In case you wanted to know but forgot to ask. She's the best thing that's happened to you since Maria. So, what are you going to do about it? What are your plans?"

I rolled my eyes back, but I had to smile at Nana's dawn offensive. "First, I'm going to finish this delicious breakfast you fixed. Then I have some dicey work to do upstairs. How's that?"

"You mustn't lose her, Alex. Don't do that," Nana advised and warned at the same time. "You won't listen to a decrepit old woman, though. What do I know about anything? I just cook and clean around here."

"And talk," I said with my mouth full. "Don't forget talk, old woman."

"Not just talk, sonny boy. Pretty sound psychological analysis, necessary cheerleading at times, and expert guidance counseling."

"I have a game plan," I said, and left it at that.

"You better have a winning game plan." Nana got the last word in. "Alex, if you lose her, you will never get over it."

The walk with the kids and even talking with Nana revitalized me. I felt clear and alert as I worked at my old rolltop for the rest of the morning.

I had started to cover the bedroom walls with notes and theories, and the beginnings of *even more theories* about Thomas Pierce. The pushpin parade had taken control. From the looks of the room, it seemed as if I knew what I was doing, but contrary to popular opinion, looks are almost always deceiving. I had hundreds of clues, and yet I didn't have a clue.

I remembered something Mr. Smith had written in

one of his messages to Pierce, which Pierce had then passed on to the FBI. *The god within us is the one that gives the laws and can change the laws. And God is within us.*

The words had seemed familiar to me, and I finally tracked down the source. The quote was from Joseph Campbell, the American mythologist and folklorist who had taught at Harvard when Pierce was a student there.

I was trying different perspectives to the puzzle. Two entry points in particular interested me.

First, Pierce was curious about language. He had studied linguistics at Harvard. He admired Noam Chomsky. What about language and words, then?

Second, Pierce was extremely organized. He had created the false impression that Mr. Smith was disorganized. He had purposely misled the FBI and Interpol.

Pierce was leaving clues from the start. Some of them were obvious.

He wants to be caught. So why doesn't he stop himself?

Murder. Punishment. Was Thomas Pierce punishing himself, or was he punishing everybody else? Right now, he was certainly punishing the hell out of me. Maybe I deserved it.

Around three o'clock, I took a stroll and picked up Damon and Jannie at the Sojourner Truth School. Not that they needed someone to walk them home. I just missed the hell out of them. I needed to see them, couldn't keep myself away.

Besides, my head ached and I wanted to get out of the house, away from all of my thoughts.

I saw Christine in the schoolyard. She was surrounded by little children. I remembered that she wanted to have kids herself. She looked so happy, and I could see that the kids loved to be around her. Who in their right mind wouldn't. She made it look so natural to be turning jump rope in a navy business suit.

She smiled when she saw me approaching across the schoolyard full of kids. The smile warmed the cockles of my heart, and all my other cockles as well.

"Look who's taking a break for air," she said, "three potato, four."

"When I was in high school," I told her as she continued to turn her end of a Day-Glo pink jump rope, "I had a girlfriend over at John Carroll. This was in my sophomore and junior years."

"Mmm, hmmm. Nice Catholic girl? White blouse, plaid skirt, saddle shoes?"

"She was very nice. Actually, she's a botanist now. See, nice? I used to walk all the way over to South Carolina Avenue just on the off chance I might see Jeanne for a couple of minutes after she finished school. I was seriously smitten."

"Must have been the saddle shoes. Are you trying to tell me that you're smitten again?" Christine laughed. The kids couldn't quite hear us, but they were laughing anyway.

"I am way beyond smitten. I am smote."

"Well that's good," she said and continued to turn the pink rope and smile at her kids, "because so am I. And when this case is over, Alex—"

"Anything you want, just say the word."

Her eyes brightened even more than was usual. "A weekend away from everything. Maybe at a country inn, but anywhere remote will do just fine."

I wanted to hold Christine so much. I wanted to kiss her right there, but that wasn't going to happen in the crowded schoolyard.

"It's a date," I said. "It's a promise."

"I'll hold you to it. *Smote,* that's good. We can try that on our weekend away."

CHAPTER 124

BACK HOME, I worked on the Pierce case until supper time. I ate a quick meal of hamburgers and summer squash with Nana and the kids. I took some more heavy heat for being an incurable and unrepentant workaholic. Nana cut me a slice of pie, and I retreated to my room again. Well fed, but deeply unsatisfied.

I couldn't help it—I was worried. Thomas Pierce might already have grabbed another victim. He could be performing an "autopsy" tonight. He could send us a message at any time.

I reread the notes I had plastered on the bedroom wall. I felt as if the answer were on the tip of my tongue and it was driving me crazy. People's lives hung in the balance.

He had "pierced" the heart of Isabella Calais.

His apartment in Cambridge was an obsessive shrine to her memory.

He had returned "home" when he went to Point Pleasant Beach. The opportunity to catch him was there—if we were smart enough, if we were as good as he was.

What were we missing, the FBI and me?

I played more word games with the assortment of clues.

He always "pierces" his victims. I wondered if he

was impotent or had become impotent, unable to have a sexual relationship with Isabella.

Mr. Smith operates like a doctor—which Pierce nearly was—which his father and his siblings are. He had failed as a doctor.

I went to bed early, around eleven, but I couldn't sleep. I guess I'd just wanted to try and turn the case off. I finally called Christine and we talked for about an hour. As we talked and I listened to the music of her voice, I couldn't help thinking about Pierce and Isabella Calais.

Pierce had loved her. Obsessive love. What would happen if I lost Christine now? What happened to Pierce after the murder? Had he gone mad?

After I got off the phone, I went back at the case again. For a while, I thought his pattern might have something to do with Homer's *Odyssey*. He was heading home after a series of tragedies and misfortunes? *No, that wasn't it.*

What the hell was the key to his code? If he wanted to drive all of us mad, it was working.

I began to play with the names of the victims, starting with Isabella and ending with Inez. *I* goes full circle to *I*? Full circle? Circles? I looked at the clock on the desk—it was almost one-thirty in the morning, but I kept at it.

I wrote—*I*.

I. Was that something? It could be a start. The personal pronoun *I?* I tried a few combinations with the letters of the names.

I-S-U . . . R
C-A-D . . .
I-A-D . . .

I stopped after the next three letters: IMU. I stared at the page. I remembered *pierced*, the obviousness of it. The simplest wordplay.

Isabella, Michaela, Ursula. Those were names of the first three victims—in order. *Jesus Christ!*

I looked at the names of all the victims—in order of the murders. I looked at the first, last, and middle names. I began mixing and matching the names. My heart was pounding. There was something here. Pierce had left us another clue, a series of clues, actually.

It was right there in front of us all the time. No one got it, because Smith's crimes appeared to be without any pattern. But Pierce had started that theory himself.

I continued to write, using either the first or last or middle names of the victims. It started IMU. Then *R*, for Robert. *D* for Dwyer. Was there a subpattern for selecting the name? It could be an arithmetic sequence.

There was a pattern to Pierce-Smith, after all. His mission began that very first night in Cambridge, Massachusetts. He *was* insane, but I had caught on to his pattern. It started with his love of wordplay.

Thomas Pierce wanted to be caught! But then something changed. He had become ambivalent about his capture. Why?

I looked at what I had assembled. "Son of a bitch," I muttered. "Isn't this something. He has a ritual."

I	Isabella Calais.
M	Stephanie Michaela Apt.
U	Ursula Davies.
R	Robert Michael Neel.
D	Brigid Dwyer.
E	Mary Ellen Klauk.
R	Robin Anne Schwartz.
E	Clark Daniel Ebel.
D	David Hale.
I	Isadore Morris.
S	Theresa Anne Secrest.
A	Elizabeth Allison Gragnano.
B	Barbara Maddalena.
E	Edwin Mueller.
L	Laurie Garnier.
L	Lewis Lavine.
A	Andrew Klauk.
C	Inspector Drew Cabot.
A	Dr. Abel Sante.
L	Simon Lewis Conklin.
A	Anthony Bruno.
I	Inez Marquez.
S	_____?

It read: I MURDERED ISABELLA CALAIS.

He had made it so easy for us. He was taunting us from the very beginning. Pierce wanted to be stopped, wanted to be caught. so why the hell hadn't he stopped himself? Why had the string of brutal murders gone on and on?

I MURDERED ISABELLA CALAIS.

The murders were a confession, and maybe Pierce was almost finished. Then what would happen? And who was *S?*

Was it Smith himself? Did S stand for Smith?

Would he symbolically murder Smith? Then Mr. Smith would disappear forever?

I called Kyle Craig and then Sampson, and I told them what I had found. It was past two in the morning, and neither of them was overjoyed to hear my voice or the news. They didn't know what to do with the word jumble and neither did I.

"I'm not sure what it gives us," Kyle said, "what it proves, Alex."

"I don't either. Not yet. It does tell us he's going to kill someone with an S in his name."

"George Steinbrenner," Kyle mumbled. "Strom Thurmond. Sting."

"Go back to sleep," I said.

My head was doing loops. Sleep wasn't an option for me. I half expected to get another message from Pierce, maybe even that night. He was mocking us. He had been from the beginning.

I wanted to get a message to him. Maybe I ought to communicate with Pierce through the newspapers or TV? We needed to get off the defensive and attack instead.

I lay in the darkness of my bedroom. *Could S be Mr. Smith?* I wondered. My head was throbbing. I was past being exhausted. I finally drifted off toward sleep. I was falling off the edge—when I grabbed hold.

I bolted up in bed. I was wide-awake now.

"S isn't Smith."

I knew who S was.

CHAPTER 125

THOMAS PIERCE was in Concord, Massachusetts.

Mr. Smith was here, too.

I was finally inside his head.

Sampson and I were ready on a cozy, picturesque side street near the house of Dr. Martin Straw, the man who had been Isabella's lover. Martin Straw was *S* in the puzzle.

The FBI had a trap set for Pierce at the house. They didn't bring huge numbers of agents this time. They were afraid of tipping off Pierce. Kyle Craig was gun-shy and he had every reason to be. Or maybe there was something else going on.

We waited for the better part of the morning and early afternoon. Concord was a self-contained, somewhat constrained town that seemed to be aging gracefully. The Thoreau and Alcott homes were here somewhere nearby. Every other house seemed to have a historical-looking plaque with a date on it.

We waited for Pierce. And then waited some more. The dreaded *stakeout in Podunk* dragged on and on. Maybe I was wrong about *S.*

A voice finally came over the radio in our car. It was Kyle. "We've spotted Pierce. He's here. But something's wrong, Alex. He's headed back toward Route

Two," Kyle said. "He's not going to Dr. Straw's. He saw something he didn't like."

Sampson looked over at me. "I told you he was careful. Good instincts. He *is* a goddamn Martian, Alex."

"He spotted something," I said. "He's as good as Kyle always said. He knows how the Bureau works, and he saw something."

Kyle and his team had wanted to let Pierce enter the Straw house before they took him down. Dr. Straw, his wife, and children had been moved from the place. We needed solid evidence against Pierce, as much as we could get. We could lose the case if we got Thomas Pierce to court without it. We definitely could lose.

A message crackled over the shortwave. "He's headed toward Route Two. Something spooked him. He's on the run!"

"He has a shortwave! He's intercepting us!" I grabbed the mike and warned Kyle. "No more talk on the radio. Pierce is listening. That's how he spotted us."

I started the engine and gunned the sedan away from the curb. I pushed the speed up to sixty on heavily populated Lowell Road. We were actually closer to Route 2 than the others. We still might be able to cut Pierce off.

A shiny, silver BMW passed us, coming from the opposite direction on the road. The driver sat on her horn as we sped by. I couldn't blame her. Sixty was a dangerous speed on the narrow village street. Everything was going crazy again, caroming out of control at the whim of a madman.

"There he is!" Sampson yelled.

Pierce's car was heading into Concord Center, the most congested area of town. He was moving way too fast.

We sped past Colonial-style houses, then upscale shops, and finally approached Monument Square. I caught glimpses of the Town House, Concord Inn, the Masons Hall—then a sign for Route 62—another for Route 2.

Our sedan whisked by car after car on the village streets. Brakes screeched around us. Other cars honked, justifiably angry and afraid of the car chase in progress.

Sampson was holding his breath and so was I. There's a joke about black men being pulled over illegally in suburban areas. The *DWB* violation. Driving while black. We were up to seventy inside the city limits.

We made it in one piece out of the town center— Walden Street—Main—then back onto Lowell Road approaching the highway.

I whipped around onto Route 2 and nearly spun out of control. The pedal was down to the floor. This was our best chance to get Thomas Pierce, maybe our last chance. Up ahead, Pierce knew this was it, too.

I was doing close to ninety now on Route 2, passing cars as if they were standing still. Pierce's Thunderbird must have been pushing eighty-five. He'd spotted us early in the chase.

"We're catching this squirrelly bastard now!" Sampson hollered at me. "Pierce goes down!"

We hit a deep pothole and the car momentarily left the road. We landed with a jarring *thud*. The wound in my side screamed. My head hurt. Sampson kept hollering in my ear about Pierce going down.

I could see his dark Thunderbird bobbing and weaving up ahead. Just a couple of car lengths separated us.

He's a planner, I warned myself. *He knew this might happen.*

I finally caught up to Pierce and pulled alongside him. Both cars were doing close to ninety. Pierce took a quick glance over at us.

I felt strangely exhilarated. Adrenaline powered through my body. *Maybe we had him.* For a second or two, I was as totally insane as Pierce.

Pierce saluted with his right hand. "Dr. Cross," he called through the open window, "we finally meet!"

CHAPTER 126

"*I KNOW about the FBI sanction!*" Pierce yelled over the whistle and roar of the wind. He looked cool and collected, oblivious to reality. "Go ahead, Cross. I want you to do it. Take me out, Cross!"

"There's no sanction order!" I yelled back. "Pull your car over! No one's going to shoot you."

Pierce grinned—his best killer smile. His blond hair was tied in a tight ponytail. He had on a black turtleneck. He looked successful—a local lawyer, shop owner, doctor. "Doc."

"Why do you think the FBI brought such a small unit," he yelled. "Terminate with prejudice. Ask your friend Kyle Craig. That's why they wanted me *inside* Straw's house!"

Was I talking to Thomas Pierce?

Or was this Mr. Smith?

Was there a difference anymore?

He threw his head back and roared with laughter. It was one of the oddest, craziest things I've ever seen. The look on his face, the body language, his calmness. He was daring us to shoot him at ninety miles an hour on Route 2 outside Concord, Massachusetts. He wanted to crash and burn.

We hit a stretch of highway with thick fir woods on either side. Two of the FBI cars caught up. They were pinned on Pierce's tail, pushing, taunting him. Had the Bureau come here planning to kill Pierce?

If they were going to take him, this was a good place—a secluded pocket away from most commuter traffic and houses.

This was the place to terminate Thomas Pierce.

Now was the time.

"You know what we have to do," Sampson said to me.

He's killed more than twenty people that we know of, I was thinking, trying to rationalize. *He'll never give up.*

"Pull over," I yelled at Pierce again.

"I murdered Isabella Calais," he screamed at me. His face was crimson. "I can't stop myself. I don't want to stop. I like it! I found out I like it, Cross!"

"Pull the hell over," Sampson's voice boomed. He had his Glock up and aimed at Pierce. "You butcher! You piece of shit!"

"I murdered Isabella Calais and I can't stop the killing. You hear what I'm saying, Cross? I murdered Isabella Calais, and I can't stop the killing."

I understood the chilling message. I'd gotten it the first time.

He was adding more letters to his list of victims. Pierce was creating a new, longer code: I murdered Isabella Calais, and I can't stop the killing. If he got away, he'd kill again and again. Maybe Thomas Pierce *wasn't* human, after all. He'd already intimated that he was his own god.

Pierce had out an automatic. He fired at us.

I yanked the steering wheel hard to the left, trying desperately to get us out of the line of fire. Our car leaned hard on its left front and rear wheels. Everything was blurred and out of focus. Sampson grabbed at the wheel. Excruciating pain shot through my wrist. I thought we were going over.

Pierce's Thunderbird shot off Route 2, rocketing down a side road. I don't know how he made the turnoff at the speed he was traveling. Maybe he didn't care whether he made it or not.

I managed to set our sedan back down on all four wheels. The FBI cars following Pierce shot past the turn. None of us could stop. Next, came a ragged ballet of skidding stops and U-turns, the screech and whine of tires and brakes. We'd lost sight of Pierce. He was behind us.

We raced back to the turnoff, then down a twisting, chevroned country road. We found the Thunderbird abandoned about two miles from Route 2.

My heart was thudding hard inside my chest. *Pierce wasn't in the car. Pierce wasn't here.*

The woods on both sides of the road were thick and offered lots of cover. Sampson and I climbed out of our car.

We hurried back into the dense thicket of fir trees, Glocks out. It was almost impossible to get through the underbrush. There was no sign of Thomas Pierce anywhere.

Pierce was gone.

CHAPTER 127

*T*HOMAS PIERCE *had vanished into thin air again. I was almost convinced he might actually live in a parallel world. Maybe he was an alien.*

Sampson and I were headed to Logan International Airport. We were going home to Washington. Rush-hour traffic in Boston wasn't cooperating with the plan.

We were still half a mile from the Callahan Tunnel, gridlocked in a line that was barely moving. Grunting and groaning cars and trucks surrounded us. Boston was rubbing our faces in our failure.

"Metaphor for our case. The whole goddamn man-hunt for Pierce," Sampson said about the traffic jumble, the mess. A good thing about Sampson—he gets either stoic or funny when things go really badly. He refuses to wallow in shit. He swims right out of it.

"I'm getting an idea," I told him, giving him some warning.

"I knew you were flying around somewhere in your private universe. Knew you weren't really here, sitting in this car with me, listening to what I'm saying."

"We'd just be stuck here in tunnel traffic if we stayed put."

Sampson nodded. "Uh-huh. We're in Boston. Don't want to have to come back tomorrow, follow up on one of your hunches then. Best to do it now. Chase those wild geese while the chasing is good."

I pulled out of the tight lane of stalled traffic. "There's just one wild goose that I can think to chase."

"You going to tell me where we're headed? I need to put my vest back on?"

"Depends on what you think of my hunches."

I followed forest green signs toward Storrow Drive, heading out of Boston the way we came. Traffic was heavy in that direction, too. There were too many people everywhere you went these days, too much crowding, and too much chaos, too much stress on everybody.

"Better put your vest back on," I told Sampson.

He didn't argue with me. Sampson reached into the backseat and fished around for our vests.

I wiggled into my own vest as I drove. "I think Thomas Pierce wants this to end. I think he's ready now. I saw it in his eyes."

"So, he had his chance back there in Concord. *'Pull off the road. Pull over, Pierce!'* You remember any of that? Sound familiar, Alex?"

I glanced at Sampson. "He needs to be in control. S was for Straw, but S is also for Smith. He has it figured out, John. He knows how he wants it to end. He always knew. It's important to him that he finish this."

Out of the corner of my eye I could see Sampson staring. "And? So? What the hell is that supposed to mean? Do you know how it ends?"

"He wants to end on S. It's magical for him. It's the

way he has it figured, the way it has to be. It's his mind game, and he plays it obsessively. He can't stop playing. He told us that. He's still playing."

Sampson was clearly having trouble with this. We had just missed capturing Pierce an hour ago. Would he put himself at risk again? "You think he's that crazy?"

"I think he's that crazy, John. I'm sure of it."

CHAPTER 128

HALF A DOZEN police squad cars were gathered on Inman Street in Cambridge. The blue-and-white cruisers were outside the apartment where Thomas Pierce and Isabella Calais had once lived, where Isabella had been murdered four years before.

EMS ambulances were parked near the gray stone front stoop. Sirens bleated and wailed. If we hadn't turned around at the Callahan Tunnel we would have missed it.

Sampson and I showed our detective shields and kept on moving forward in a hurry. Nobody stopped us. Nobody could have.

Pierce was upstairs.

So was Mr. Smith.

The game had come full circle.

"Somebody called in a homicide in progress," one of the Cambridge uniforms told us on the way up the stone front stairs. "I hear they got the guy cornered upstairs. Wackadoo of the first order."

"We know all about him," Sampson said.

Sampson and I took the stairs to the second floor.

"You think Pierce called all this heat on himself?" Sampson asked as we hurried up the stairs. I was beyond being out of breath, beyond pain, beyond shock or surprise.

This is how he wants it to end.

I didn't know what to make of Thomas Pierce. He had numbed me, and all the rest of us. I was drifting beyond thought, at least logical ideas. There had never been a killer like Pierce. Not even close. He was the most *alienated* human being I'd ever met. Not alien, *alienated*.

"You still with me, Alex?" I felt Sampson's hand gripping my shoulder.

"Sorry," I said. "At first, I thought Pierce couldn't feel anything, that he was just another psychopath. Cold rage, arbitrary murders."

"And now?"

I was inside Pierce's head.

"Now I'm wondering whether Pierce maybe feels *everything*. I think that's what drove him mad. This one can *feel*."

The Cambridge police were gathered everywhere in the hallway. The local cops looked shell-shocked and wild-eyed. A photograph of Isabella stared out from the foyer. She looked beautiful, almost regal, and so very sad.

"Welcome to the wild, wacky world of Thomas Pierce," Sampson said.

A Cambridge detective explained the situation to us. He had silver-blond hair, an ageless hatchet face. He spoke in a low, confidential tone, almost a whisper. "Pierce is in the bedroom at the far end of the hall. Barricaded himself in there."

"The master bedroom, his and Isabella's room," I said.

The detective nodded. "Right, the master bedroom. I worked the original murder. I hate the prick. I saw what he did to her."

"What's he doing in the bedroom?" I asked.

The detective shook his head. "We think he's going to kill himself. He doesn't care to explain himself to us peons. He's got a gun. The powers that be are trying to decide whether to go in."

"He hurt anybody?" Sampson spoke up.

The Cambridge detective shook his head. "No, not that we know of. Not yet."

Sampson's eyes narrowed. "Then maybe we shouldn't interfere."

We walked down the narrow hallway to where several more detectives were talking among themselves. A couple of them were arguing and pointing toward the bedroom.

This is how he wants it. He's still in control.

"I'm Alex Cross," I told the detective-lieutenant on the scene. He knew who I was. "What has he said so far?"

The lieutenant was sweating. He was a bruiser, and a good thirty pounds over his fighting weight. "Told us that he killed Isabella Calais, confessed. I think we knew that already. Said he was going to kill himself." He rubbed his chin with his left hand. "We're trying to decide if we care. The FBI is on the way."

I pulled away from the lieutenant.

"Pierce," I called down the hallway. The talking going

on outside the bedroom suddenly stopped. "Pierce! It's Alex Cross," I called again. "I want to come in, Pierce!"

I felt a chill. It was too quiet. Not a sound. Then I heard Pierce from the bedroom. He sounded tired and weak. Maybe it was an act. Who knew what he would pull next?

"Come in if you want. Just you, Cross."

"Let him go," Sampson whispered from behind. "Alex, let it go for once."

I turned to him. "I wish I could."

I pushed through the group of policemen at the end of the hallway. I remembered the poster that hung there: *Without God, We Are Condemned to Be Free.* Was that what this was about?

I took out my gun and slowly inched open the bedroom door. I wasn't prepared for what I saw.

Thomas Pierce was sprawled on the bed he had once shared with Isabella Calais.

He held a gleaming, razor-sharp scalpel in his hand.

CHAPTER 129

*T*HOMAS PIERCE'S CHEST *was cut wide open.* He had ripped himself apart as he would a corpse at an autopsy. He was still alive, but barely. It was incredible that he was conscious and alert.

Pierce spoke to me. I don't know how, but he did. "You've never seen Mr. Smith's handiwork before?"

I shook my head in disbelief. I had never seen anything like this, not in all my years in Violent Crimes or Homicide. Flaps of skin hung over Pierce's rib cage, exposing translucent muscle and tendons. I was afraid, repulsed, shocked—all at the same time.

Thomas Pierce was Mr. Smith's victim. His last?

"Don't come any closer. Just stay there," he said. It was a command.

"Who am I talking to? Thomas Pierce, or Mr. Smith?"

Pierce shrugged. "Don't play shrink games with me. I'm smarter than you are."

I nodded. Why argue with him—with Pierce, or was it Mr. Smith?

"I murdered Isabella Calais," he said slowly. His eyes became hooded. He almost looked in a trance. "I murdered Isabella Calais."

He pressed the scalpel to his chest, ready to stab himself again, to *pierce*. I wanted to turn away, but I couldn't.

This man wants to cut into his own heart, I thought to myself. *Everything has come full circle to this. Is Mr. Smith S? Of course he is.*

"You never got rid of any of Isabella's things," I said. "You kept her pictures up."

Pierce nodded. "Yes, Dr. Cross. I was mourning her, wasn't I?"

"That's what I thought at first. It's what the people at the Behavioral Science Unit at Quantico believed. But then I finally got it."

"What did you get? Tell me all about myself." Pierce mocked. He was lucid. His mind still worked quickly.

"The other murders—you didn't want to kill any of them, did you?"

Thomas Pierce glared. He focused on me with a sheer act of will. His arrogance reminded me of Soneji. "So why did I?"

"You were punishing yourself. Each murder was a reenactment of Isabella's death. You repeated the ritual over and over. You suffered her death each time you killed."

Thomas Pierce moaned. "Ohhh, ohhh. I murdered her here. In this bed! . . . Can you imagine? Of course you can't. No one can."

He raised the scalpel above his body.

"Pierce, don't!"

I had to do something. I rushed him. I threw myself at him, and the scalpel jammed into my right palm. I screamed in pain as Pierce pulled it out.

I grabbed at the folded yellow-and-white-flowered comforter and pressed it against Pierce's chest. He was fighting me, flopping around like a man having a seizure.

"Alex, no. Alex, look out!" I heard Sampson call out from behind me. I could see him out of the corner of my eye. He was moving fast toward the bed. "Alex, the scalpel!" he yelled.

Pierce was still struggling beneath me. He screamed obscenities. His strength was amazing. I didn't know where the scalpel was, or if he still had it.

"Let Smith kill Pierce!" he screeched.

"No," I yelled back. "I want you alive."

Then the unthinkable—again.

Sampson fired from point-blank range. The explosion was deafening in the small bedroom. Thomas Pierce's body convulsed on the bed. Both his legs kicked high in the air. He screeched like a badly wounded animal. He sounded inhuman—like an *alien*.

Sampson fired a second time. A strange guttural sound came from Pierce's throat. His eyes rolled way back in his head. The whites showed. The scalpel dropped from his hand.

I shook my head. "No, John. No more. Pierce is dead. Mr. Smith is dead, too. May he rest in hell."

Epilogue
Home Again, Home Again

CHAPTER 130

I WAS DRAINED of all feeling, slightly wounded and bandaged, but at least I got home safe and sound and in time to say good night to the kids. Damon and Jannie now had their own rooms. They both wanted it that way. Nana had given Jannie her room on the second floor. Nana had moved down to the smaller bedroom near the kitchen, which suited her fine.

I was so glad to be there, to be home again.

"Somebody's been decorating in here," I said as I peeked into Jannie's new digs. It surprised her that I was home from the wars. Her face lit up like a jack-o'-lantern on Halloween.

"I did it myself." Jannie pumped up her arms and "made muscles" for me. "Nana helped me hang the new curtains, though. We made them on the sewing machine. You like?"

"You're the hostess with the mostes'. I guess I missed all the fun," I told her.

"You sure did," Jannie said and laughed. "C'mere you," she said.

I went over to my little girl, and she gave me one of the sweetest hugs in the long and sometimes illustrious history of fathers and daughters. I felt so safe in her arms.

Then I went to Damon's room, and because it had

been both Damon and Jannie's room for so long, I was taken aback, shook up with the change.

Damon had chosen a sporting decor with monster and comedy movie accents. Manly, yet sensitive. I liked what he'd done to his room. It was pure Damon.

"You've got to help me with *my* room," I told him.

"We missed our boxing lesson tonight," he said, not in the tone of a major complaint, just setting the record straight.

We settled for wrestling on his bed, but I also had to agree to a double boxing lesson in the basement the following night. Actually, I couldn't wait. Damon was growing up too fast. So was Jannie. I couldn't have been happier with either of them.

I was a lucky man.

I had made it home again.

CHAPTER 131

I WAS TRYING to live my life differently, but it's hard to change old habits. I had a saying I really liked: *heart leads head.*

I was working on that too. I was going for it tonight.

Christine was still living out in Mitchellville, but not in her old house. She told me that staying there was too painful after her husband's murder during the "Jack and Jill" case. She had moved to a condo and fixed it up nicely.

I turned off the John Hanson Highway, and a few blocks later I saw the porch light of her place up ahead. I stopped my car and sat in the dark with the motor running.

The porch light and also a single light in the living room were on, but the place was mostly dark. I glanced at my watch: almost quarter to eleven. *I should have called her first.*

I finally climbed out of my old Porsche and headed to the front door.

I rang the bell and waited. I was feeling vulnerable in the harsh light of the front porch.

Heart leads head.

Christine was taking a long time answering the doorbell, and I started to worry about her. It was one of those old bad habits. The dragonslayer never sleeps.

Maybe something was wrong inside the house. I was wearing my Glock. I have to, according to the law.

I could smell flowers outside in the night air. The natural fragrance reminded me of the perfume Christine sometimes wore, Gardenia Passion. I called it "Gardenia Ambush" as a joke.

I was about to ring the bell a second time when the door suddenly swung open.

"What a surprise!" Christine said. She broke into a brilliant smile. Her brown eyes went down to my bandage. "What happened to your hand?"

I shrugged. "It's nothing, really. Just a scratch."

"Won't even make your highlight film reel, right?"

I laughed. "That's probably true."

Christine was wearing faded jeans and a plain white T-shirt tied at the waist. Her feet were bare. I had never seen her when she didn't look good to me, when she didn't make me feel a little light-headed.

"Are you really okay? Alex? I was out in the garden. I thought that maybe you were back from Boston. Now I'm having prescient feelings, premonitions, just like you."

I reached out and took Christine into my arms and suddenly everything was right. I felt whole again. I felt connected to the eternal river and all that good stuff. I had missed that feeling for too many years of my life.

"This was part of my premonition," she whispered. "I willed you here, Alex. I willed you into my arms."

We kissed and pressed against each other and it seemed as if we were merging, getting closer and closer. I loved the touch of her mouth against mine, the feel of her body, the way we fit. We were both strong, and yet we could be gentle together. I passionately believe in soulmates. I guess I always have. The best thing I had ever done in my life was to be in love. I missed it and was finally ready to love again.

"I missed you too much this time," I whispered against the softness of her cheek.

"I missed you," she said. "That's why I couldn't sleep. I knew you would come."

She's the one, I was thinking. I didn't have any doubt of it.

Heart leads head.

I cupped her face gently in my hands. She felt so precious to me.

"I love you more than I ever loved anything in my life. I love you so much. Marry me, Christine."

closer. I loved the touch of her mouth against mine, the feel of her body, the way we fit. We were both strong, and yet he could be gentle, tender; I passionate, be there in tenderness. I guess I always have. The last thing I had ever done, in my, life, was to be in love. I missed it and was finally ready, to love again.

"I missed you too much, this time," I whispered against the softness of her cheek.

"I missed you," she said. "That's why I couldn't sleep, I knew you would come."

She's the one, I was thinking. I didn't have any doubt of it.

Her eyes lit up.

I cupped her face gently in my hands. She felt so precious to me.

"I love you more than I ever loved anything in my life. I love you so much. I love you. Oh, love."

More
James Patterson!

Please turn this page
for a
bonus excerpt from

WHEN THE WIND BLOWS,

arriving in stores
November 1998.

More
James Patterson!

Please turn this page
for a
bonus excerpt from

WHEN THE WIND BLOWS,

arriving in stores
November 1998.

ONE

"Somebody please help me! Somebody please! Can anybody hear me?"

Max's screams pierced the clear mountain air. Her throat and lungs were beginning to hurt, to burn.

The eleven-year-old girl was running as fast as she could from the hateful, despicable School. She was strong, but she was beginning to tire. As she ran, her long blond hair flared behind her like a beautiful silk scarf. She was pretty, even though there were dark plum-colored circles under her eyes.

She knew the men were coming to kill her. She could hear them hurrying through the woods behind her.

She glanced over her right shoulder, painfully twisting her neck. She flashed a mental picture of her little brother, Matthew. Where was he? The two of them had separated just outside the School, both running and screaming.

She was afraid Matthew was already dead. Uncle Thomas probably got him. Thomas had betrayed them and that hurt so much she couldn't stand to think about it.

Tears rolled down her cheeks. The hunters were closing in. She could feel their heavy footsteps thumping hard and fast against the crust of the earth.

A throbbing orange-and-red ball of sun was sinking below the horizon. Soon it would be pitch-black and cold out here in the Front Range of the Rockies. All she wore was a simple tube of white cotton, sleeveless, loosely drawn together at the neckline and waist. Her feet were wrapped in thin-soled ballet slippers.

Move. She urged her aching, tired body on. She could go faster than this. She knew she could.

The twisting path narrowed, then wound around a great mossy-green shoulder of rock. She clawed and struggled forward through more thick tangles of branches and brush.

The girl suddenly stopped. She could go no farther.

A huge, high fence loomed above the bushes. It was easily ten feet. Rows of razor-sharp concertina wire were tangled and coiled across the top.

A metal sign warned: *Extreme danger! Electrified fence. Extreme danger!*

Max bent over and cupped her hands over her bare knees. She was blowing out air, wheezing hard, trying to keep from weeping.

The hunters were almost there. She could hear, smell, sense their awful presence.

With a sudden flourish, she unfurled her wings. They were white and silver tipped and appeared to have been unhinged. The wings sailed to a point above her head, seemingly of their own accord. Their span was nine feet. The sun glinted off the full array of her plumage.

Max started to run again, flapping her wings hard and fast. Her slippered feet lifted off the hardscrabble.

She flew over the high barbed wire like a bird.

TWO

Five armed men ran quietly and easily through the ageless boulders and towering aspens and ponderosa pines. They didn't see her yet, but they knew it wouldn't be long before they caught up with the girl.

They were jogging rapidly, but every so often the man in front picked up the pace a significant notch or two. All of them were competent trackers, good at this, but he was the best, a natural leader. He was more focused, more controlled, the best hunter.

The men appeared calm on the outside, but inside it was a different story. This was a critical time. The girl had to be captured and brought back. She shouldn't have gotten out here in the first place. Discretion was critical; it always had been, but never more than right now.

The girl was only eleven, but she had "gifts," and that could present a formidable problem outdoors. Her senses were acute; she was incredibly strong for her size, her age, her gender; and of course, there was the possibility that she might try to fly.

Suddenly, they could see her up ahead: she was

5

clearly visible against the deep blue background of the sky.

"Tinkerbell. Northwest, fifty degrees," the group leader called out.

She was called Tinkerbell, but he knew she hated the name. The only name she answered to was Max, which wasn't short for Maxine, or Maximillian, but for Maximum. Maybe because she always gave her all. She always went for it. Just as she was doing right now.

There she was, in all her glory! She was running at full speed, and she was very close to the perimeter fence. She had no way of knowing that. She'd never been this far from home before.

Every eye was on her. None of them could look away, not for an instant. Her long hair streamed behind her, and she seemed to flow up the steep, rocky hillside. She was in great shape; she could really move for such a young girl. She was a force to reckon with out here in the open.

The man running in front suddenly pulled up. Harding Thomas stopped short. He threw up his arm to halt the others. They didn't understand at first, because they thought they had her now.

Then, almost as if he'd known she would—she took off. She flew. She was going over the concertina wire of the ten-foot-high perimeter fence.

The men watched in complete silence and awe. Their eyes widened. Blood rushed to their brains and made a pounding sound in their ears.

She opened to a full wingspan and the movement seemed effortless. She was a beautiful, natural flyer. She flapped her white and silver wings up and down, up and down. The air actually seemed to carry her along, like a leaf on the wind.

"I knew she'd try to go over," Thomas turned to the others and spit out the words. "Too bad."

He lifted his rifle to his shoulder. The girl was about to disappear over the nearest edge of the canyon wall. Another second or two and she'd be gone from sight.

He pulled the trigger.

The men watched in complete silence and awe. Their eyes widened. Blood rushed to their brains and made a pounding sound in their ears.

She opened to a full wingspan and the movement seemed effortless. She was a beautiful aerial flyer. She flapped her white and silver wings up and down, up and down. The air actually seemed to carry her along, like a leaf on the wind.

"I knew she'd try to go over," Thomas turned to the others and spit out the words. "Too bad."

He lifted his rifle to his shoulder. The girl was about to disappear over the nearest edge of the canyon wall. Another second or two and she'd be gone from sight.

He pulled the trigger.

THREE

Kit Harrison was headed to Denver from Boston. He was good looking enough to draw looks on the airplane: trim, six foot two, sandy blond hair. He was a graduate of N.Y.U. Law School. And yet he felt like such a loser.

He was perspiring badly in the crammed and claustrophobic middle-aisle airplane seat of an American Airlines 747. He was so obviously pathetic that the pleasant and accommodating flight attendant stopped and asked if he was feeling all right. Was he ill?

Kit told her that he was just fine, but it was another lie, the mother of all lies. His condition was called post-traumatic stress disorder and sometimes featured nasty anxiety attacks that left him feeling he could die right there. He'd been suffering from the disorder for close to four years.

So yeah, I am ill, Madame Flight Attendant. Only it's a little worse than that.

See, I'm not supposed to be going to Colorado. I'm supposed to be on vacation in Nantucket. Actually, I'm supposed to be taking some time off, getting my head screwed on straight, getting used to maybe being fired from my job of twelve years.

Getting used to not being an FBI agent anymore, not being on the fast track at the Bureau, not being much of anything.

The name computer-printed on his plane ticket read Kit Harrison, but it wasn't his real name. His name was Thomas Anthony Brennan. He had been senior FBI agent Brennan, a shooting star at one time. He was thirty-eight, and lately, he felt he was feeling his age for the first time in his life.

From this moment on, he would forget the old name. Forget his old job, too.

I'm Kit Harrison. I'm going to Colorado to hunt and fish in the Rockies. I'll keep to that simple story. That simple lie.

Kit, Tom, whoever the hell he was, hadn't been up in an airplane in nearly four years. Not since August 9, 1994. He didn't want to think about that now.

So Kit pretended he was asleep as the sweat continued to trickle down his face and neck, as the fear inside him built way past the danger level. He couldn't get his mind to rest, even for just a few minutes. He *had* to be on this plane.

He *had* to travel to Colorado.

It was all connected to August 9, wasn't it? Sure

it was. That was when the stress disorder had begun. This was for Kim and for Tommy and for Michael—little Mike the Tyke.

And oh yeah, it also happened to be hugely beneficial for just about everybody else on the planet. Very strange—but that last outrageous bit was absolutely true, scarily true. In his opinion, nothing in history was more important than what he'd come here to investigate.

Unless he was crazy.

Which was a distinct possibility.